STEALTH™

CREATED BY **ROBERT KIRKMAN** & **MARC SILVESTRI**

MIKE COSTA
writer

NATE BELLEGARDE
artist

TAMRA BONVILLAIN
colorist

SAL CIPRIANO
letterer

JASON HOWARD
cover

SEAN MACKIEWICZ
editor

ANDRES JUAREZ
logo design

CARINA TAYLOR
production design

CORY WALKER
stealth character redesign

created by
ROBERT KIRKMAN
and **MARC SILVESTRI**

SKYBOUND.

ROBERT KIRKMAN Chairman | DAVID ALPERT CEO | SEAN MACKIEWICZ SVP, Editor-in-Chief | SHAWN KIRKHAM SVP, Business Development | BRIAN HUNTINGTON VP, Online Content | SHAUNA WYNNE Publicity Director | ANDRES JUAREZ Art Director | ALEX ANTONE Senior Editor | JON MOISAN Editor | ARIELLE BASICH Associate Editor | CARINA TAYLOR Graphic Designer | PAUL SHIN Business Development Manager | JOHNNY O'DELL Social Media Manager | DAN PETERSEN Sr. Director of Operations & Events | Foreign Rights Inquiries ag@sequentialrights.com | Other Licensing Inquiries contact@skybound.com | www.skybound.com

IMAGE COMICS, INC. | TODD McFARLANE President | JIM VALENTINO Vice President | MARC SILVESTRI Chief Executive Officer | ERIK LARSEN Chief Financial Officer | ROBERT KIRKMAN Chief Operating Officer | ERIC STEPHENSON Publisher / Chief Creative Officer | SHANNA MATUSZAK Editorial Coordinator | MARLA EIZIK Talent Liaison | NICOLE LAPALME Controller | LEANNA CAUNTER Accounting Analyst | SUE KORPELA Accounting & HR Manager | JEFF BOISON Director of Sales & Publishing Planning | DIRK WOOD Director of International Sales & Licensing | ALEX COX Director of Direct Market & Speciality Sales | CHLOE RAMOS-PETERSON Book Market & Library Sales Manager | EMILIO BAUTISTA Digital Sales Coordinator | KAT SALAZAR Director of PR & Marketing | DREW FITZGERALD Marketing Content Associate | HEATHER DOORNINK Production Director | DREW GILL Art Director | HILARY DILORETO Print Manager | TRICIA RAMOS Traffic Manager | ERIKA SCHNATZ Senior Production Artist | RYAN BREWER Production Artist | DEANNA PHELPS Production Artist | www.imagecomics.com

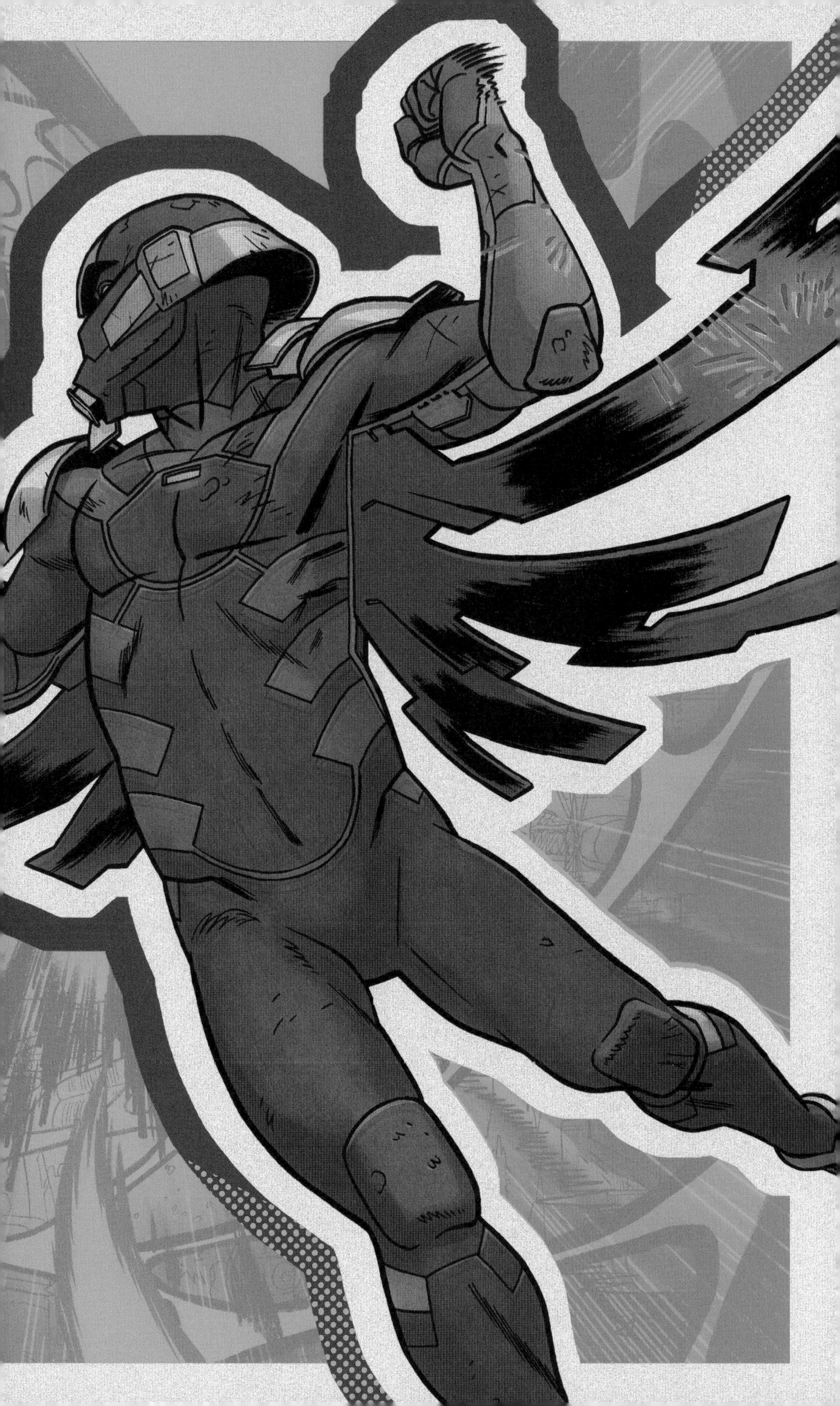

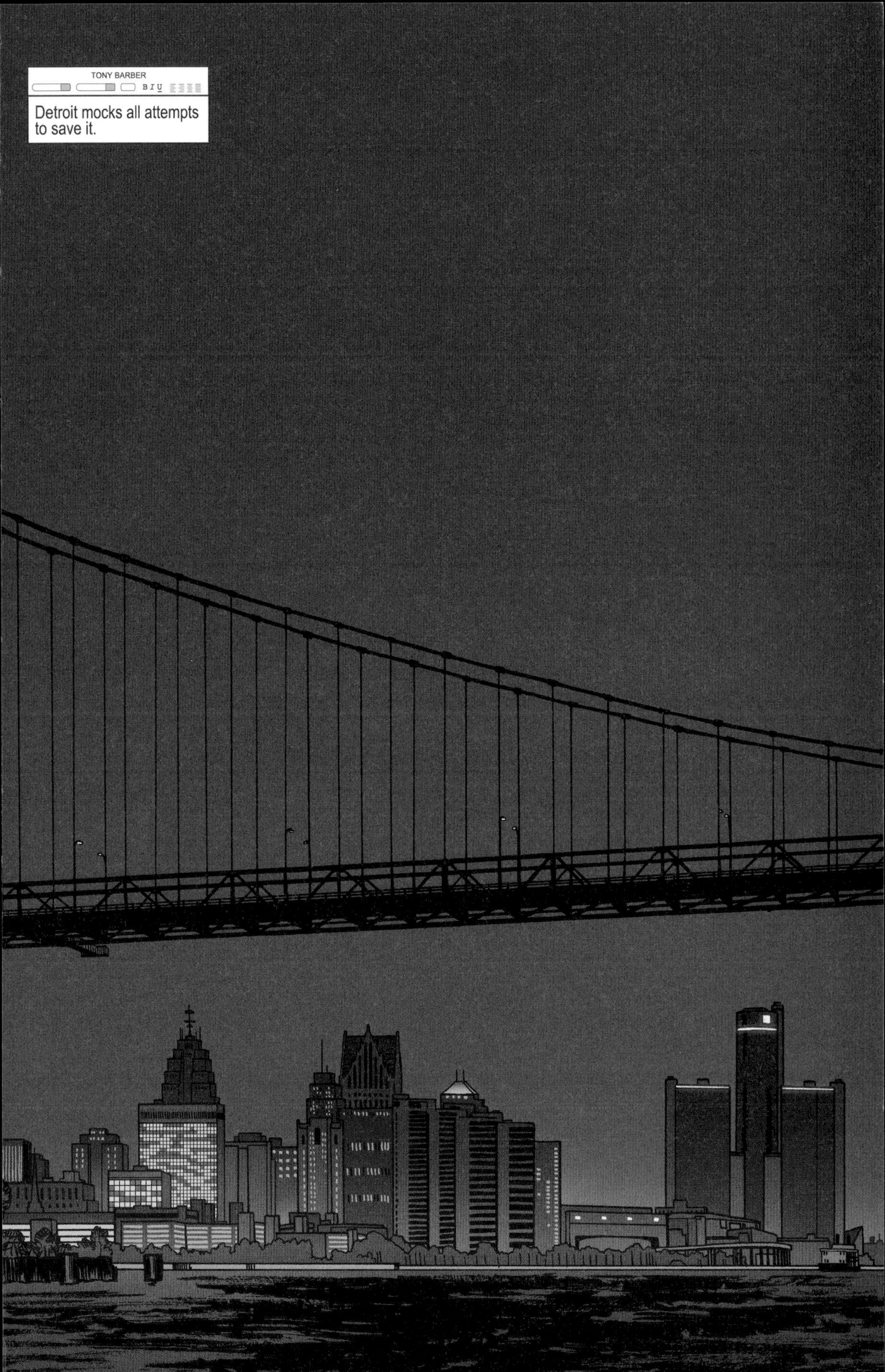
TONY BARBER
B I U
Detroit mocks all attempts to save it.

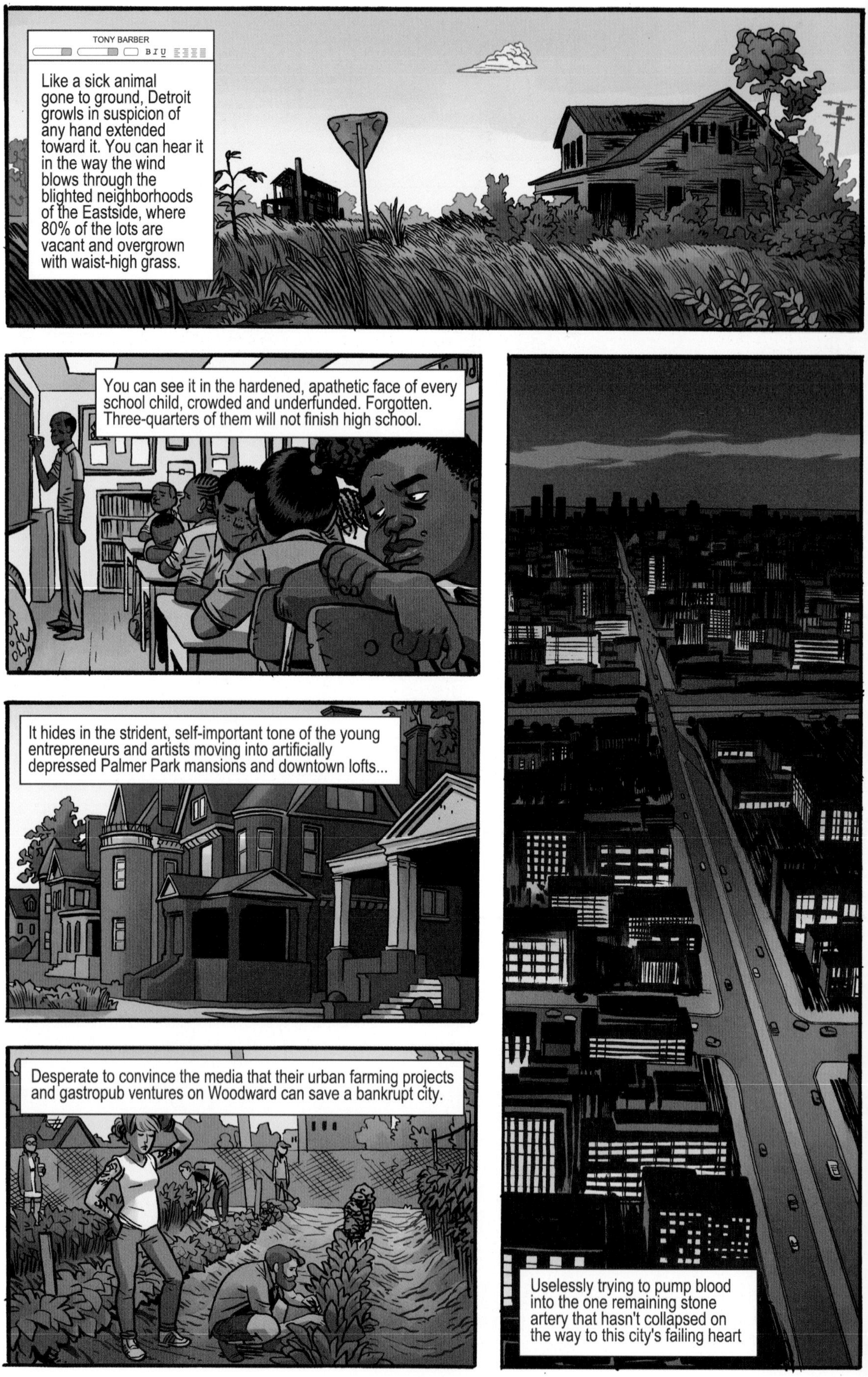
TONY BARBER
Like a sick animal gone to ground, Detroit growls in suspicion of any hand extended toward it. You can hear it in the way the wind blows through the blighted neighborhoods of the Eastside, where 80% of the lots are vacant and overgrown with waist-high grass.
You can see it in the hardened, apathetic face of every school child, crowded and underfunded. Forgotten. Three-quarters of them will not finish high school.
It hides in the strident, self-important tone of the young entrepreneurs and artists moving into artificially depressed Palmer Park mansions and downtown lofts...
Desperate to convince the media that their urban farming projects and gastropub ventures on Woodward can save a bankrupt city.
Uselessly trying to pump blood into the one remaining stone artery that hasn't collapsed on the way to this city's failing heart

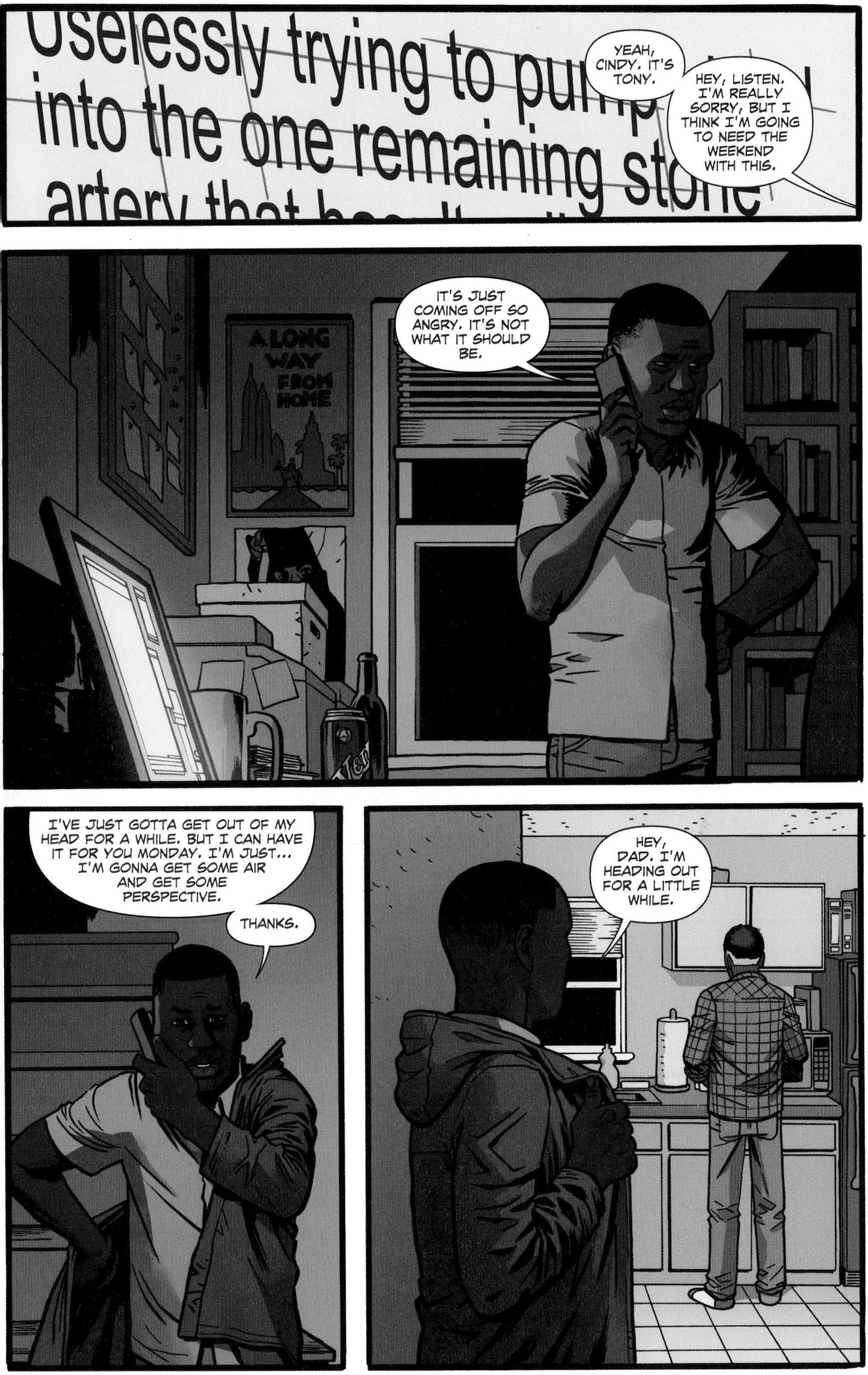

Uselessly trying to
into the one remaining stone
YEAH, CINDY. IT'S TONY.
HEY, LISTEN. I'M REALLY SORRY, BUT I THINK I'M GOING TO NEED THE WEEKEND WITH THIS.
A LONG WAY FROM HOME
IT'S JUST COMING OFF SO ANGRY. IT'S NOT WHAT IT SHOULD BE.
I'VE JUST GOTTA GET OUT OF MY HEAD FOR A WHILE. BUT I CAN HAVE IT FOR YOU MONDAY. I'M JUST... I'M GONNA GET SOME AIR AND GET SOME PERSPECTIVE.
THANKS.
HEY, DAD. I'M HEADING OUT FOR A LITTLE WHILE.

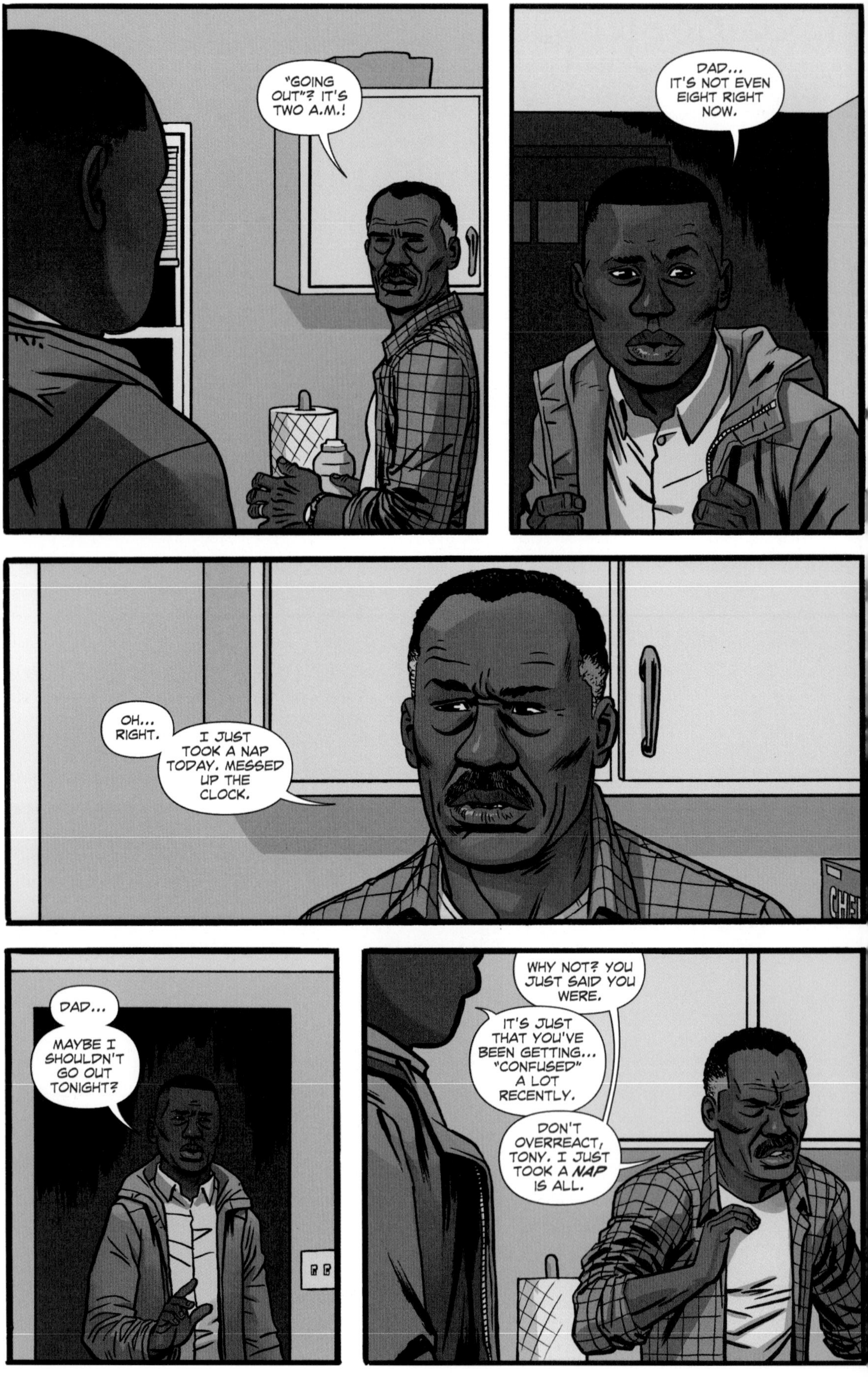
"GOING OUT"? IT'S TWO A.M.!
DAD... IT'S NOT EVEN EIGHT RIGHT NOW.
OH... RIGHT.
I JUST TOOK A NAP TODAY. MESSED UP THE CLOCK.
DAD...
MAYBE I SHOULDN'T GO OUT TONIGHT?
WHY NOT? YOU JUST SAID YOU WERE.
IT'S JUST THAT YOU'VE BEEN GETTING... "CONFUSED" A LOT RECENTLY.
DON'T OVERREACT, TONY. I JUST TOOK A *NAP* IS ALL.

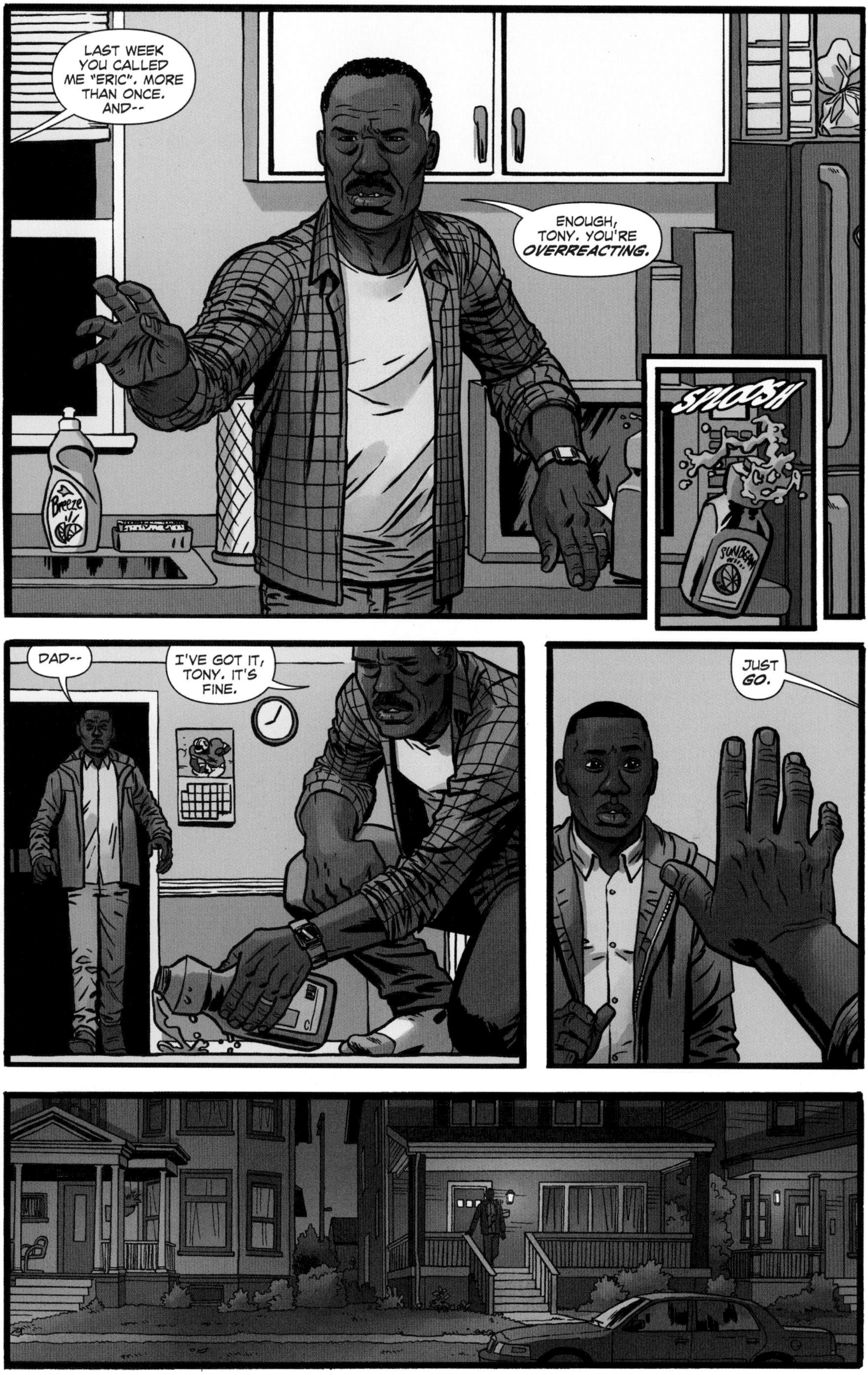
LAST WEEK YOU CALLED ME "ERIC". MORE THAN ONCE. AND--
ENOUGH, TONY. YOU'RE *OVERREACTING.*
SPLOOSH
DAD--
I'VE GOT IT, TONY. IT'S FINE.
JUST *GO.*

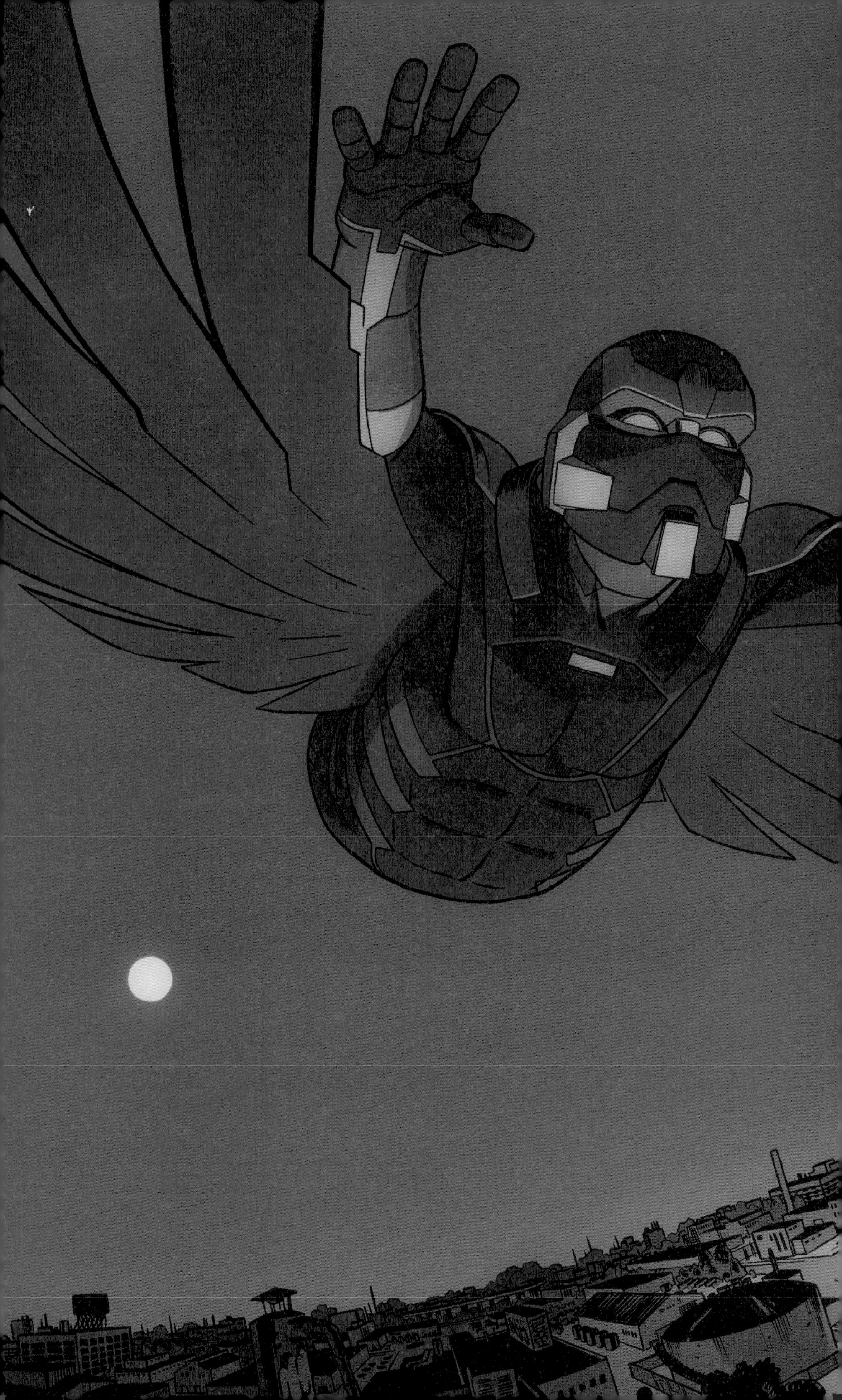

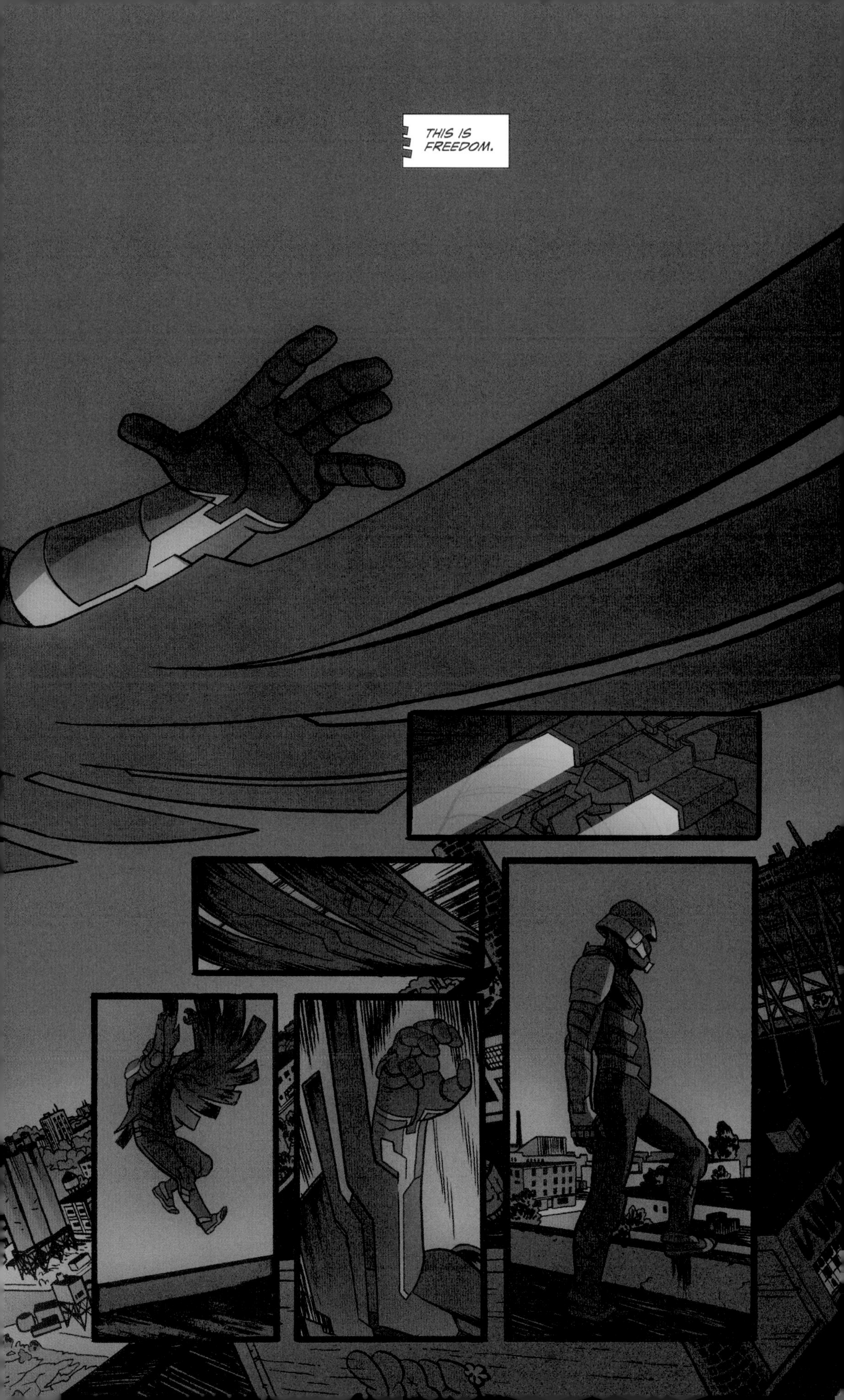
THIS IS FREEDOM.

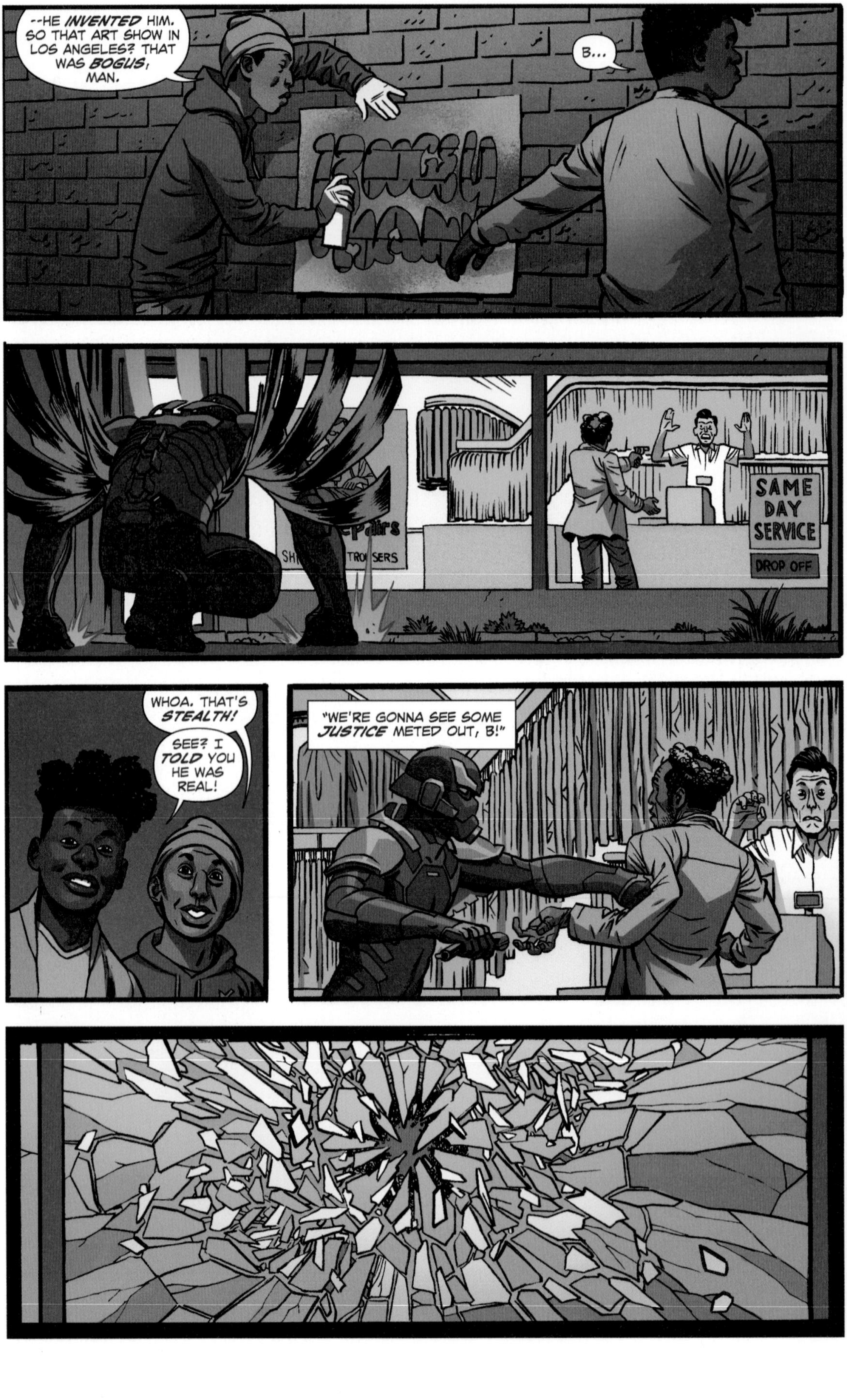
--HE *INVENTED* HIM. SO THAT ART SHOW IN LOS ANGELES? THAT WAS *BOGUS*, MAN.
B...
SAME DAY SERVICE
DROP OFF
TROUSERS
WHOA. THAT'S *STEALTH!*
SEE? I *TOLD* YOU HE WAS REAL!
"WE'RE GONNA SEE SOME *JUSTICE* METED OUT, B!"

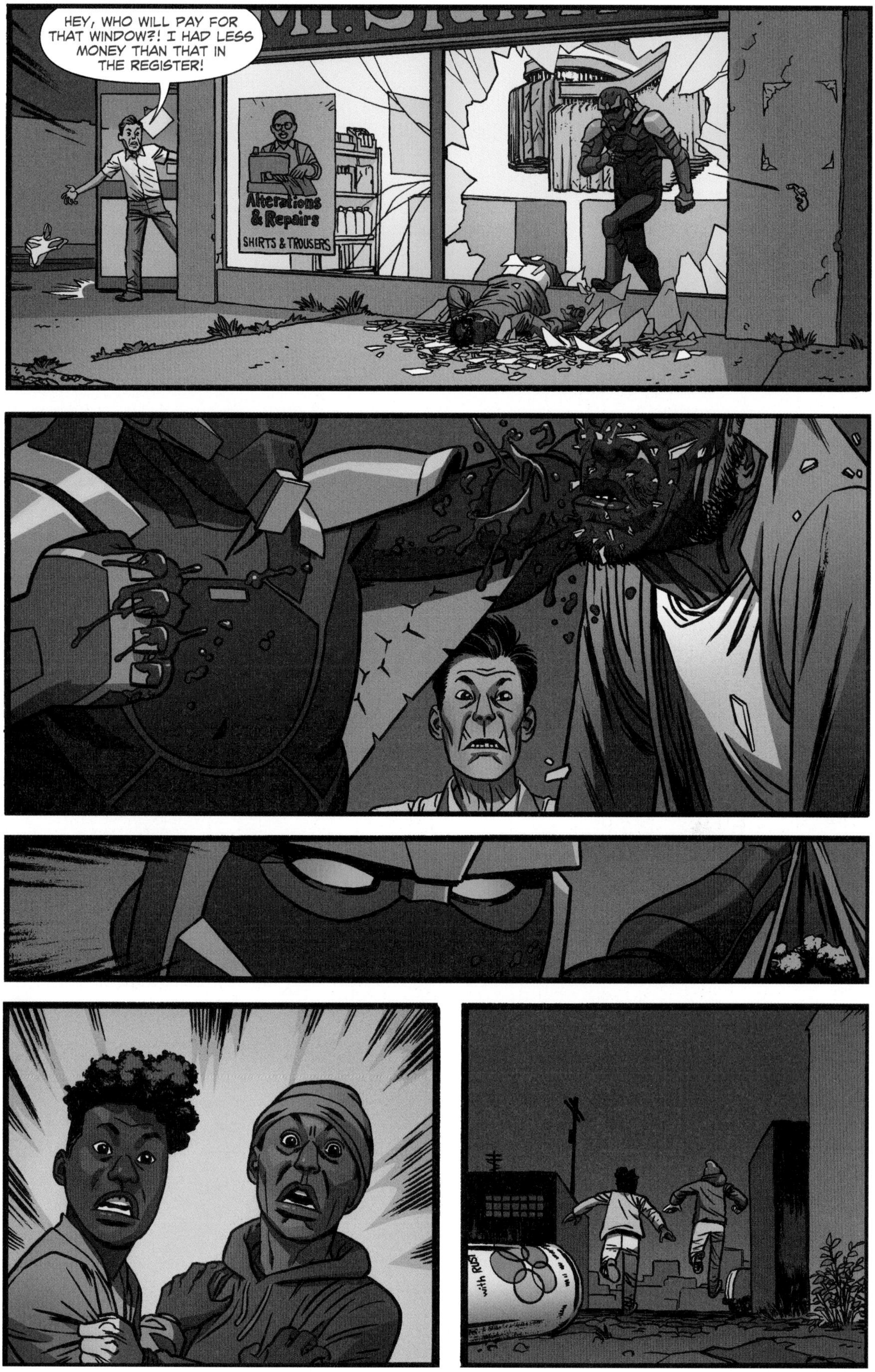
HEY, WHO WILL PAY FOR THAT WINDOW?! I HAD LESS MONEY THAN THAT IN THE REGISTER!
Alterations & Repairs
SHIRTS & TROUSERS

DAD?
YOU STILL UP?
SORRY I'M SO
LATE, BUT--

DAD!

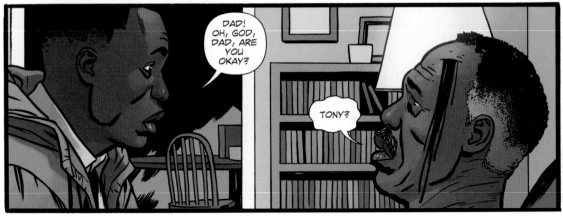

DAD!
OH, GOD,
DAD, ARE
YOU
OKAY?

TONY?

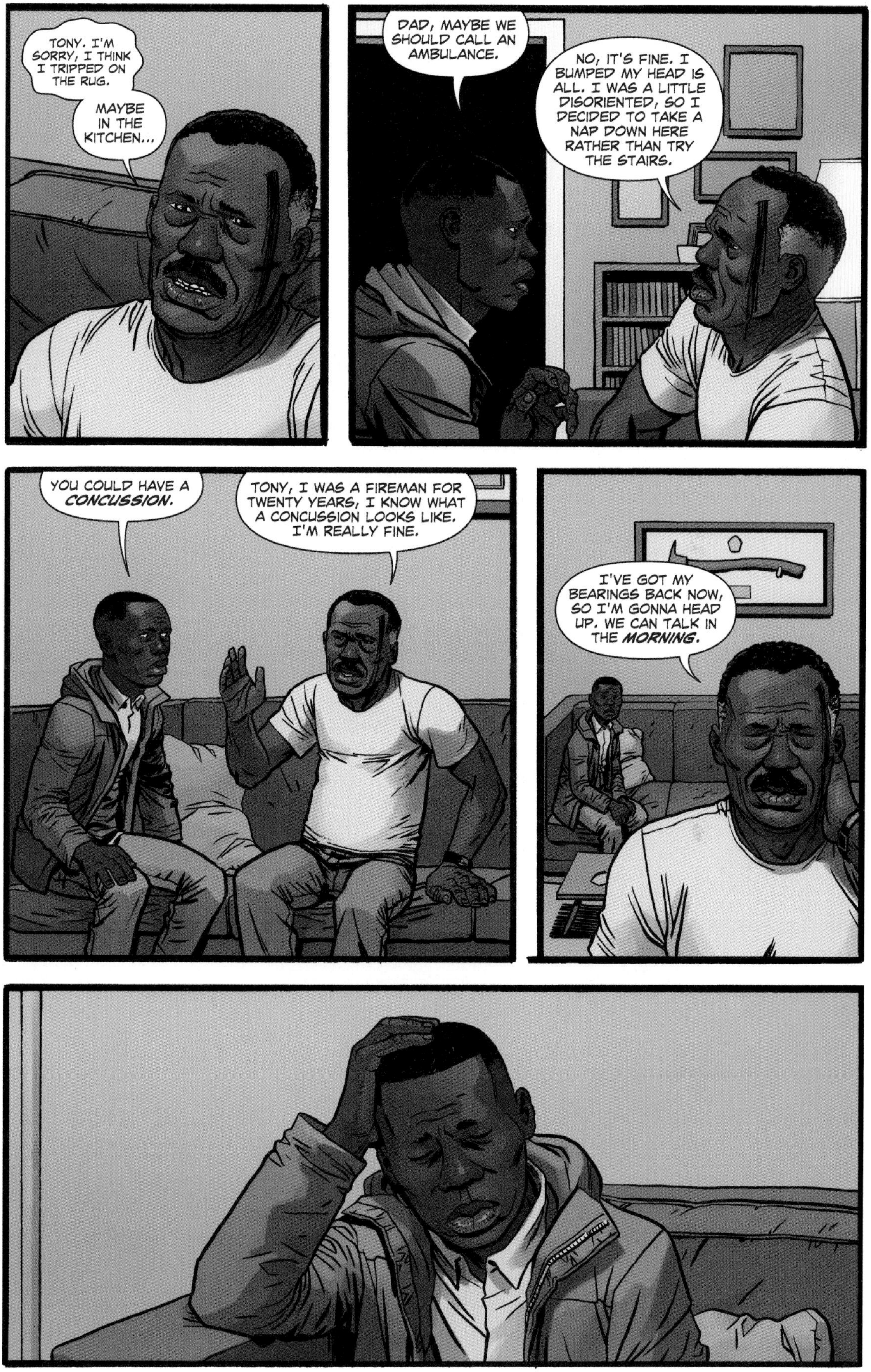
TONY. I'M SORRY, I THINK I TRIPPED ON THE RUG.
MAYBE IN THE KITCHEN...
DAD, MAYBE WE SHOULD CALL AN AMBULANCE.
NO, IT'S FINE. I BUMPED MY HEAD IS ALL. I WAS A LITTLE DISORIENTED, SO I DECIDED TO TAKE A NAP DOWN HERE RATHER THAN TRY THE STAIRS.
YOU COULD HAVE A *CONCUSSION*.
TONY, I WAS A FIREMAN FOR TWENTY YEARS, I KNOW WHAT A CONCUSSION LOOKS LIKE. I'M REALLY FINE.
I'VE GOT MY BEARINGS BACK NOW, SO I'M GONNA HEAD UP. WE CAN TALK IN THE *MORNING*.

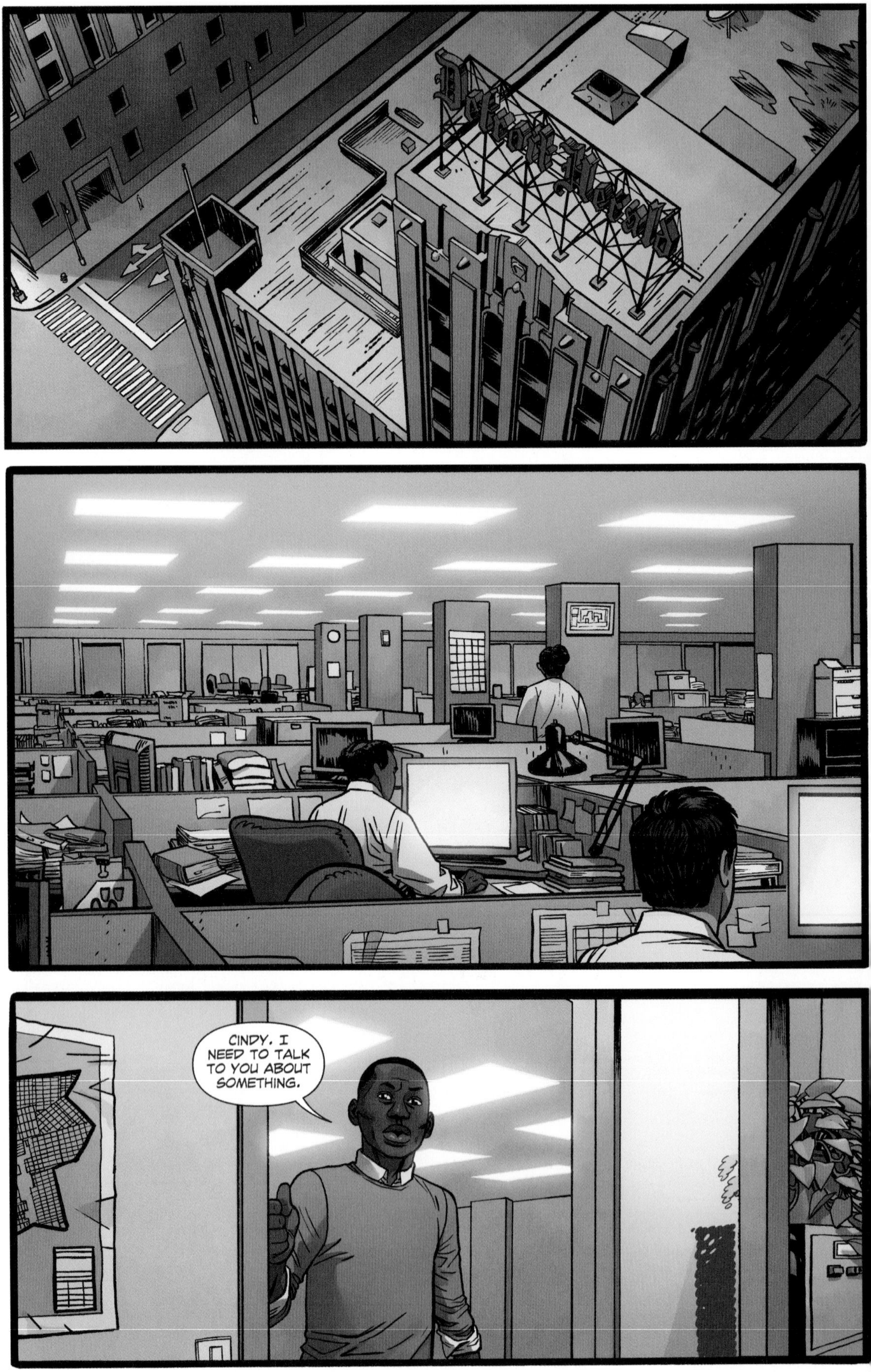
Detroit Herald
CINDY. I NEED TO TALK TO YOU ABOUT SOMETHING.

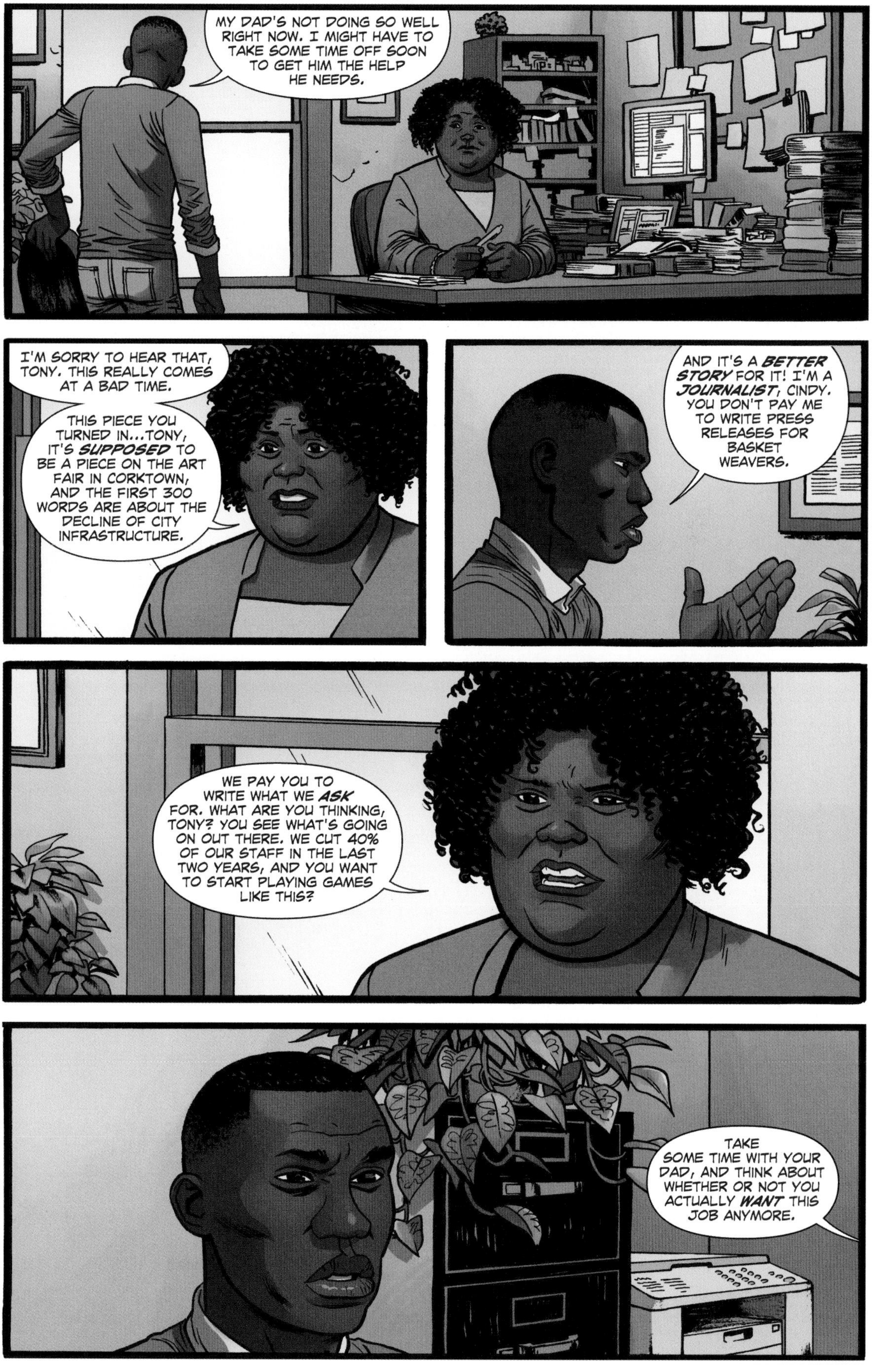
MY DAD'S NOT DOING SO WELL RIGHT NOW. I MIGHT HAVE TO TAKE SOME TIME OFF SOON TO GET HIM THE HELP HE NEEDS.
I'M SORRY TO HEAR THAT, TONY. THIS REALLY COMES AT A BAD TIME.
THIS PIECE YOU TURNED IN...TONY, IT'S SUPPOSED TO BE A PIECE ON THE ART FAIR IN CORKTOWN, AND THE FIRST 300 WORDS ARE ABOUT THE DECLINE OF CITY INFRASTRUCTURE.
AND IT'S A BETTER STORY FOR IT! I'M A JOURNALIST, CINDY. YOU DON'T PAY ME TO WRITE PRESS RELEASES FOR BASKET WEAVERS.
WE PAY YOU TO WRITE WHAT WE ASK FOR. WHAT ARE YOU THINKING, TONY? YOU SEE WHAT'S GOING ON OUT THERE. WE CUT 40% OF OUR STAFF IN THE LAST TWO YEARS, AND YOU WANT TO START PLAYING GAMES LIKE THIS?
TAKE SOME TIME WITH YOUR DAD, AND THINK ABOUT WHETHER OR NOT YOU ACTUALLY WANT THIS JOB ANYMORE.

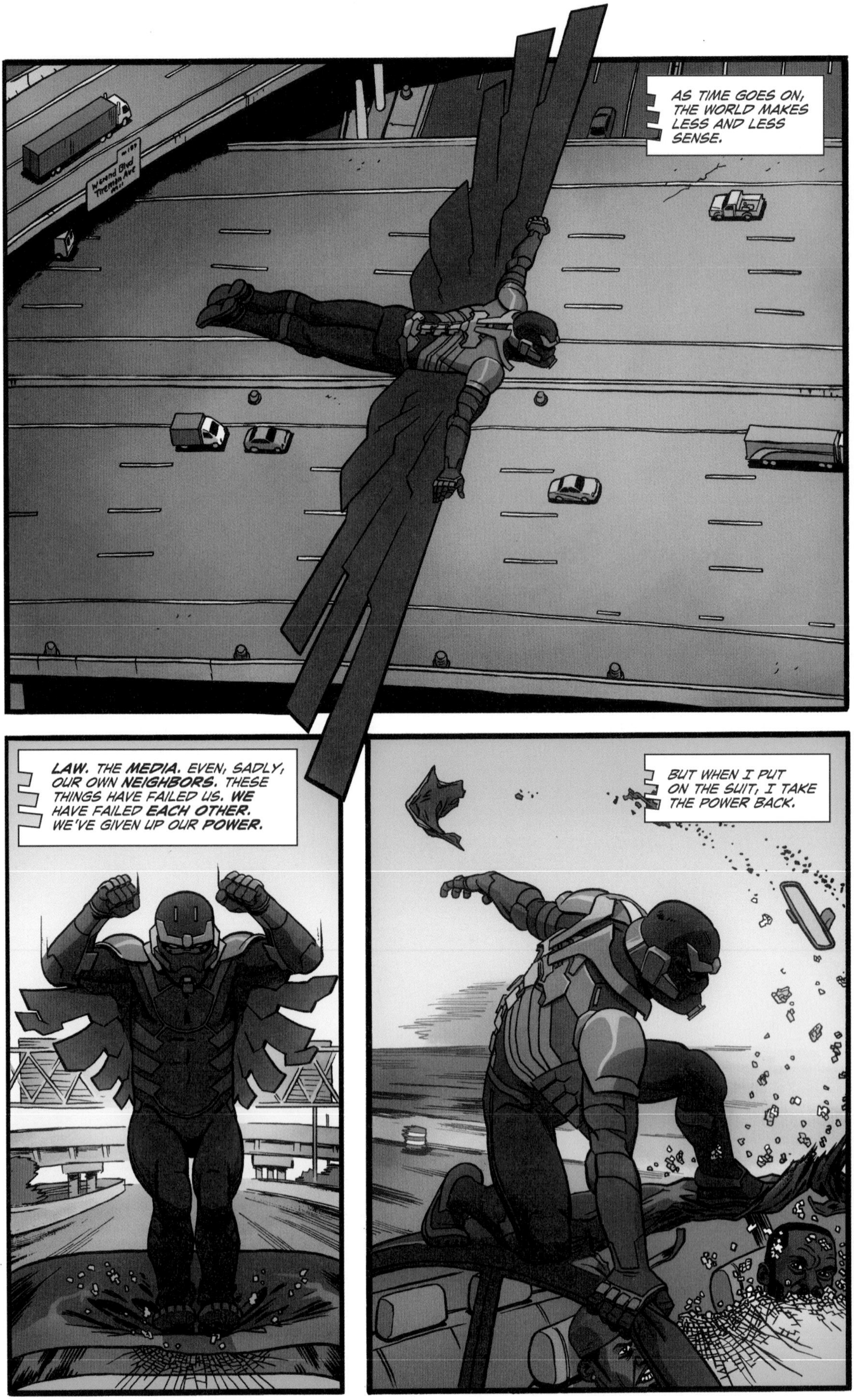
AS TIME GOES ON, THE WORLD MAKES LESS AND LESS SENSE.
LAW. THE MEDIA. EVEN, SADLY, OUR OWN NEIGHBORS. THESE THINGS HAVE FAILED US. WE HAVE FAILED EACH OTHER. WE'VE GIVEN UP OUR POWER.
BUT WHEN I PUT ON THE SUIT, I TAKE THE POWER BACK.

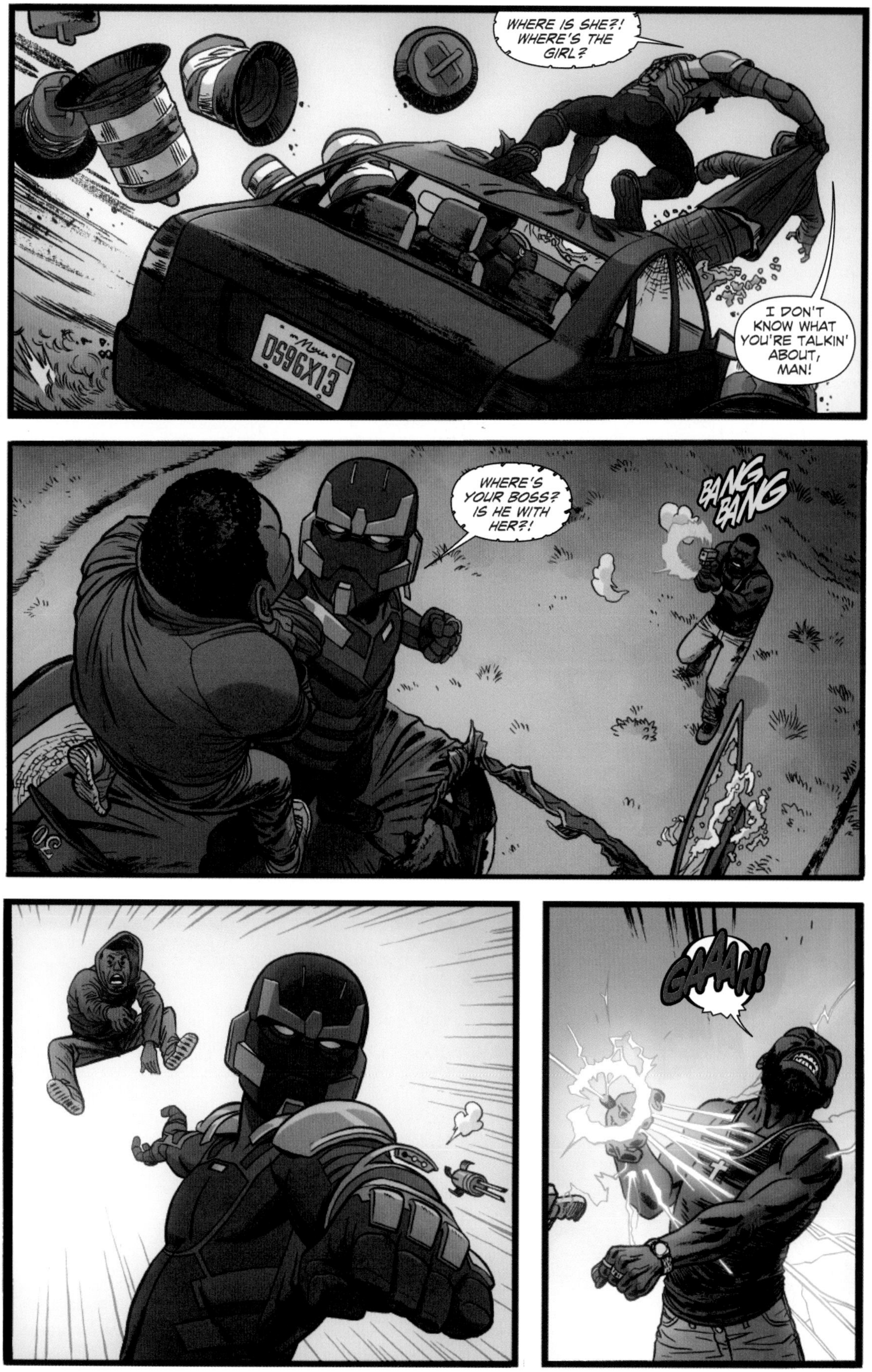
WHERE IS SHE?! WHERE'S THE GIRL?
I DON'T KNOW WHAT YOU'RE TALKIN' ABOUT, MAN!
DS96X13
WHERE'S YOUR BOSS? IS HE WITH HER?!
BANG BANG
GAAAH!

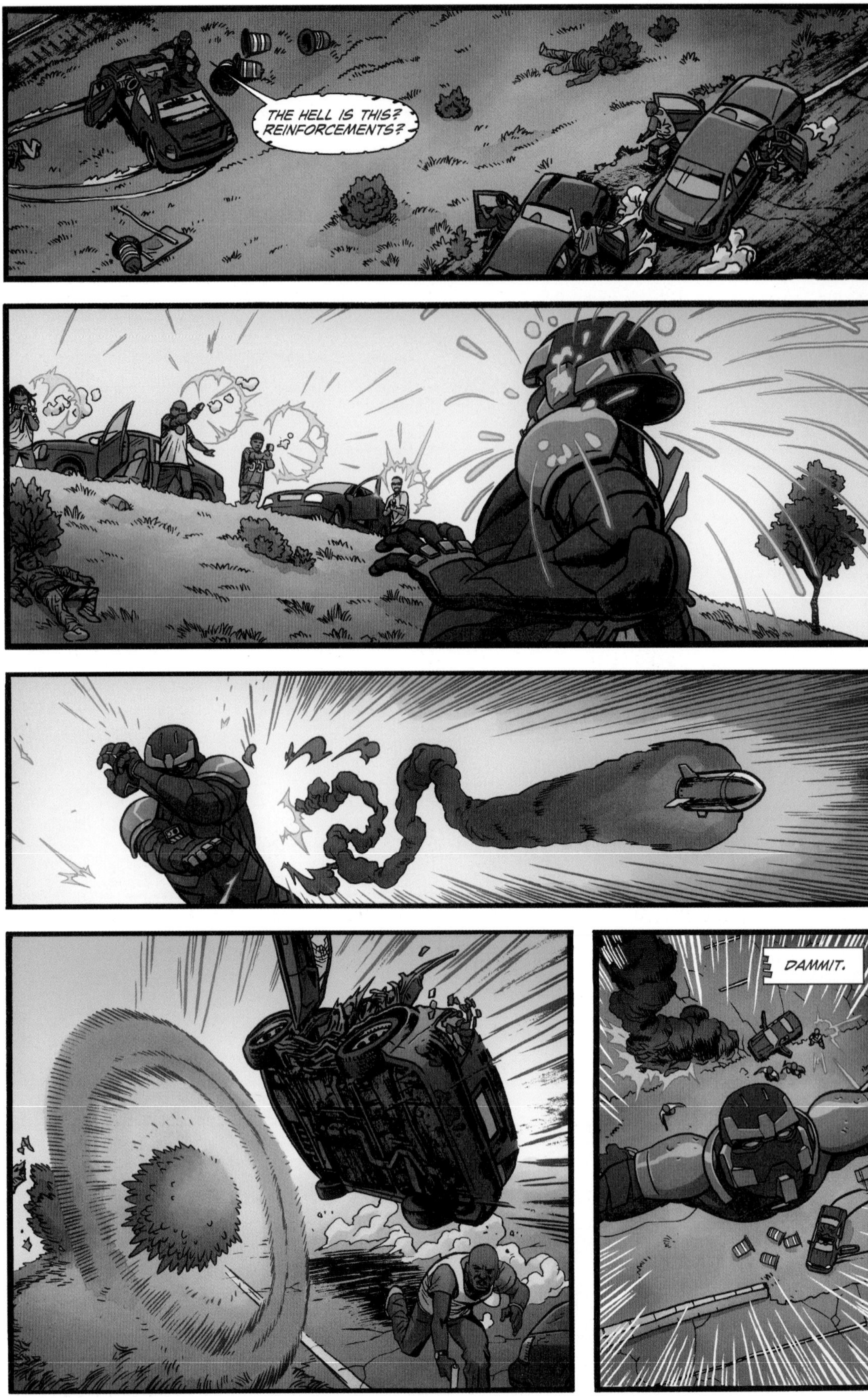
THE HELL IS THIS? REINFORCEMENTS?
DAMMIT.

CHRIST, WHAT A DAY...

--BRINGING YOU MORE ON THIS STORY AS IT DEVELOPS. RIGHT NOW, WE KNOW VERY LITTLE.

DAD? ARE YOU UPSTAIRS? YOU LEFT THE TV ON.

ONCE AGAIN-- IT APPEARS AS THOUGH THE VIGILANTE STEALTH ATTACKED A POLICE CAR ON THE LODGE FREEWAY THIS AFTERNOON, RESULTING IN A FIREFIGHT WITH POLICE. FIVE OFFICERS WERE INJURED.

WHAT THE HELL ARE THEY TALKING ABOUT?

CRASH KA-THUMP

DAD?

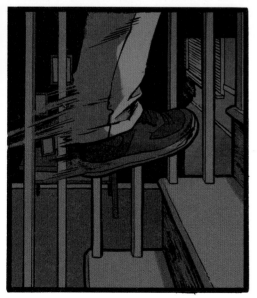

DAD? ARE YOU OKAY?

DAD...?

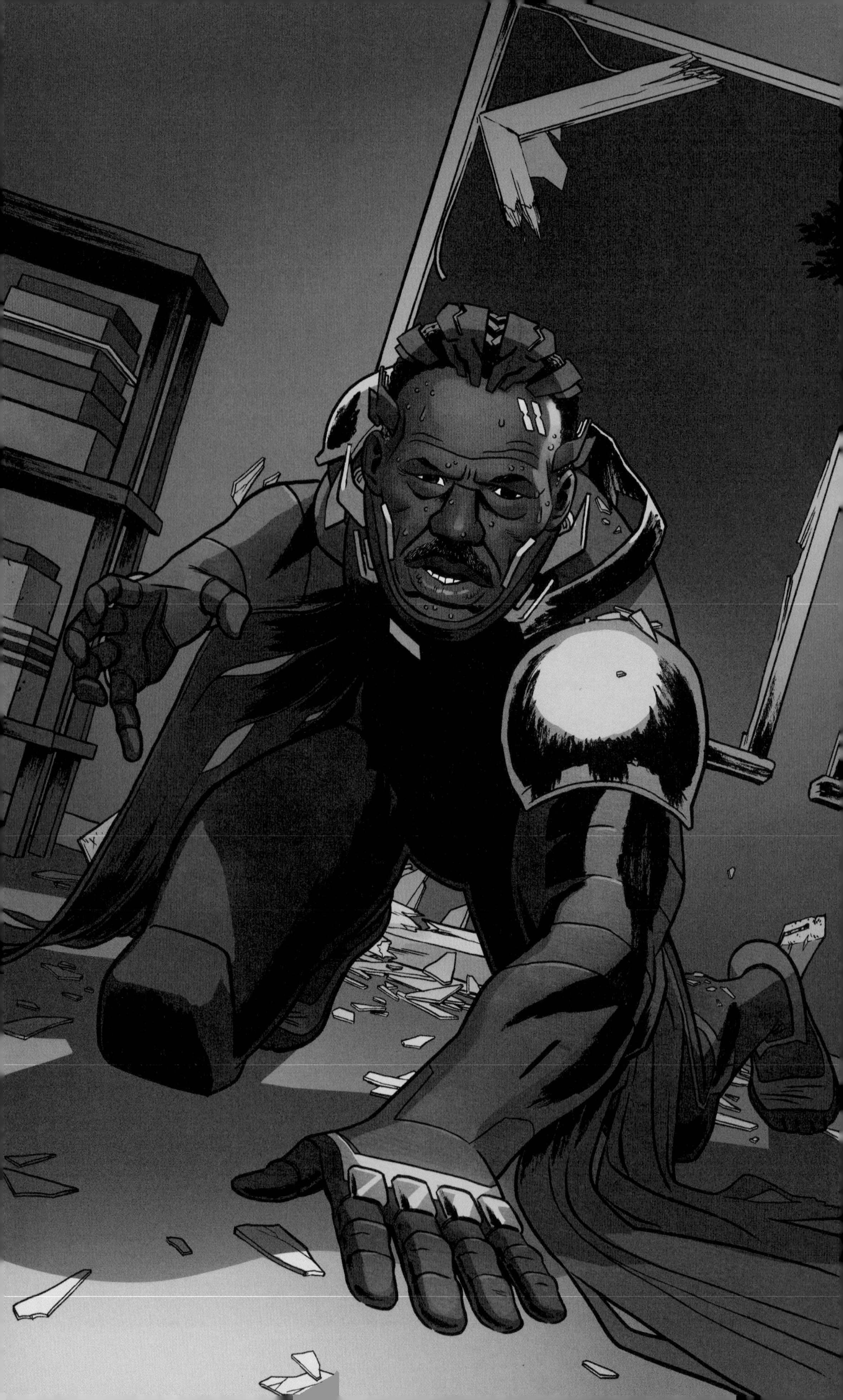

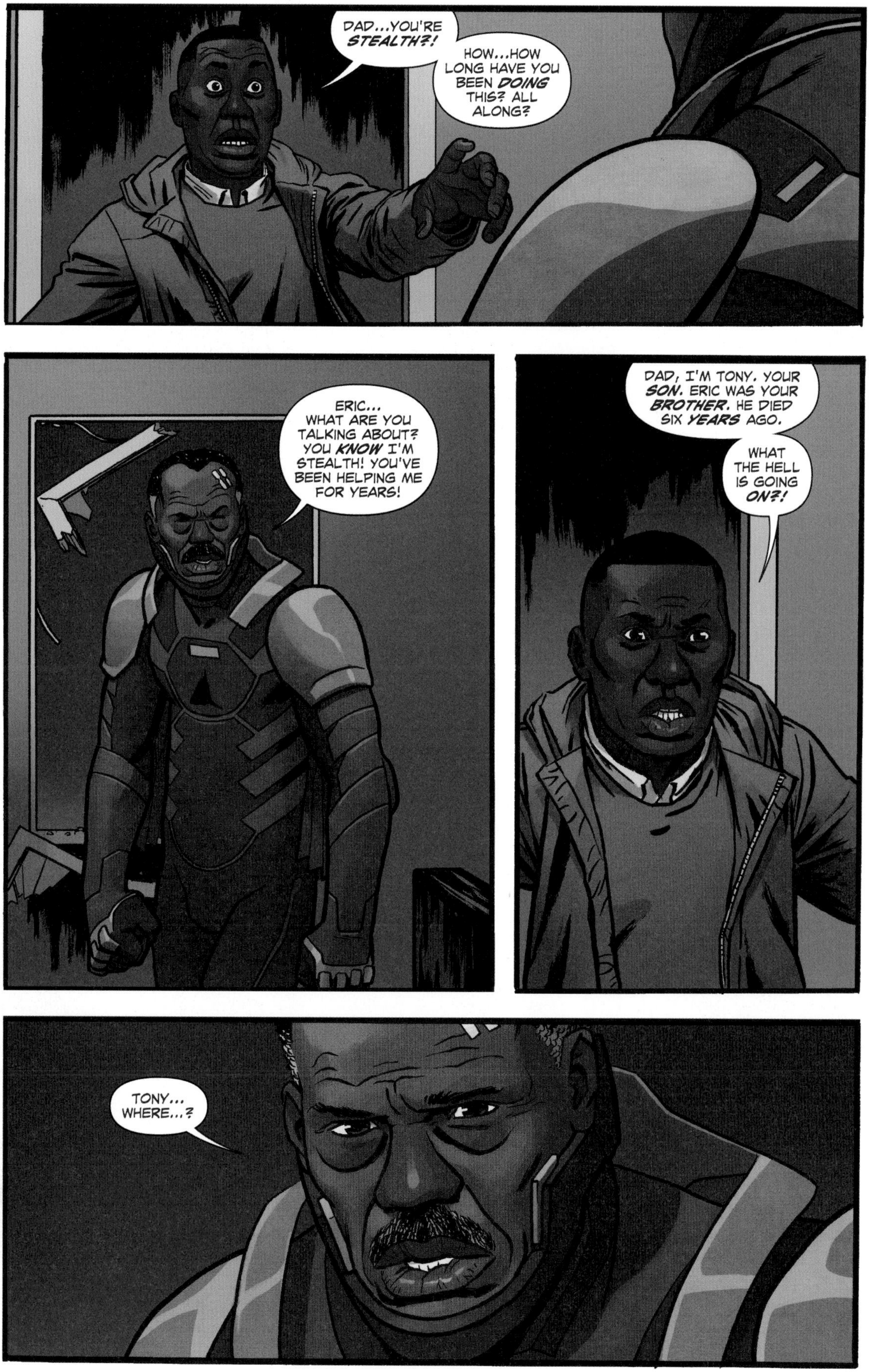

DAD...YOU'RE STEALTH?!
HOW...HOW LONG HAVE YOU BEEN DOING THIS? ALL ALONG?
ERIC... WHAT ARE YOU TALKING ABOUT? YOU KNOW I'M STEALTH! YOU'VE BEEN HELPING ME FOR YEARS!
DAD, I'M TONY. YOUR SON. ERIC WAS YOUR BROTHER. HE DIED SIX YEARS AGO.
WHAT THE HELL IS GOING ON?!
TONY... WHERE...?

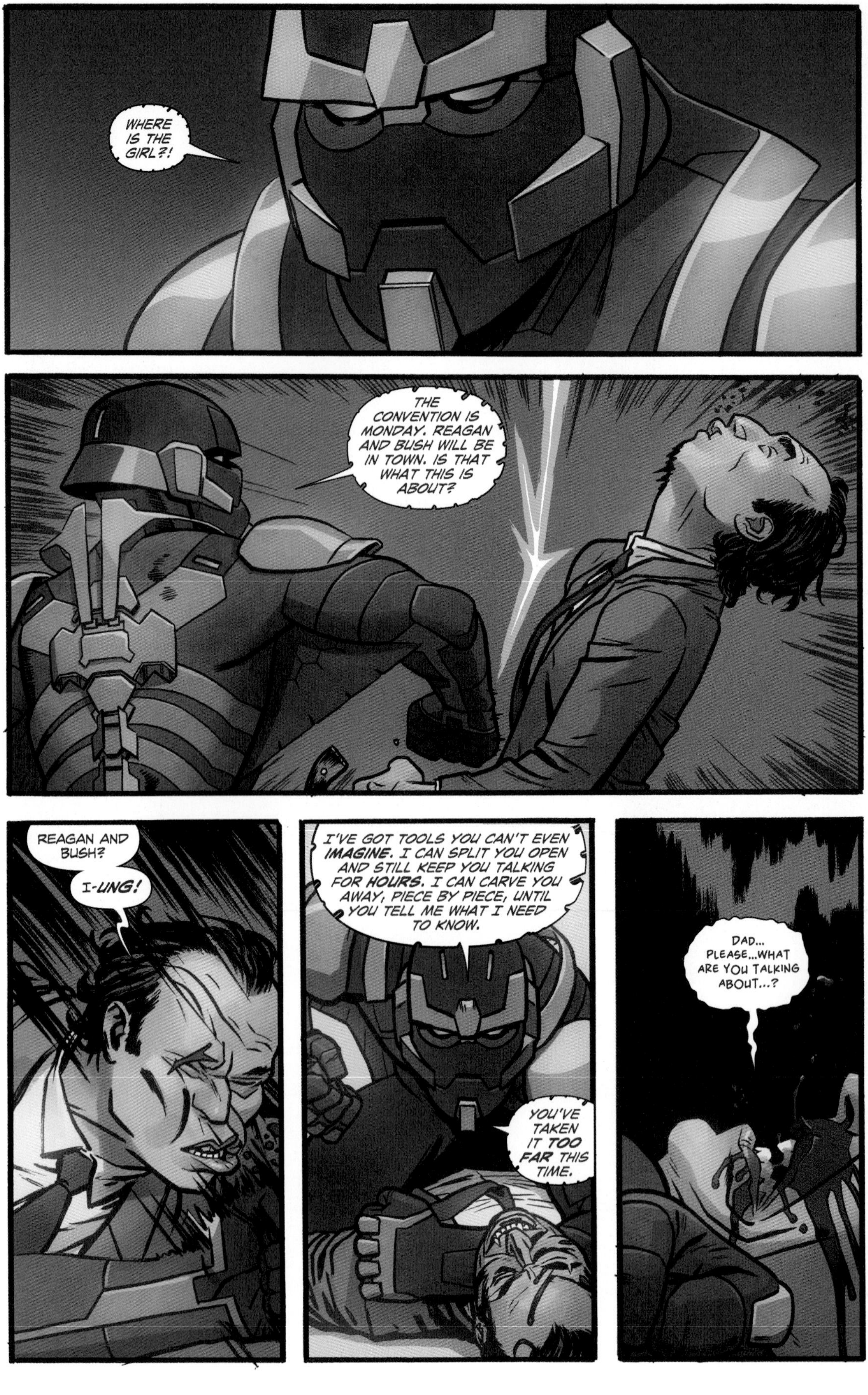
WHERE IS THE GIRL?!
THE CONVENTION IS MONDAY. REAGAN AND BUSH WILL BE IN TOWN. IS THAT WHAT THIS IS ABOUT?
REAGAN AND BUSH?
I-UNG!
I'VE GOT TOOLS YOU CAN'T EVEN IMAGINE. I CAN SPLIT YOU OPEN AND STILL KEEP YOU TALKING FOR HOURS. I CAN CARVE YOU AWAY, PIECE BY PIECE, UNTIL YOU TELL ME WHAT I NEED TO KNOW.
YOU'VE TAKEN IT TOO FAR THIS TIME.
DAD... PLEASE...WHAT ARE YOU TALKING ABOUT...?

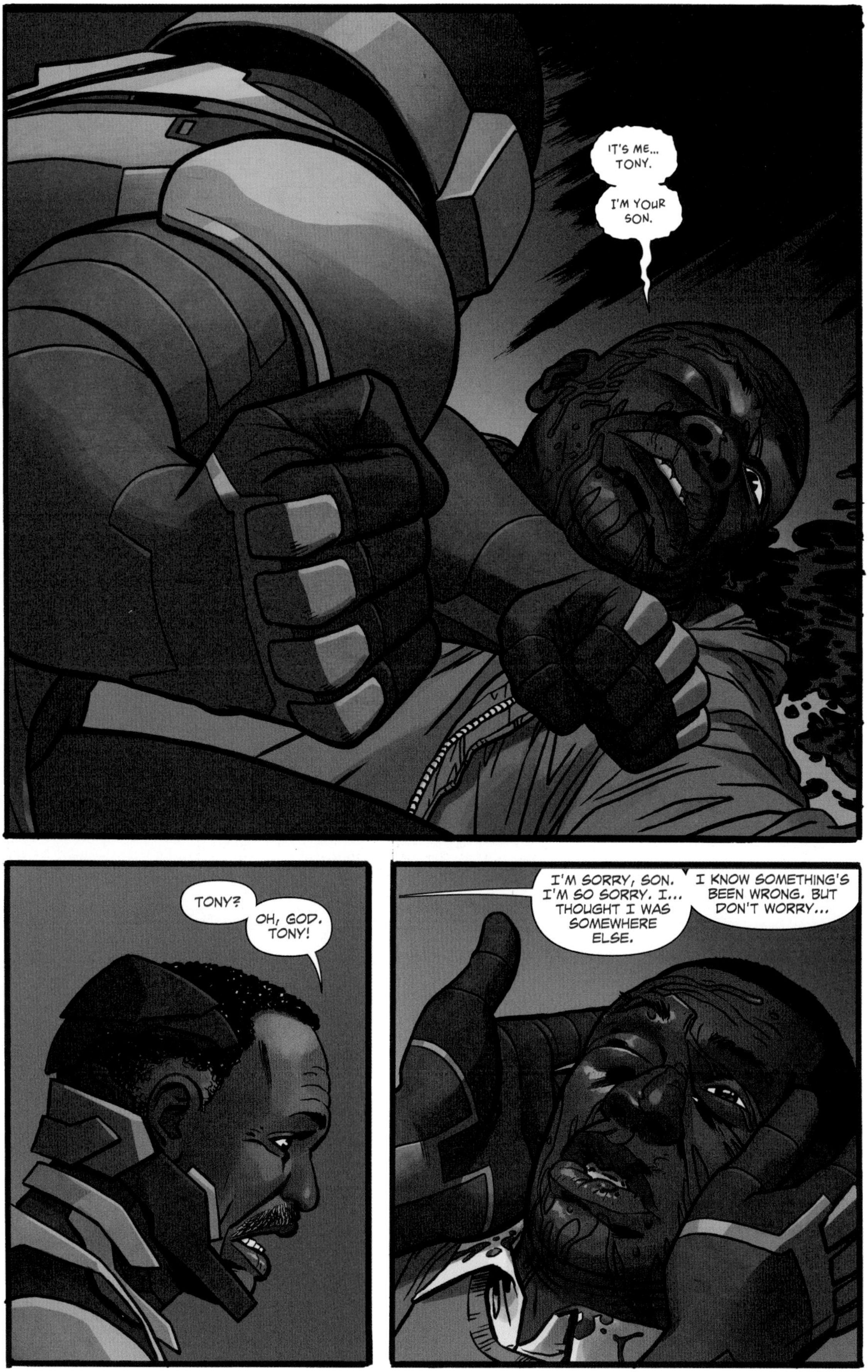
IT'S ME... TONY.
I'M YOUR SON.
TONY?
OH, GOD. TONY!
I'M SORRY, SON. I'M SO SORRY. I... THOUGHT I WAS SOMEWHERE ELSE.
I KNOW SOMETHING'S BEEN WRONG. BUT DON'T WORRY...

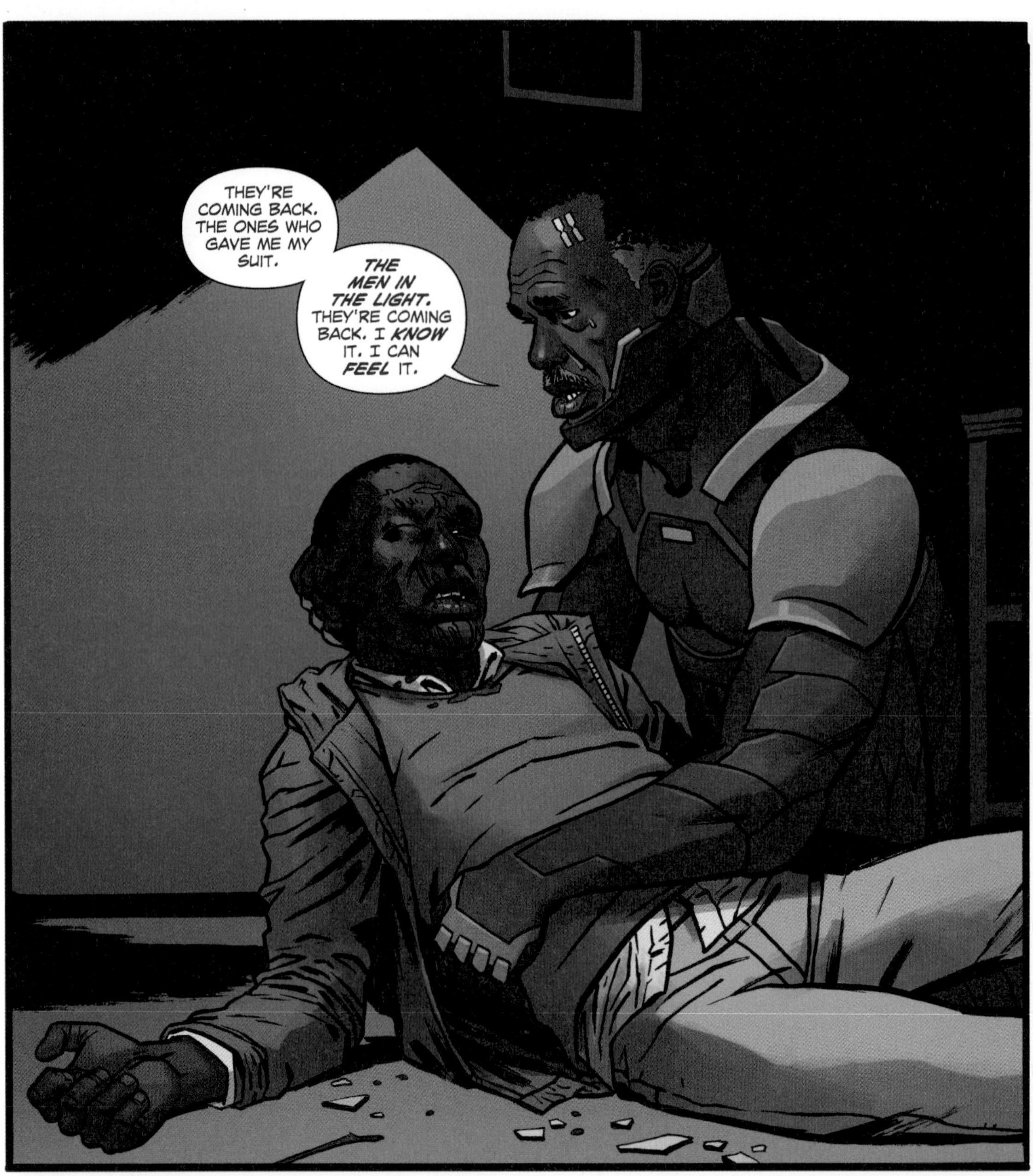
THEY'RE COMING BACK. THE ONES WHO GAVE ME MY SUIT.
THE MEN IN THE LIGHT. THEY'RE COMING BACK. I *KNOW* IT. I CAN *FEEL* IT.

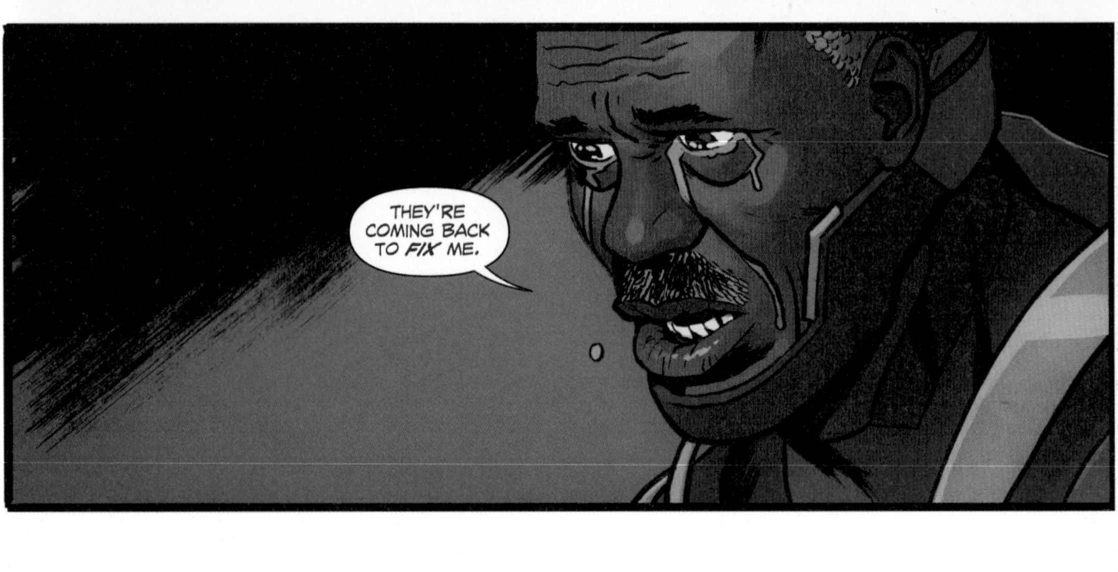
THEY'RE COMING BACK TO *FIX* ME.

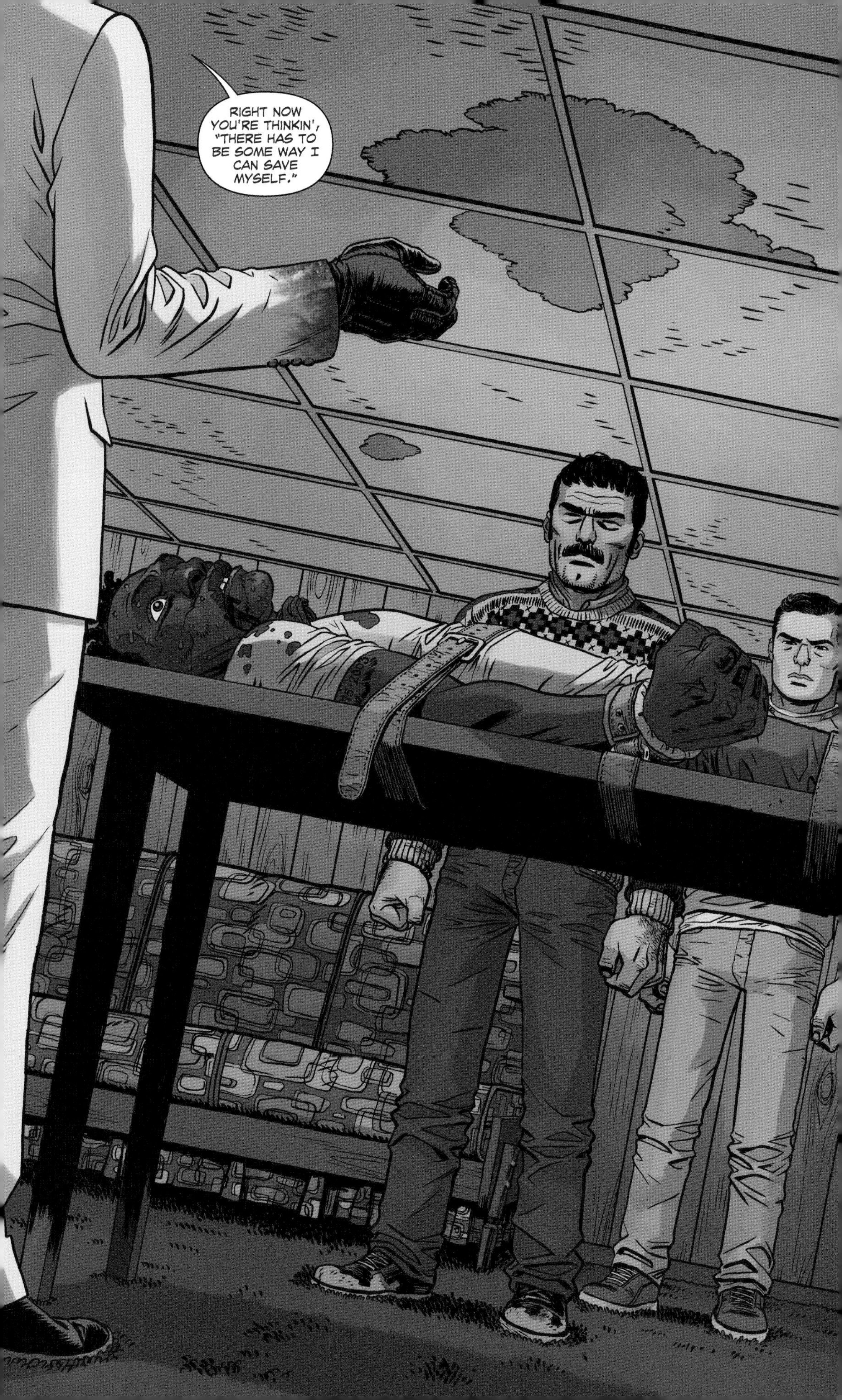
RIGHT NOW YOU'RE THINKIN', "THERE HAS TO BE SOME WAY I CAN SAVE MYSELF."

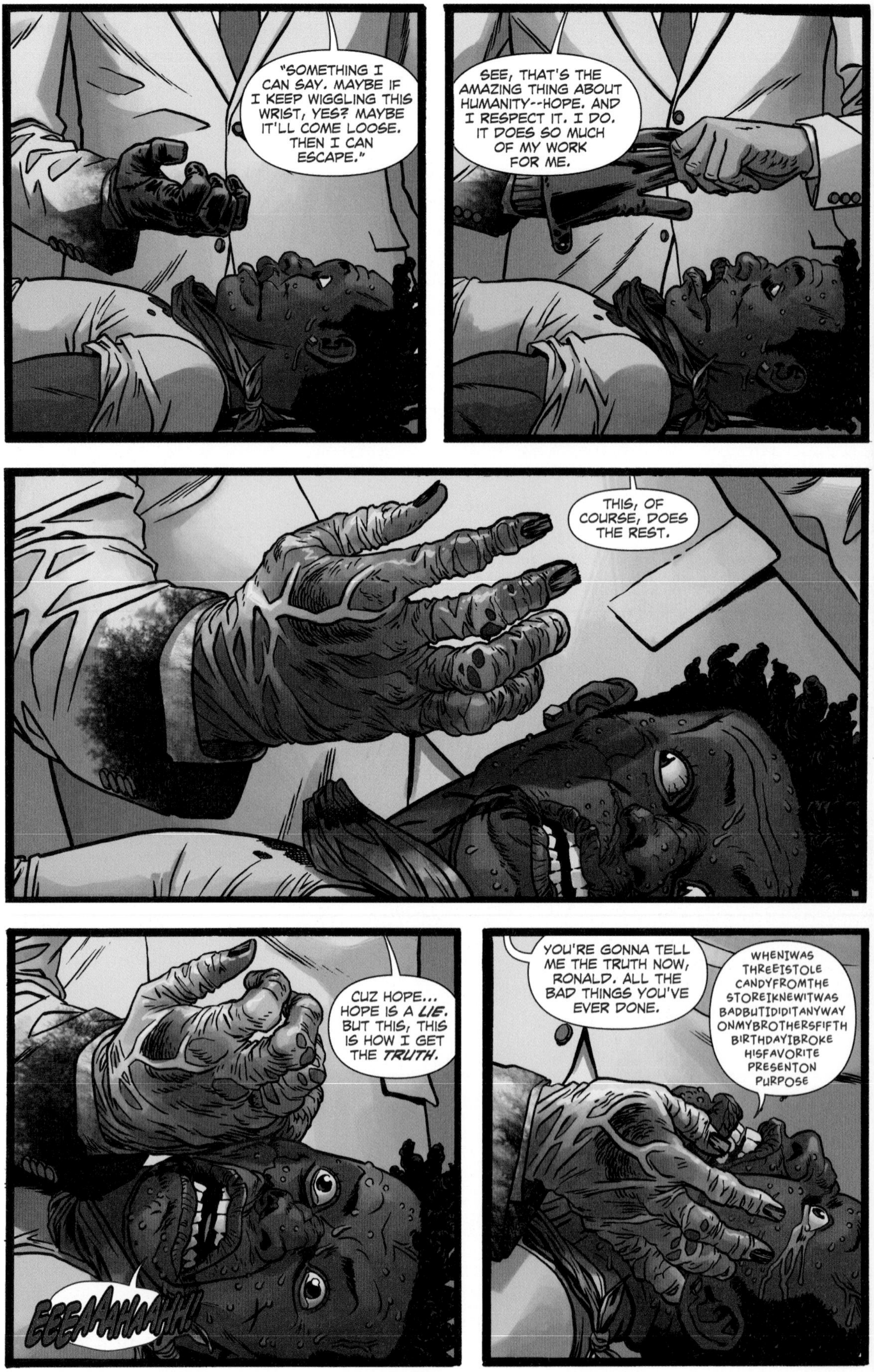
"SOMETHING I CAN SAY. MAYBE IF I KEEP WIGGLING THIS WRIST, YES? MAYBE IT'LL COME LOOSE. THEN I CAN ESCAPE."
SEE, THAT'S THE AMAZING THING ABOUT HUMANITY--HOPE. AND I RESPECT IT. I DO. IT DOES SO MUCH OF MY WORK FOR ME.
THIS, OF COURSE, DOES THE REST.
CUZ HOPE... HOPE IS A *LIE*. BUT THIS, THIS IS HOW I GET THE *TRUTH*.
EEEAAAHAAAHH!
YOU'RE GONNA TELL ME THE TRUTH NOW, RONALD. ALL THE BAD THINGS YOU'VE EVER DONE.
WHENIWAS THREEISTOLE CANDYFROMTHE STOREIKNEWITWAS BADBUTIDIDITANYWAY ONMYBROTHERSFIFTH BIRTHDAYIBROKE HISFAVORITE PRESENTON PURPOSE

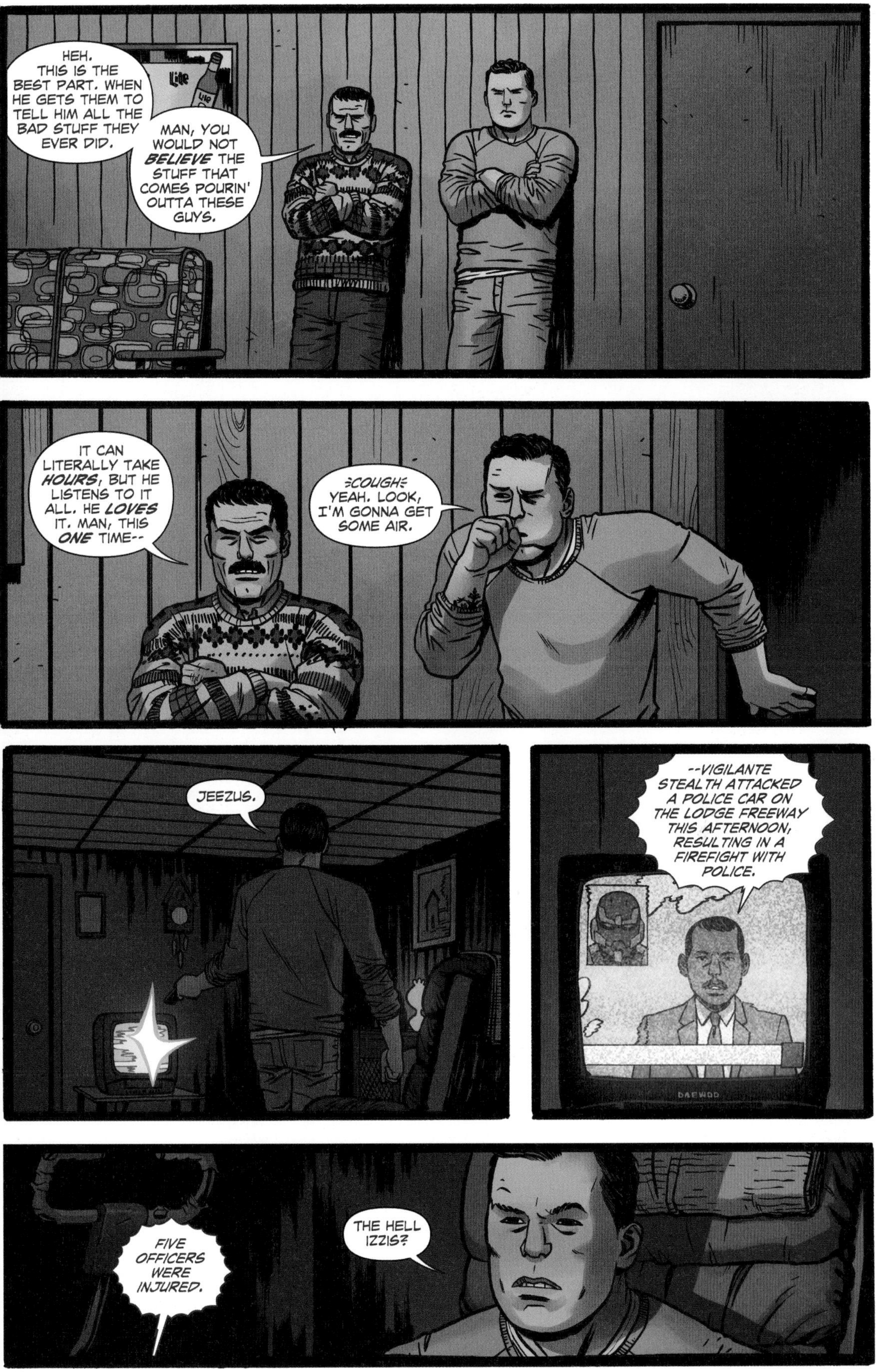
HEH. THIS IS THE BEST PART. WHEN HE GETS THEM TO TELL HIM ALL THE BAD STUFF THEY EVER DID.
MAN, YOU WOULD NOT BELIEVE THE STUFF THAT COMES POURIN' OUTTA THESE GUYS.
IT CAN LITERALLY TAKE HOURS, BUT HE LISTENS TO IT ALL. HE LOVES IT. MAN, THIS ONE TIME--
COUGH YEAH. LOOK, I'M GONNA GET SOME AIR.
JEEZUS.
--VIGILANTE STEALTH ATTACKED A POLICE CAR ON THE LODGE FREEWAY THIS AFTERNOON, RESULTING IN A FIREFIGHT WITH POLICE.
DAEWOO
FIVE OFFICERS WERE INJURED.
THE HELL IZZIS?

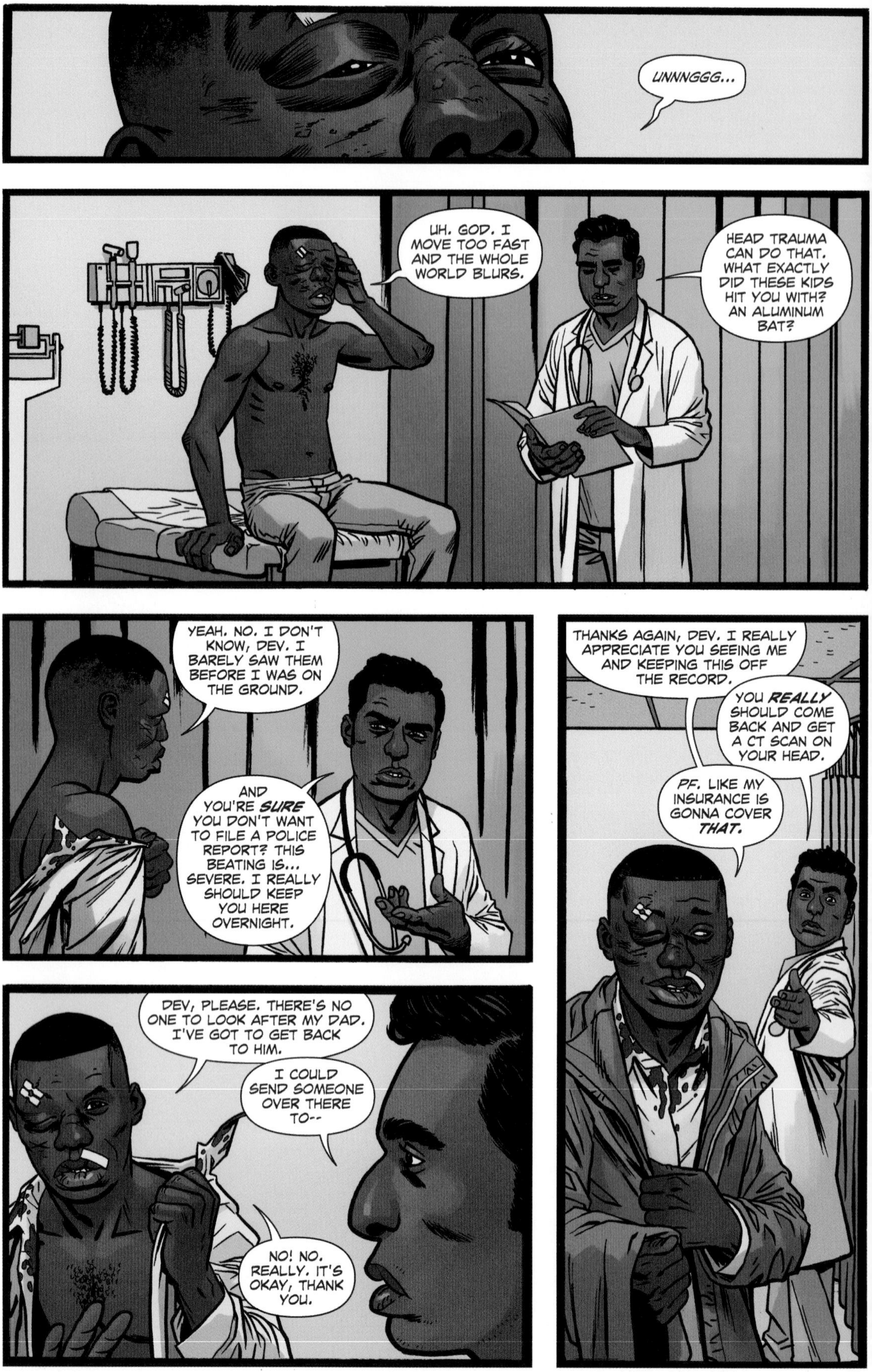
UNNNGGG...
UH. GOD. I MOVE TOO FAST AND THE WHOLE WORLD BLURS.
HEAD TRAUMA CAN DO THAT. WHAT EXACTLY DID THESE KIDS HIT YOU WITH? AN ALUMINUM BAT?
YEAH. NO. I DON'T KNOW, DEV. I BARELY SAW THEM BEFORE I WAS ON THE GROUND.
AND YOU'RE SURE YOU DON'T WANT TO FILE A POLICE REPORT? THIS BEATING IS... SEVERE. I REALLY SHOULD KEEP YOU HERE OVERNIGHT.
DEV, PLEASE. THERE'S NO ONE TO LOOK AFTER MY DAD. I'VE GOT TO GET BACK TO HIM.
I COULD SEND SOMEONE OVER THERE TO--
NO! NO. REALLY. IT'S OKAY, THANK YOU.
THANKS AGAIN, DEV. I REALLY APPRECIATE YOU SEEING ME AND KEEPING THIS OFF THE RECORD.
YOU REALLY SHOULD COME BACK AND GET A CT SCAN ON YOUR HEAD.
PF. LIKE MY INSURANCE IS GONNA COVER THAT.

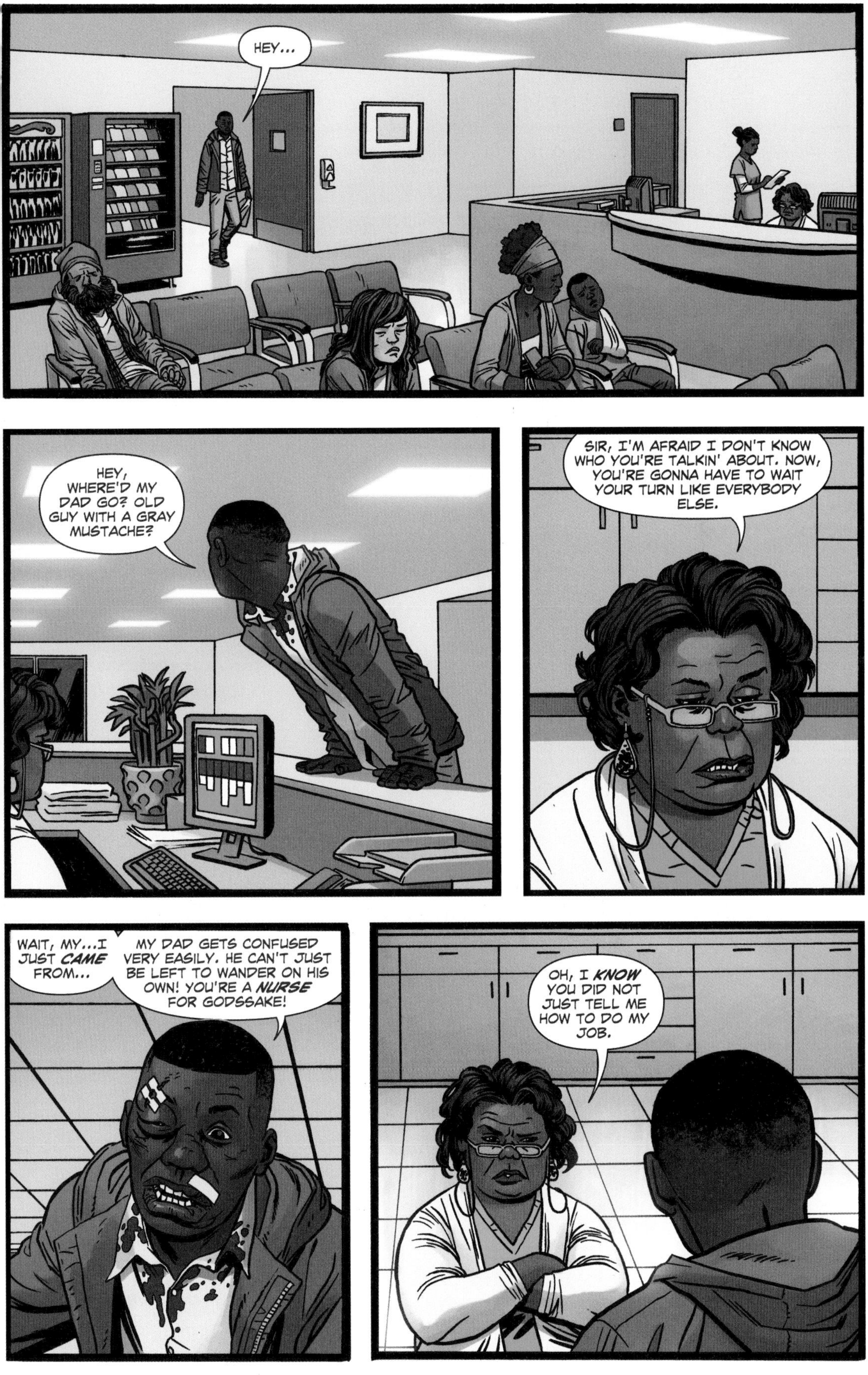
HEY...
HEY, WHERE'D MY DAD GO? OLD GUY WITH A GRAY MUSTACHE?
SIR, I'M AFRAID I DON'T KNOW WHO YOU'RE TALKIN' ABOUT. NOW, YOU'RE GONNA HAVE TO WAIT YOUR TURN LIKE EVERYBODY ELSE.
WAIT, MY...I JUST CAME FROM...
MY DAD GETS CONFUSED VERY EASILY. HE CAN'T JUST BE LEFT TO WANDER ON HIS OWN! YOU'RE A NURSE FOR GODSSAKE!
OH, I KNOW YOU DID NOT JUST TELL ME HOW TO DO MY JOB.

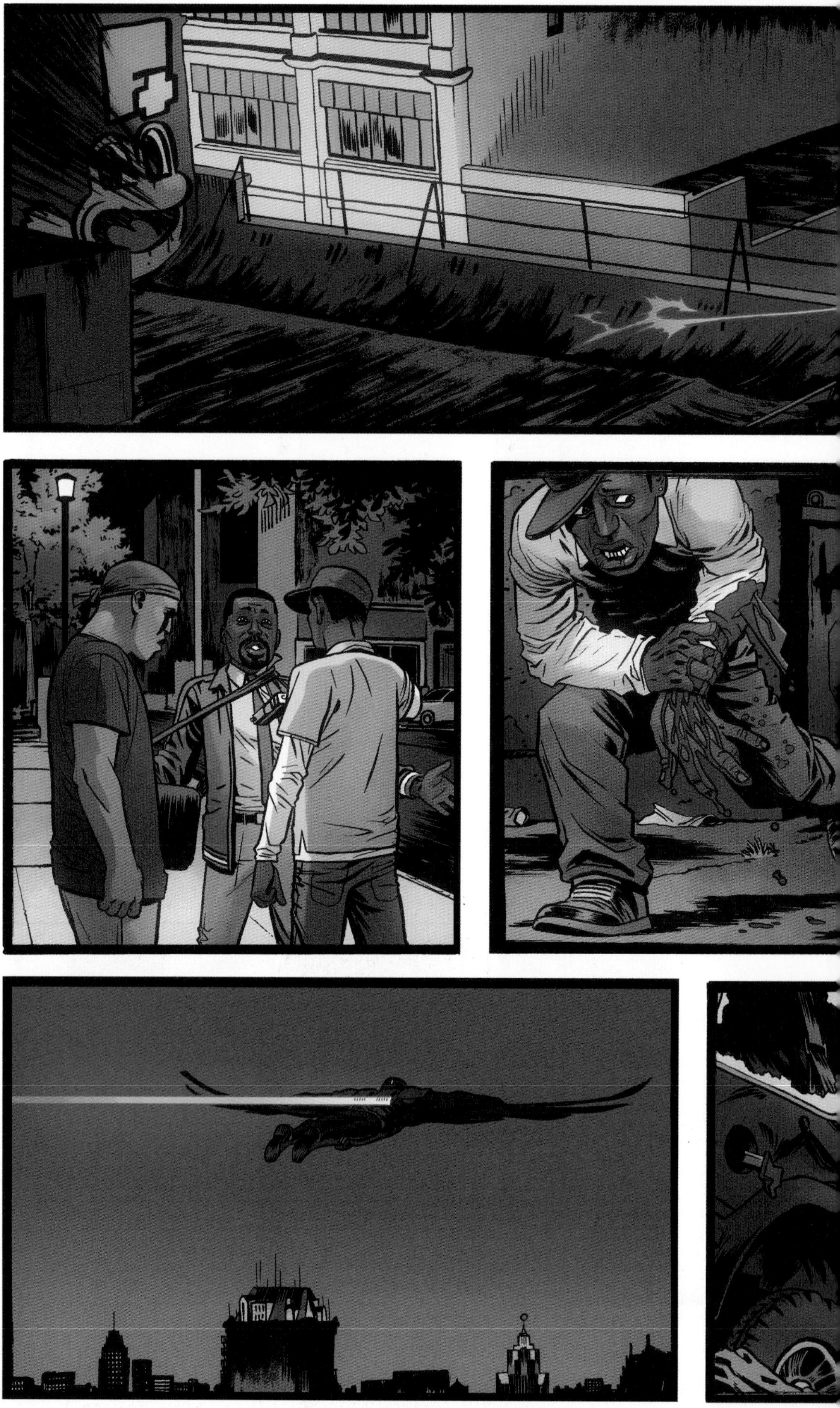

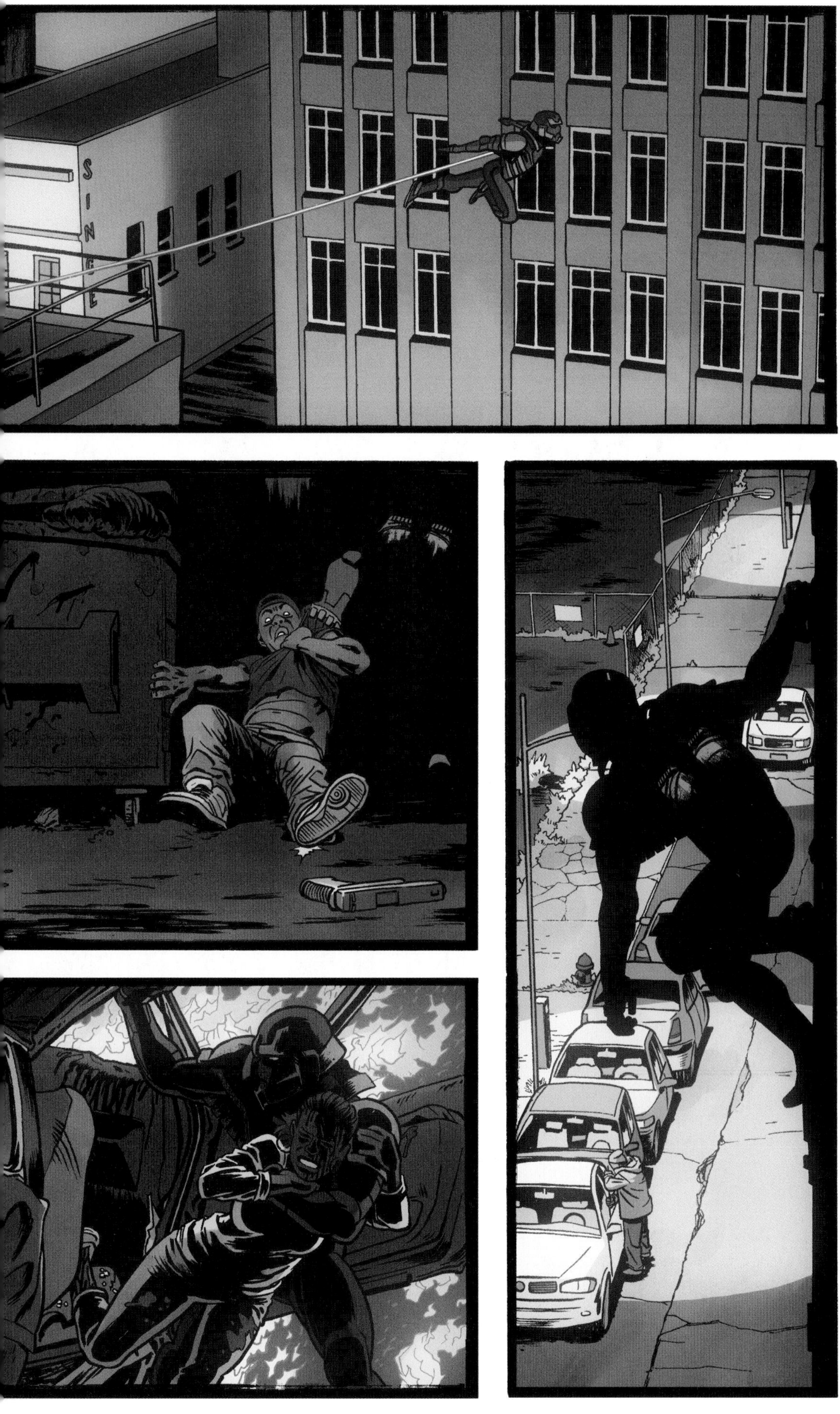
SINGE

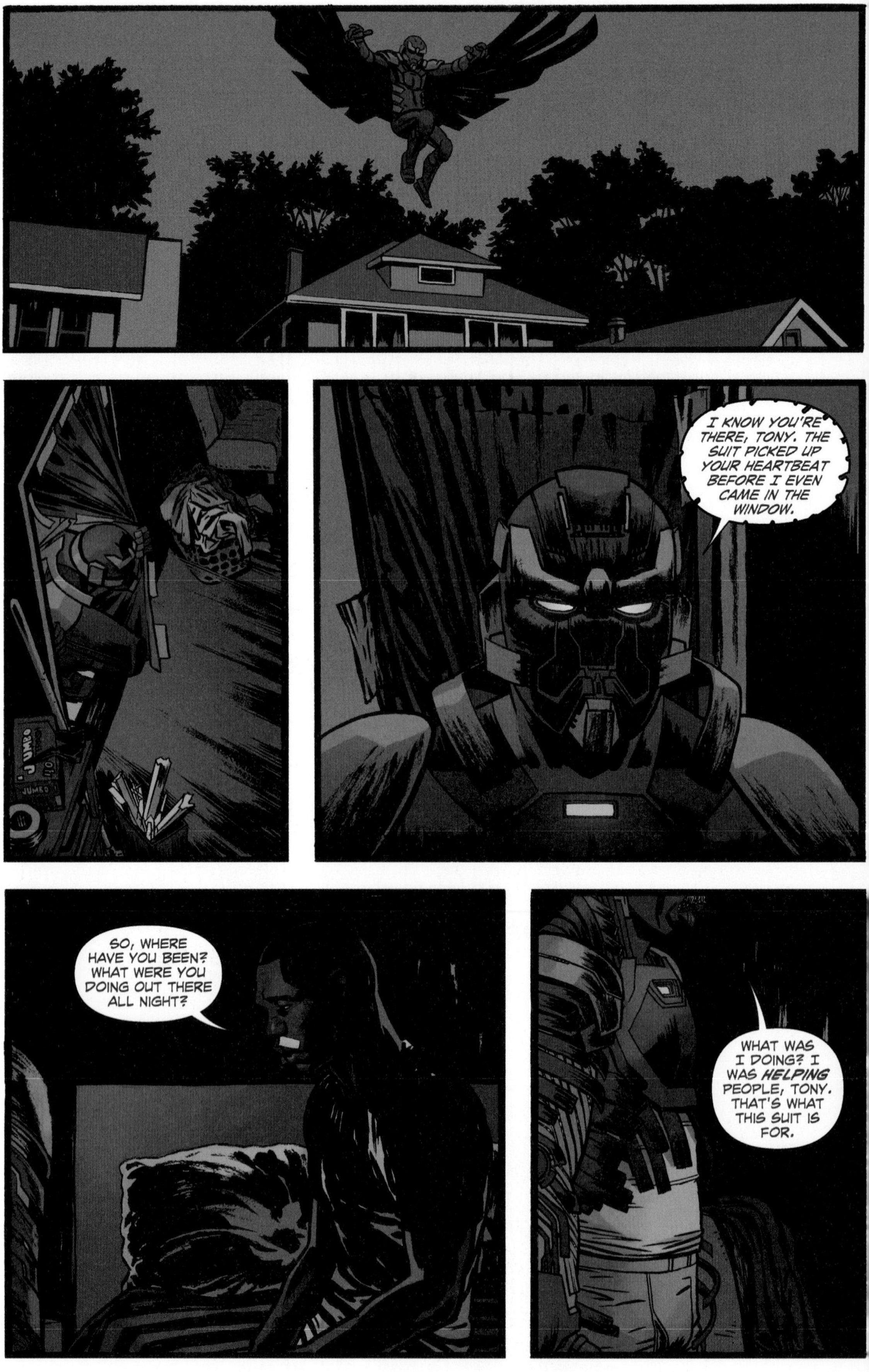
I KNOW YOU'RE THERE, TONY. THE SUIT PICKED UP YOUR HEARTBEAT BEFORE I EVEN CAME IN THE WINDOW.
SO, WHERE HAVE YOU BEEN? WHAT WERE YOU DOING OUT THERE ALL NIGHT?
WHAT WAS I DOING? I WAS *HELPING* PEOPLE, TONY. THAT'S WHAT THIS SUIT IS FOR.

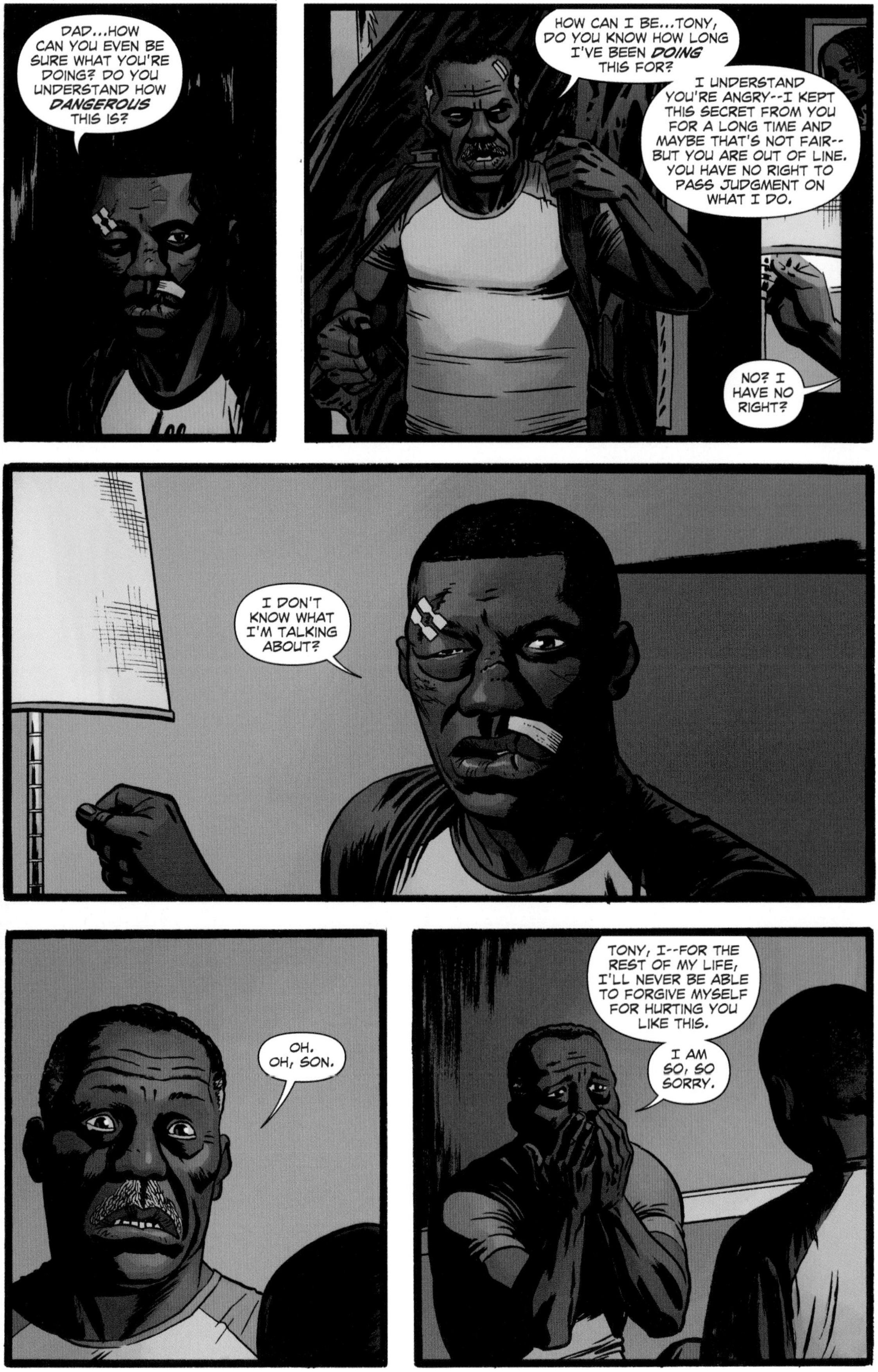
DAD...HOW CAN YOU EVEN BE SURE WHAT YOU'RE DOING? DO YOU UNDERSTAND HOW DANGEROUS THIS IS?
HOW CAN I BE...TONY, DO YOU KNOW HOW LONG I'VE BEEN DOING THIS FOR?
I UNDERSTAND YOU'RE ANGRY--I KEPT THIS SECRET FROM YOU FOR A LONG TIME AND MAYBE THAT'S NOT FAIR--BUT YOU ARE OUT OF LINE. YOU HAVE NO RIGHT TO PASS JUDGMENT ON WHAT I DO.
NO? I HAVE NO RIGHT?
I DON'T KNOW WHAT I'M TALKING ABOUT?
OH. OH, SON.
TONY, I--FOR THE REST OF MY LIFE, I'LL NEVER BE ABLE TO FORGIVE MYSELF FOR HURTING YOU LIKE THIS.
I AM SO, SO SORRY.

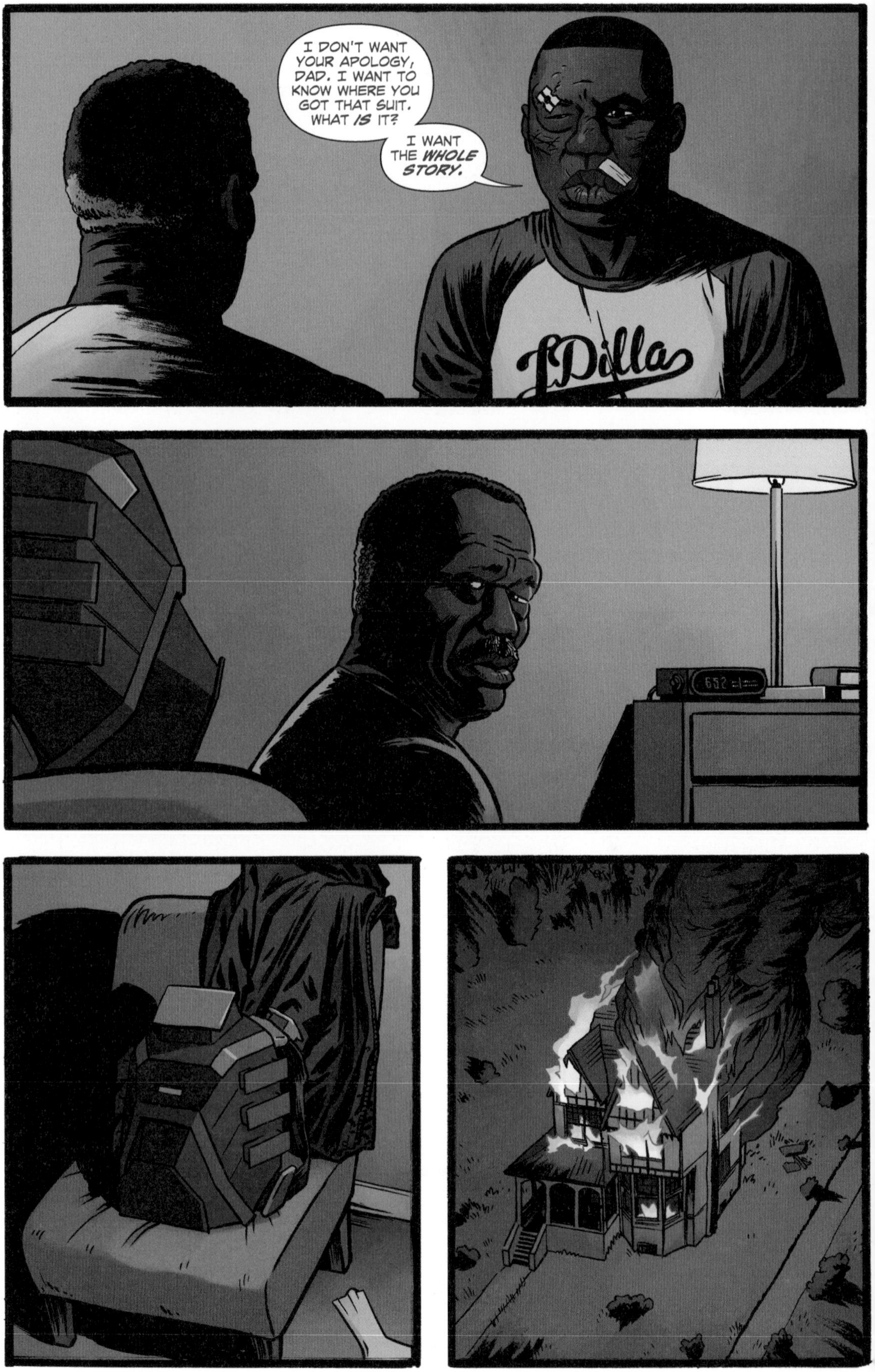
I DON'T WANT YOUR APOLOGY, DAD. I WANT TO KNOW WHERE YOU GOT THAT SUIT. WHAT *IS* IT?
I WANT THE *WHOLE STORY.*
J Dilla

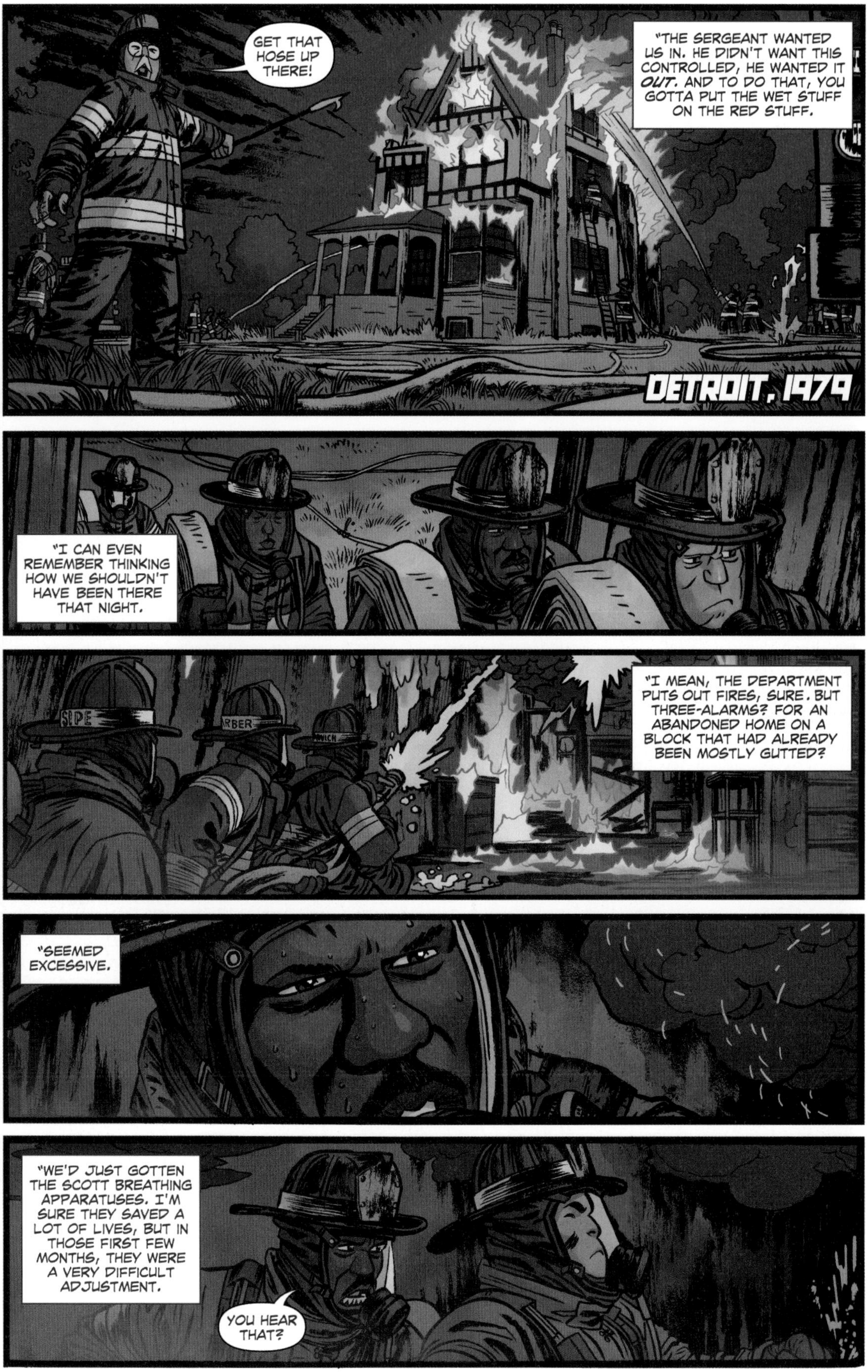
GET THAT HOSE UP THERE!
"THE SERGEANT WANTED US IN. HE DIDN'T WANT THIS CONTROLLED, HE WANTED IT *OUT*. AND TO DO THAT, YOU GOTTA PUT THE WET STUFF ON THE RED STUFF.
DETROIT, 1979
"I CAN EVEN REMEMBER THINKING HOW WE SHOULDN'T HAVE BEEN THERE THAT NIGHT.
"I MEAN, THE DEPARTMENT PUTS OUT FIRES, SURE. BUT THREE-ALARMS? FOR AN ABANDONED HOME ON A BLOCK THAT HAD ALREADY BEEN MOSTLY GUTTED?
"SEEMED EXCESSIVE.
"WE'D JUST GOTTEN THE SCOTT BREATHING APPARATUSES. I'M SURE THEY SAVED A LOT OF LIVES, BUT IN THOSE FIRST FEW MONTHS, THEY WERE A VERY DIFFICULT ADJUSTMENT.
YOU HEAR THAT?

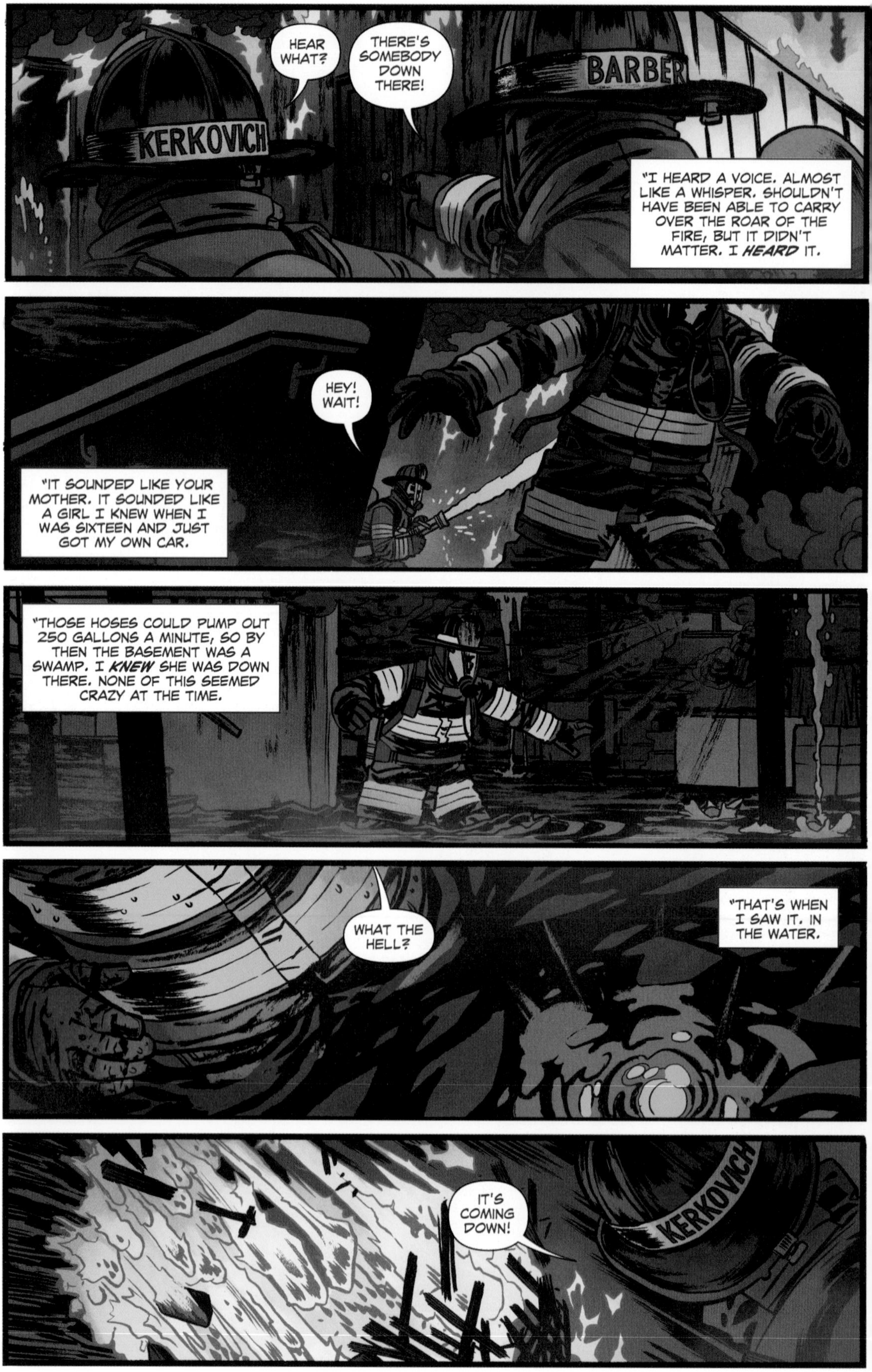
KERKOVICH
BARBER
HEAR WHAT?
THERE'S SOMEBODY DOWN THERE!
"I HEARD A VOICE. ALMOST LIKE A WHISPER. SHOULDN'T HAVE BEEN ABLE TO CARRY OVER THE ROAR OF THE FIRE, BUT IT DIDN'T MATTER. I HEARD IT.
HEY! WAIT!
"IT SOUNDED LIKE YOUR MOTHER. IT SOUNDED LIKE A GIRL I KNEW WHEN I WAS SIXTEEN AND JUST GOT MY OWN CAR.
"THOSE HOSES COULD PUMP OUT 250 GALLONS A MINUTE, SO BY THEN THE BASEMENT WAS A SWAMP. I KNEW SHE WAS DOWN THERE. NONE OF THIS SEEMED CRAZY AT THE TIME.
WHAT THE HELL?
"THAT'S WHEN I SAW IT. IN THE WATER.
IT'S COMING DOWN!
KERKOVICH

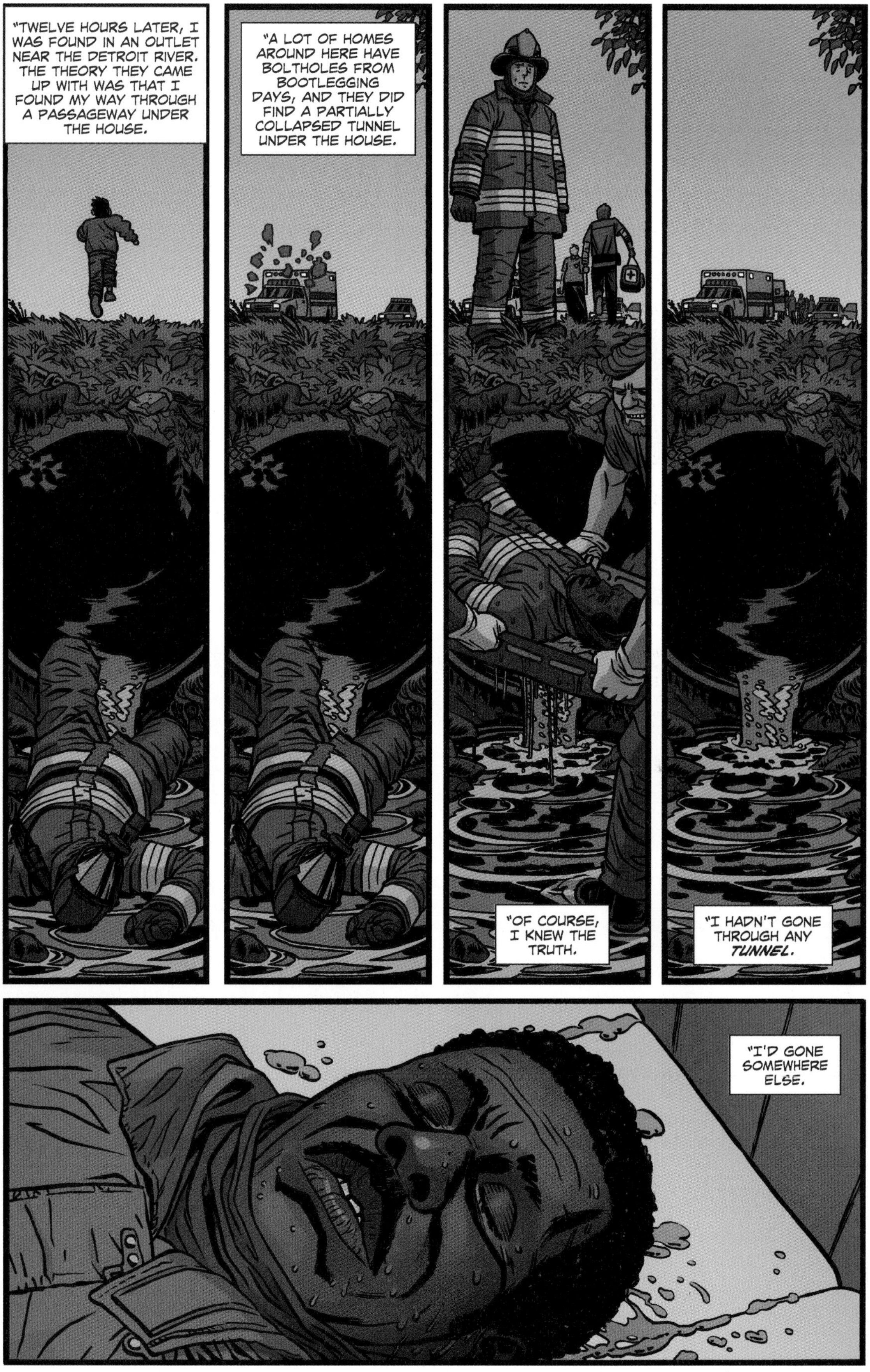
"TWELVE HOURS LATER, I WAS FOUND IN AN OUTLET NEAR THE DETROIT RIVER. THE THEORY THEY CAME UP WITH WAS THAT I FOUND MY WAY THROUGH A PASSAGEWAY UNDER THE HOUSE.
"A LOT OF HOMES AROUND HERE HAVE BOLTHOLES FROM BOOTLEGGING DAYS, AND THEY DID FIND A PARTIALLY COLLAPSED TUNNEL UNDER THE HOUSE.
"OF COURSE, I KNEW THE TRUTH.
"I HADN'T GONE THROUGH ANY *TUNNEL*.
"I'D GONE SOMEWHERE ELSE.

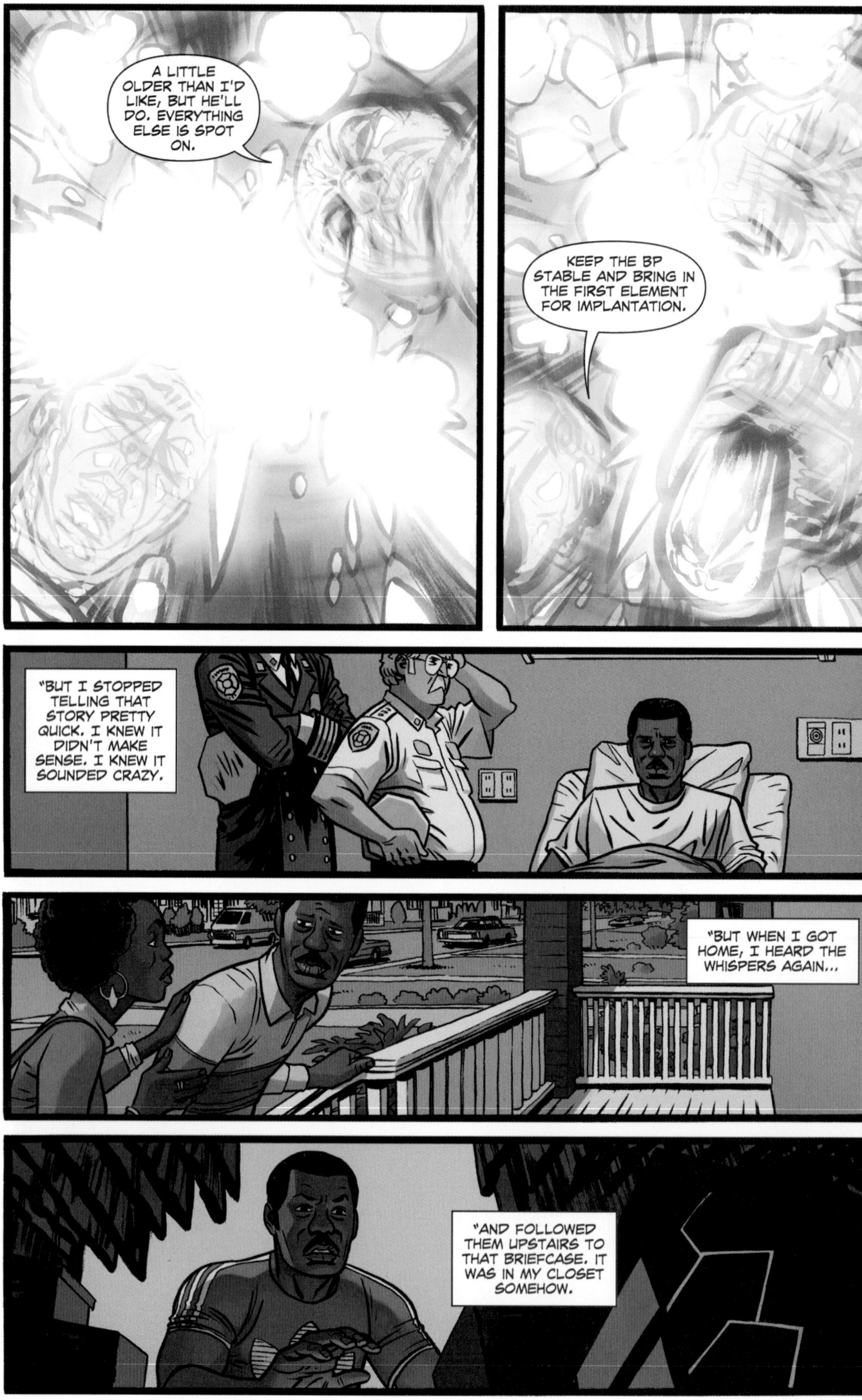
A LITTLE OLDER THAN I'D LIKE, BUT HE'LL DO. EVERYTHING ELSE IS SPOT ON.
KEEP THE BP STABLE AND BRING IN THE FIRST ELEMENT FOR IMPLANTATION.
"BUT I STOPPED TELLING THAT STORY PRETTY QUICK. I KNEW IT DIDN'T MAKE SENSE. I KNEW IT SOUNDED CRAZY.
"BUT WHEN I GOT HOME, I HEARD THE WHISPERS AGAIN...
"AND FOLLOWED THEM UPSTAIRS TO THAT BRIEFCASE. IT WAS IN MY CLOSET SOMEHOW.

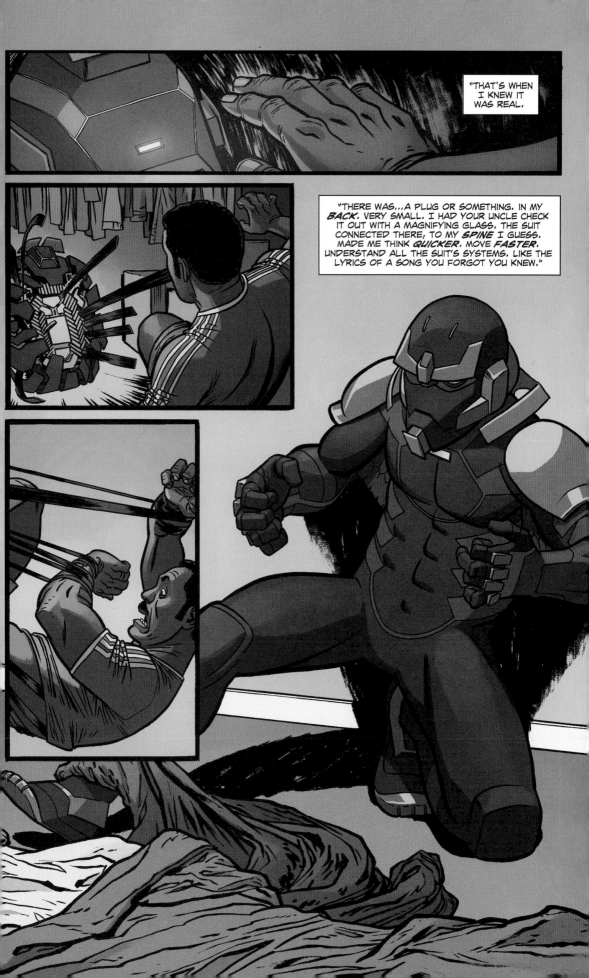

"THAT'S WHEN I KNEW IT WAS REAL."

"THERE WAS...A PLUG OR SOMETHING. IN MY *BACK*. VERY SMALL. I HAD YOUR UNCLE CHECK IT OUT WITH A MAGNIFYING GLASS. THE SUIT CONNECTED THERE, TO MY *SPINE* I GUESS. MADE ME THINK *QUICKER*. MOVE *FASTER*. UNDERSTAND ALL THE SUIT'S SYSTEMS. LIKE THE LYRICS OF A SONG YOU FORGOT YOU KNEW."

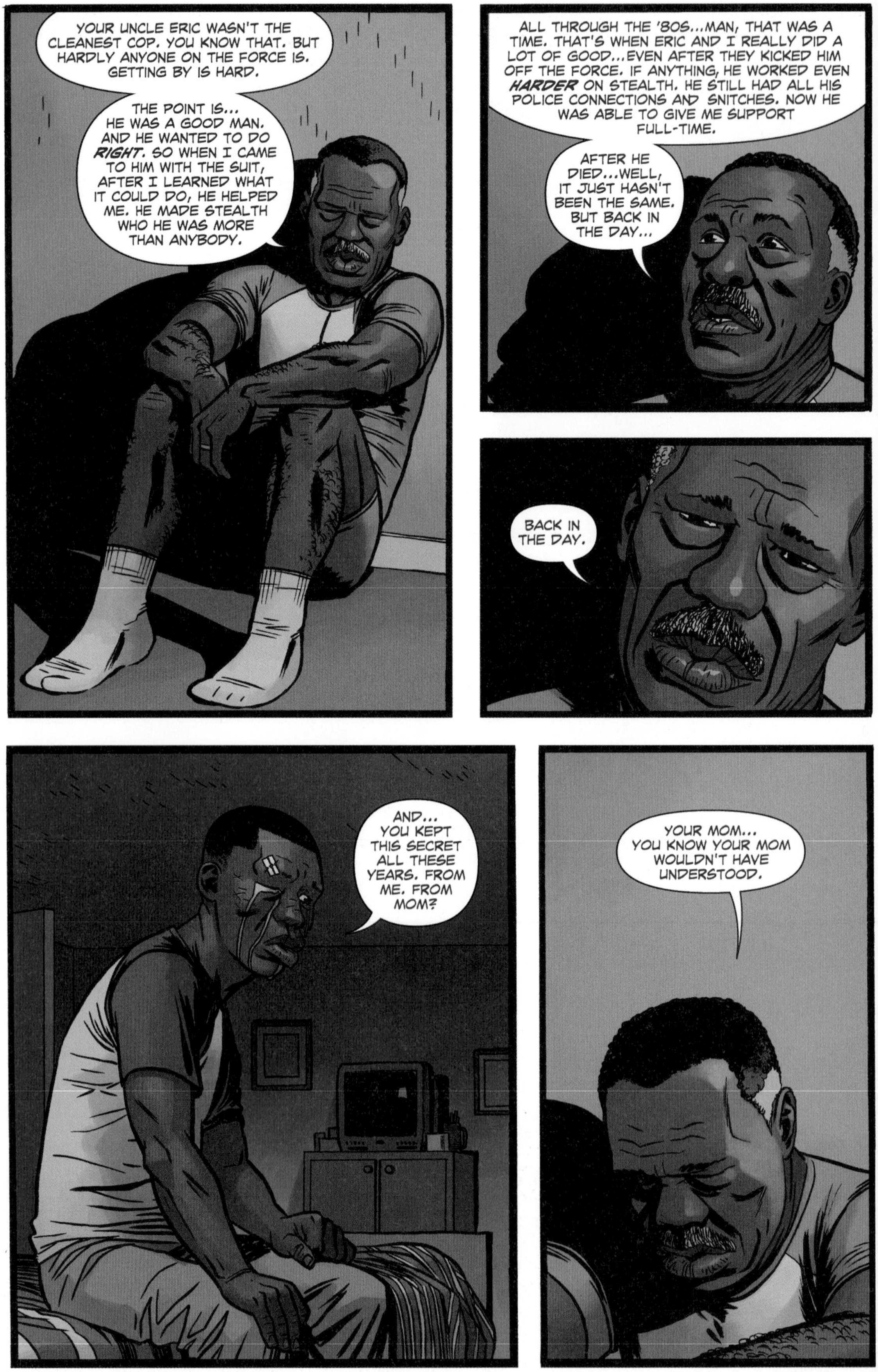
YOUR UNCLE ERIC WASN'T THE CLEANEST COP. YOU KNOW THAT. BUT HARDLY ANYONE ON THE FORCE IS. GETTING BY IS HARD.
THE POINT IS... HE WAS A GOOD MAN. AND HE WANTED TO DO RIGHT. SO WHEN I CAME TO HIM WITH THE SUIT, AFTER I LEARNED WHAT IT COULD DO, HE HELPED ME. HE MADE STEALTH WHO HE WAS MORE THAN ANYBODY.
ALL THROUGH THE '80S...MAN, THAT WAS A TIME. THAT'S WHEN ERIC AND I REALLY DID A LOT OF GOOD...EVEN AFTER THEY KICKED HIM OFF THE FORCE. IF ANYTHING, HE WORKED EVEN HARDER ON STEALTH. HE STILL HAD ALL HIS POLICE CONNECTIONS AND SNITCHES. NOW HE WAS ABLE TO GIVE ME SUPPORT FULL-TIME.
AFTER HE DIED...WELL, IT JUST HASN'T BEEN THE SAME. BUT BACK IN THE DAY...
BACK IN THE DAY.
AND... YOU KEPT THIS SECRET ALL THESE YEARS. FROM ME. FROM MOM?
YOUR MOM... YOU KNOW YOUR MOM WOULDN'T HAVE UNDERSTOOD.

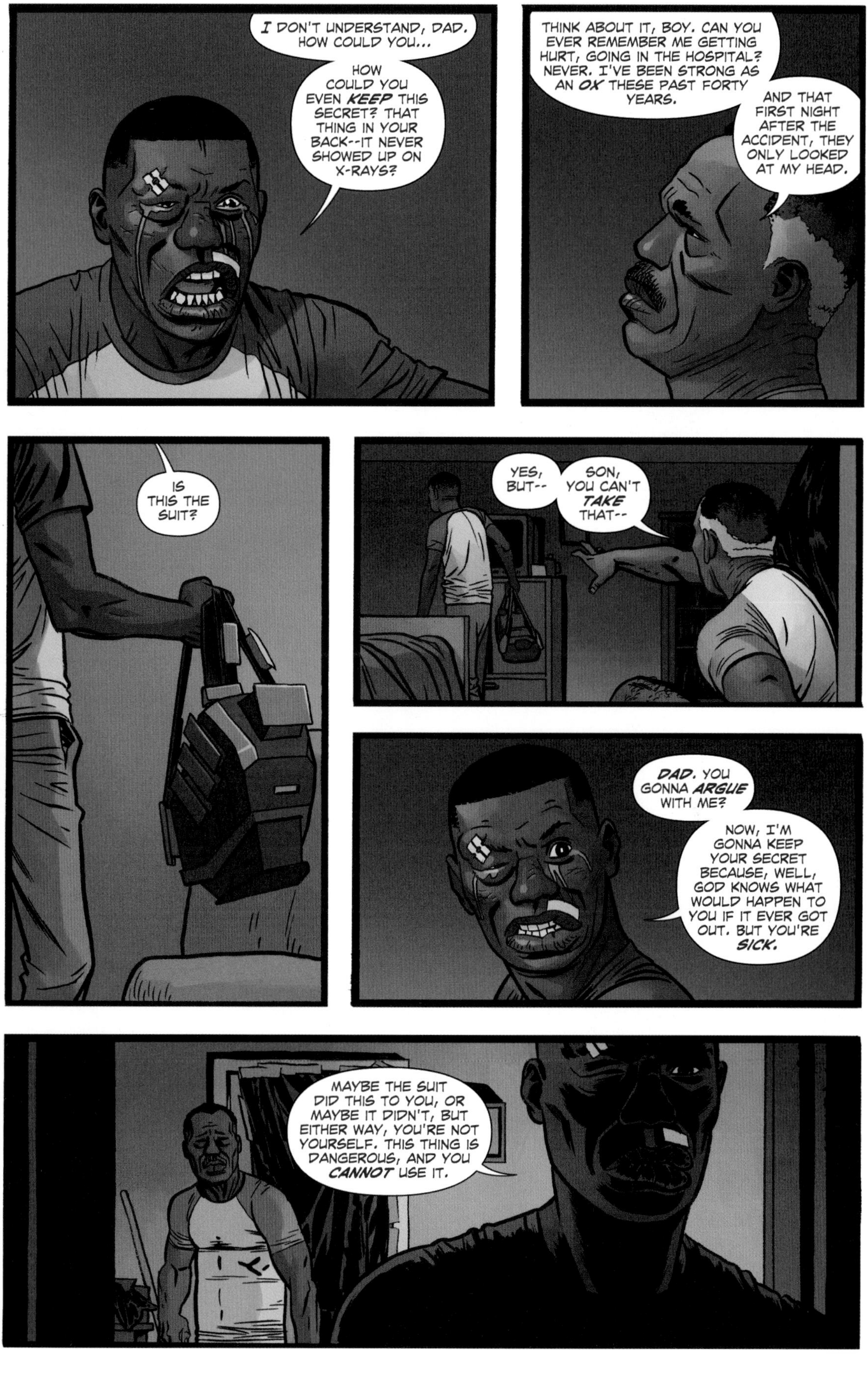
I DON'T UNDERSTAND, DAD. HOW COULD YOU...
HOW COULD YOU EVEN KEEP THIS SECRET? THAT THING IN YOUR BACK--IT NEVER SHOWED UP ON X-RAYS?
THINK ABOUT IT, BOY. CAN YOU EVER REMEMBER ME GETTING HURT, GOING IN THE HOSPITAL? NEVER. I'VE BEEN STRONG AS AN OX THESE PAST FORTY YEARS.
AND THAT FIRST NIGHT AFTER THE ACCIDENT, THEY ONLY LOOKED AT MY HEAD.
IS THIS THE SUIT?
YES, BUT--
SON, YOU CAN'T TAKE THAT--
DAD. YOU GONNA ARGUE WITH ME?
NOW, I'M GONNA KEEP YOUR SECRET BECAUSE, WELL, GOD KNOWS WHAT WOULD HAPPEN TO YOU IF IT EVER GOT OUT. BUT YOU'RE SICK.
MAYBE THE SUIT DID THIS TO YOU, OR MAYBE IT DIDN'T, BUT EITHER WAY, YOU'RE NOT YOURSELF. THIS THING IS DANGEROUS, AND YOU CANNOT USE IT.

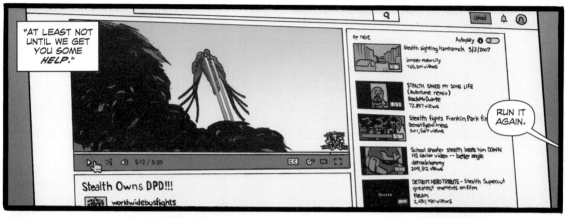

"AT LEAST NOT UNTIL WE GET YOU SOME *HELP*."

Stealth Owns DPD!!!

worldwidebusfights

Up next

Stealth sighting Hamtramck 5/3/2007
jumper motorcity
765,201 views

STEALTH SAVED MY SONS LIFE
(autotune remix)
BlackMrDuarte
72,857 views

Stealth fights Franklin Park fil
DetroitByewitness
501,567 views

School shooter stealth beats him DOWN
HS savior video -- better angle
detrockhammy
209,312 views

DETROIT HERO TRIBUTE - Stealth Supercut
greatest moments on film
fleam
2,680,790 views

RUN IT AGAIN.

THIS IS UNBELIEVABLE.

LOOK AT THIS--HE'S USING *ORDINANCE* ON THESE GUYS, ON *COPS*.

WHAT DO YOU THINK, BOSS? HE FINALLY HAD ENOUGH OF COPS GETTING IN HIS WAY? OR MAYBE THEY WERE DIRTY?

DIRTY? NO. I DON'T KNOW THEM. AND EVEN IF THEY *WERE* DOIN' THE DIRT FOR SOME OTHER MICKEY MOUSE CREW, HE GETS INTO IT WITH THE OTHER COPS THAT ROLL IN FOR BACK-UP. NO WAY THEY'RE ALL ON THE TAKE.

AND NO, I DON'T THINK HE'D JUST TURN AGAINST COPS EITHER. WE HAVE GUYS ON THE FORCE THAT USED TO BE CONVINCED HE *WAS* A COP BASED ON THE THINGS HE'D KNOW.

HE'S NEVER RAISED A HAND AGAINST THEM BEFORE. AND NOW? IN BROAD DAYLIGHT?

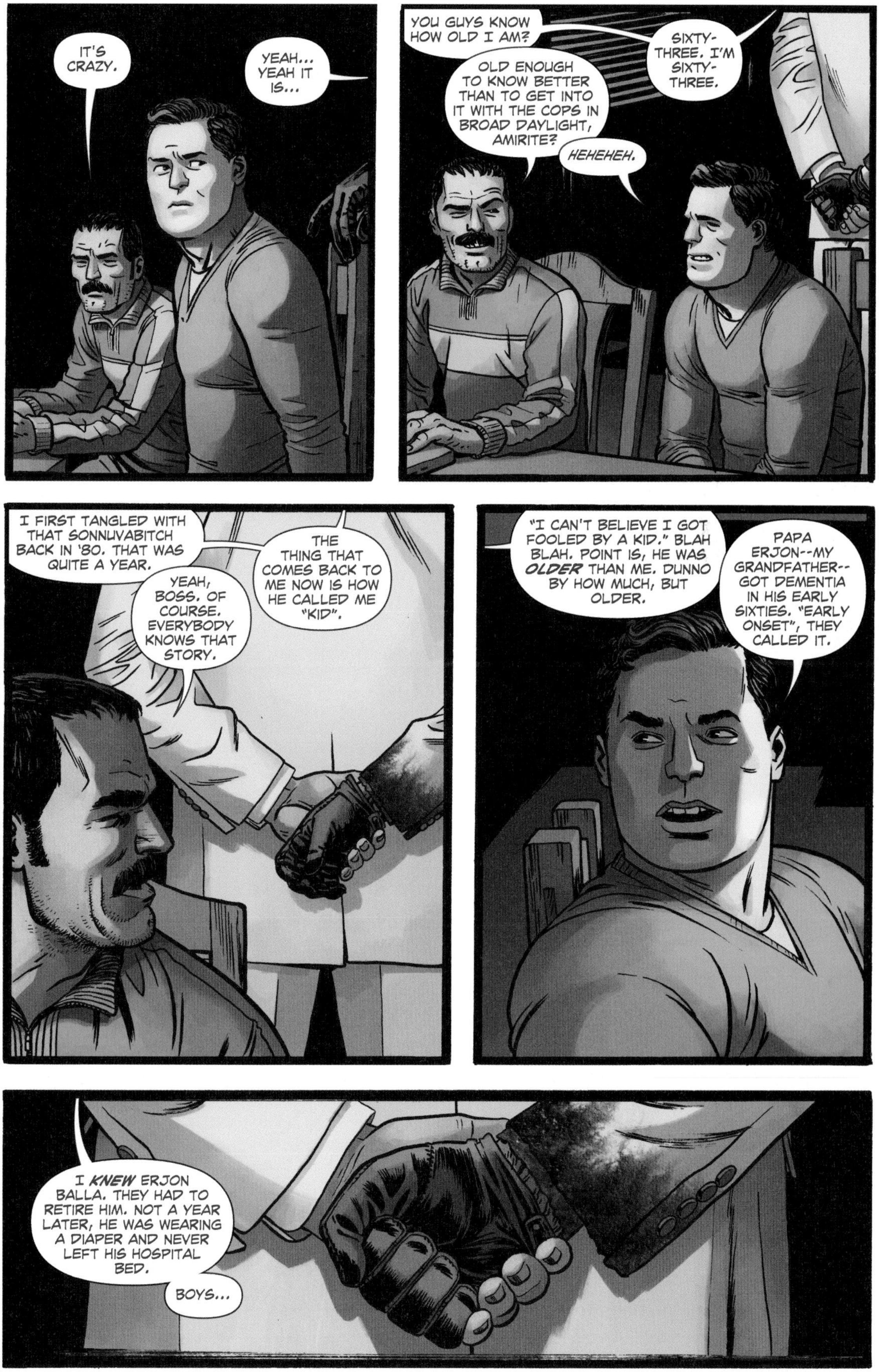
IT'S CRAZY.
YEAH... YEAH IT IS...
YOU GUYS KNOW HOW OLD I AM?
SIXTY-THREE. I'M SIXTY-THREE.
OLD ENOUGH TO KNOW BETTER THAN TO GET INTO IT WITH THE COPS IN BROAD DAYLIGHT, AMIRITE?
HEHEHEH.
I FIRST TANGLED WITH THAT SONNUVABITCH BACK IN '80. THAT WAS QUITE A YEAR.
YEAH, BOSS. OF COURSE. EVERYBODY KNOWS THAT STORY.
THE THING THAT COMES BACK TO ME NOW IS HOW HE CALLED ME "KID".
"I CAN'T BELIEVE I GOT FOOLED BY A KID." BLAH BLAH. POINT IS, HE WAS OLDER THAN ME. DUNNO BY HOW MUCH, BUT OLDER.
PAPA ERJON--MY GRANDFATHER--GOT DEMENTIA IN HIS EARLY SIXTIES. "EARLY ONSET", THEY CALLED IT.
I KNEW ERJON BALLA. THEY HAD TO RETIRE HIM. NOT A YEAR LATER, HE WAS WEARING A DIAPER AND NEVER LEFT HIS HOSPITAL BED.
BOYS...

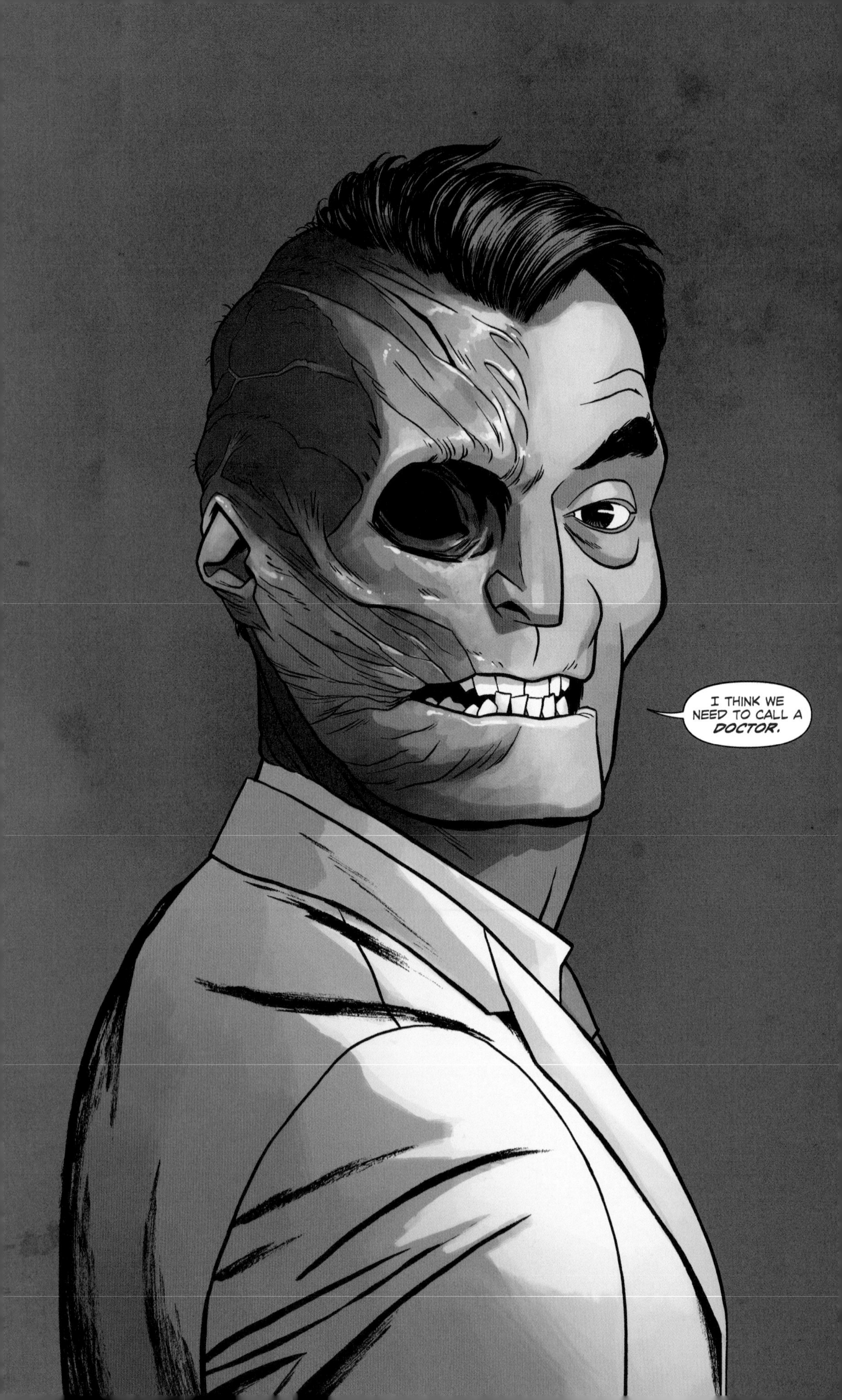
I THINK WE NEED TO CALL A DOCTOR.

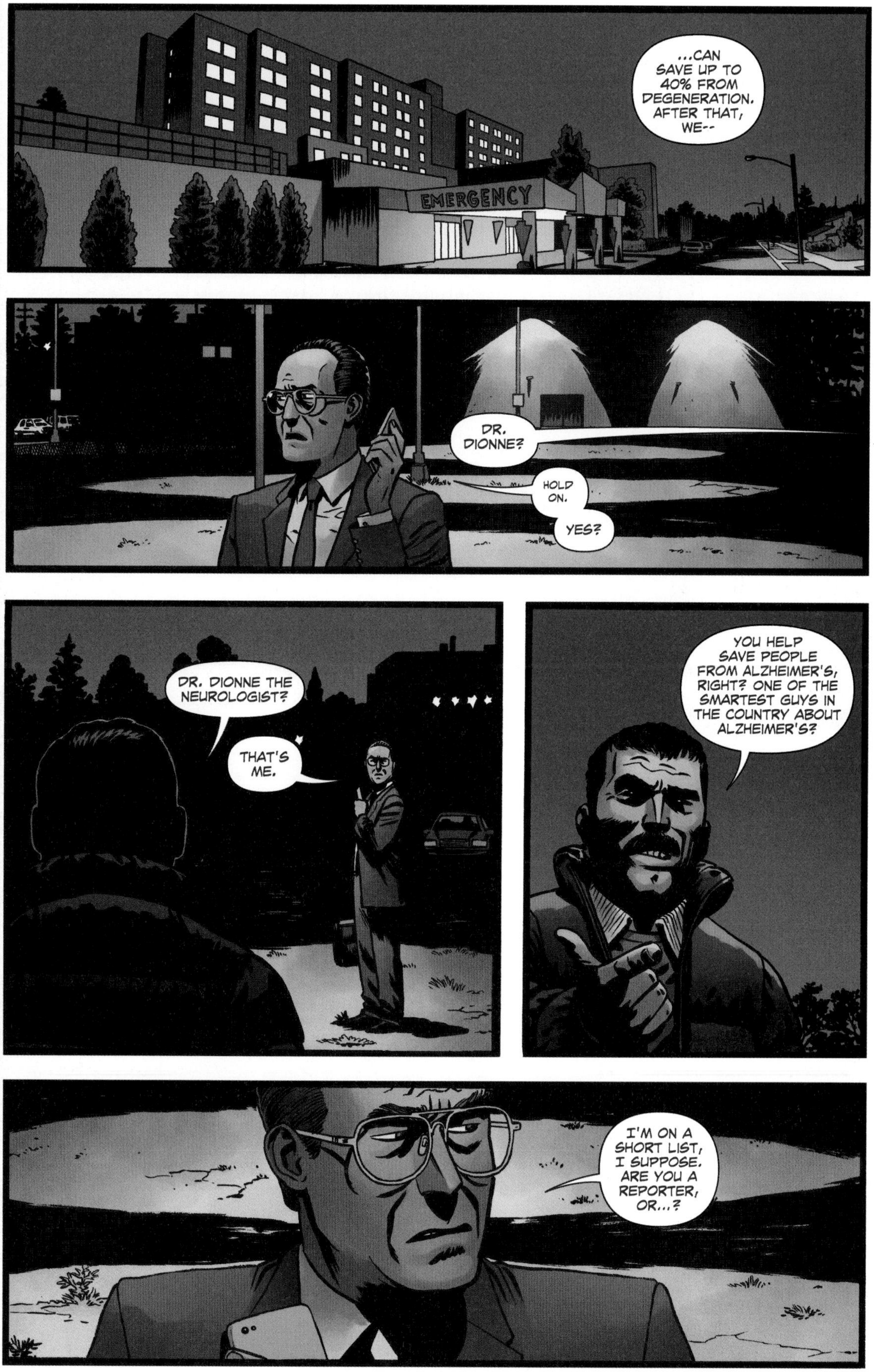
...CAN SAVE UP TO 40% FROM DEGENERATION. AFTER THAT, WE--
EMERGENCY
DR. DIONNE?
HOLD ON.
YES?
DR. DIONNE THE NEUROLOGIST?
THAT'S ME.
YOU HELP SAVE PEOPLE FROM ALZHEIMER'S, RIGHT? ONE OF THE SMARTEST GUYS IN THE COUNTRY ABOUT ALZHEIMER'S?
I'M ON A SHORT LIST, I SUPPOSE. ARE YOU A REPORTER, OR...?

HA, NO. BUT THIS IS DEFINITELY GOING TO MAKE THE NEWS.

BLAM

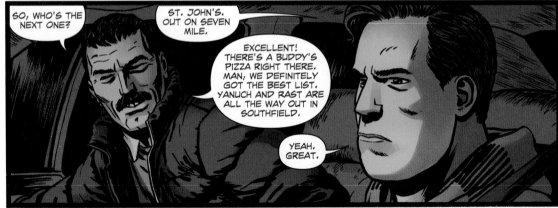

SO, WHO'S THE NEXT ONE?

ST. JOHN'S. OUT ON SEVEN MILE.

EXCELLENT! THERE'S A BUDDY'S PIZZA RIGHT THERE. MAN, WE DEFINITELY GOT THE BEST LIST. YANUCH AND RAST ARE ALL THE WAY OUT IN SOUTHFIELD.

YEAH. GREAT.

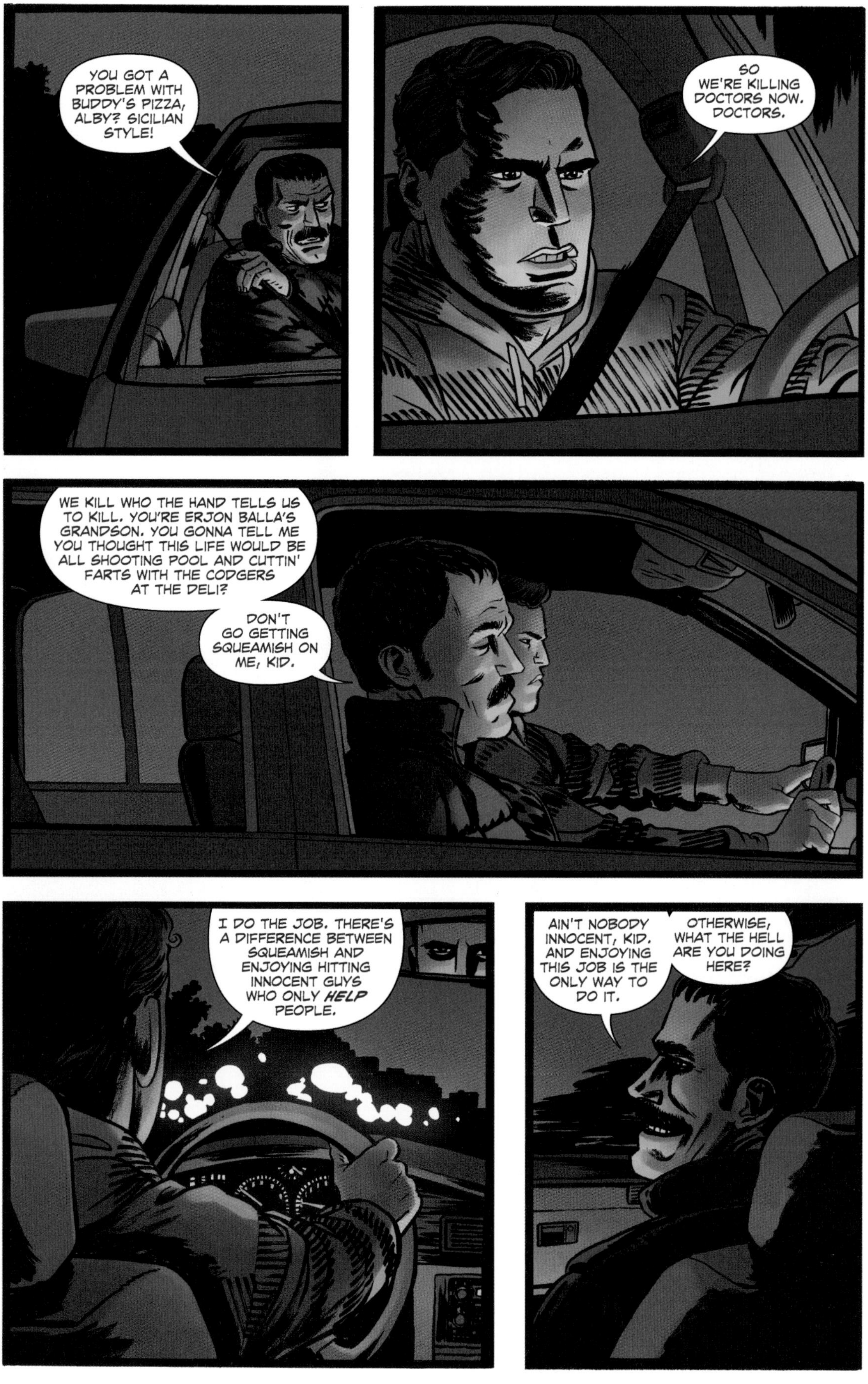
YOU GOT A PROBLEM WITH BUDDY'S PIZZA, ALBY? SICILIAN STYLE!
SO WE'RE KILLING DOCTORS NOW. DOCTORS.
WE KILL WHO THE HAND TELLS US TO KILL. YOU'RE ERJON BALLA'S GRANDSON. YOU GONNA TELL ME YOU THOUGHT THIS LIFE WOULD BE ALL SHOOTING POOL AND CUTTIN' FARTS WITH THE CODGERS AT THE DELI?
DON'T GO GETTING SQUEAMISH ON ME, KID.
I DO THE JOB. THERE'S A DIFFERENCE BETWEEN SQUEAMISH AND ENJOYING HITTING INNOCENT GUYS WHO ONLY *HELP* PEOPLE.
AIN'T NOBODY INNOCENT, KID. AND ENJOYING THIS JOB IS THE ONLY WAY TO DO IT.
OTHERWISE, WHAT THE HELL ARE YOU DOING HERE?

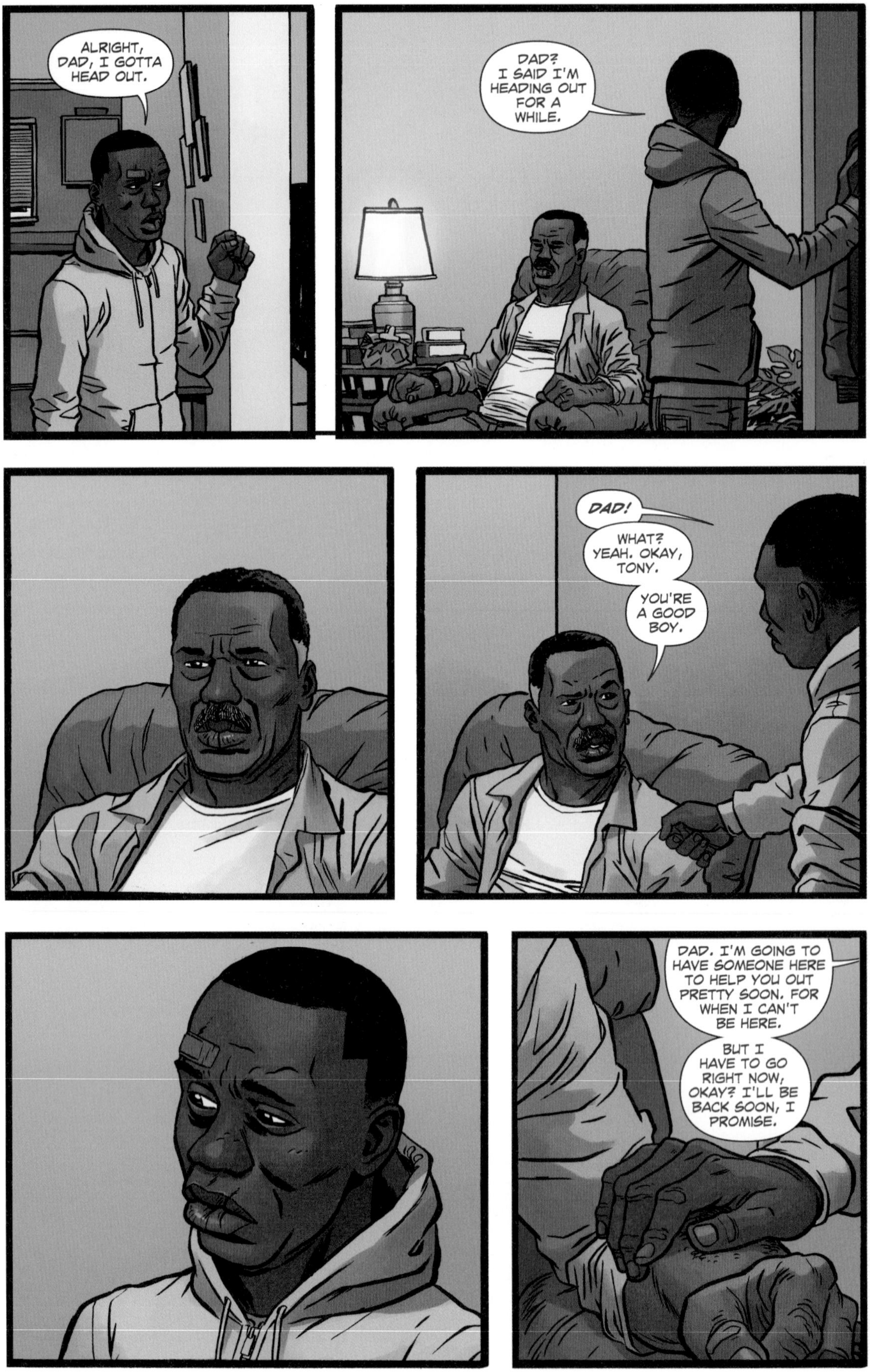
ALRIGHT, DAD, I GOTTA HEAD OUT.
DAD? I SAID I'M HEADING OUT FOR A WHILE.
DAD!
WHAT? YEAH. OKAY, TONY.
YOU'RE A GOOD BOY.
DAD. I'M GOING TO HAVE SOMEONE HERE TO HELP YOU OUT PRETTY SOON. FOR WHEN I CAN'T BE HERE.
BUT I HAVE TO GO RIGHT NOW, OKAY? I'LL BE BACK SOON, I PROMISE.

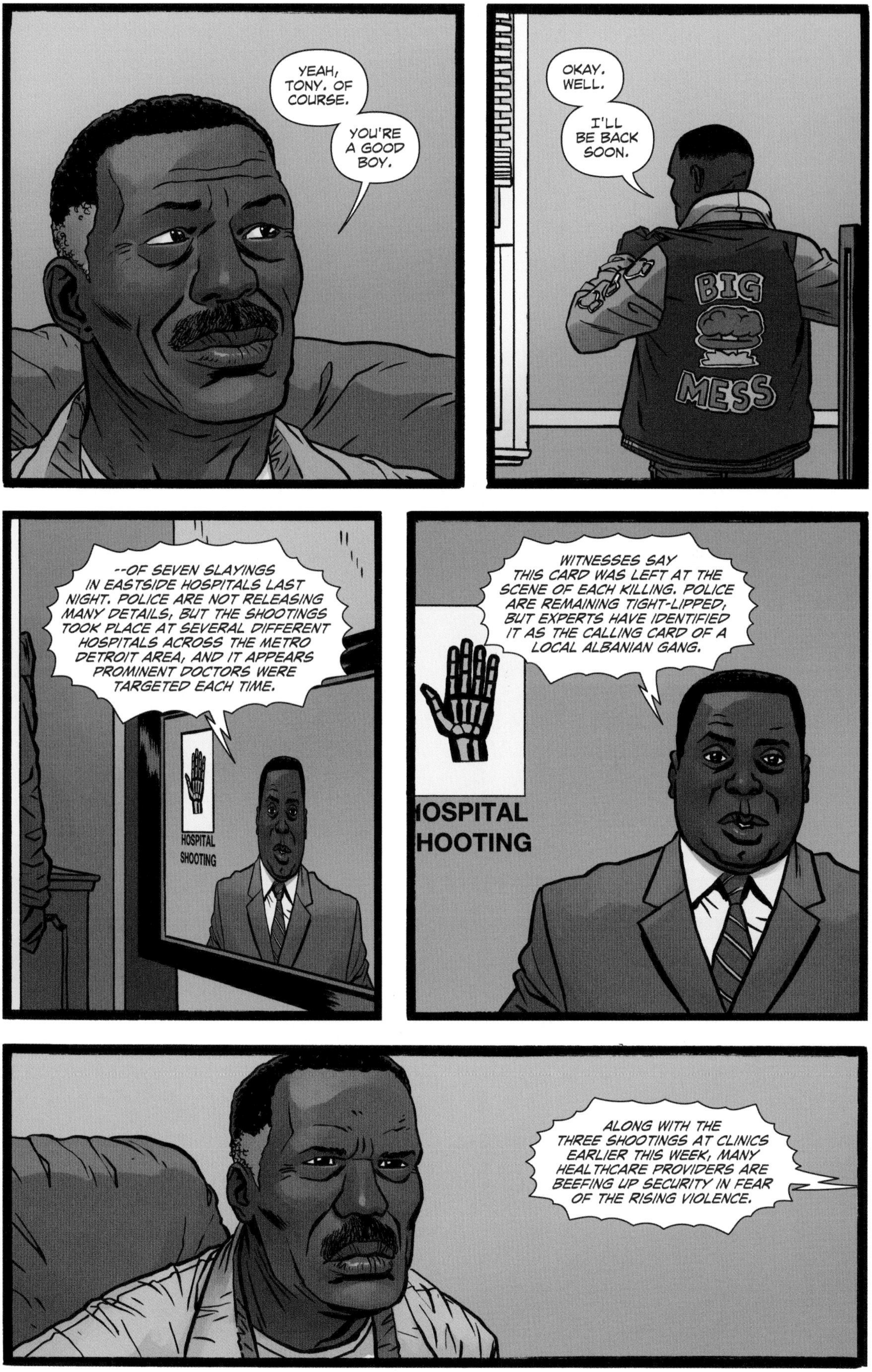
YEAH, TONY. OF COURSE.
YOU'RE A GOOD BOY.
OKAY. WELL.
I'LL BE BACK SOON.
BIG MESS
--OF SEVEN SLAYINGS IN EASTSIDE HOSPITALS LAST NIGHT. POLICE ARE NOT RELEASING MANY DETAILS, BUT THE SHOOTINGS TOOK PLACE AT SEVERAL DIFFERENT HOSPITALS ACROSS THE METRO DETROIT AREA, AND IT APPEARS PROMINENT DOCTORS WERE TARGETED EACH TIME.
HOSPITAL SHOOTING
WITNESSES SAY THIS CARD WAS LEFT AT THE SCENE OF EACH KILLING. POLICE ARE REMAINING TIGHT-LIPPED, BUT EXPERTS HAVE IDENTIFIED IT AS THE CALLING CARD OF A LOCAL ALBANIAN GANG.
HOSPITAL SHOOTING
ALONG WITH THE THREE SHOOTINGS AT CLINICS EARLIER THIS WEEK, MANY HEALTHCARE PROVIDERS ARE BEEFING UP SECURITY IN FEAR OF THE RISING VIOLENCE.

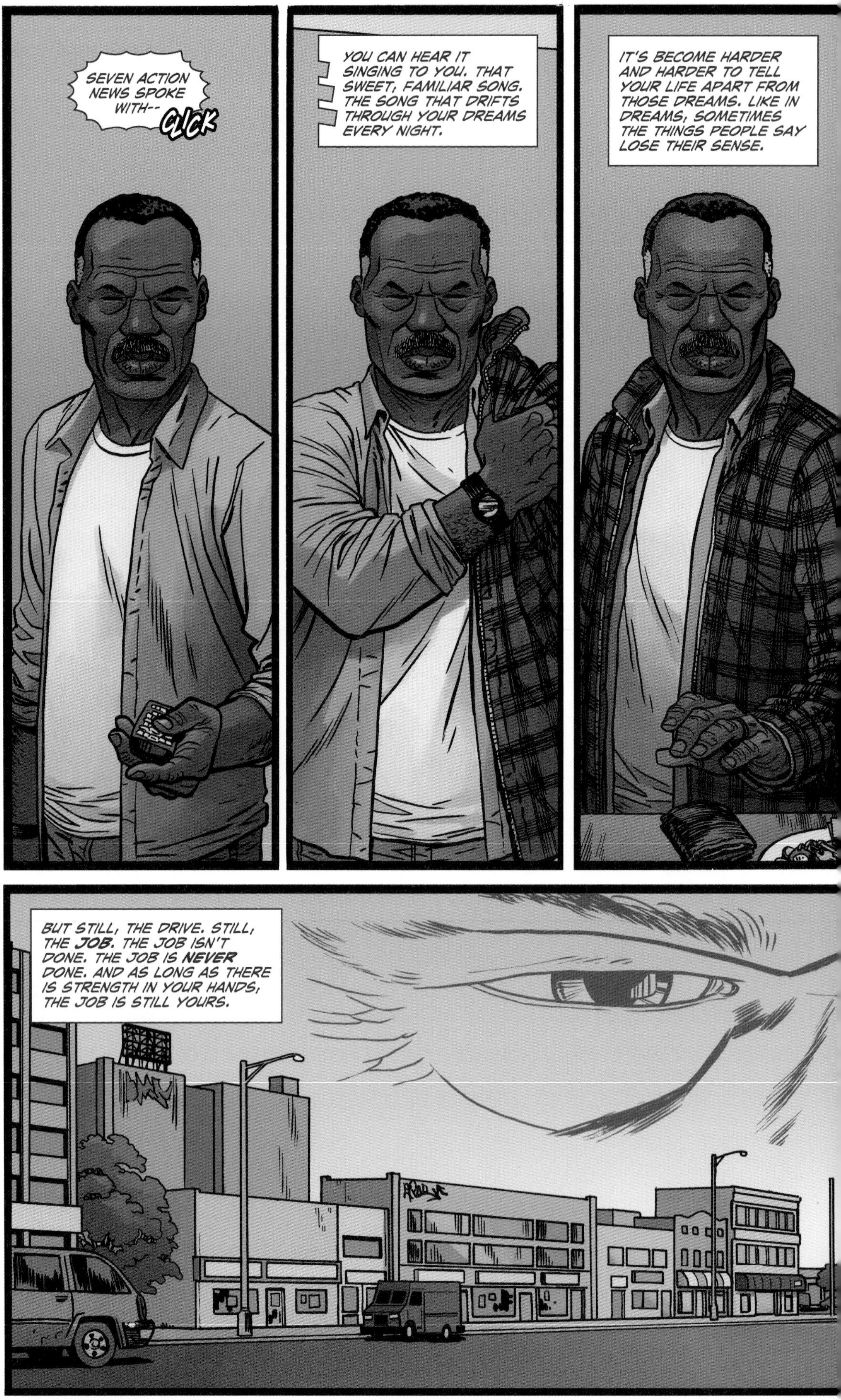
SEVEN ACTION NEWS SPOKE WITH--
CLICK
YOU CAN HEAR IT SINGING TO YOU. THAT SWEET, FAMILIAR SONG. THE SONG THAT DRIFTS THROUGH YOUR DREAMS EVERY NIGHT.
IT'S BECOME HARDER AND HARDER TO TELL YOUR LIFE APART FROM THOSE DREAMS. LIKE IN DREAMS, SOMETIMES THE THINGS PEOPLE SAY LOSE THEIR SENSE.
BUT STILL, THE DRIVE. STILL, THE JOB. THE JOB ISN'T DONE. THE JOB IS NEVER DONE. AND AS LONG AS THERE IS STRENGTH IN YOUR HANDS, THE JOB IS STILL YOURS.

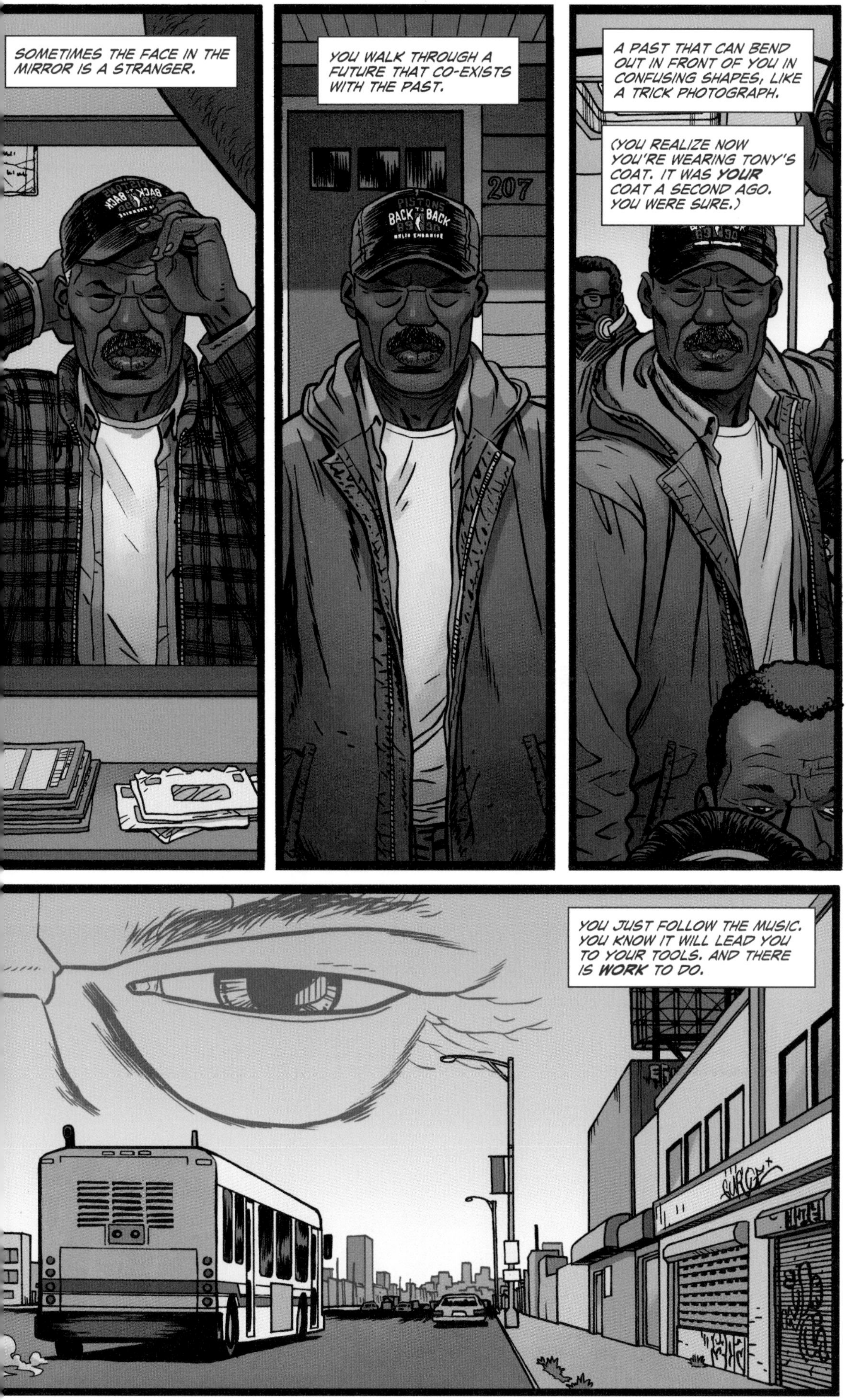

SOMETIMES THE FACE IN THE MIRROR IS A STRANGER.
YOU WALK THROUGH A FUTURE THAT CO-EXISTS WITH THE PAST.
PISTONS
BACK TO BACK
207
A PAST THAT CAN BEND OUT IN FRONT OF YOU IN CONFUSING SHAPES, LIKE A TRICK PHOTOGRAPH.
(YOU REALIZE NOW YOU'RE WEARING TONY'S COAT. IT WAS **YOUR** COAT A SECOND AGO. YOU WERE SURE.)
YOU JUST FOLLOW THE MUSIC. YOU KNOW IT WILL LEAD YOU TO YOUR TOOLS. AND THERE IS **WORK** TO DO.

YOU...I REMEMBER YOU.

SIR?

WHEN I...

WHEN STEALTH STOPPED A ROBBERY HERE FIVE YEARS AGO... SIX YEARS AGO?

YOU WERE THE GUARD WHO SAVED THAT WOMAN. RISKED YOUR LIFE AND GOT WINGED BY A BULLET. BUT YOU SAVED THAT WOMAN.

THAT WAS ALMOST TEN YEARS AGO, ACTUALLY. BUT YES, THAT WAS ME.

HOW DID YOU KNOW THAT?

I...READ THE POLICE REPORT. BECAUSE... UH...

AH! OKAY.

I'M A REPORTER FOR THE HERALD, AND I'M WRITING A BOOK ON STEALTH.

HOW'D YOU LIKE ME TO TELL YOUR STORY?

Anthony Barber
Reporter

Detroit Herald

321 W Lafayette
Detroit, MI 48

T 313-222
E barber

AND THIS IS THE SAFE DEPOSIT ROOM WHERE THE PERPS TIED UP THE HOSTAGES.

YOU STEPPED IN FRONT OF THAT BULLET RIGHT OVER THERE, RIGHT?

YEAH. WOW, THAT WAS A PRETTY DETAILED REPORT.

JUST FOR THE RECORD, I KNOW THERE ARE PEOPLE IN THIS CITY WHO ARE DISGUSTED BY STEALTH OR THINK IT'S A SIGN THE SYSTEM IS BROKEN.

BUT I'VE ACTUALLY SEEN HIM IN ACTION, AND I CAN TELL YOU, HE'S A HERO. AND IF HE HADN'T SET THE EXAMPLE, I MIGHT NOT HAVE THIS SCAR ON MY SHOULDER TODAY.

THAT AIN'T A BROKEN SYSTEM.

COULD YOU DO AN OLD MAN A FAVOR AND GET ME A CUP OF WATER? I GOT THE DIABEETUS, AND IT DOES MAKE A MAN THIRSTY.

SIR...I REALLY CAN'T LEAVE YOU ALONE BACK HERE.

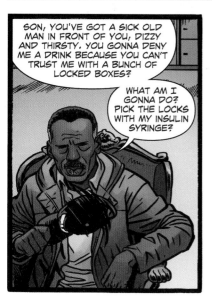

SON, YOU'VE GOT A SICK OLD MAN IN FRONT OF YOU, DIZZY AND THIRSTY. YOU GONNA DENY ME A DRINK BECAUSE YOU CAN'T TRUST ME WITH A BUNCH OF LOCKED BOXES?

WHAT AM I GONNA DO? PICK THE LOCKS WITH MY INSULIN SYRINGE?

I... ER...

ALRIGHT. BUT PLEASE STAY HERE IN THAT CHAIR. I'LL BE RIGHT BACK.

THANK YOU, TONY.

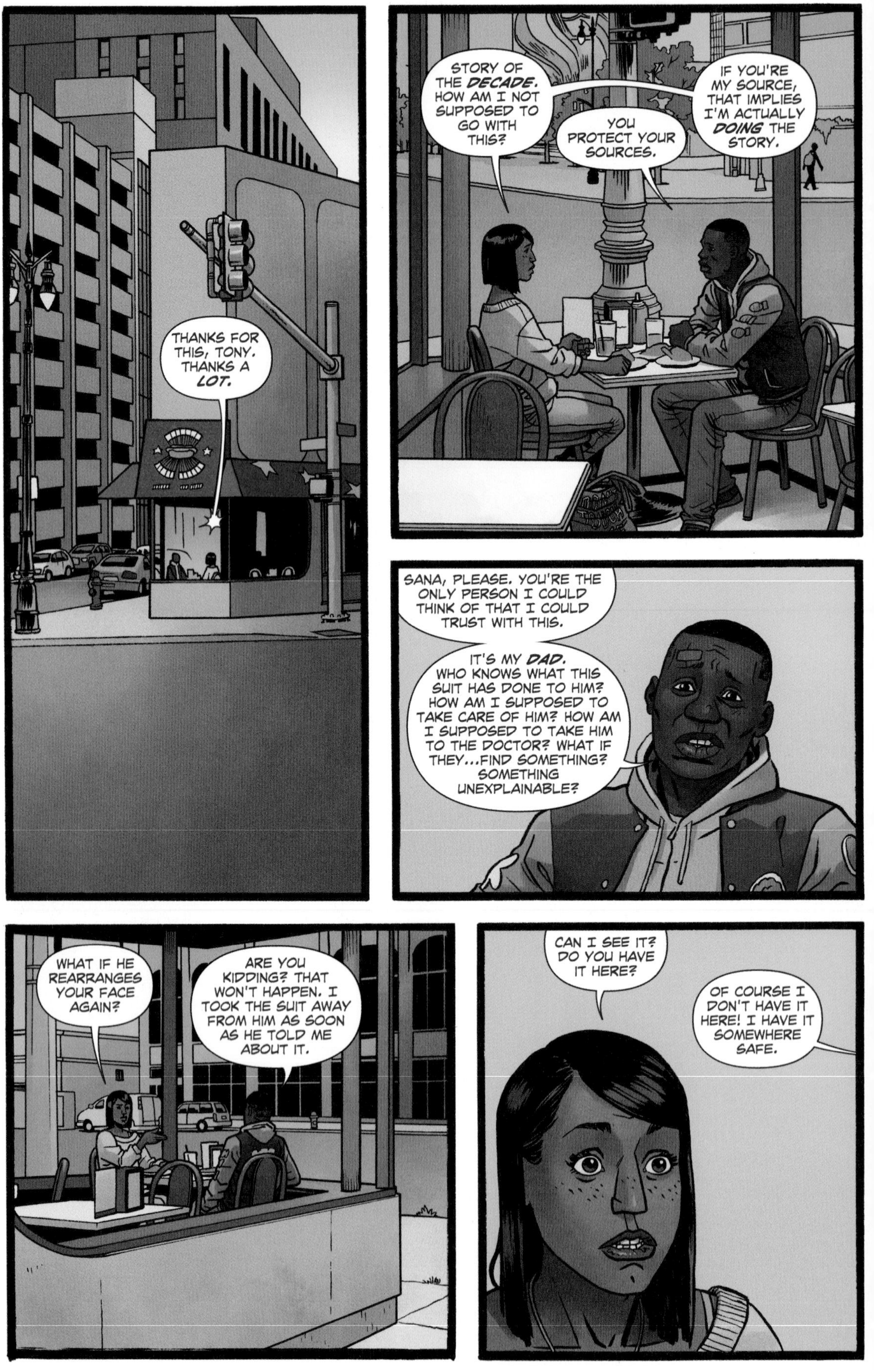
THANKS FOR THIS, TONY. THANKS A LOT.
STORY OF THE DECADE. HOW AM I NOT SUPPOSED TO GO WITH THIS?
YOU PROTECT YOUR SOURCES.
IF YOU'RE MY SOURCE, THAT IMPLIES I'M ACTUALLY DOING THE STORY.
SANA, PLEASE. YOU'RE THE ONLY PERSON I COULD THINK OF THAT I COULD TRUST WITH THIS.
IT'S MY DAD. WHO KNOWS WHAT THIS SUIT HAS DONE TO HIM? HOW AM I SUPPOSED TO TAKE CARE OF HIM? HOW AM I SUPPOSED TO TAKE HIM TO THE DOCTOR? WHAT IF THEY...FIND SOMETHING? SOMETHING UNEXPLAINABLE?
WHAT IF HE REARRANGES YOUR FACE AGAIN?
ARE YOU KIDDING? THAT WON'T HAPPEN. I TOOK THE SUIT AWAY FROM HIM AS SOON AS HE TOLD ME ABOUT IT.
CAN I SEE IT? DO YOU HAVE IT HERE?
OF COURSE I DON'T HAVE IT HERE! I HAVE IT SOMEWHERE SAFE.

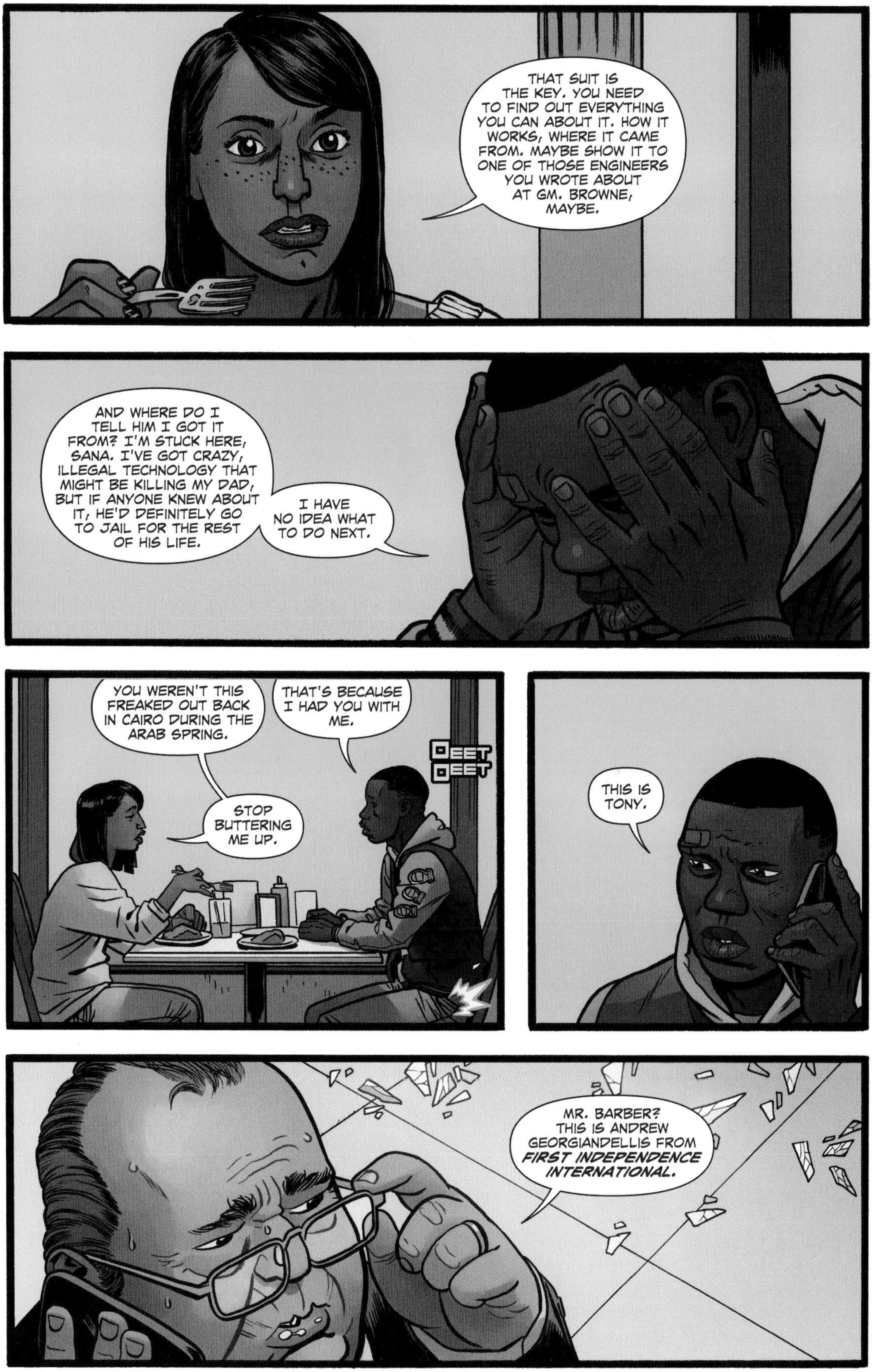
THAT SUIT IS THE KEY. YOU NEED TO FIND OUT EVERYTHING YOU CAN ABOUT IT. HOW IT WORKS, WHERE IT CAME FROM. MAYBE SHOW IT TO ONE OF THOSE ENGINEERS YOU WROTE ABOUT AT GM. BROWNE, MAYBE.
AND WHERE DO I TELL HIM I GOT IT FROM? I'M STUCK HERE, SANA. I'VE GOT CRAZY, ILLEGAL TECHNOLOGY THAT MIGHT BE KILLING MY DAD, BUT IF ANYONE KNEW ABOUT IT, HE'D DEFINITELY GO TO JAIL FOR THE REST OF HIS LIFE.
I HAVE NO IDEA WHAT TO DO NEXT.
YOU WEREN'T THIS FREAKED OUT BACK IN CAIRO DURING THE ARAB SPRING.
THAT'S BECAUSE I HAD YOU WITH ME.
STOP BUTTERING ME UP.
DEET DEET
THIS IS TONY.
MR. BARBER? THIS IS ANDREW GEORGIANDELLIS FROM *FIRST INDEPENDENCE INTERNATIONAL.*

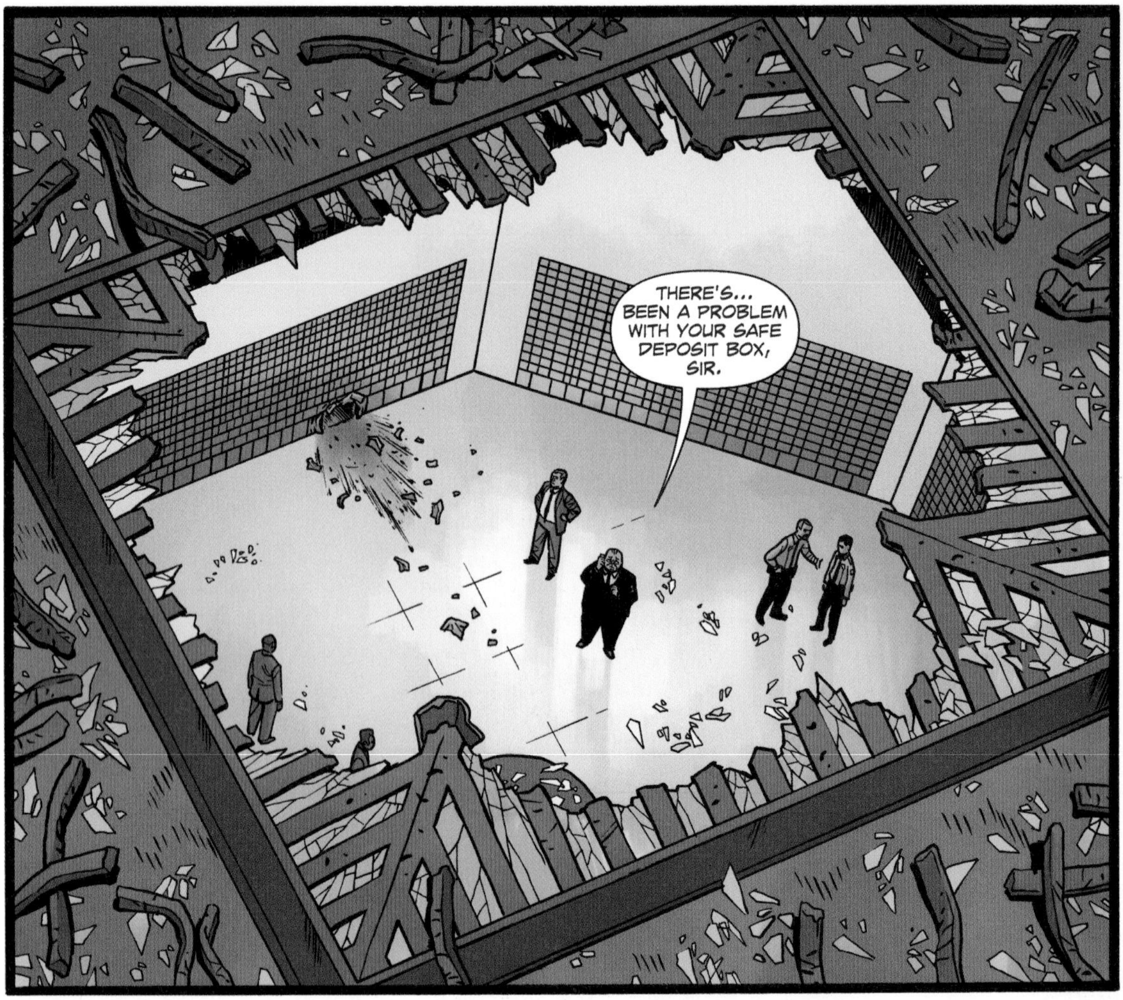
THERE'S... BEEN A PROBLEM WITH YOUR SAFE DEPOSIT BOX, SIR.

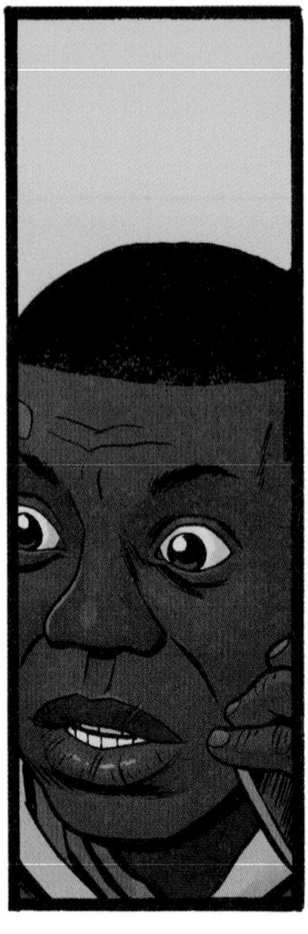

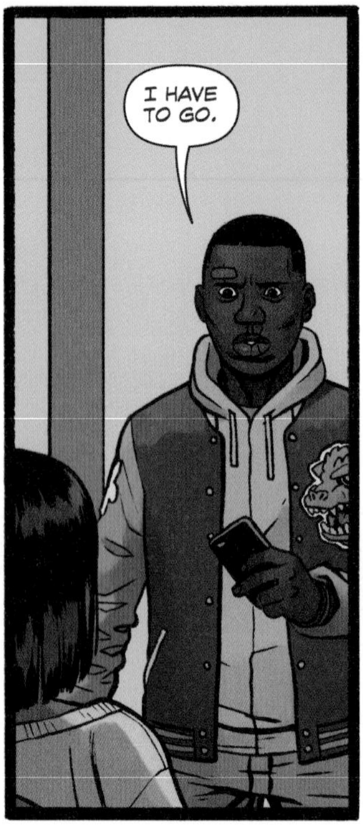
I HAVE TO GO.

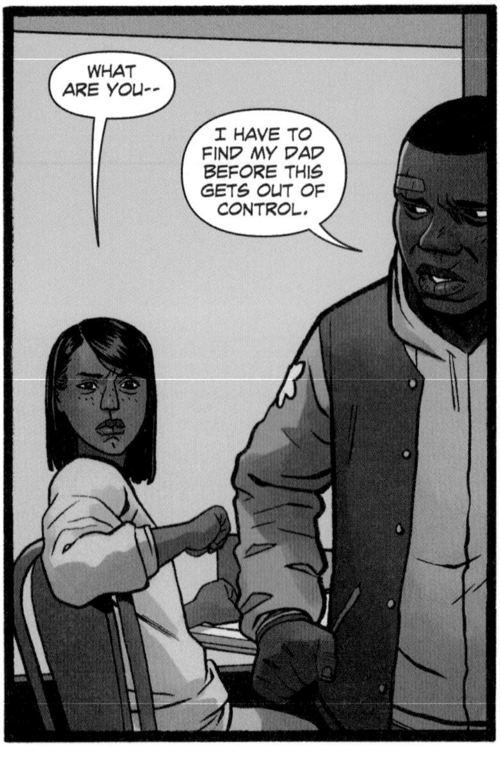
WHAT ARE YOU--
I HAVE TO FIND MY DAD BEFORE THIS GETS OUT OF CONTROL.

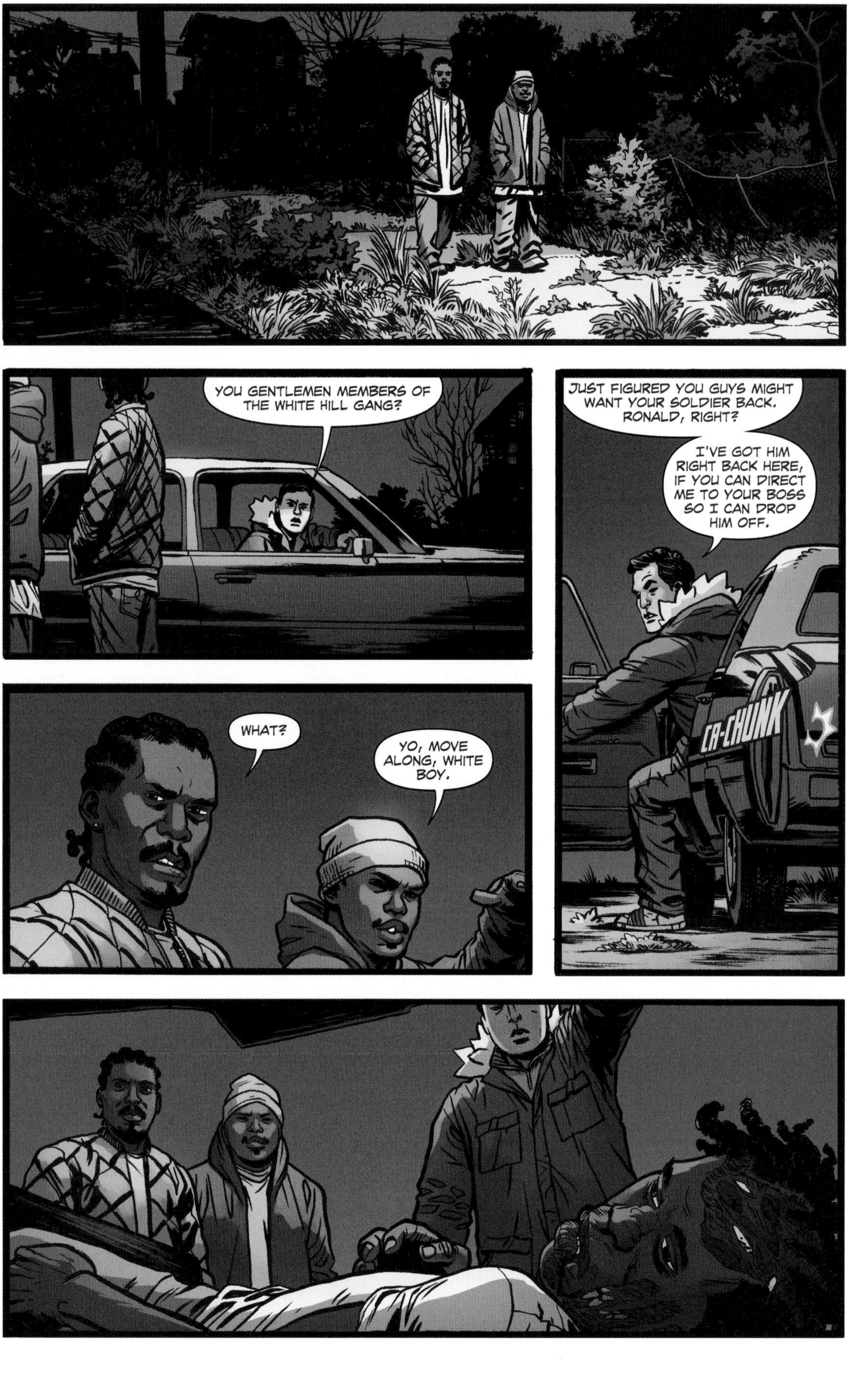
YOU GENTLEMEN MEMBERS OF THE WHITE HILL GANG?
JUST FIGURED YOU GUYS MIGHT WANT YOUR SOLDIER BACK. RONALD, RIGHT?
I'VE GOT HIM RIGHT BACK HERE, IF YOU CAN DIRECT ME TO YOUR BOSS SO I CAN DROP HIM OFF.
CA-CHUNK
WHAT?
YO, MOVE ALONG, WHITE BOY.

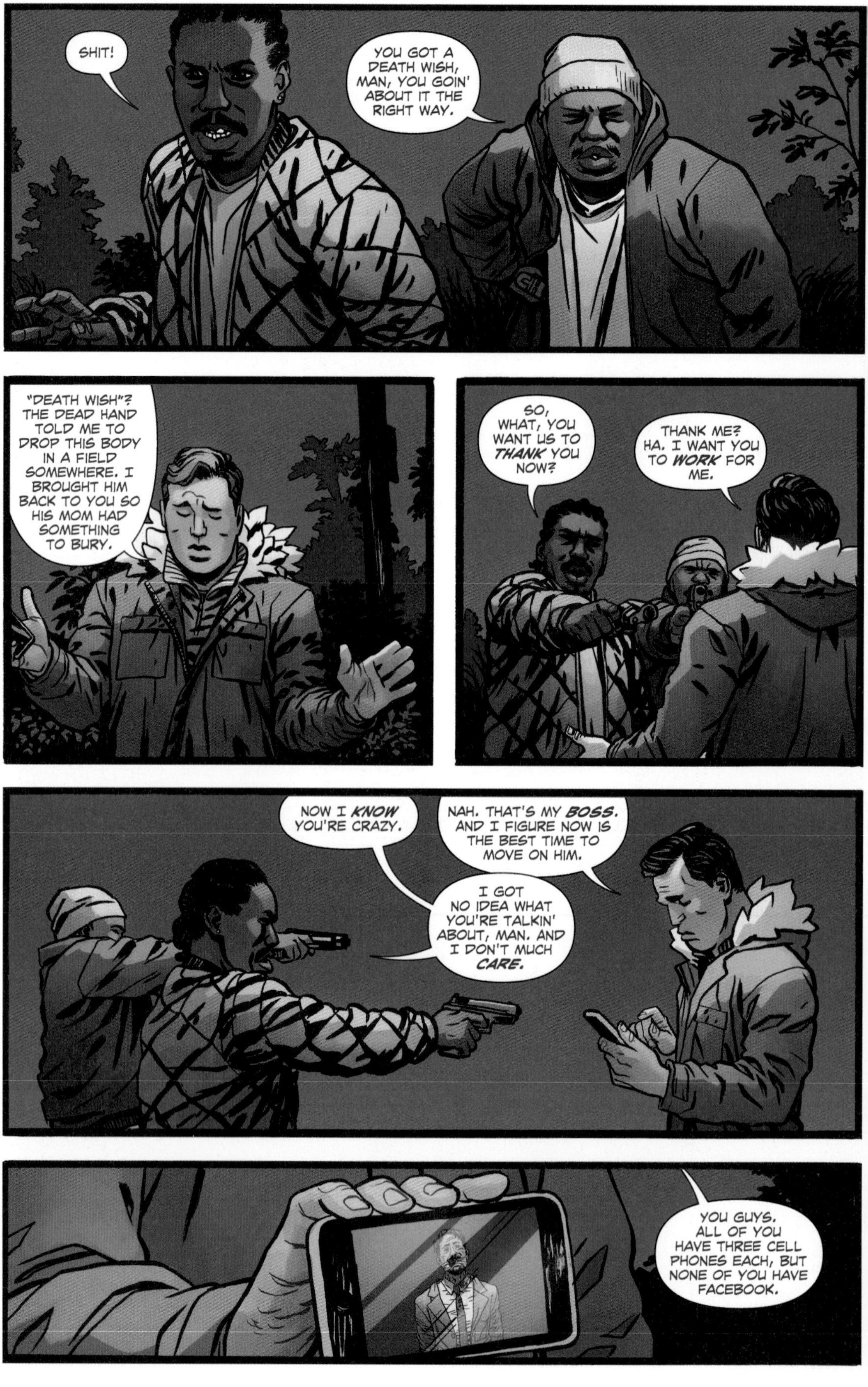
SHIT!
YOU GOT A DEATH WISH, MAN, YOU GOIN' ABOUT IT THE RIGHT WAY.
"DEATH WISH"? THE DEAD HAND TOLD ME TO DROP THIS BODY IN A FIELD SOMEWHERE. I BROUGHT HIM BACK TO YOU SO HIS MOM HAD SOMETHING TO BURY.
SO, WHAT, YOU WANT US TO THANK YOU NOW?
THANK ME? HA. I WANT YOU TO WORK FOR ME.
NOW I KNOW YOU'RE CRAZY.
NAH. THAT'S MY BOSS. AND I FIGURE NOW IS THE BEST TIME TO MOVE ON HIM.
I GOT NO IDEA WHAT YOU'RE TALKIN' ABOUT, MAN. AND I DON'T MUCH CARE.
YOU GUYS. ALL OF YOU HAVE THREE CELL PHONES EACH, BUT NONE OF YOU HAVE FACEBOOK.

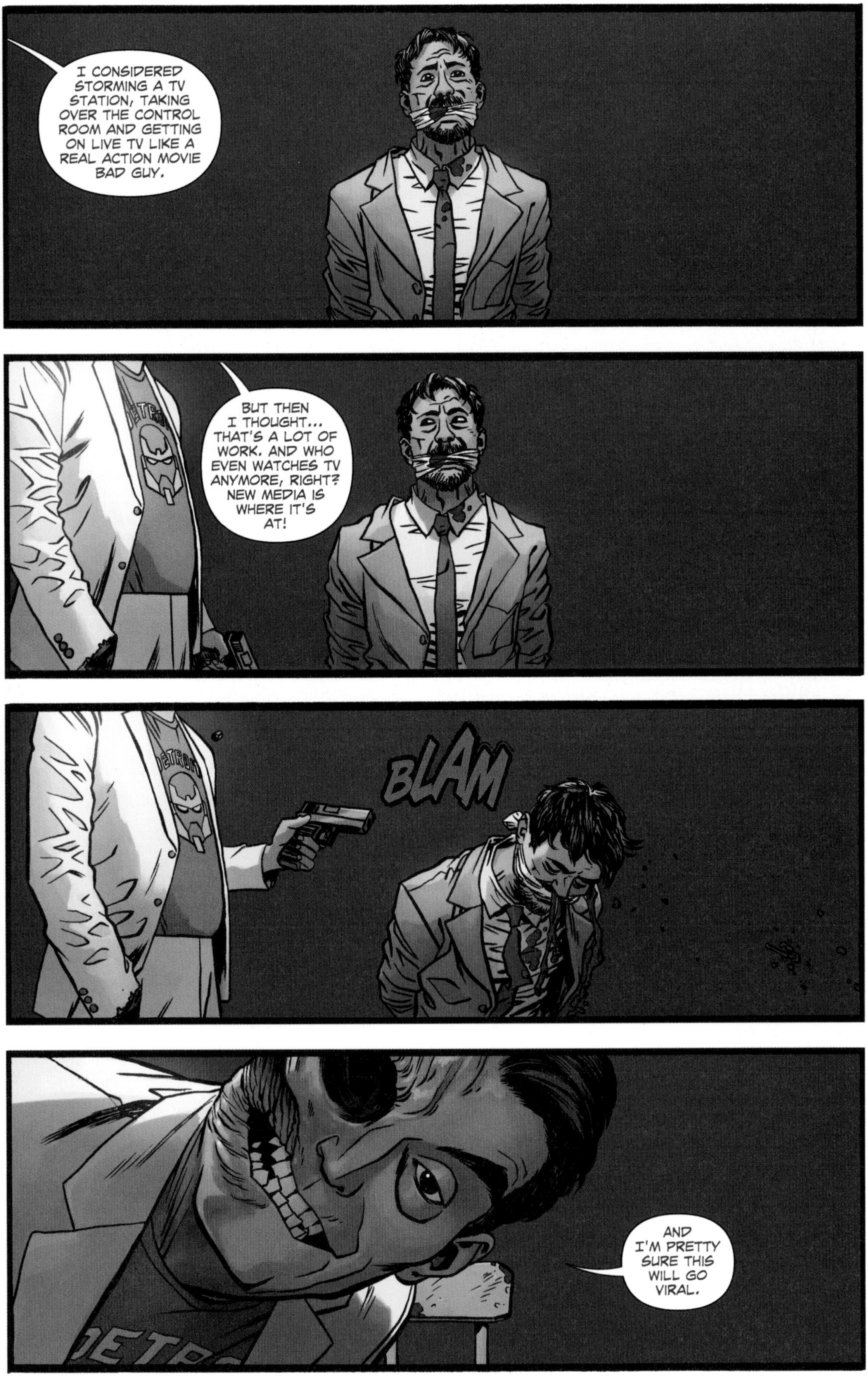
I CONSIDERED STORMING A TV STATION, TAKING OVER THE CONTROL ROOM AND GETTING ON LIVE TV LIKE A REAL ACTION MOVIE BAD GUY.
BUT THEN I THOUGHT... THAT'S A LOT OF WORK. AND WHO EVEN WATCHES TV ANYMORE, RIGHT? NEW MEDIA IS WHERE IT'S AT!
BLAM
AND I'M PRETTY SURE THIS WILL GO VIRAL.

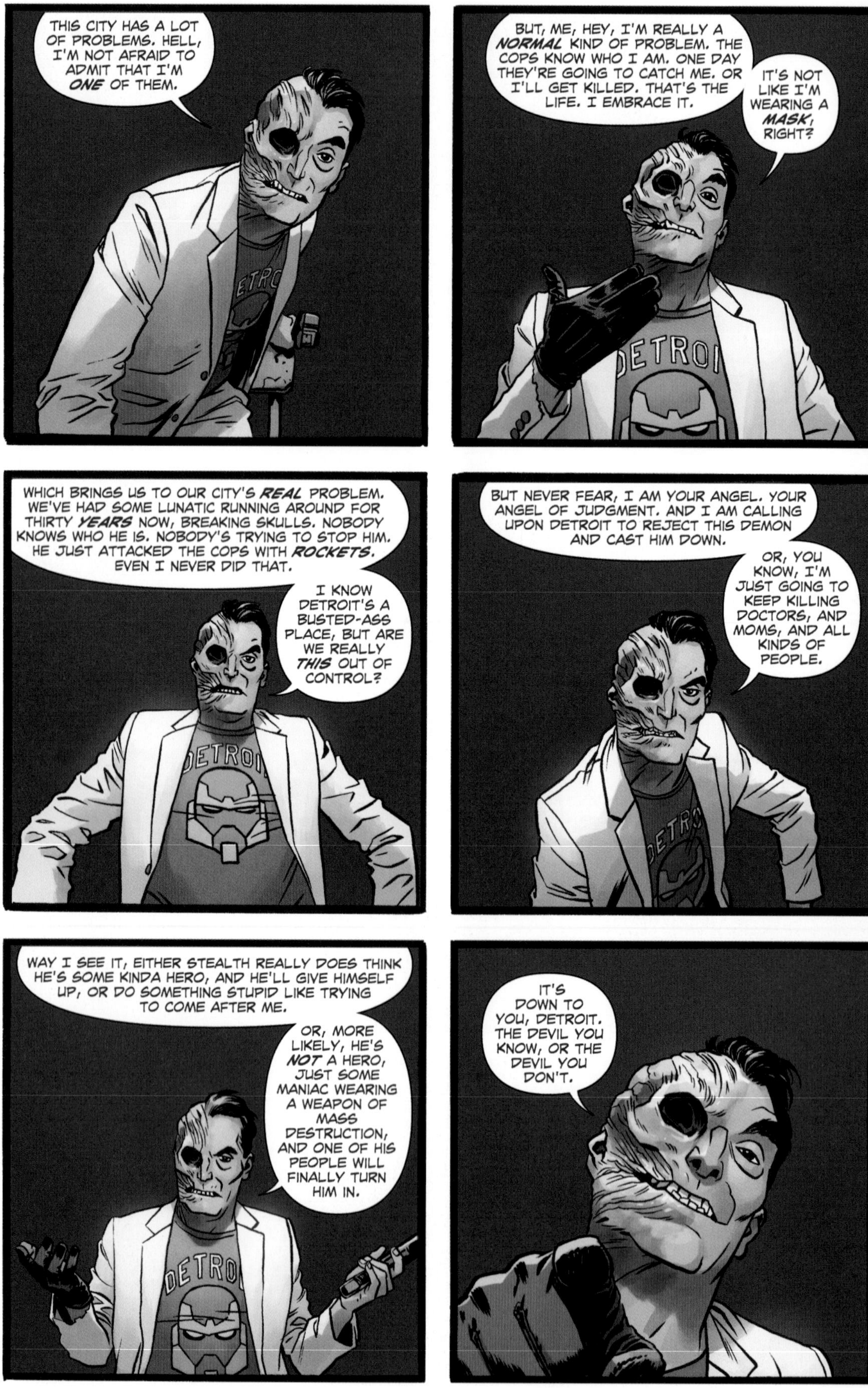
THIS CITY HAS A LOT OF PROBLEMS. HELL, I'M NOT AFRAID TO ADMIT THAT I'M ONE OF THEM.
BUT, ME, HEY, I'M REALLY A NORMAL KIND OF PROBLEM. THE COPS KNOW WHO I AM. ONE DAY THEY'RE GOING TO CATCH ME. OR I'LL GET KILLED. THAT'S THE LIFE. I EMBRACE IT.
IT'S NOT LIKE I'M WEARING A MASK, RIGHT?
DETROIT
WHICH BRINGS US TO OUR CITY'S REAL PROBLEM. WE'VE HAD SOME LUNATIC RUNNING AROUND FOR THIRTY YEARS NOW, BREAKING SKULLS. NOBODY KNOWS WHO HE IS. NOBODY'S TRYING TO STOP HIM. HE JUST ATTACKED THE COPS WITH ROCKETS. EVEN I NEVER DID THAT.
I KNOW DETROIT'S A BUSTED-ASS PLACE, BUT ARE WE REALLY THIS OUT OF CONTROL?
BUT NEVER FEAR, I AM YOUR ANGEL. YOUR ANGEL OF JUDGMENT. AND I AM CALLING UPON DETROIT TO REJECT THIS DEMON AND CAST HIM DOWN.
OR, YOU KNOW, I'M JUST GOING TO KEEP KILLING DOCTORS, AND MOMS, AND ALL KINDS OF PEOPLE.
WAY I SEE IT, EITHER STEALTH REALLY DOES THINK HE'S SOME KINDA HERO, AND HE'LL GIVE HIMSELF UP, OR DO SOMETHING STUPID LIKE TRYING TO COME AFTER ME.
OR, MORE LIKELY, HE'S NOT A HERO, JUST SOME MANIAC WEARING A WEAPON OF MASS DESTRUCTION, AND ONE OF HIS PEOPLE WILL FINALLY TURN HIM IN.
IT'S DOWN TO YOU, DETROIT. THE DEVIL YOU KNOW, OR THE DEVIL YOU DON'T.

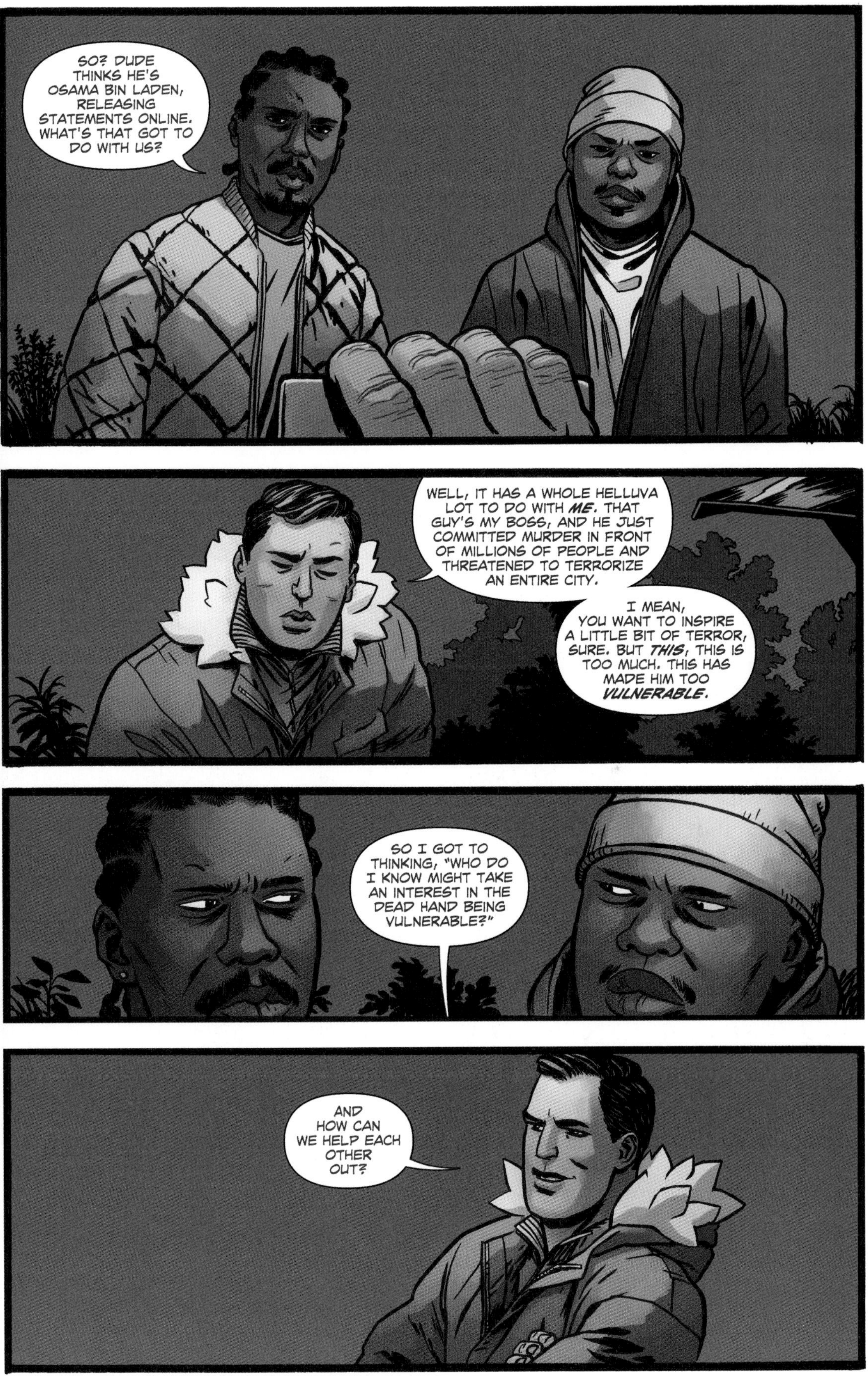
SO? DUDE THINKS HE'S OSAMA BIN LADEN, RELEASING STATEMENTS ONLINE. WHAT'S THAT GOT TO DO WITH US?
WELL, IT HAS A WHOLE HELLUVA LOT TO DO WITH *ME*. THAT GUY'S MY BOSS, AND HE JUST COMMITTED MURDER IN FRONT OF MILLIONS OF PEOPLE AND THREATENED TO TERRORIZE AN ENTIRE CITY.
I MEAN, YOU WANT TO INSPIRE A LITTLE BIT OF TERROR, SURE. BUT *THIS*, THIS IS TOO MUCH. THIS HAS MADE HIM TOO *VULNERABLE*.
SO I GOT TO THINKING, "WHO DO I KNOW MIGHT TAKE AN INTEREST IN THE DEAD HAND BEING VULNERABLE?"
AND HOW CAN WE HELP EACH OTHER OUT?

THE BEWICK SAFE HOUSE. THE THIRD SAFE HOUSE? SECOND.

NO. IT'S THE THIRD. DEFINITELY THE THIRD.

IT WAS THE SECOND ONE THAT WAS DISCOVERED. ON TRUMBULL. YOU FOUGHT THE 313 MAFIA BY WAYNE STATE. A BAD FIGHT.

BEWICK IS STILL SAFE AND YOU HAVE TO HOLE UP. YOU CAN'T GO BACK HOME BECAUSE TONY KNOWS YOUR SECRET.

BUT HOW CAN TONY KNOW YOUR SECRET? HE'S ONLY A BOY.

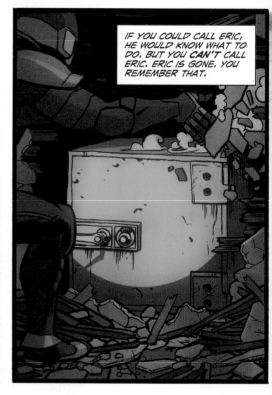

IF YOU COULD CALL ERIC, HE WOULD KNOW WHAT TO DO. BUT YOU **CAN'T** CALL ERIC. ERIC IS GONE. YOU REMEMBER THAT.

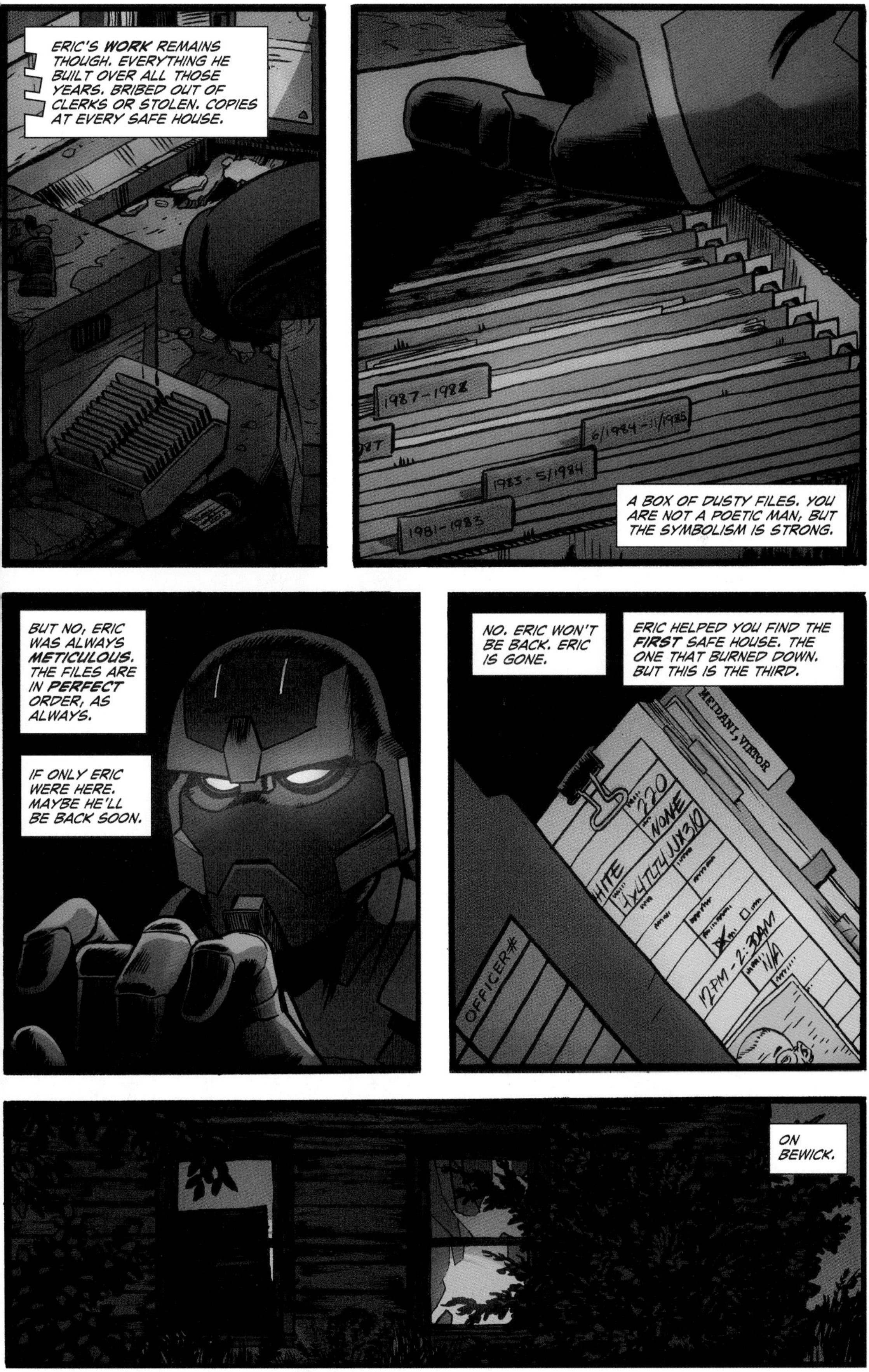
ERIC'S **WORK** REMAINS THOUGH. EVERYTHING HE BUILT OVER ALL THOSE YEARS. BRIBED OUT OF CLERKS OR STOLEN. COPIES AT EVERY SAFE HOUSE.
1987-1988
6/1984-11/1985
1983-5/1984
1981-1983
A BOX OF DUSTY FILES. YOU ARE NOT A POETIC MAN, BUT THE SYMBOLISM IS STRONG.
BUT NO, ERIC WAS ALWAYS **METICULOUS**. THE FILES ARE IN **PERFECT** ORDER, AS ALWAYS.
IF ONLY ERIC WERE HERE. MAYBE HE'LL BE BACK SOON.
NO. ERIC WON'T BE BACK. ERIC IS GONE.
ERIC HELPED YOU FIND THE **FIRST** SAFE HOUSE. THE ONE THAT BURNED DOWN. BUT THIS IS THE THIRD.
OFFICER#
ON BEWICK.

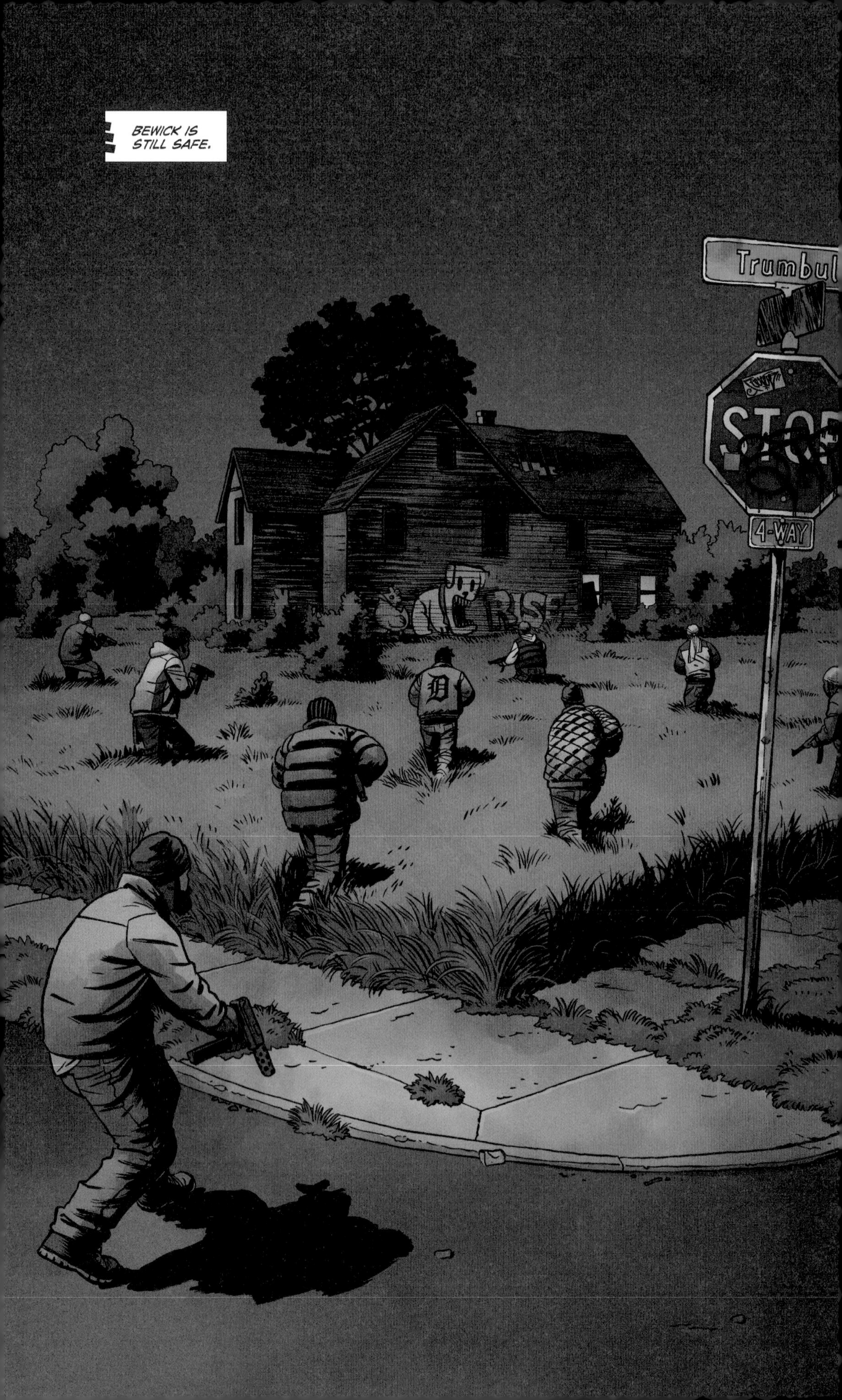
BEWICK IS STILL SAFE.
Trumbul
STOP
4-WAY

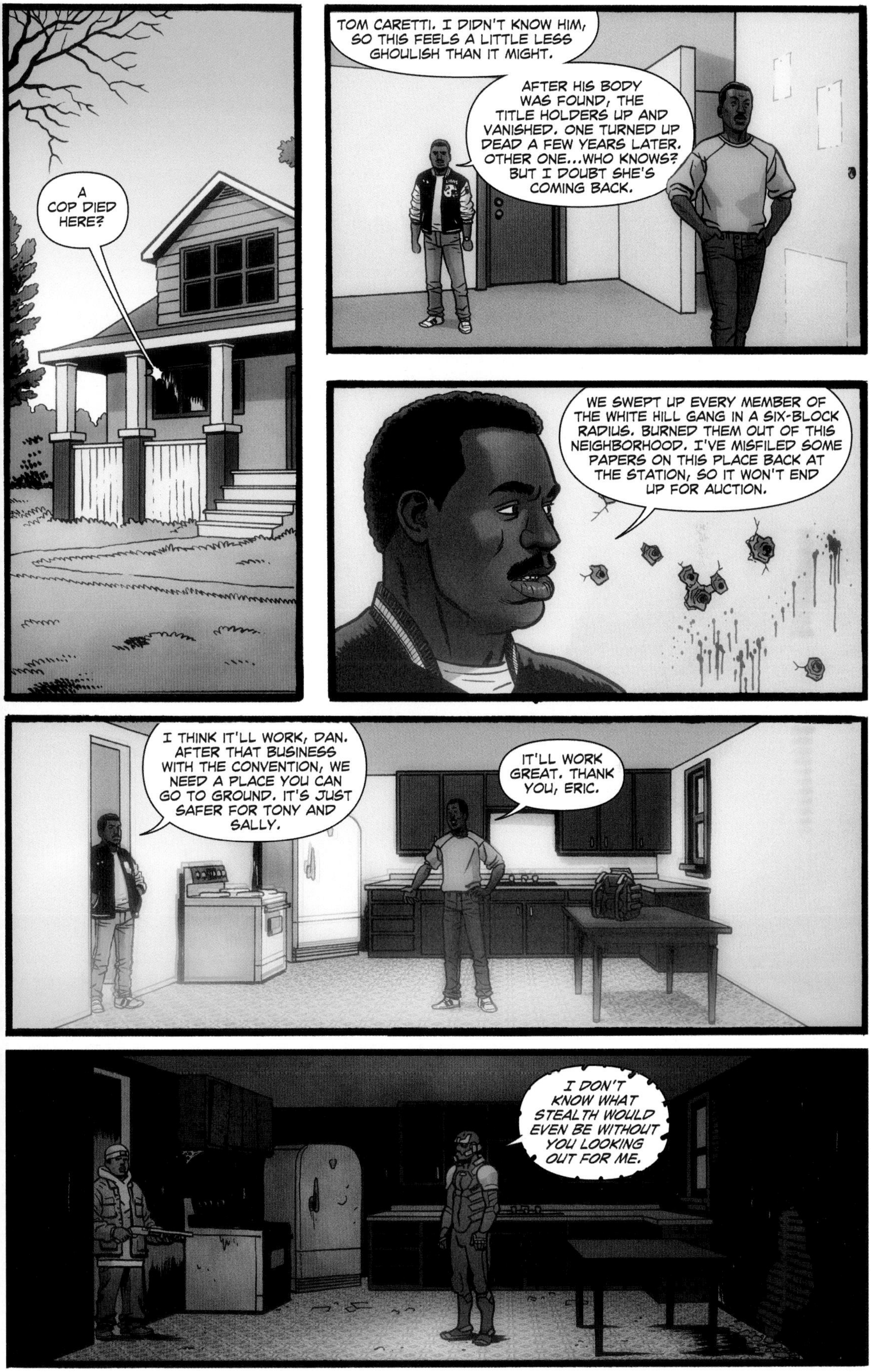
A COP DIED HERE?
TOM CARETTI. I DIDN'T KNOW HIM, SO THIS FEELS A LITTLE LESS GHOULISH THAN IT MIGHT.
AFTER HIS BODY WAS FOUND, THE TITLE HOLDERS UP AND VANISHED. ONE TURNED UP DEAD A FEW YEARS LATER. OTHER ONE...WHO KNOWS? BUT I DOUBT SHE'S COMING BACK.
WE SWEPT UP EVERY MEMBER OF THE WHITE HILL GANG IN A SIX-BLOCK RADIUS. BURNED THEM OUT OF THIS NEIGHBORHOOD. I'VE MISFILED SOME PAPERS ON THIS PLACE BACK AT THE STATION, SO IT WON'T END UP FOR AUCTION.
I THINK IT'LL WORK, DAN. AFTER THAT BUSINESS WITH THE CONVENTION, WE NEED A PLACE YOU CAN GO TO GROUND. IT'S JUST SAFER FOR TONY AND SALLY.
IT'LL WORK GREAT. THANK YOU, ERIC.
I DON'T KNOW WHAT STEALTH WOULD EVEN BE WITHOUT YOU LOOKING OUT FOR ME.

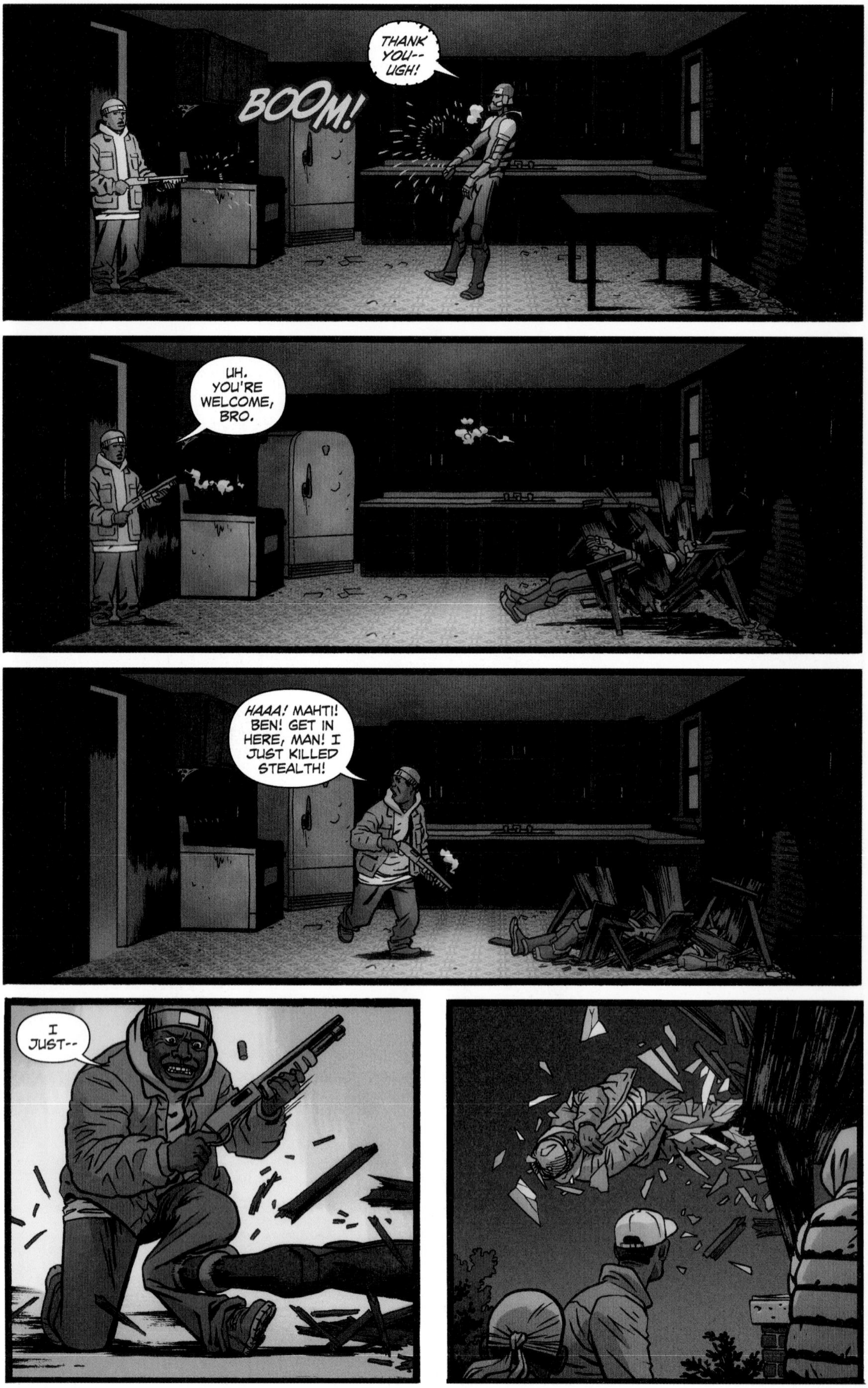

THANK YOU-- UGH!
BOOM!
UH. YOU'RE WELCOME, BRO.
HAAA! MAHTI! BEN! GET IN HERE, MAN! I JUST KILLED STEALTH!
I JUST--

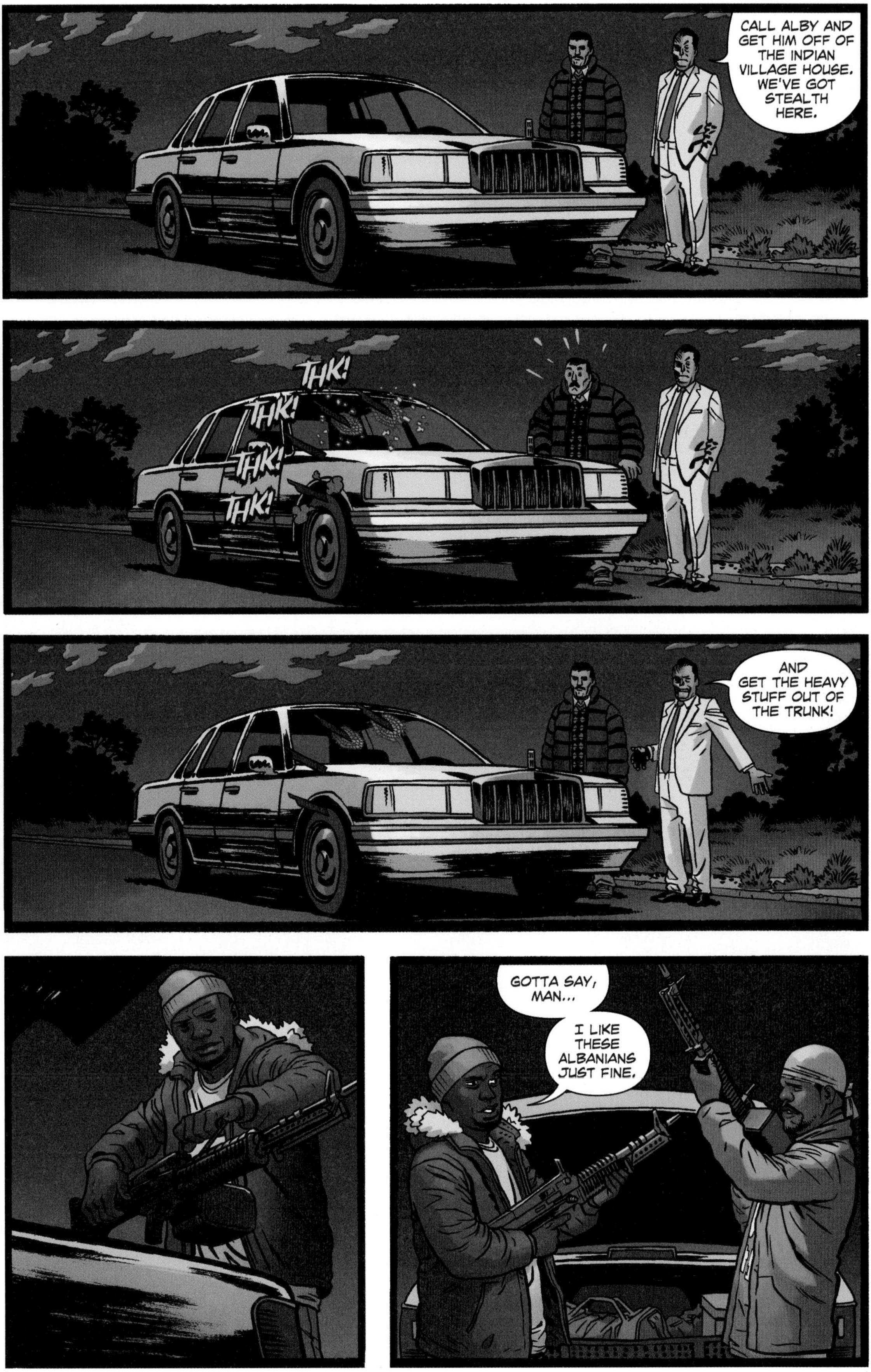
CALL ALBY AND GET HIM OFF OF THE INDIAN VILLAGE HOUSE. WE'VE GOT STEALTH HERE.
THK!
THK!
THK!
THK!
AND GET THE HEAVY STUFF OUT OF THE TRUNK!
GOTTA SAY, MAN...
I LIKE THESE ALBANIANS JUST FINE.

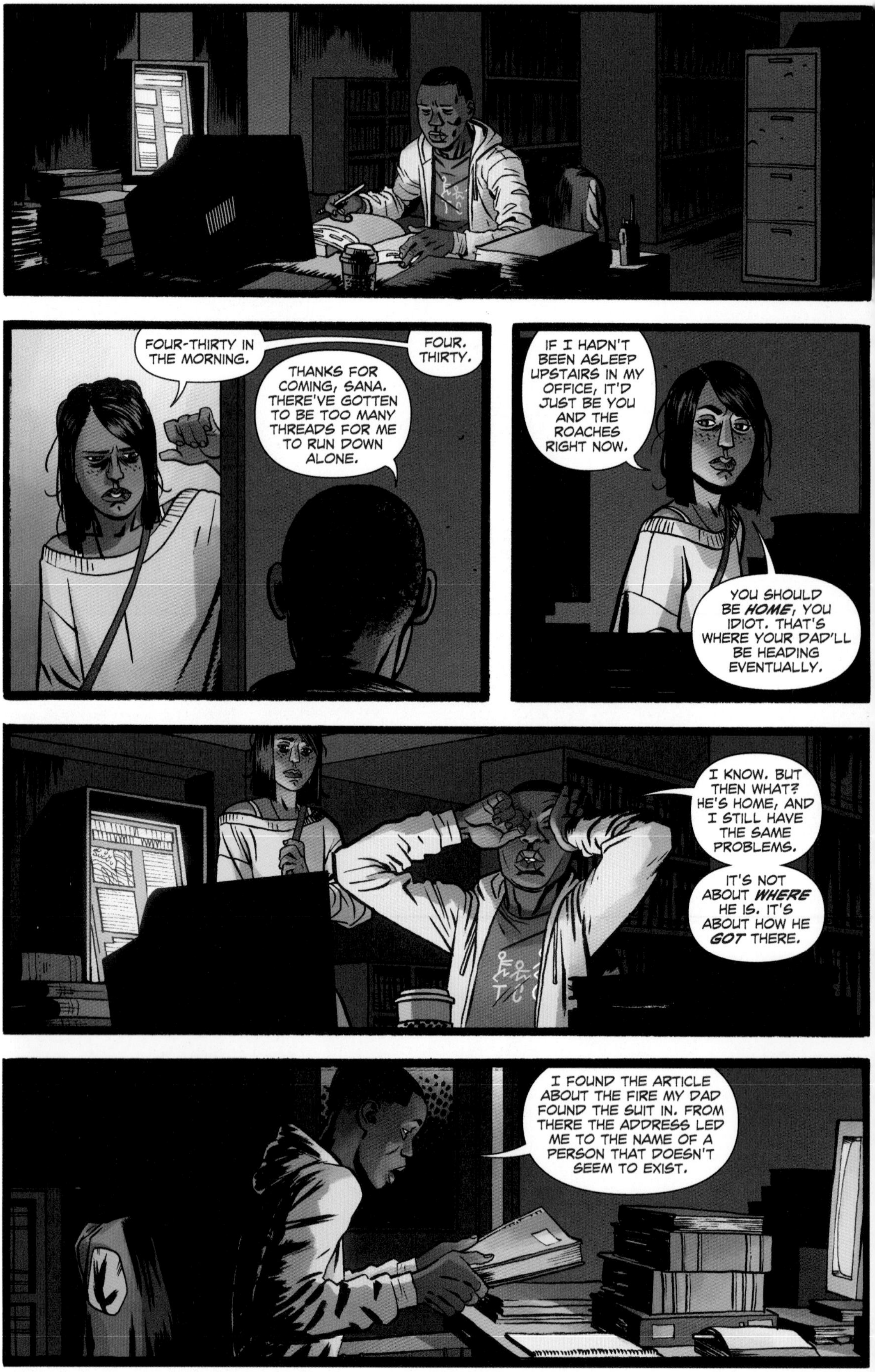
FOUR-THIRTY IN THE MORNING.
FOUR. THIRTY.
THANKS FOR COMING, SANA. THERE'VE GOTTEN TO BE TOO MANY THREADS FOR ME TO RUN DOWN ALONE.
IF I HADN'T BEEN ASLEEP UPSTAIRS IN MY OFFICE, IT'D JUST BE YOU AND THE ROACHES RIGHT NOW.
YOU SHOULD BE ***HOME***, YOU IDIOT. THAT'S WHERE YOUR DAD'LL BE HEADING EVENTUALLY.
I KNOW. BUT THEN WHAT? HE'S HOME, AND I STILL HAVE THE SAME PROBLEMS.
IT'S NOT ABOUT ***WHERE*** HE IS. IT'S ABOUT HOW HE ***GOT*** THERE.
I FOUND THE ARTICLE ABOUT THE FIRE MY DAD FOUND THE SUIT IN. FROM THERE THE ADDRESS LED ME TO THE NAME OF A PERSON THAT DOESN'T SEEM TO EXIST.

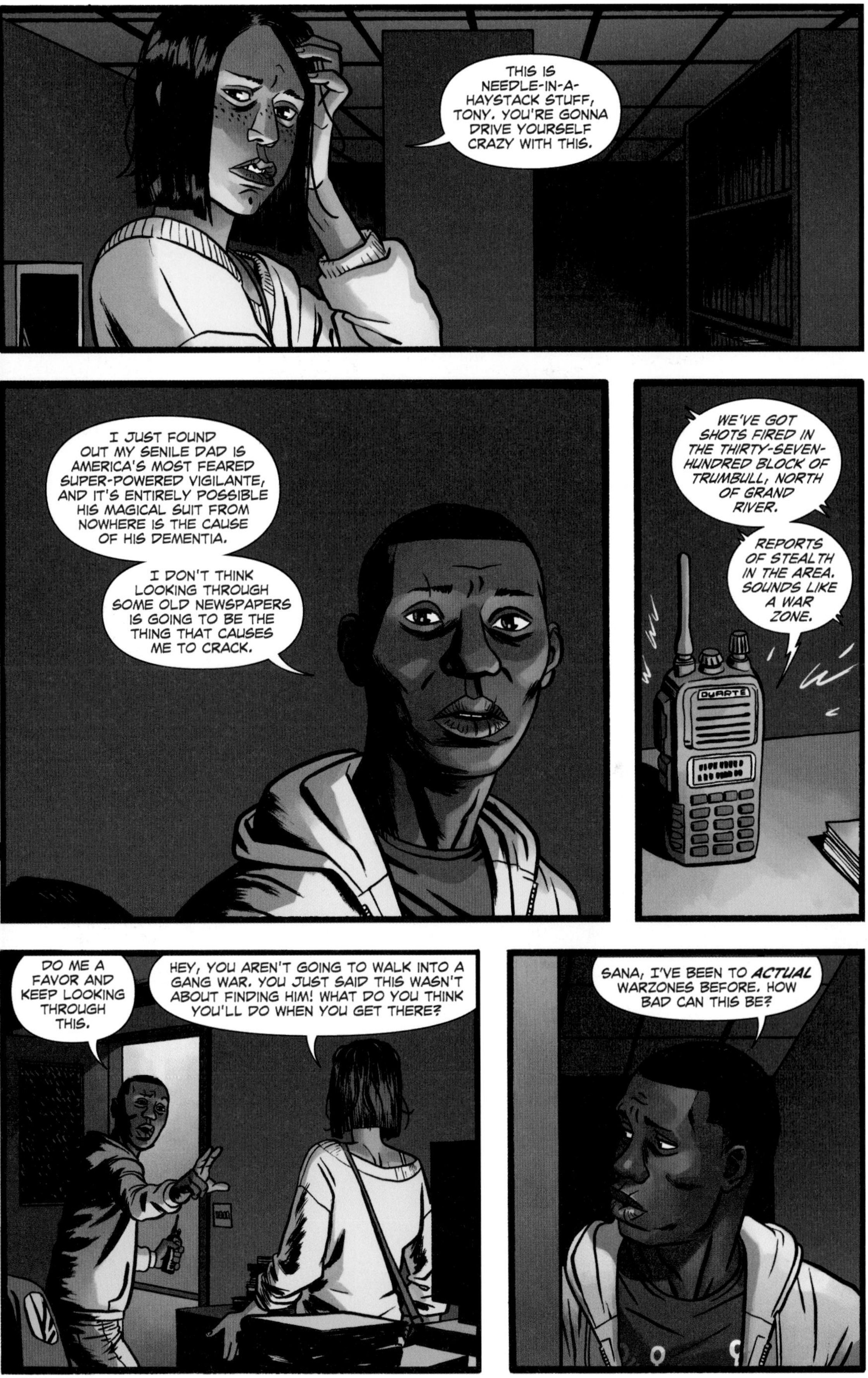
THIS IS NEEDLE-IN-A-HAYSTACK STUFF, TONY. YOU'RE GONNA DRIVE YOURSELF CRAZY WITH THIS.
I JUST FOUND OUT MY SENILE DAD IS AMERICA'S MOST FEARED SUPER-POWERED VIGILANTE, AND IT'S ENTIRELY POSSIBLE HIS MAGICAL SUIT FROM NOWHERE IS THE CAUSE OF HIS DEMENTIA.
I DON'T THINK LOOKING THROUGH SOME OLD NEWSPAPERS IS GOING TO BE THE THING THAT CAUSES ME TO CRACK.
WE'VE GOT SHOTS FIRED IN THE THIRTY-SEVEN-HUNDRED BLOCK OF TRUMBULL, NORTH OF GRAND RIVER.
REPORTS OF STEALTH IN THE AREA. SOUNDS LIKE A WAR ZONE.
DUARTE
DO ME A FAVOR AND KEEP LOOKING THROUGH THIS.
HEY, YOU AREN'T GOING TO WALK INTO A GANG WAR. YOU JUST SAID THIS WASN'T ABOUT FINDING HIM! WHAT DO YOU THINK YOU'LL DO WHEN YOU GET THERE?
SANA, I'VE BEEN TO *ACTUAL* WARZONES BEFORE. HOW BAD CAN THIS BE?

WHERE THE HELL IS ALBY WITH THE REST OF THE GUYS?

DON'T STAND AROUND CRINGING! GET THE HELL IN THERE!

CORNERED. CAN'T GET OUT THROUGH THE ROOF, HOUSE MIGHT COLLAPSE, AND THERE ARE KIDS HERE.

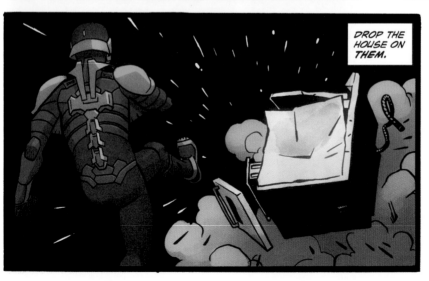

DROP THE HOUSE ON *THEM.*

DEFINITELY FEELS LIKE THE GAS BILL WAS JUST PAID.

GRENADES!

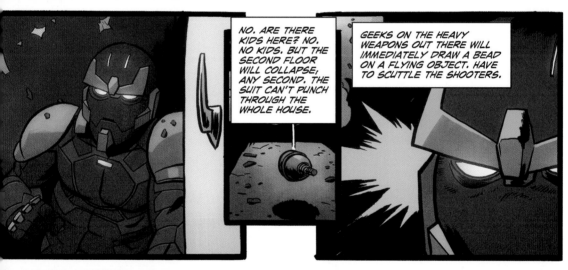

NO. ARE THERE KIDS HERE? NO. NO KIDS. BUT THE SECOND FLOOR WILL COLLAPSE, ANY SECOND. THE SUIT CAN'T PUNCH THROUGH THE WHOLE HOUSE.

GEEKS ON THE HEAVY WEAPONS OUT THERE WILL IMMEDIATELY DRAW A BEAD ON A FLYING OBJECT. HAVE TO SCUTTLE THE SHOOTERS.

PLEASE DON'T LET THAT BE A MEMORY FROM TWENTY YEARS AGO.

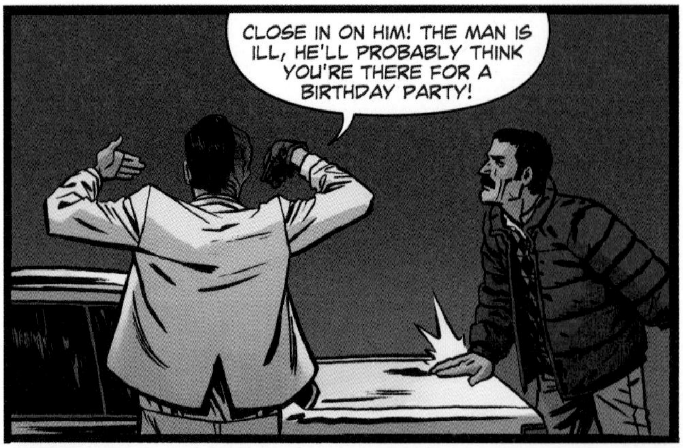
CLOSE IN ON HIM! THE MAN IS ILL, HE'LL PROBABLY THINK YOU'RE THERE FOR A BIRTHDAY PARTY!

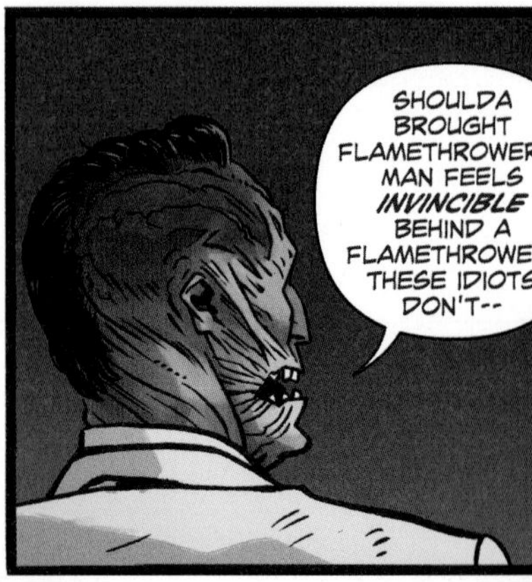
SHOULDA BROUGHT FLAMETHROWERS. MAN FEELS *INVINCIBLE* BEHIND A FLAMETHROWER. THESE IDIOTS DON'T--

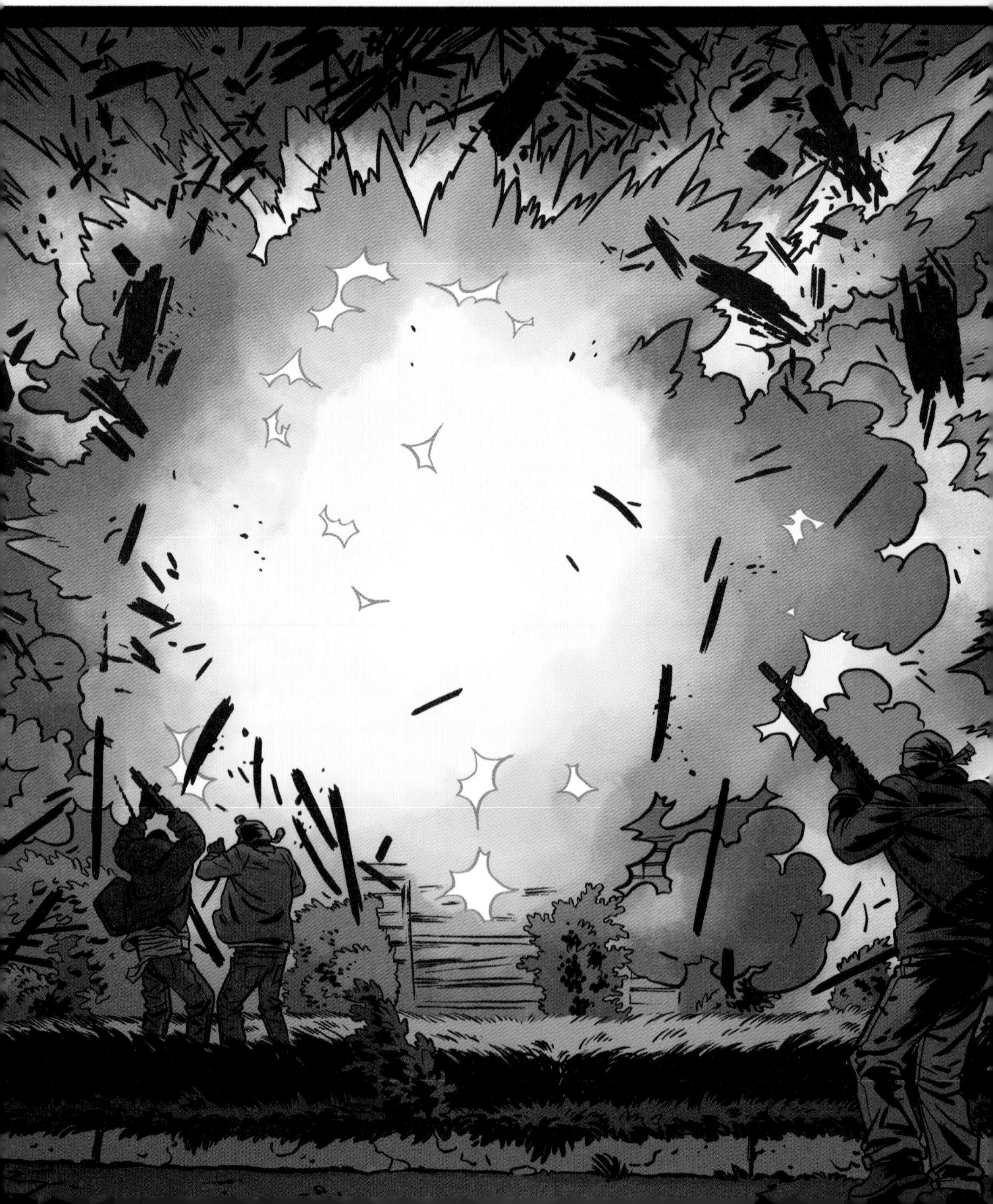

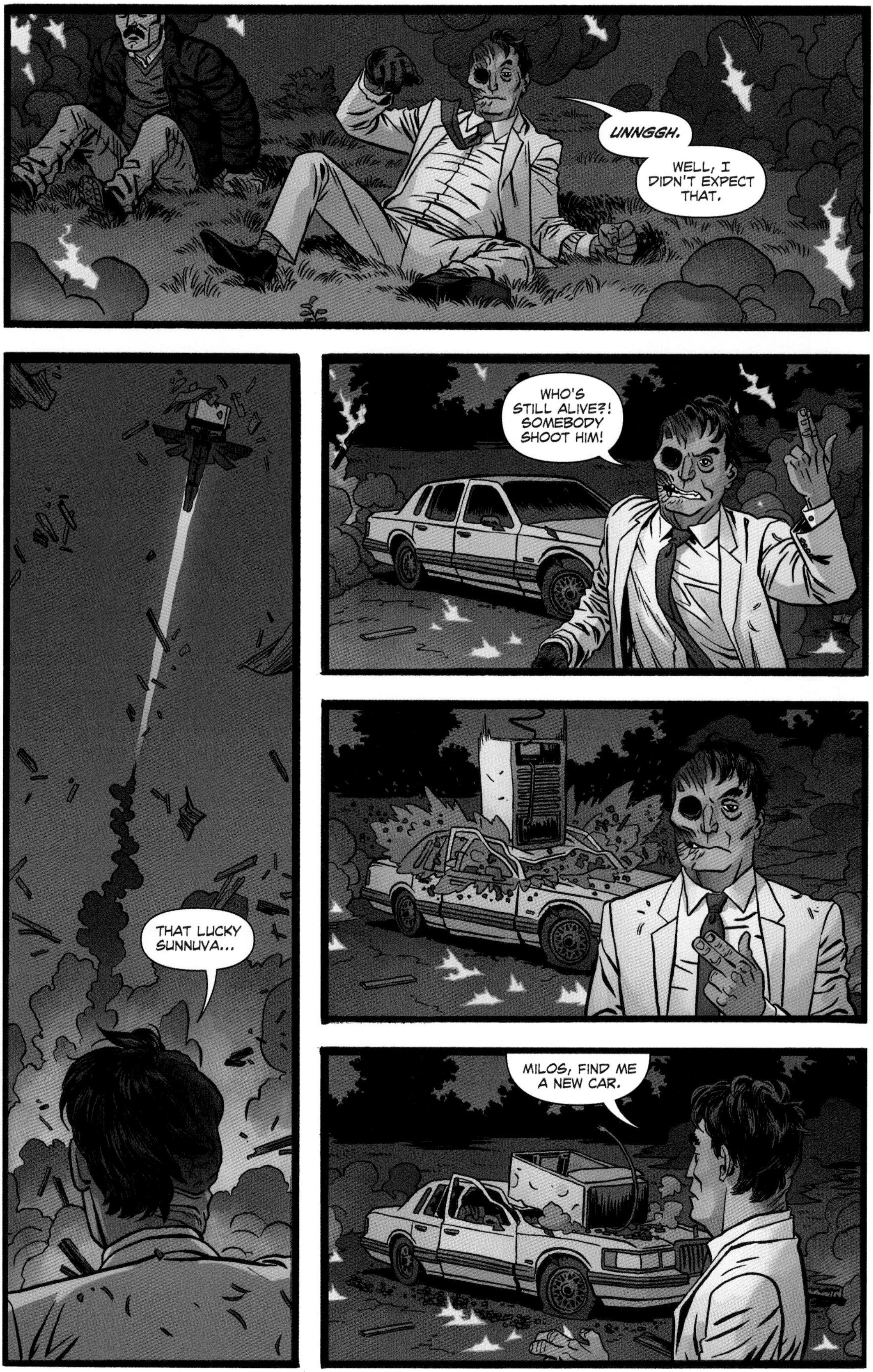
UNNGGH.
WELL, I DIDN'T EXPECT THAT.
THAT LUCKY SUNNUVA...
WHO'S STILL ALIVE?! SOMEBODY SHOOT HIM!
MILOS, FIND ME A NEW CAR.

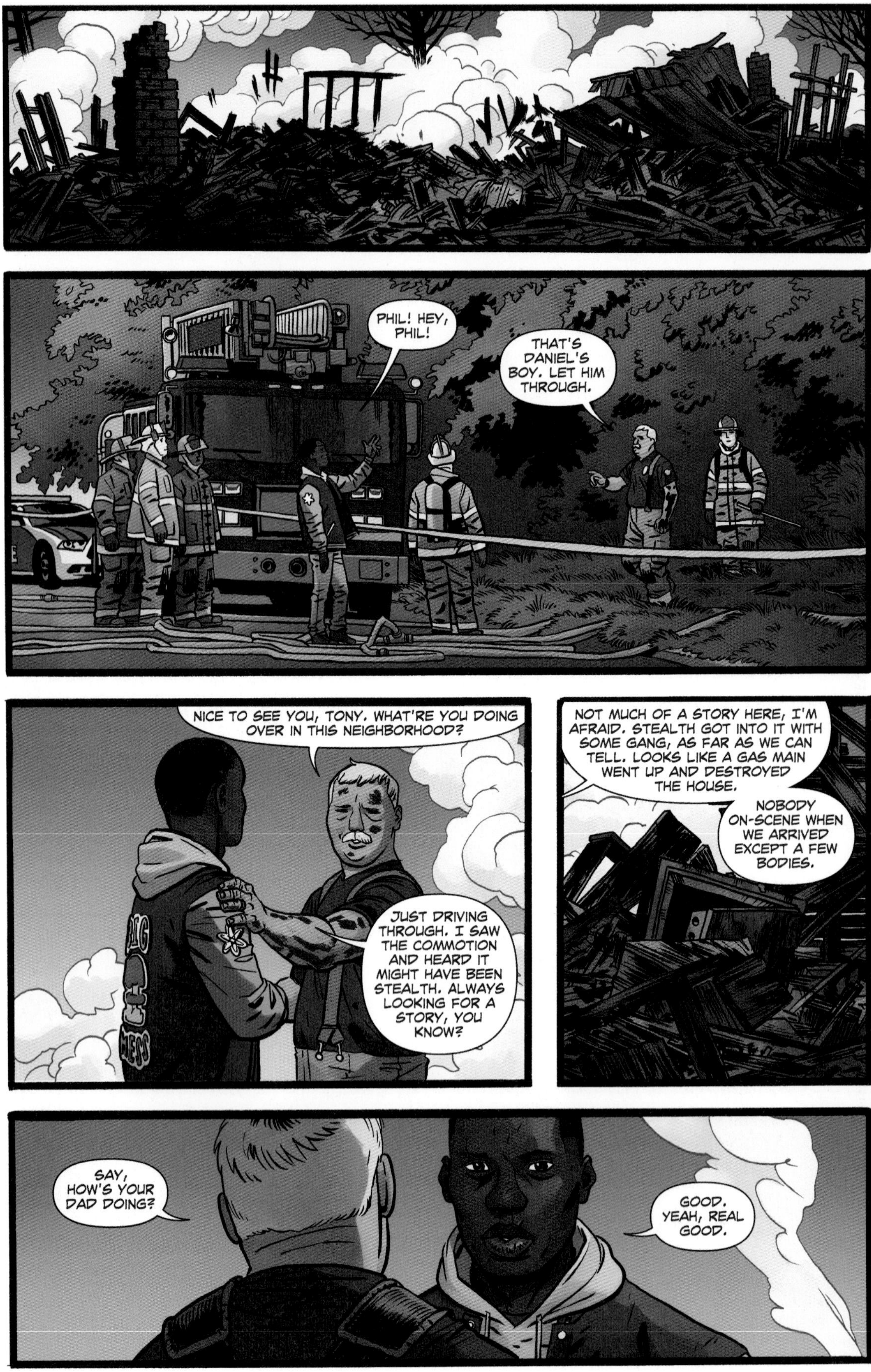
PHIL! HEY, PHIL!
THAT'S DANIEL'S BOY. LET HIM THROUGH.
NICE TO SEE YOU, TONY. WHAT'RE YOU DOING OVER IN THIS NEIGHBORHOOD?
JUST DRIVING THROUGH. I SAW THE COMMOTION AND HEARD IT MIGHT HAVE BEEN STEALTH. ALWAYS LOOKING FOR A STORY, YOU KNOW?
NOT MUCH OF A STORY HERE, I'M AFRAID. STEALTH GOT INTO IT WITH SOME GANG, AS FAR AS WE CAN TELL. LOOKS LIKE A GAS MAIN WENT UP AND DESTROYED THE HOUSE.
NOBODY ON-SCENE WHEN WE ARRIVED EXCEPT A FEW BODIES.
SAY, HOW'S YOUR DAD DOING?
GOOD. YEAH, REAL GOOD.

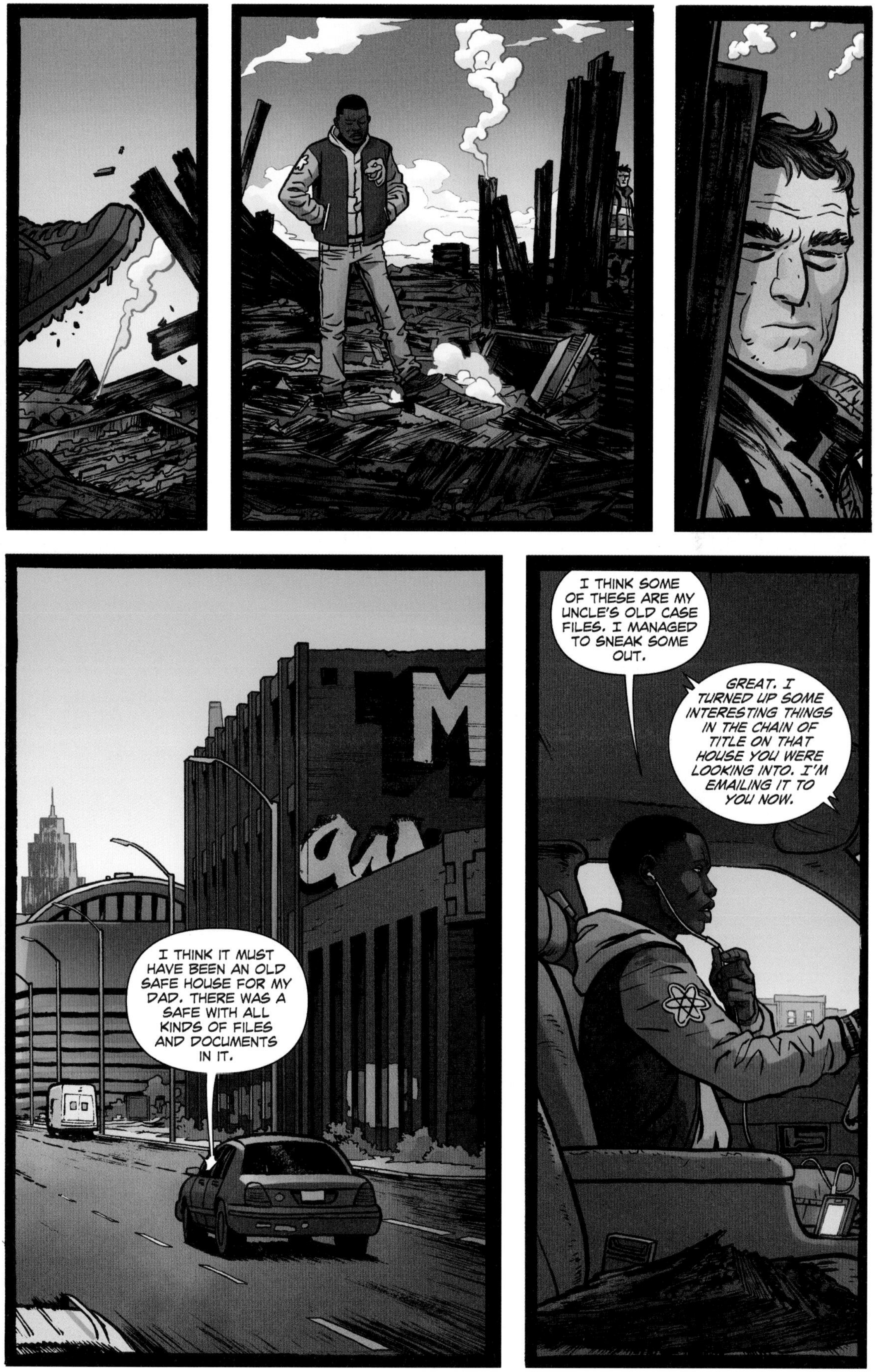
I THINK IT MUST HAVE BEEN AN OLD SAFE HOUSE FOR MY DAD. THERE WAS A SAFE WITH ALL KINDS OF FILES AND DOCUMENTS IN IT.
I THINK SOME OF THESE ARE MY UNCLE'S OLD CASE FILES. I MANAGED TO SNEAK SOME OUT.
GREAT. I TURNED UP SOME INTERESTING THINGS IN THE CHAIN OF TITLE ON THAT HOUSE YOU WERE LOOKING INTO. I'M EMAILING IT TO YOU NOW.

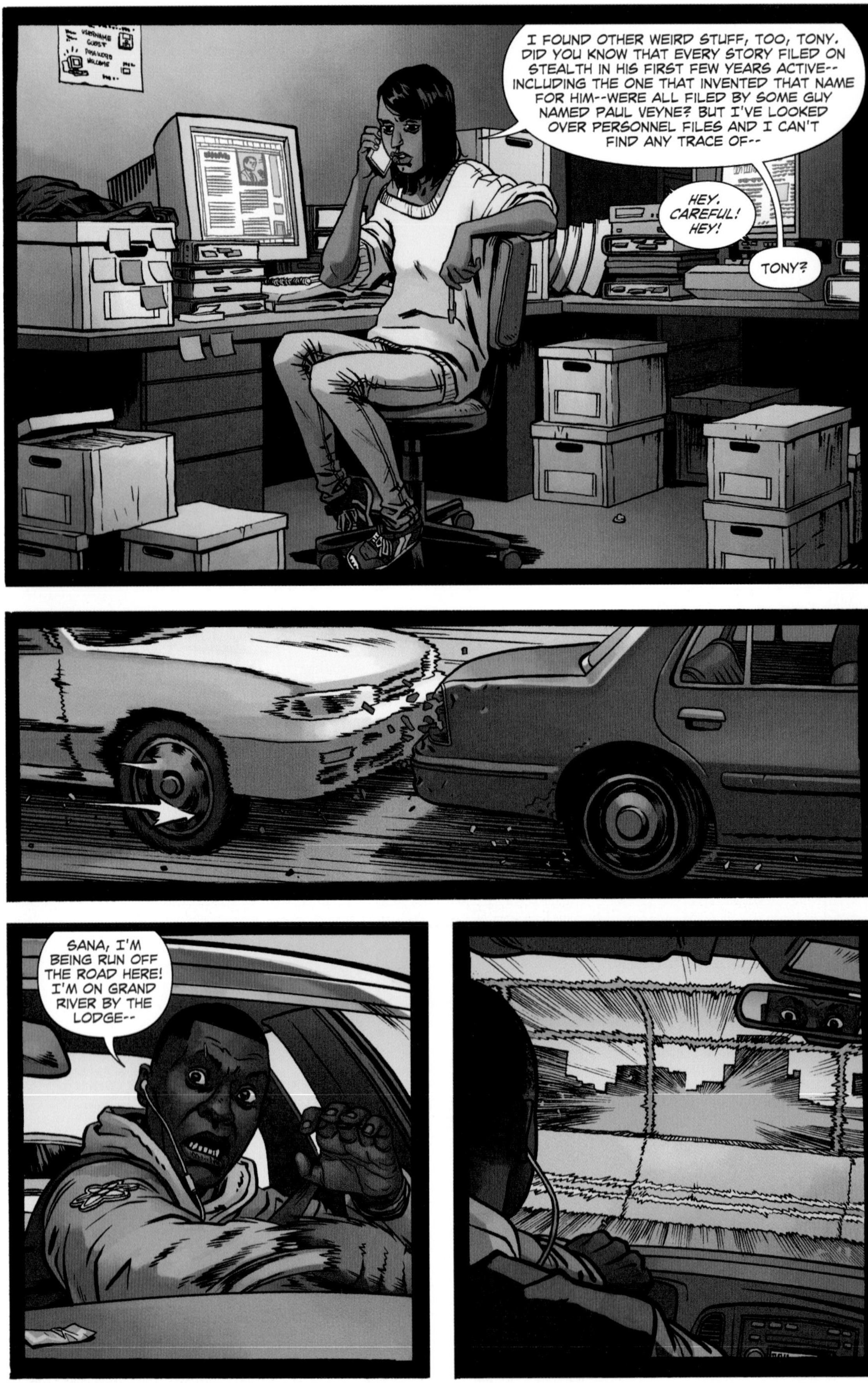

I FOUND OTHER WEIRD STUFF, TOO, TONY. DID YOU KNOW THAT EVERY STORY FILED ON STEALTH IN HIS FIRST FEW YEARS ACTIVE--INCLUDING THE ONE THAT INVENTED THAT NAME FOR HIM--WERE ALL FILED BY SOME GUY NAMED PAUL VEYNE? BUT I'VE LOOKED OVER PERSONNEL FILES AND I CAN'T FIND ANY TRACE OF--
HEY. CAREFUL! HEY!
TONY?
SANA, I'M BEING RUN OFF THE ROAD HERE! I'M ON GRAND RIVER BY THE LODGE--

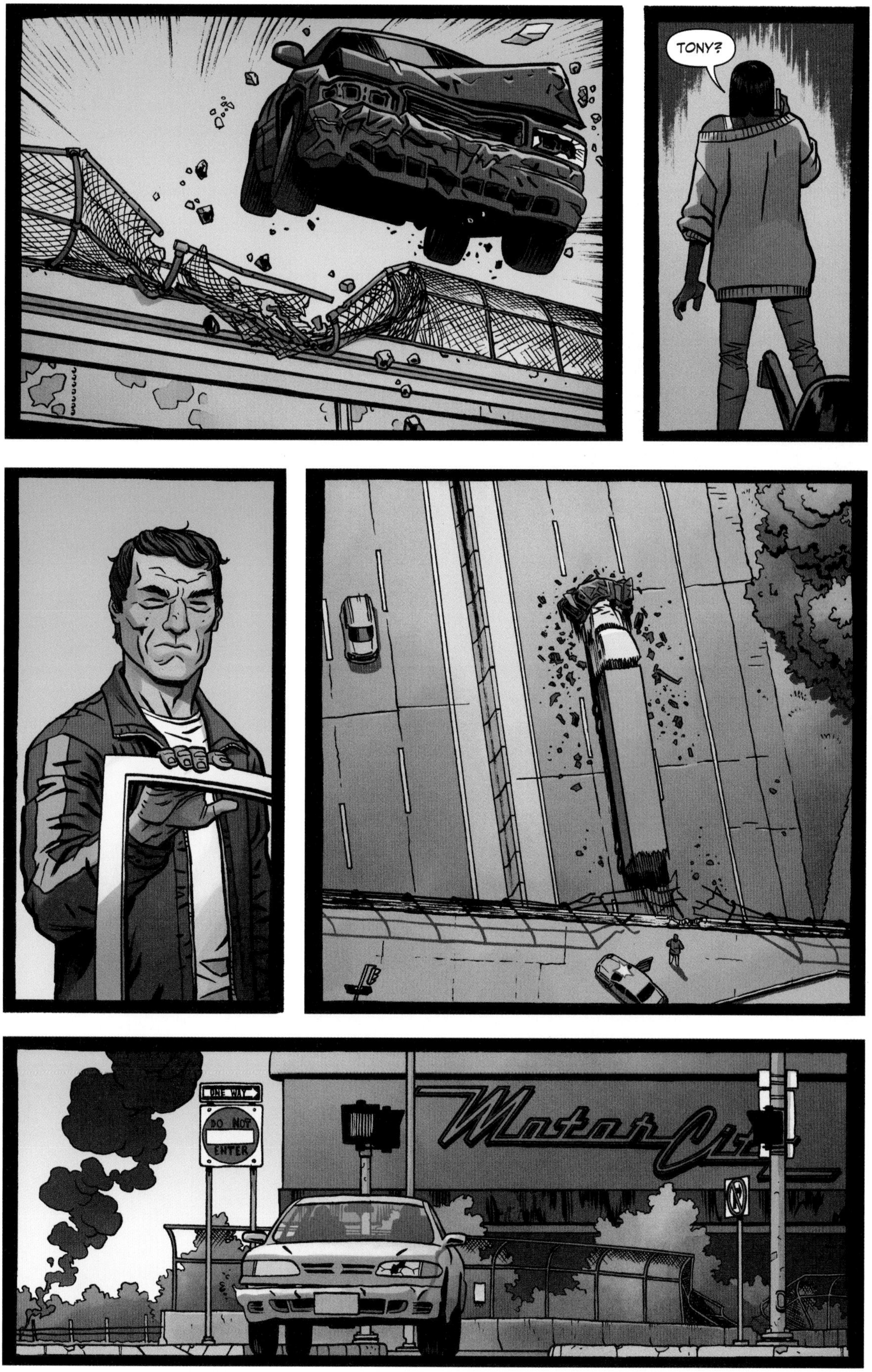
TONY?
ONE WAY
DO NOT
ENTER

TONY?!

I'M HERE, SANA.

SOMEONE RAN ME OFF AN OVERPASS. I GOT OUT OF THE CAR BEFORE IT WAS HIT BY ONCOMING TRAFFIC.

YOU WERE RUN OFF AN OVERPASS AND YOU GOT OUT OF THE CAR? WHO ARE YOU, BRUCE WILLIS?

MY WINDOW BROKE OUT. I MANAGED TO CRAWL OUT. I DON'T KNOW, MY BELL GOT RUNG, I'M A LITTLE FUZZY.

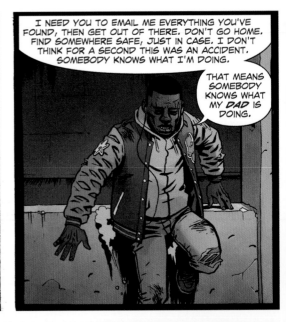

I NEED YOU TO EMAIL ME EVERYTHING YOU'VE FOUND, THEN GET OUT OF THERE. DON'T GO HOME. FIND SOMEWHERE SAFE, JUST IN CASE. I DON'T THINK FOR A SECOND THIS WAS AN ACCIDENT. SOMEBODY KNOWS WHAT I'M DOING.

THAT MEANS SOMEBODY KNOWS WHAT MY DAD IS DOING.

WHICH MEANS THEY PROBABLY HAVE THE ANSWERS I WANT.

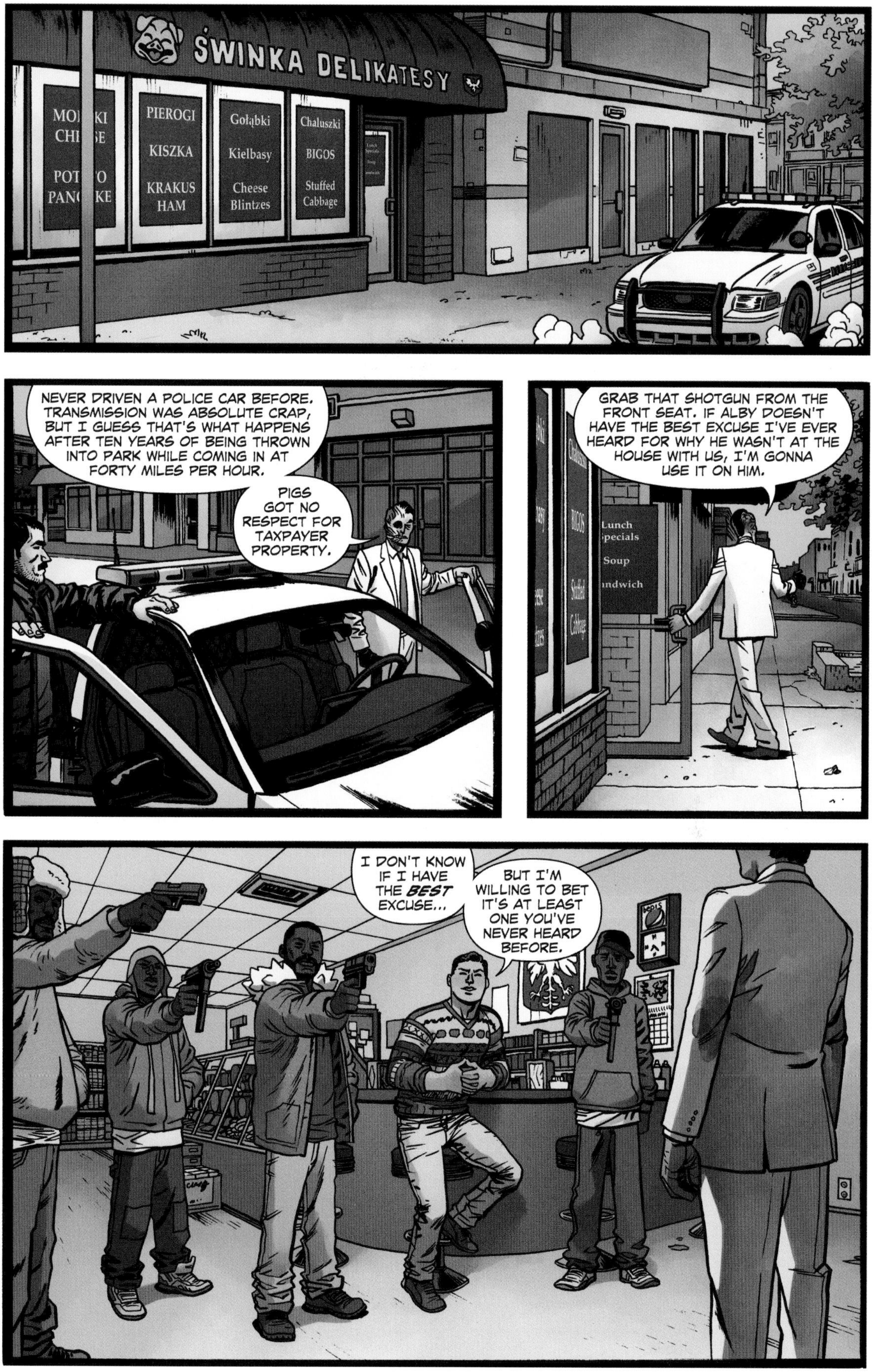
ŚWINKA DELIKATESY
PIEROGI KISZKA KRAKUS HAM
Gołąbki Kielbasy Cheese Blintzes
Chaluszki BIGOS Stuffed Cabbage
NEVER DRIVEN A POLICE CAR BEFORE. TRANSMISSION WAS ABSOLUTE CRAP, BUT I GUESS THAT'S WHAT HAPPENS AFTER TEN YEARS OF BEING THROWN INTO PARK WHILE COMING IN AT FORTY MILES PER HOUR.
PIGS GOT NO RESPECT FOR TAXPAYER PROPERTY.
GRAB THAT SHOTGUN FROM THE FRONT SEAT. IF ALBY DOESN'T HAVE THE BEST EXCUSE I'VE EVER HEARD FOR WHY HE WASN'T AT THE HOUSE WITH US, I'M GONNA USE IT ON HIM.
I DON'T KNOW IF I HAVE THE *BEST* EXCUSE...
BUT I'M WILLING TO BET IT'S AT LEAST ONE YOU'VE NEVER HEARD BEFORE.

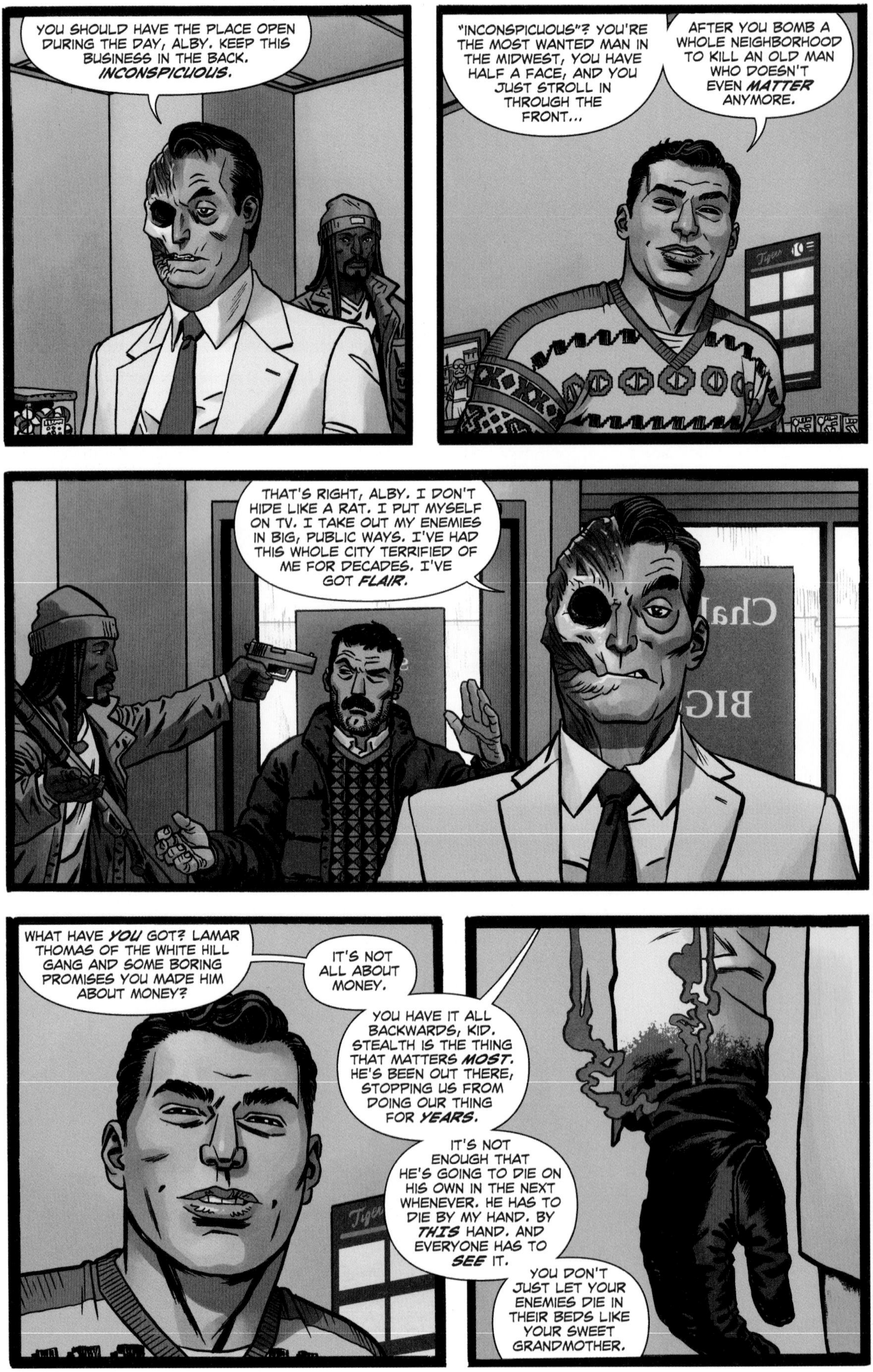
YOU SHOULD HAVE THE PLACE OPEN DURING THE DAY, ALBY. KEEP THIS BUSINESS IN THE BACK. *INCONSPICUOUS.*
"INCONSPICUOUS"? YOU'RE THE MOST WANTED MAN IN THE MIDWEST, YOU HAVE HALF A FACE, AND YOU JUST STROLL IN THROUGH THE FRONT...
AFTER YOU BOMB A WHOLE NEIGHBORHOOD TO KILL AN OLD MAN WHO DOESN'T EVEN *MATTER* ANYMORE.
THAT'S RIGHT, ALBY. I DON'T HIDE LIKE A RAT. I PUT MYSELF ON TV. I TAKE OUT MY ENEMIES IN BIG, PUBLIC WAYS. I'VE HAD THIS WHOLE CITY TERRIFIED OF ME FOR DECADES. I'VE GOT *FLAIR.*
WHAT HAVE *YOU* GOT? LAMAR THOMAS OF THE WHITE HILL GANG AND SOME BORING PROMISES YOU MADE HIM ABOUT MONEY?
IT'S NOT ALL ABOUT MONEY.
YOU HAVE IT ALL BACKWARDS, KID. STEALTH IS THE THING THAT MATTERS *MOST.* HE'S BEEN OUT THERE, STOPPING US FROM DOING OUR THING FOR *YEARS.*
IT'S NOT ENOUGH THAT HE'S GOING TO DIE ON HIS OWN IN THE NEXT WHENEVER. HE HAS TO DIE BY MY HAND. BY *THIS* HAND. AND EVERYONE HAS TO *SEE* IT.
YOU DON'T JUST LET YOUR ENEMIES DIE IN THEIR BEDS LIKE YOUR SWEET GRANDMOTHER.

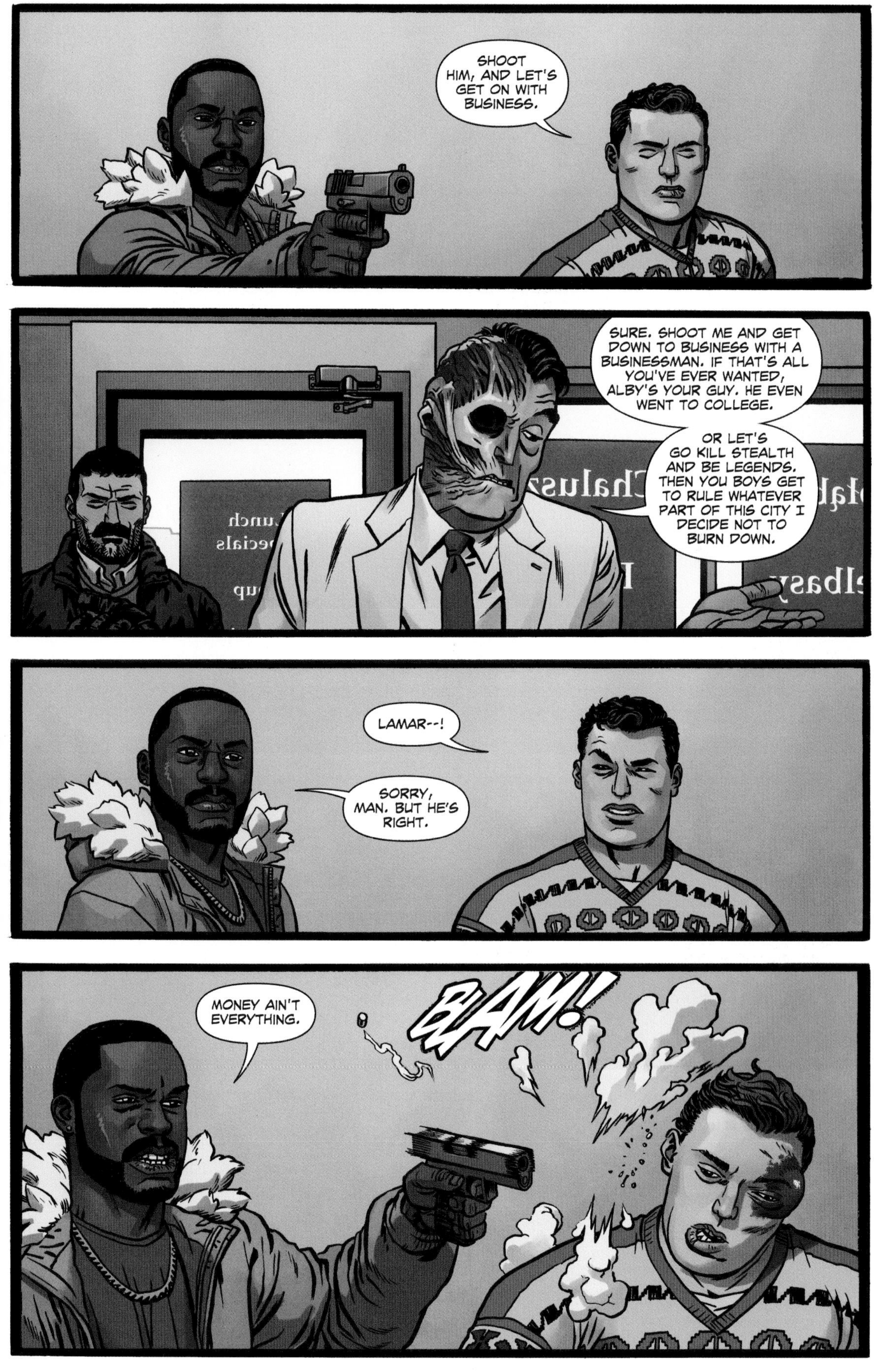
SHOOT HIM, AND LET'S GET ON WITH BUSINESS.
SURE. SHOOT ME AND GET DOWN TO BUSINESS WITH A BUSINESSMAN. IF THAT'S ALL YOU'VE EVER WANTED, ALBY'S YOUR GUY. HE EVEN WENT TO COLLEGE.
OR LET'S GO KILL STEALTH AND BE LEGENDS. THEN YOU BOYS GET TO RULE WHATEVER PART OF THIS CITY I DECIDE NOT TO BURN DOWN.
LAMAR--!
SORRY, MAN. BUT HE'S RIGHT.
MONEY AIN'T EVERYTHING.
BLAM!

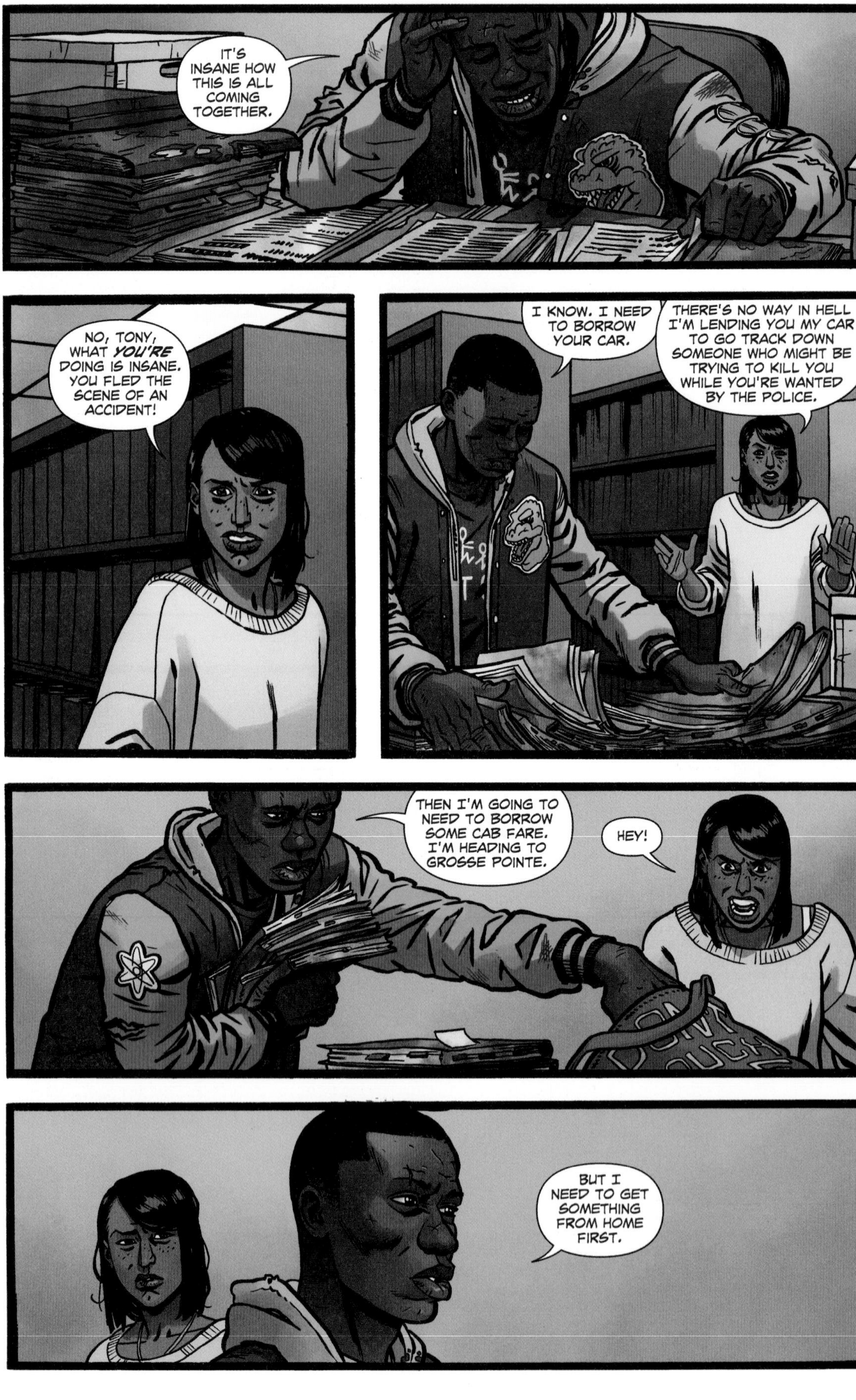
IT'S INSANE HOW THIS IS ALL COMING TOGETHER.
NO, TONY, WHAT *YOU'RE* DOING IS INSANE. YOU FLED THE SCENE OF AN ACCIDENT!
I KNOW. I NEED TO BORROW YOUR CAR.
THERE'S NO WAY IN HELL I'M LENDING YOU MY CAR TO GO TRACK DOWN SOMEONE WHO MIGHT BE TRYING TO KILL YOU WHILE YOU'RE WANTED BY THE POLICE.
THEN I'M GOING TO NEED TO BORROW SOME CAB FARE. I'M HEADING TO GROSSE POINTE.
HEY!
BUT I NEED TO GET SOMETHING FROM HOME FIRST.

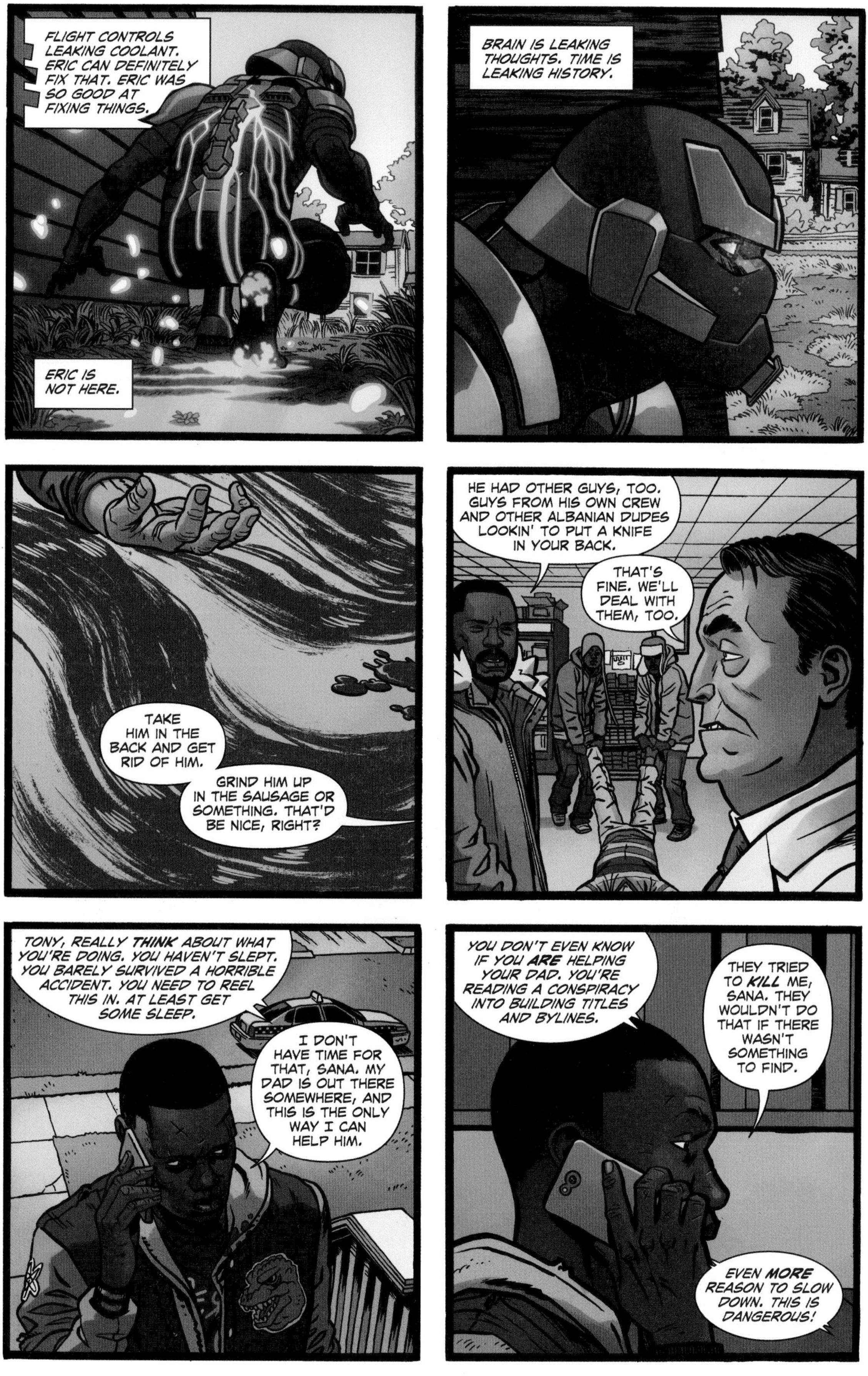
FLIGHT CONTROLS LEAKING COOLANT. ERIC CAN DEFINITELY FIX THAT. ERIC WAS SO GOOD AT FIXING THINGS.
ERIC IS NOT HERE.
BRAIN IS LEAKING THOUGHTS. TIME IS LEAKING HISTORY.
TAKE HIM IN THE BACK AND GET RID OF HIM.
GRIND HIM UP IN THE SAUSAGE OR SOMETHING. THAT'D BE NICE, RIGHT?
HE HAD OTHER GUYS, TOO. GUYS FROM HIS OWN CREW AND OTHER ALBANIAN DUDES LOOKIN' TO PUT A KNIFE IN YOUR BACK.
THAT'S FINE. WE'LL DEAL WITH THEM, TOO.
TONY, REALLY THINK ABOUT WHAT YOU'RE DOING. YOU HAVEN'T SLEPT. YOU BARELY SURVIVED A HORRIBLE ACCIDENT. YOU NEED TO REEL THIS IN. AT LEAST GET SOME SLEEP.
I DON'T HAVE TIME FOR THAT, SANA. MY DAD IS OUT THERE SOMEWHERE, AND THIS IS THE ONLY WAY I CAN HELP HIM.
YOU DON'T EVEN KNOW IF YOU ARE HELPING YOUR DAD. YOU'RE READING A CONSPIRACY INTO BUILDING TITLES AND BYLINES.
THEY TRIED TO KILL ME, SANA. THEY WOULDN'T DO THAT IF THERE WASN'T SOMETHING TO FIND.
EVEN MORE REASON TO SLOW DOWN. THIS IS DANGEROUS!

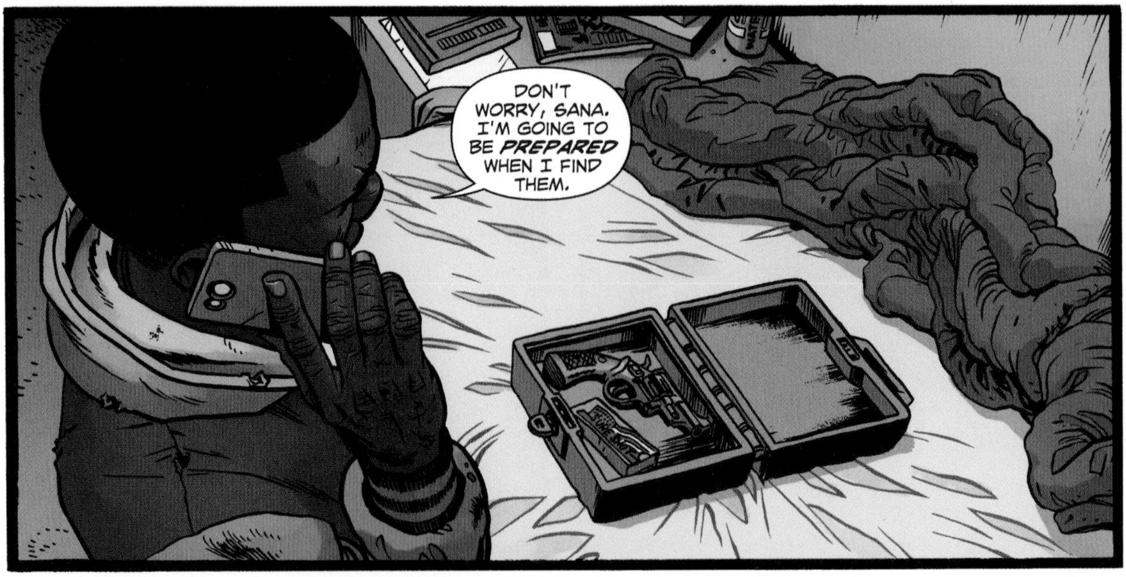
DON'T WORRY, SANA. I'M GOING TO BE PREPARED WHEN I FIND THEM.

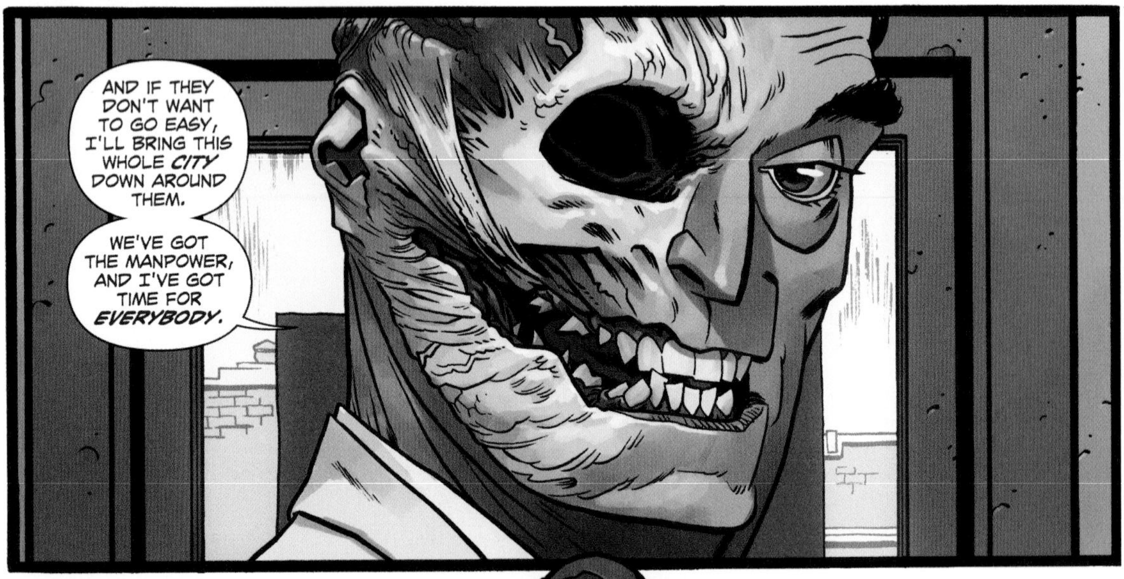
AND IF THEY DON'T WANT TO GO EASY, I'LL BRING THIS WHOLE CITY DOWN AROUND THEM.
WE'VE GOT THE MANPOWER, AND I'VE GOT TIME FOR EVERYBODY.

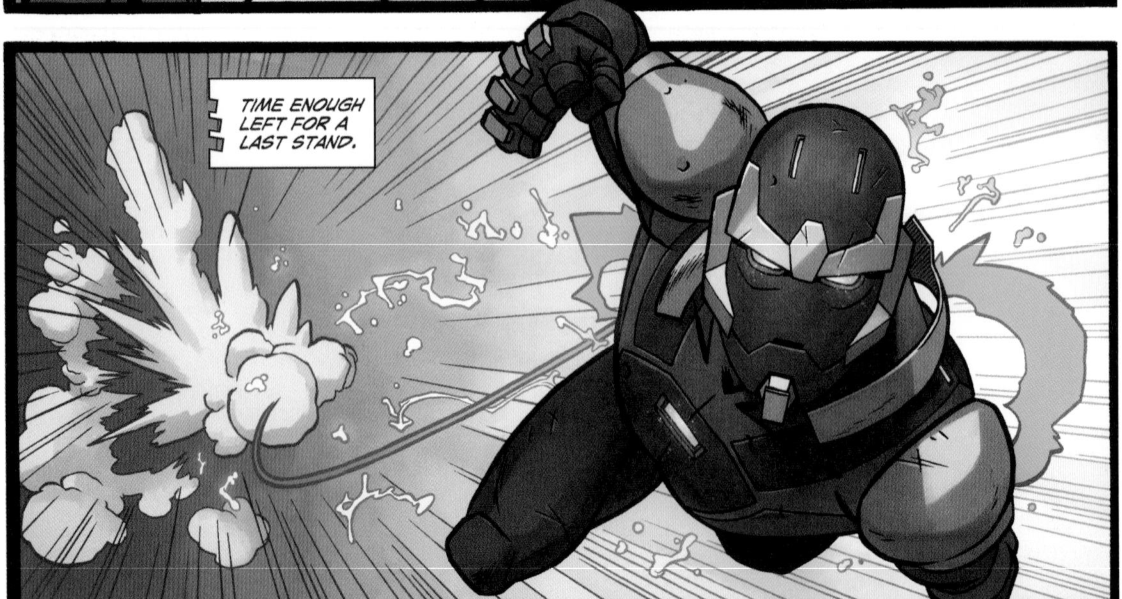
TIME ENOUGH LEFT FOR A LAST STAND.

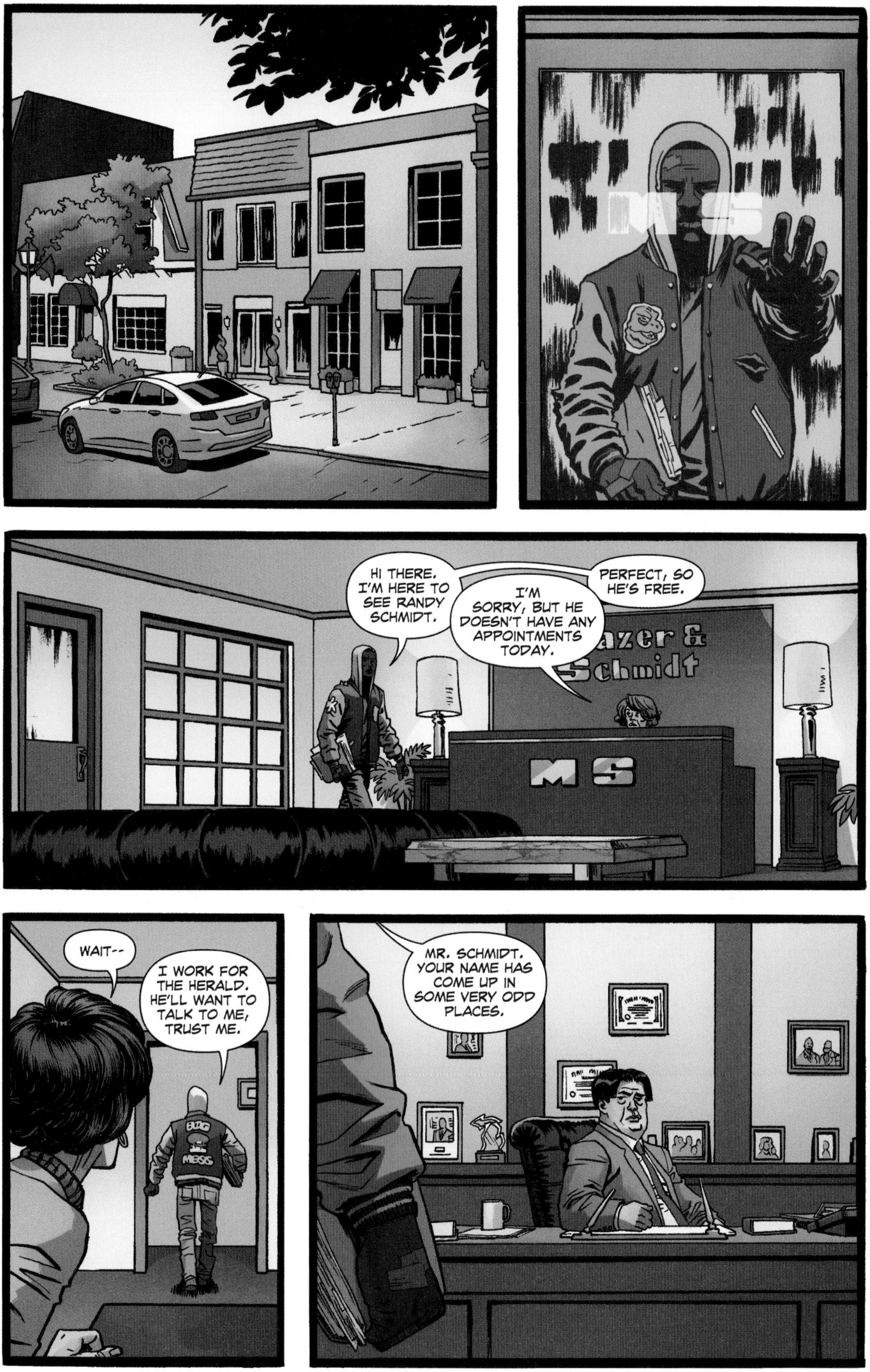
HI THERE. I'M HERE TO SEE RANDY SCHMIDT.
I'M SORRY, BUT HE DOESN'T HAVE ANY APPOINTMENTS TODAY.
PERFECT, SO HE'S FREE.
WAIT--
I WORK FOR THE HERALD. HE'LL WANT TO TALK TO ME, TRUST ME.
MR. SCHMIDT. YOUR NAME HAS COME UP IN SOME VERY ODD PLACES.

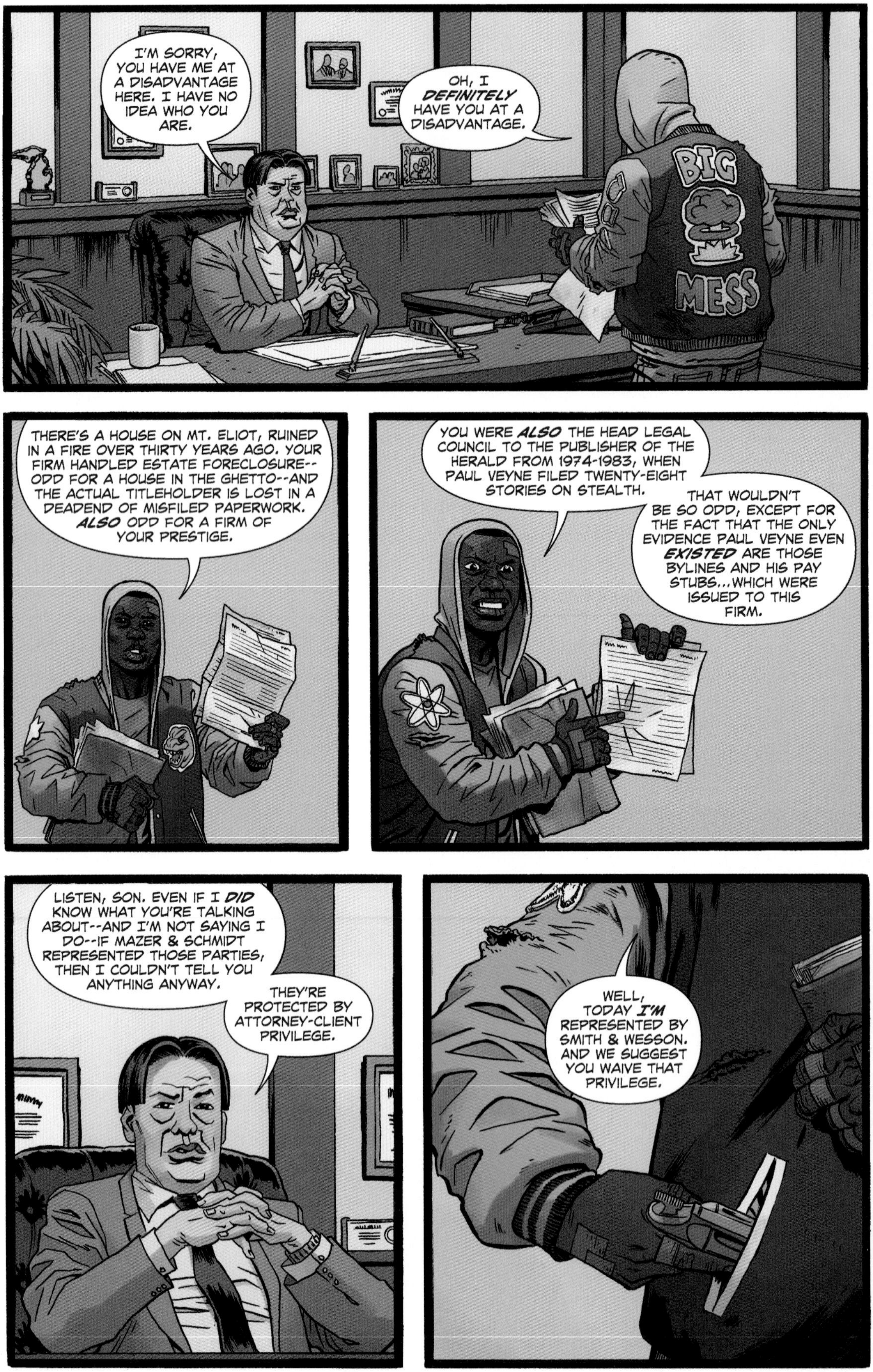
I'M SORRY, YOU HAVE ME AT A DISADVANTAGE HERE. I HAVE NO IDEA WHO YOU ARE.
OH, I *DEFINITELY* HAVE YOU AT A DISADVANTAGE.
BIG MESS
THERE'S A HOUSE ON MT. ELIOT, RUINED IN A FIRE OVER THIRTY YEARS AGO. YOUR FIRM HANDLED ESTATE FORECLOSURE--ODD FOR A HOUSE IN THE GHETTO--AND THE ACTUAL TITLEHOLDER IS LOST IN A DEADEND OF MISFILED PAPERWORK. *ALSO* ODD FOR A FIRM OF YOUR PRESTIGE.
YOU WERE *ALSO* THE HEAD LEGAL COUNCIL TO THE PUBLISHER OF THE HERALD FROM 1974-1983, WHEN PAUL VEYNE FILED TWENTY-EIGHT STORIES ON STEALTH.
THAT WOULDN'T BE SO ODD, EXCEPT FOR THE FACT THAT THE ONLY EVIDENCE PAUL VEYNE EVEN *EXISTED* ARE THOSE BYLINES AND HIS PAY STUBS...WHICH WERE ISSUED TO THIS FIRM.
LISTEN, SON. EVEN IF I *DID* KNOW WHAT YOU'RE TALKING ABOUT--AND I'M NOT SAYING I DO--IF MAZER & SCHMIDT REPRESENTED THOSE PARTIES, THEN I COULDN'T TELL YOU ANYTHING ANYWAY.
THEY'RE PROTECTED BY ATTORNEY-CLIENT PRIVILEGE.
WELL, TODAY *I'M* REPRESENTED BY SMITH & WESSON. AND WE SUGGEST YOU WAIVE THAT PRIVILEGE.

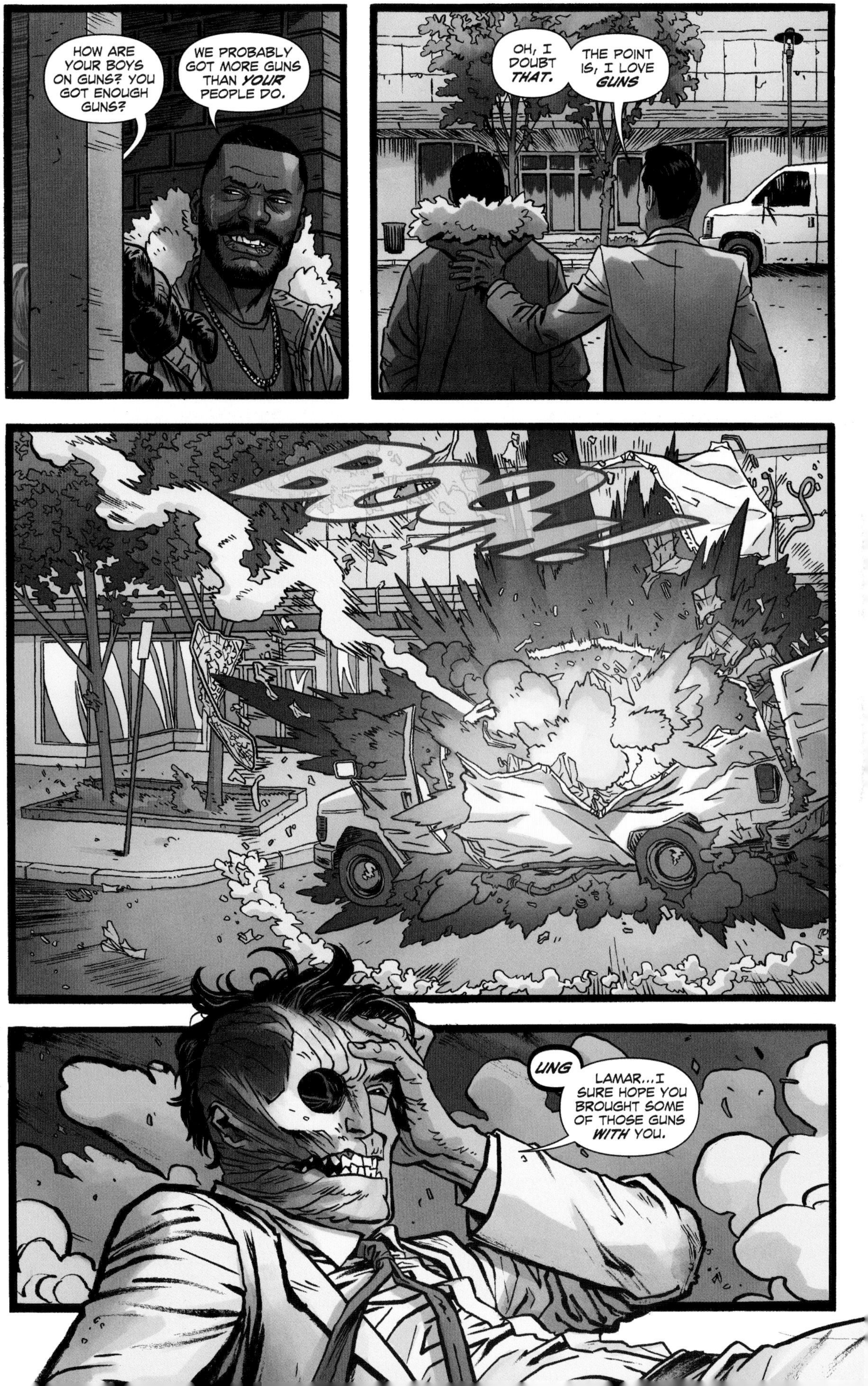

HOW ARE YOUR BOYS ON GUNS? YOU GOT ENOUGH GUNS?
WE PROBABLY GOT MORE GUNS THAN *YOUR* PEOPLE DO.
OH, I DOUBT *THAT.*
THE POINT IS, I LOVE *GUNS*
UNG
LAMAR...I SURE HOPE YOU BROUGHT SOME OF THOSE GUNS *WITH* YOU.

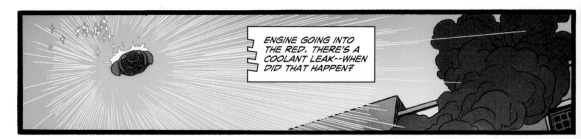

ENGINE GOING INTO THE RED. THERE'S A COOLANT LEAK--WHEN DID THAT HAPPEN?

DOESN'T MATTER. IT GOT YOU HERE. YOU TRACKED HIM ALL THE WAY FROM BELLE ISLE. OR WAS IT THE PLACE IN SOUTHFIELD?

WHAT'S HAPPENING HERE? WHEN DID THE WHITE HILL GANG START WORKING WITH THE ALBANIANS?

ŚWINKA DELIKATESY

Detroit Police

WHEN DID THE WHOLE WORLD START GOING CRAZY?

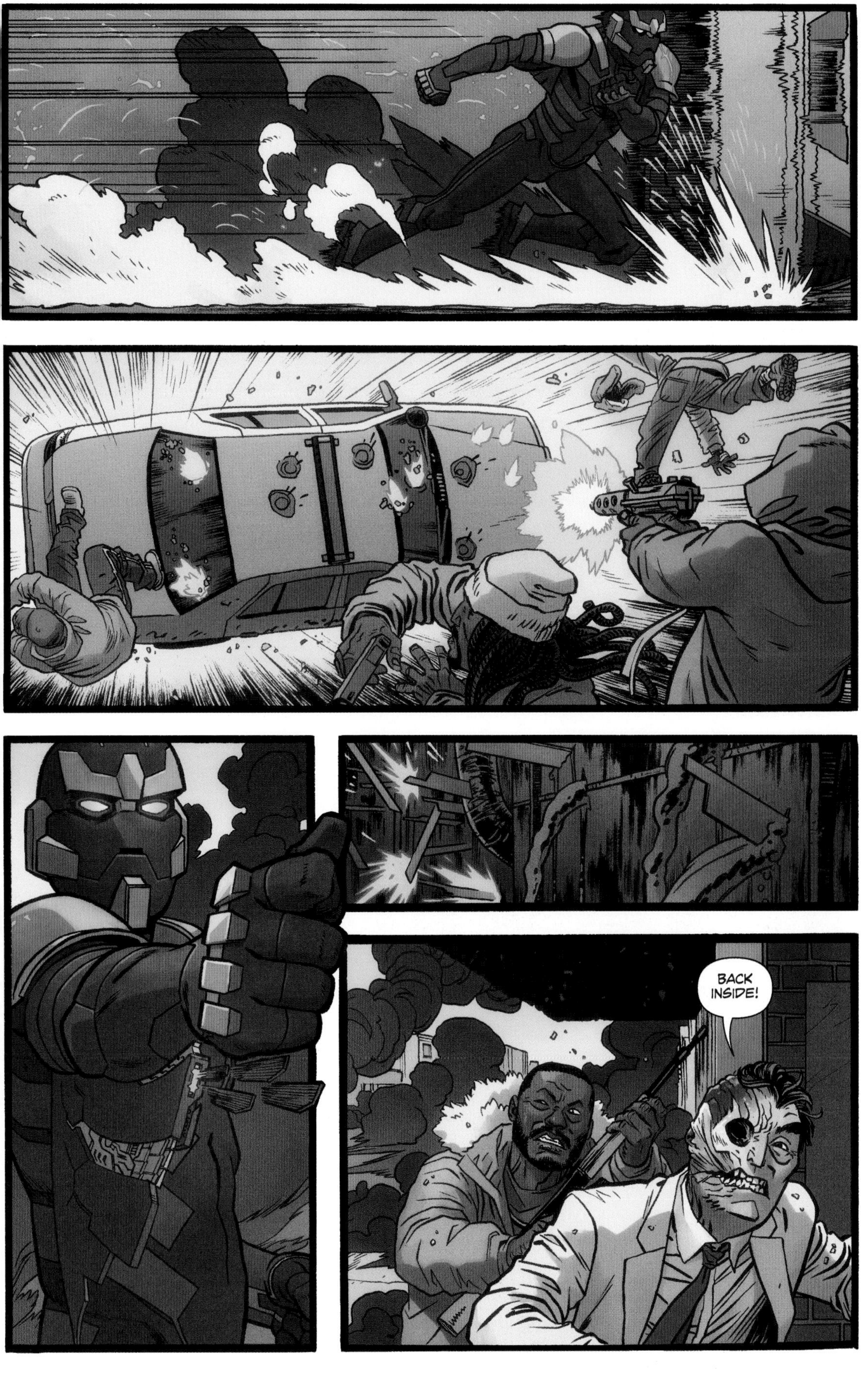
BACK INSIDE!

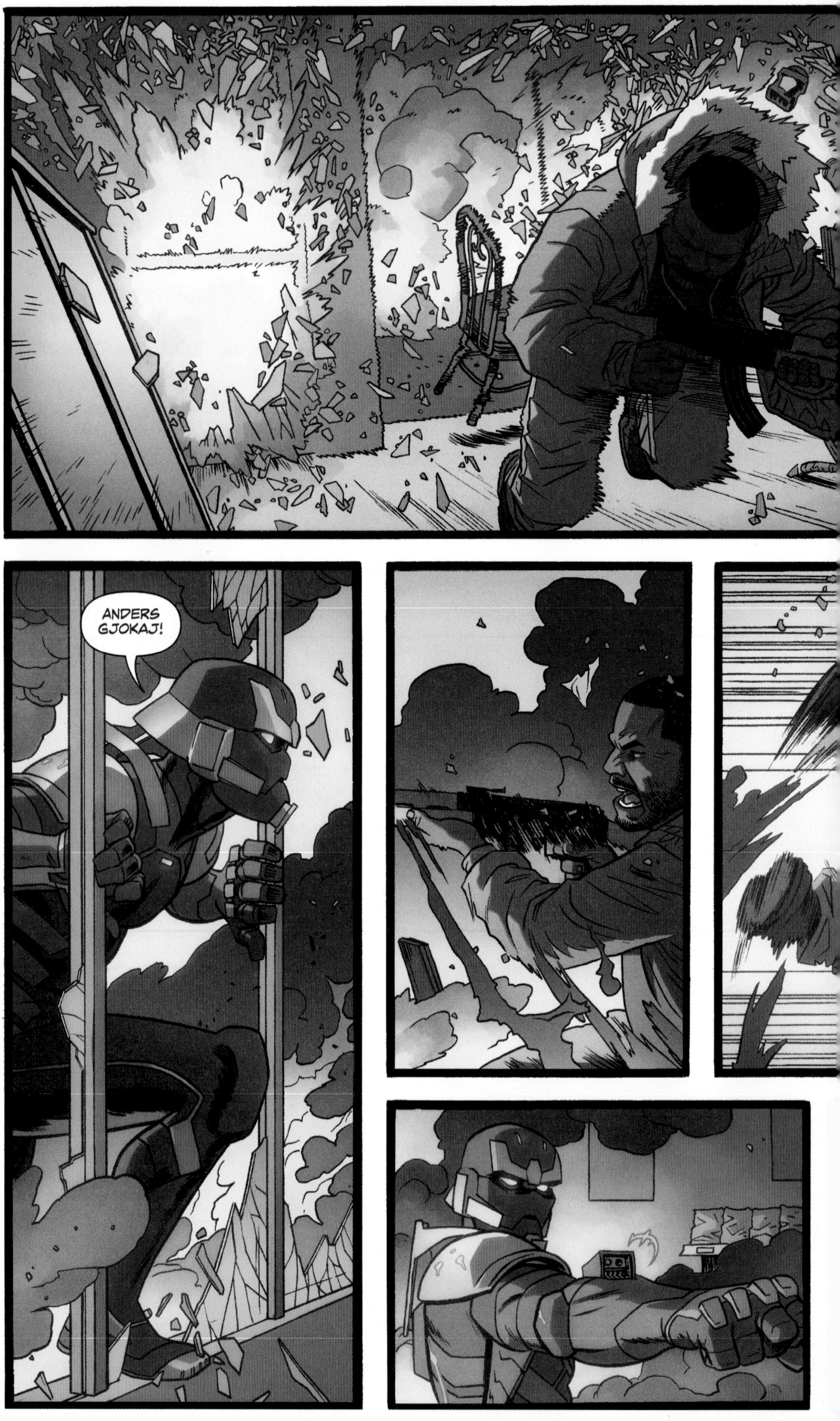
ANDERS GJOKAJ!

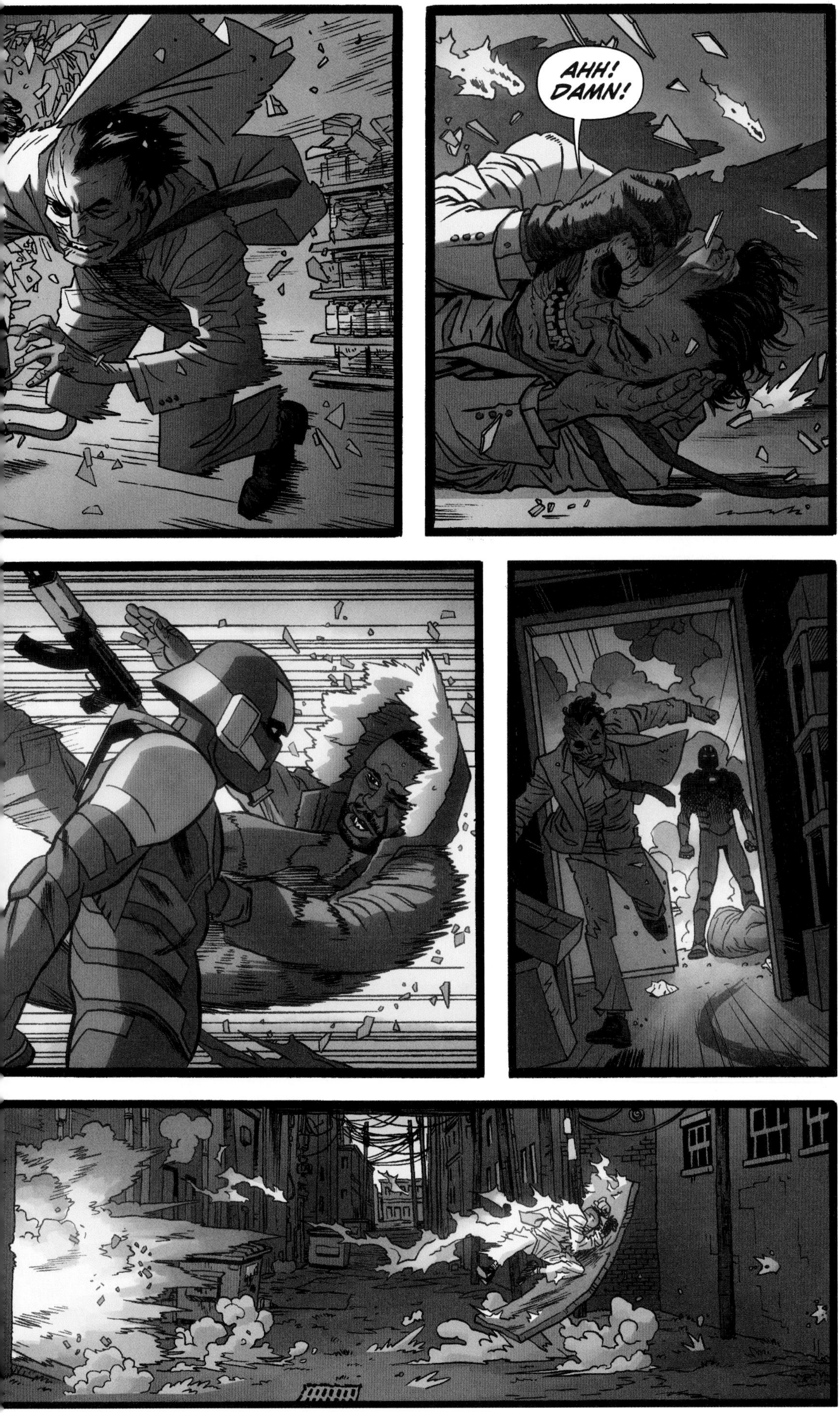
AHH! DAMN!

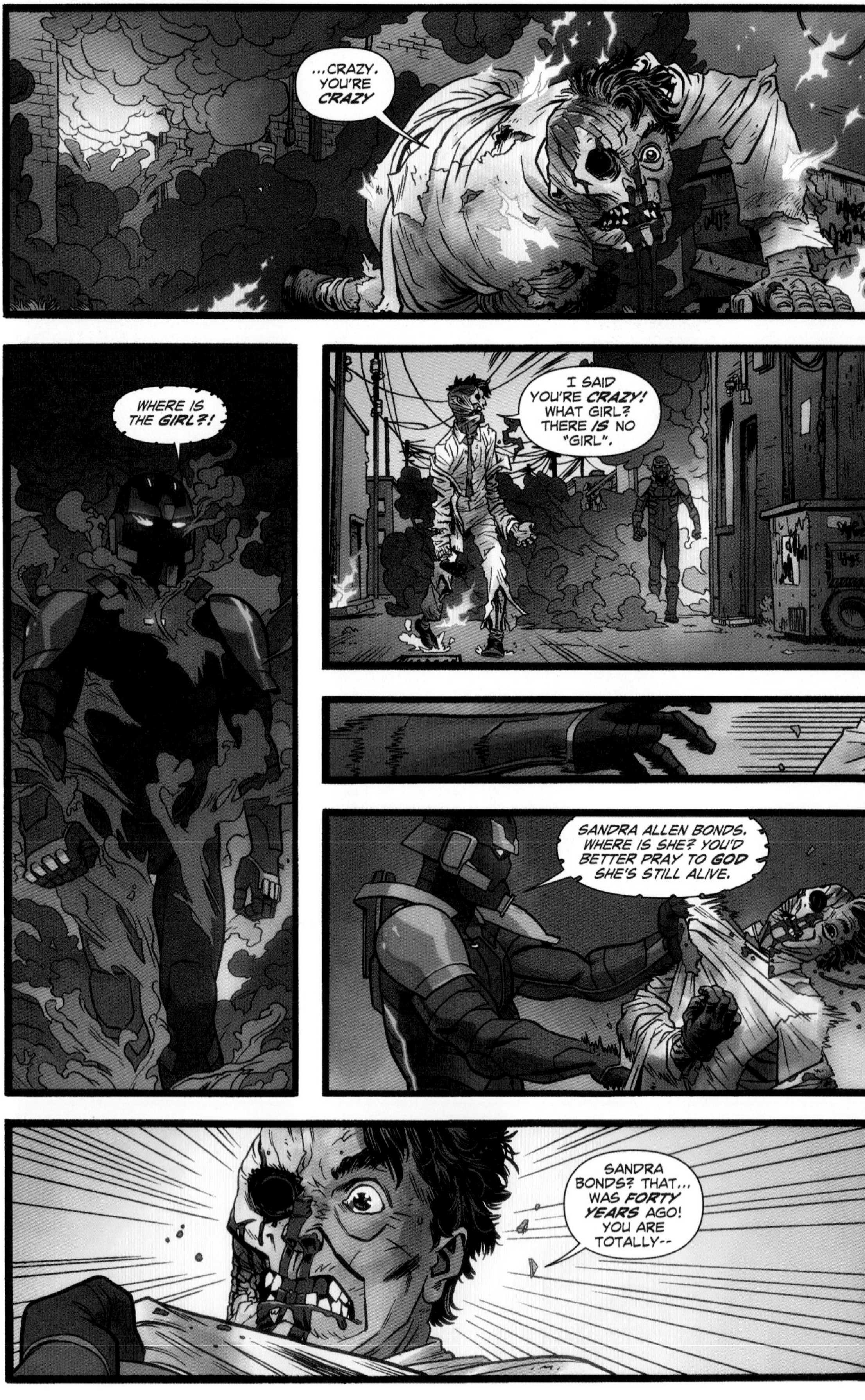
...CRAZY. YOU'RE CRAZY
WHERE IS THE GIRL?!
I SAID YOU'RE CRAZY! WHAT GIRL? THERE IS NO "GIRL".
SANDRA ALLEN BONDS. WHERE IS SHE? YOU'D BETTER PRAY TO GOD SHE'S STILL ALIVE.
SANDRA BONDS? THAT... WAS FORTY YEARS AGO! YOU ARE TOTALLY--

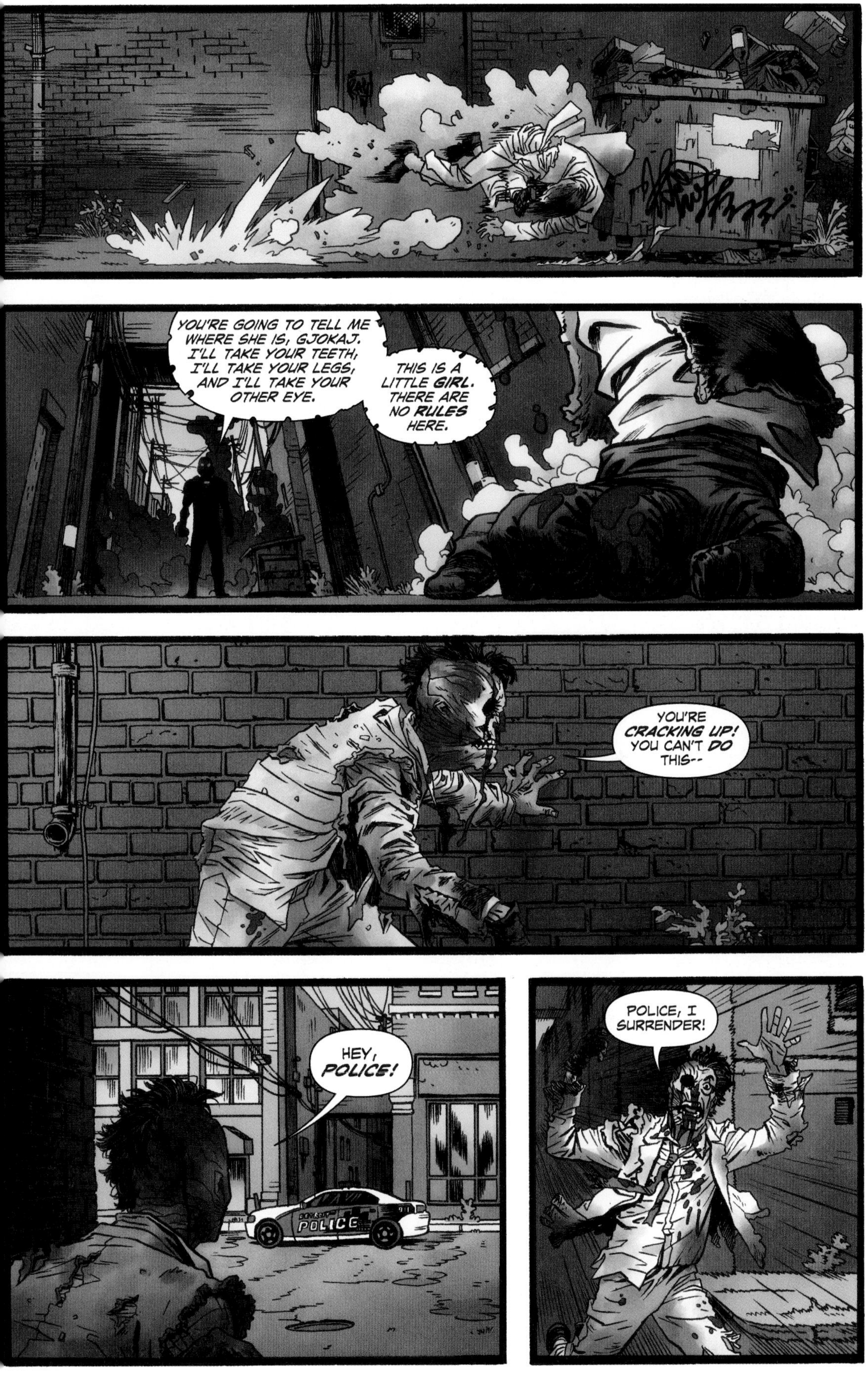
YOU'RE GOING TO TELL ME WHERE SHE IS, GJOKAJ. I'LL TAKE YOUR TEETH, I'LL TAKE YOUR LEGS, AND I'LL TAKE YOUR OTHER EYE.
THIS IS A LITTLE GIRL. THERE ARE NO RULES HERE.
YOU'RE CRACKING UP! YOU CAN'T DO THIS--
POLICE
HEY, POLICE!
POLICE, I SURRENDER!

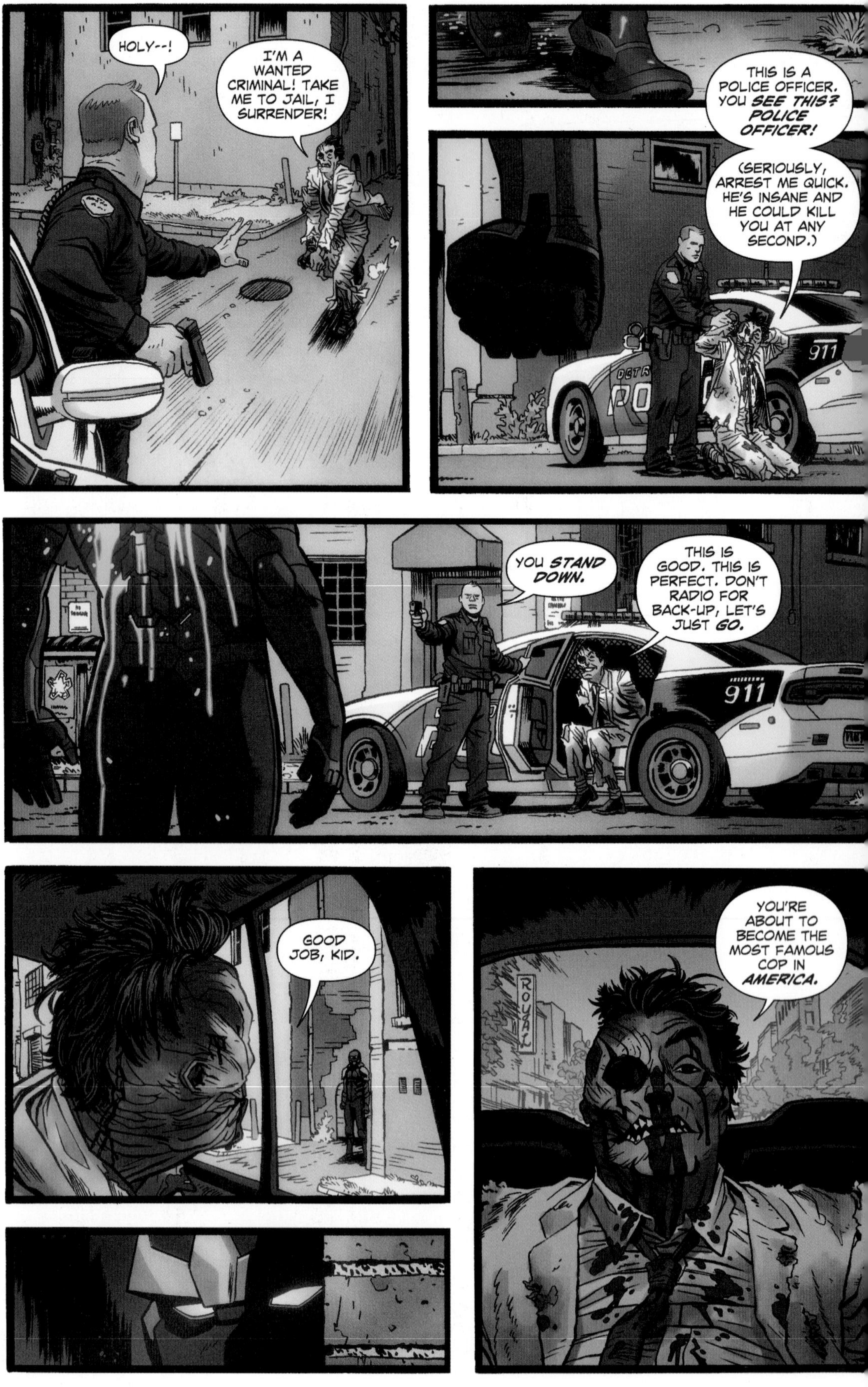
HOLY--!
I'M A WANTED CRIMINAL! TAKE ME TO JAIL, I SURRENDER!
THIS IS A POLICE OFFICER. YOU SEE THIS? POLICE OFFICER!
(SERIOUSLY, ARREST ME QUICK. HE'S INSANE AND HE COULD KILL YOU AT ANY SECOND.)
911
YOU STAND DOWN.
THIS IS GOOD. THIS IS PERFECT. DON'T RADIO FOR BACK-UP, LET'S JUST GO.
911
GOOD JOB, KID.
YOU'RE ABOUT TO BECOME THE MOST FAMOUS COP IN AMERICA.

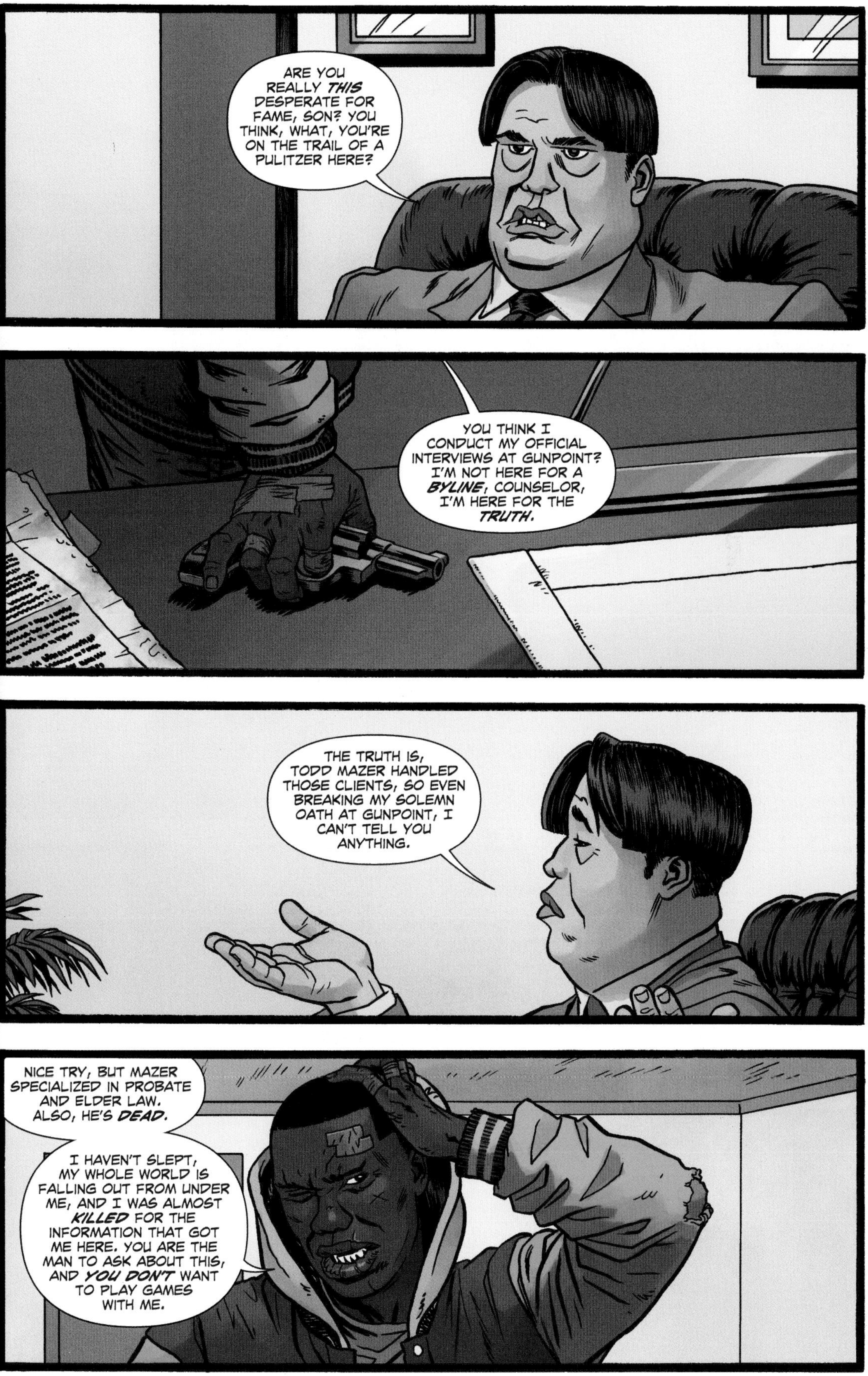
ARE YOU REALLY THIS DESPERATE FOR FAME, SON? YOU THINK, WHAT, YOU'RE ON THE TRAIL OF A PULITZER HERE?
YOU THINK I CONDUCT MY OFFICIAL INTERVIEWS AT GUNPOINT? I'M NOT HERE FOR A BYLINE, COUNSELOR, I'M HERE FOR THE TRUTH.
THE TRUTH IS, TODD MAZER HANDLED THOSE CLIENTS, SO EVEN BREAKING MY SOLEMN OATH AT GUNPOINT, I CAN'T TELL YOU ANYTHING.
NICE TRY, BUT MAZER SPECIALIZED IN PROBATE AND ELDER LAW. ALSO, HE'S DEAD.
I HAVEN'T SLEPT, MY WHOLE WORLD IS FALLING OUT FROM UNDER ME, AND I WAS ALMOST KILLED FOR THE INFORMATION THAT GOT ME HERE. YOU ARE THE MAN TO ASK ABOUT THIS, AND YOU DON'T WANT TO PLAY GAMES WITH ME.

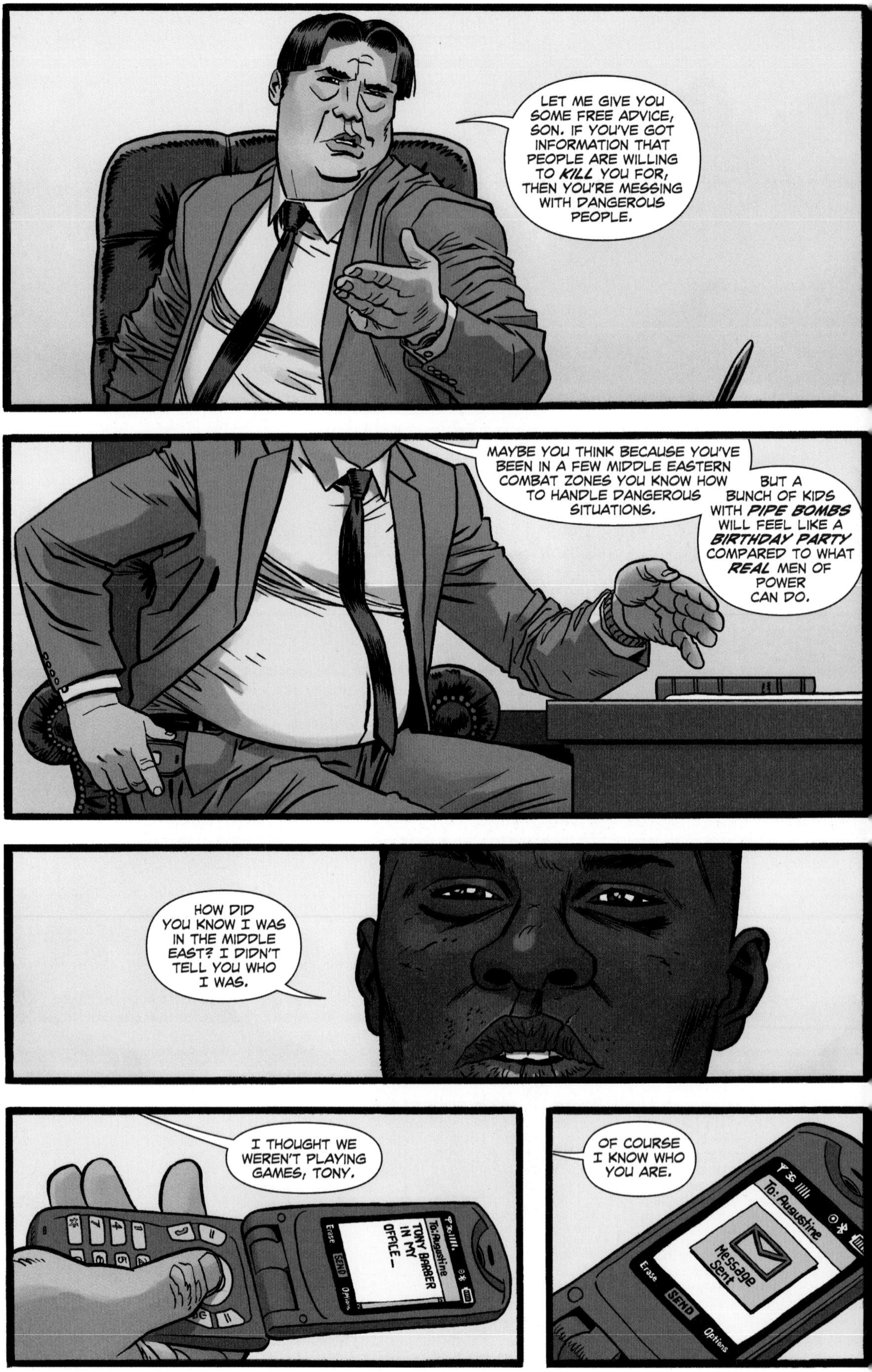

LET ME GIVE YOU SOME FREE ADVICE, SON. IF YOU'VE GOT INFORMATION THAT PEOPLE ARE WILLING TO KILL YOU FOR, THEN YOU'RE MESSING WITH DANGEROUS PEOPLE.
MAYBE YOU THINK BECAUSE YOU'VE BEEN IN A FEW MIDDLE EASTERN COMBAT ZONES YOU KNOW HOW TO HANDLE DANGEROUS SITUATIONS.
BUT A BUNCH OF KIDS WITH PIPE BOMBS WILL FEEL LIKE A BIRTHDAY PARTY COMPARED TO WHAT REAL MEN OF POWER CAN DO.
HOW DID YOU KNOW I WAS IN THE MIDDLE EAST? I DIDN'T TELL YOU WHO I WAS.
I THOUGHT WE WEREN'T PLAYING GAMES, TONY.
To: Augustine
TONY BARBER IN MY OFFICE—
Erase
SEND
Options
OF COURSE I KNOW WHO YOU ARE.
To: Augustine
Message Sent
Erase
SEND
Options

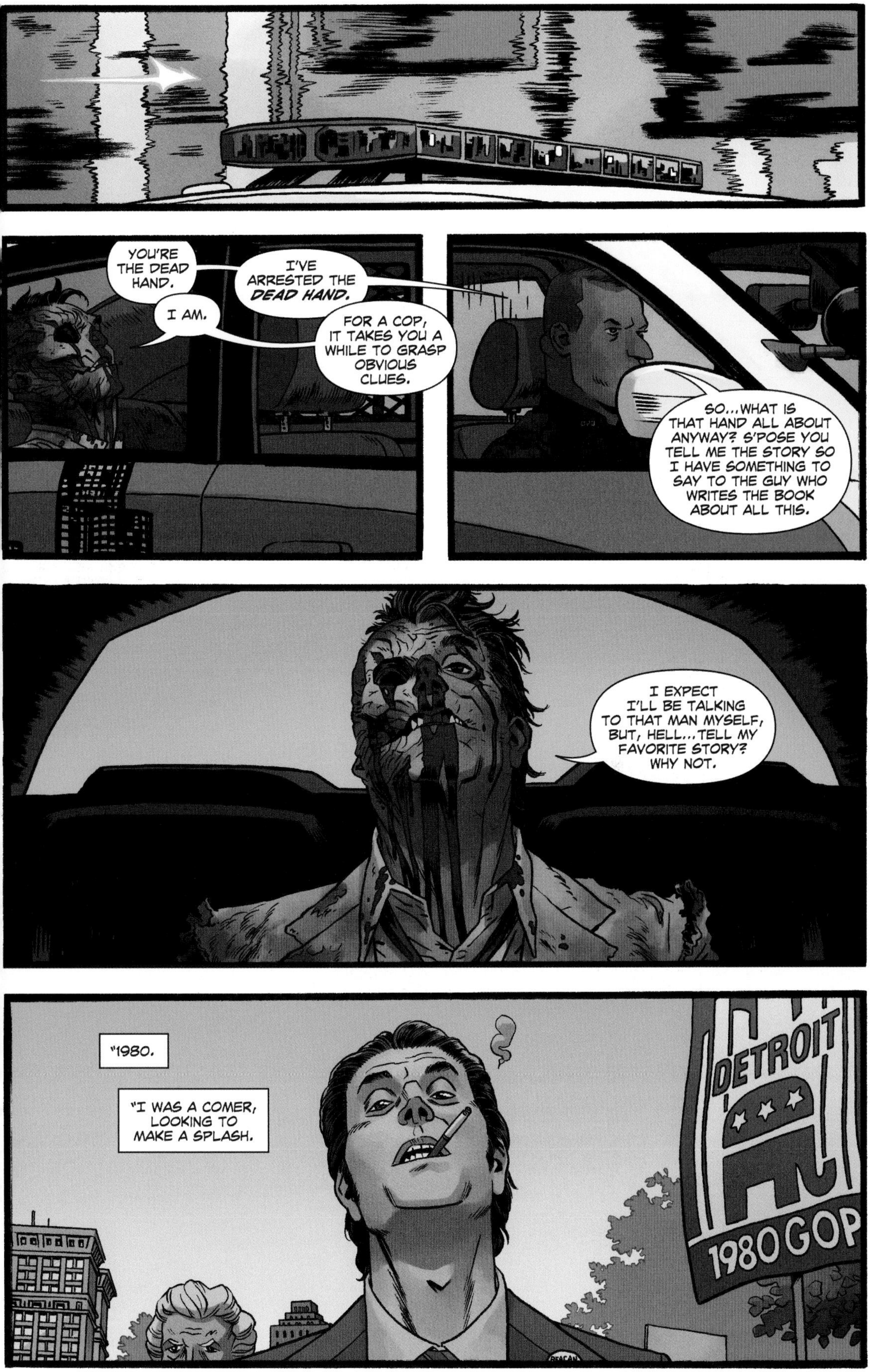
YOU'RE THE DEAD HAND.
I'VE ARRESTED THE *DEAD HAND.*
I AM.
FOR A COP, IT TAKES YOU A WHILE TO GRASP OBVIOUS CLUES.
SO...WHAT IS THAT HAND ALL ABOUT ANYWAY? S'POSE YOU TELL ME THE STORY SO I HAVE SOMETHING TO SAY TO THE GUY WHO WRITES THE BOOK ABOUT ALL THIS.
I EXPECT I'LL BE TALKING TO THAT MAN MYSELF, BUT, HELL...TELL MY FAVORITE STORY? WHY NOT.
"1980.
"I WAS A COMER, LOOKING TO MAKE A SPLASH.
DETROIT
1980 GOP

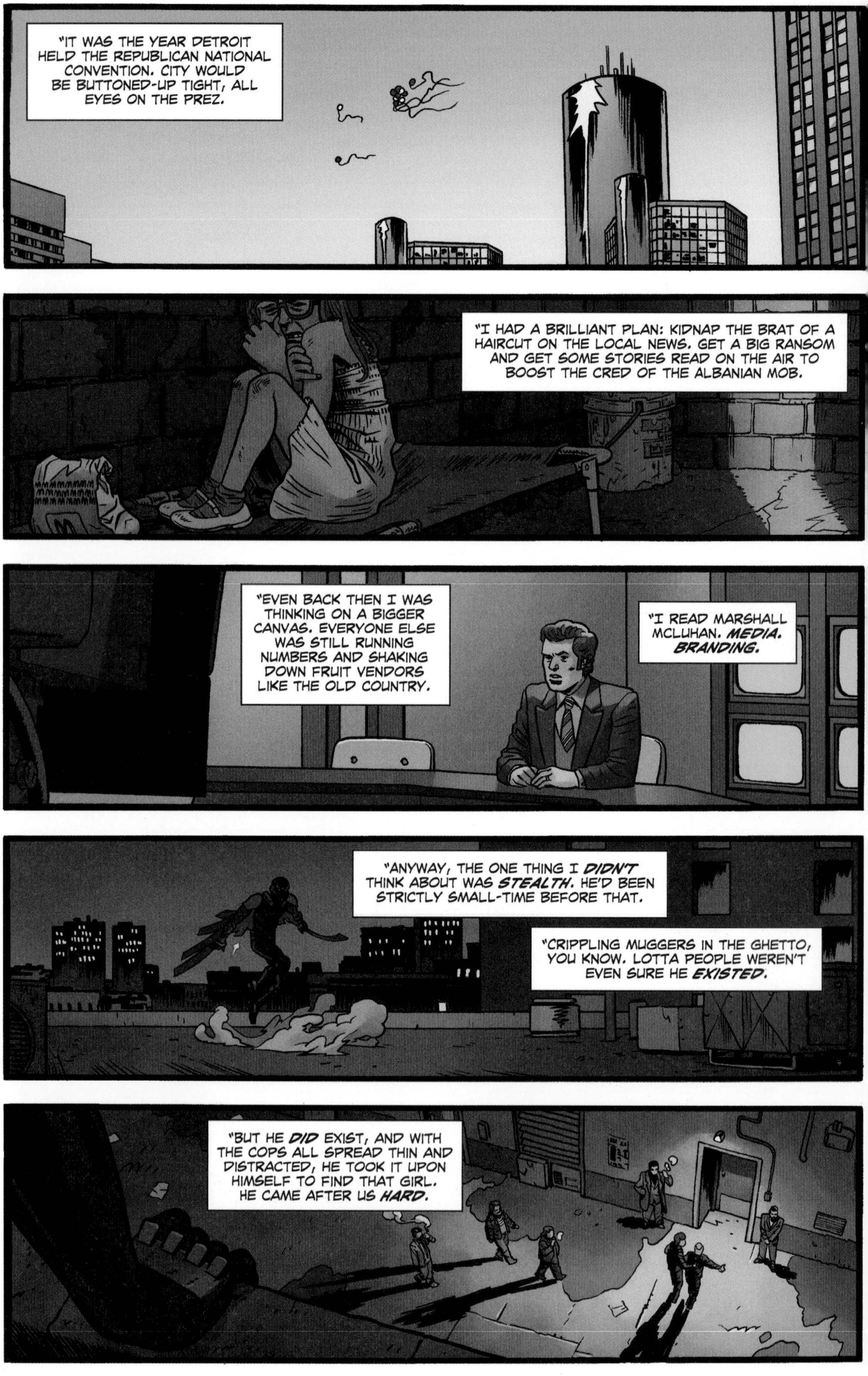
"IT WAS THE YEAR DETROIT HELD THE REPUBLICAN NATIONAL CONVENTION. CITY WOULD BE BUTTONED-UP TIGHT, ALL EYES ON THE PREZ.
"I HAD A BRILLIANT PLAN: KIDNAP THE BRAT OF A HAIRCUT ON THE LOCAL NEWS. GET A BIG RANSOM AND GET SOME STORIES READ ON THE AIR TO BOOST THE CRED OF THE ALBANIAN MOB.
"EVEN BACK THEN I WAS THINKING ON A BIGGER CANVAS. EVERYONE ELSE WAS STILL RUNNING NUMBERS AND SHAKING DOWN FRUIT VENDORS LIKE THE OLD COUNTRY.
"I READ MARSHALL MCLUHAN. *MEDIA. BRANDING.*
"ANYWAY, THE ONE THING I *DIDN'T* THINK ABOUT WAS *STEALTH*. HE'D BEEN STRICTLY SMALL-TIME BEFORE THAT.
"CRIPPLING MUGGERS IN THE GHETTO, YOU KNOW. LOTTA PEOPLE WEREN'T EVEN SURE HE *EXISTED*.
"BUT HE *DID* EXIST, AND WITH THE COPS ALL SPREAD THIN AND DISTRACTED, HE TOOK IT UPON HIMSELF TO FIND THAT GIRL. HE CAME AFTER US *HARD*.

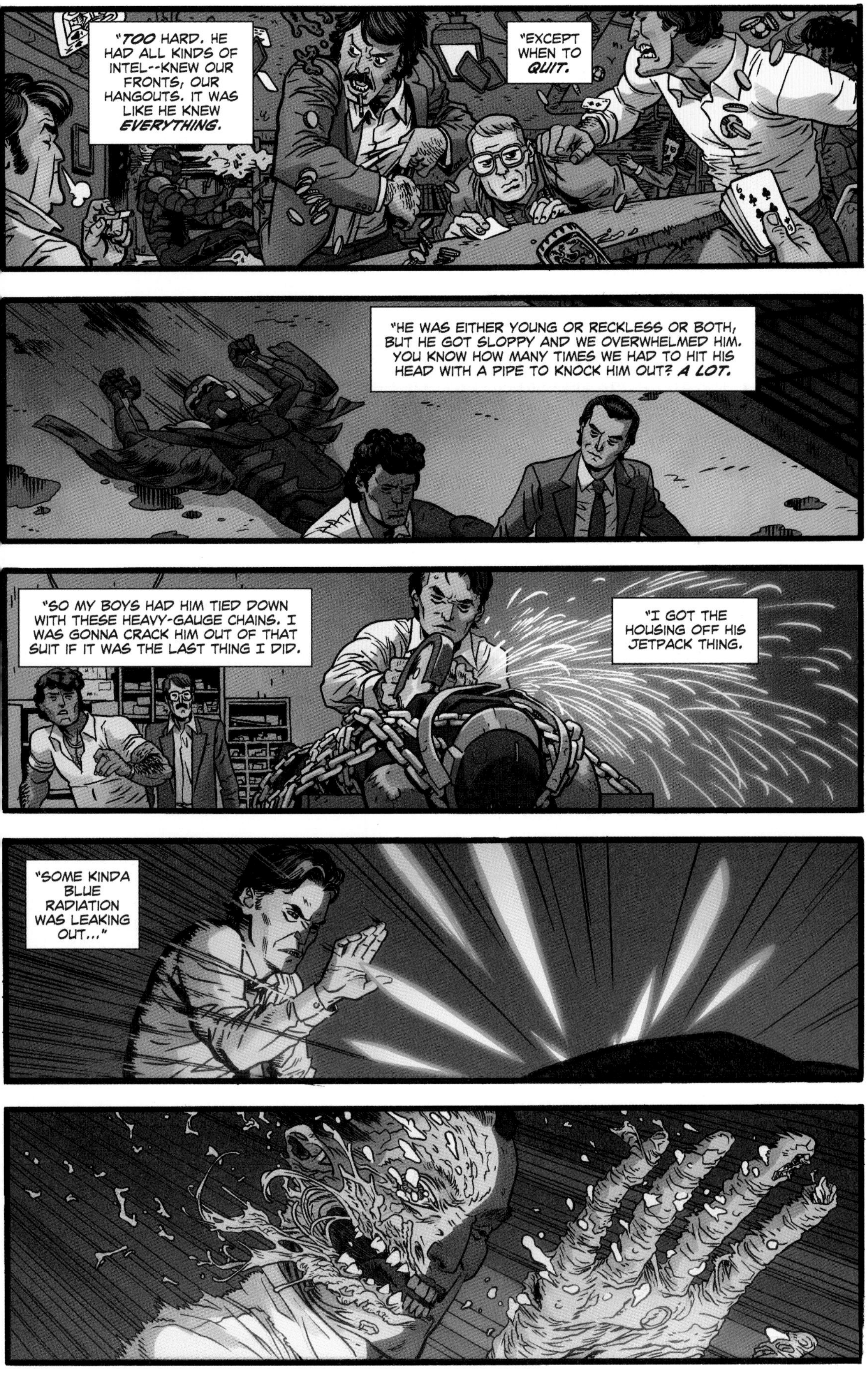
"TOO HARD. HE HAD ALL KINDS OF INTEL--KNEW OUR FRONTS, OUR HANGOUTS. IT WAS LIKE HE KNEW EVERYTHING.
"EXCEPT WHEN TO QUIT.
"HE WAS EITHER YOUNG OR RECKLESS OR BOTH, BUT HE GOT SLOPPY AND WE OVERWHELMED HIM. YOU KNOW HOW MANY TIMES WE HAD TO HIT HIS HEAD WITH A PIPE TO KNOCK HIM OUT? A LOT.
"SO MY BOYS HAD HIM TIED DOWN WITH THESE HEAVY-GAUGE CHAINS. I WAS GONNA CRACK HIM OUT OF THAT SUIT IF IT WAS THE LAST THING I DID.
"I GOT THE HOUSING OFF HIS JETPACK THING.
"SOME KINDA BLUE RADIATION WAS LEAKING OUT..."

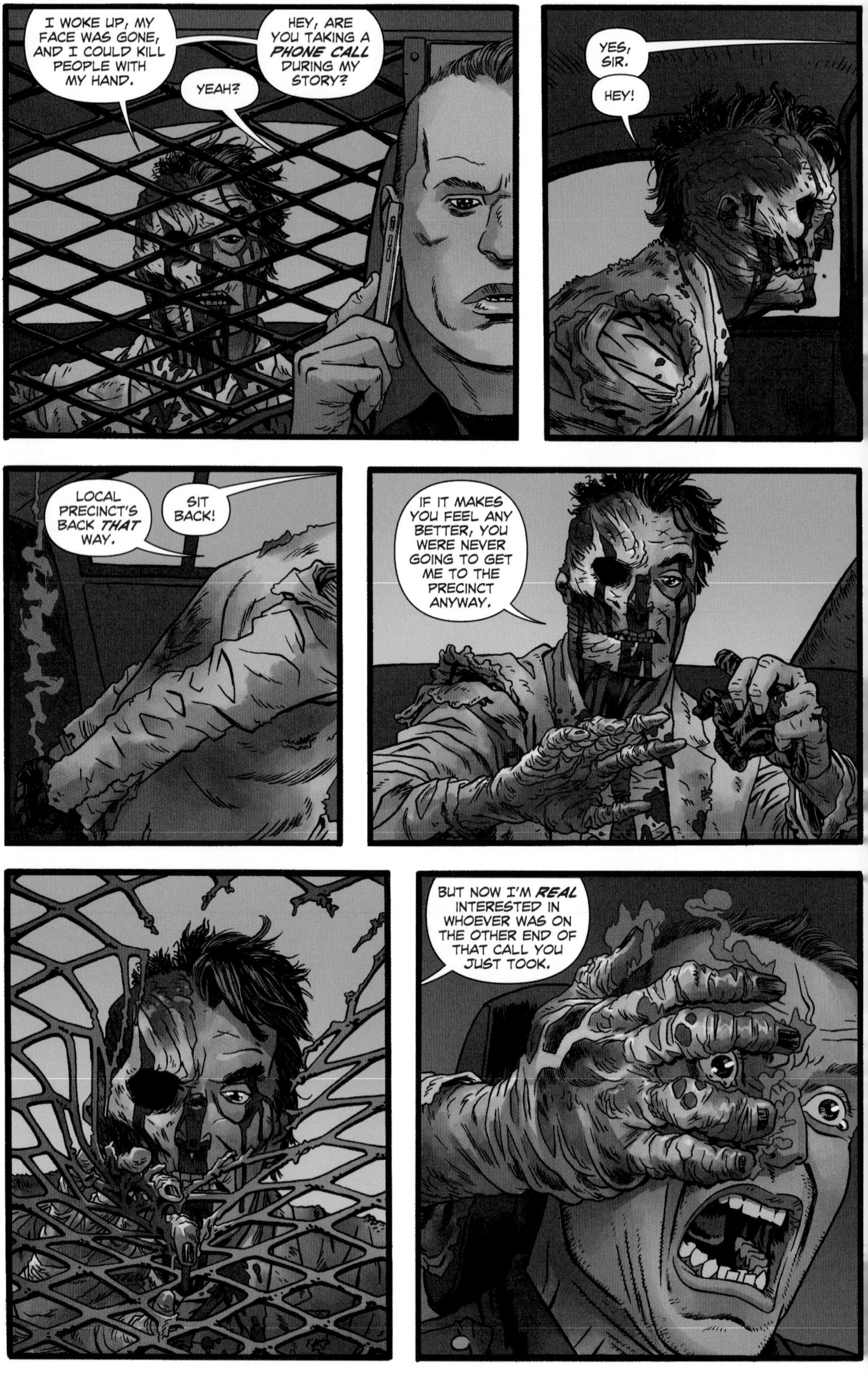
I WOKE UP, MY FACE WAS GONE, AND I COULD KILL PEOPLE WITH MY HAND.
HEY, ARE YOU TAKING A PHONE CALL DURING MY STORY?
YEAH?
YES, SIR.
HEY!
LOCAL PRECINCT'S BACK THAT WAY.
SIT BACK!
IF IT MAKES YOU FEEL ANY BETTER, YOU WERE NEVER GOING TO GET ME TO THE PRECINCT ANYWAY.
BUT NOW I'M REAL INTERESTED IN WHOEVER WAS ON THE OTHER END OF THAT CALL YOU JUST TOOK.

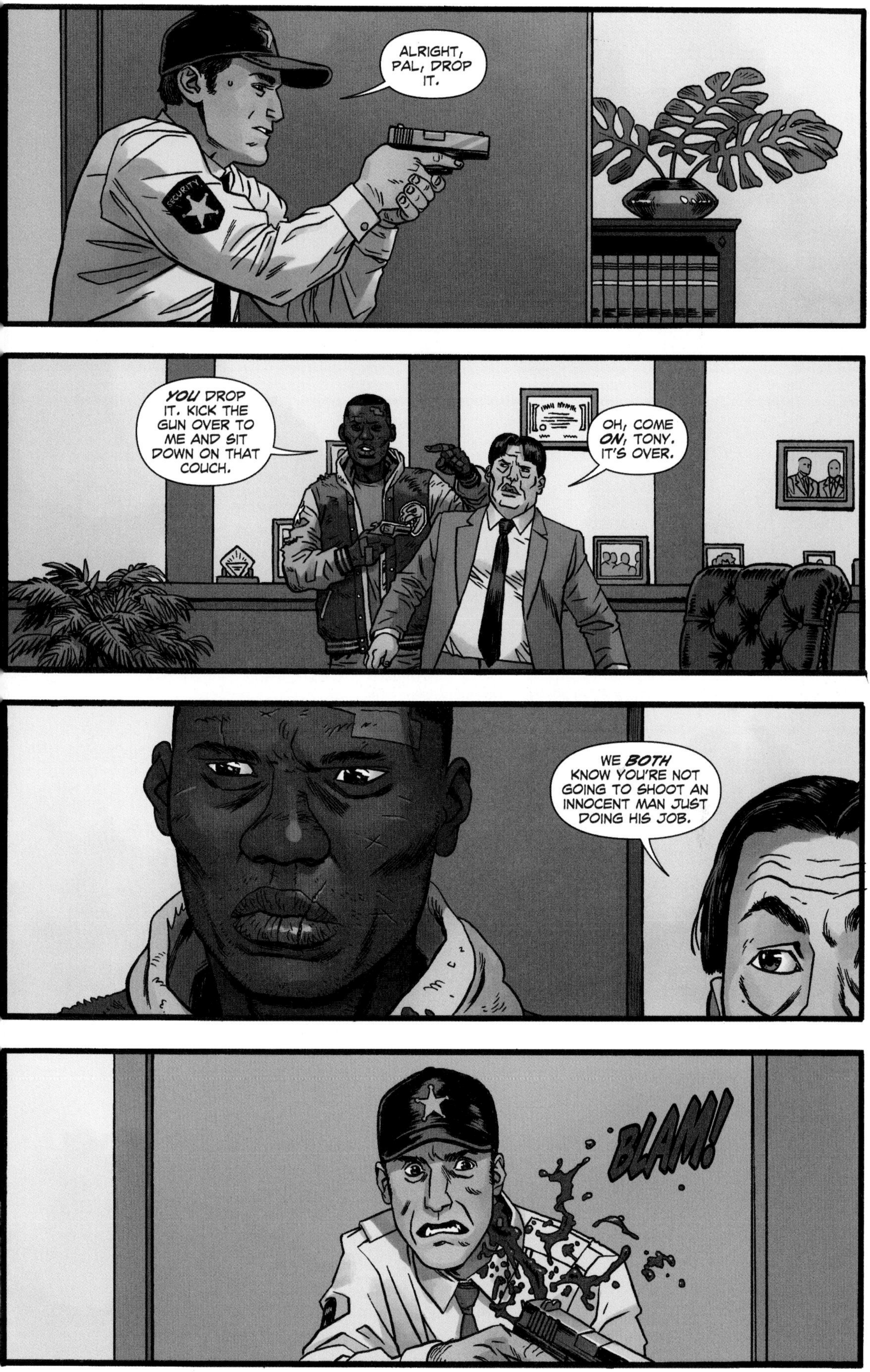
ALRIGHT, PAL, DROP IT.
YOU DROP IT. KICK THE GUN OVER TO ME AND SIT DOWN ON THAT COUCH.
OH, COME ON, TONY. IT'S OVER.
WE BOTH KNOW YOU'RE NOT GOING TO SHOOT AN INNOCENT MAN JUST DOING HIS JOB.
BLAM!

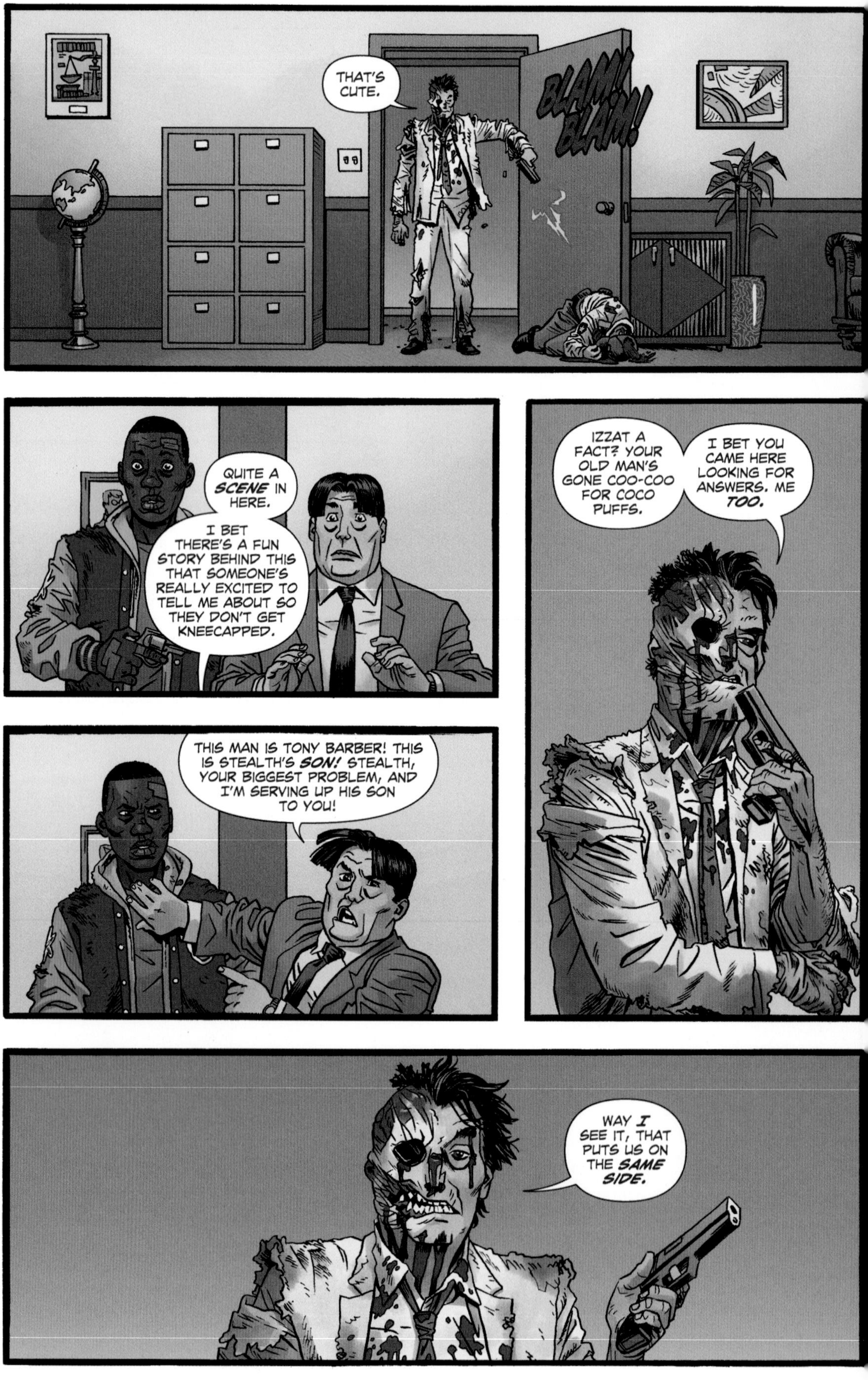
THAT'S CUTE.
BLAM! BLAM!
QUITE A SCENE IN HERE.
I BET THERE'S A FUN STORY BEHIND THIS THAT SOMEONE'S REALLY EXCITED TO TELL ME ABOUT SO THEY DON'T GET KNEECAPPED.
THIS MAN IS TONY BARBER! THIS IS STEALTH'S SON! STEALTH, YOUR BIGGEST PROBLEM, AND I'M SERVING UP HIS SON TO YOU!
IZZAT A FACT? YOUR OLD MAN'S GONE COO-COO FOR COCO PUFFS.
I BET YOU CAME HERE LOOKING FOR ANSWERS. ME TOO.
WAY I SEE IT, THAT PUTS US ON THE SAME SIDE.

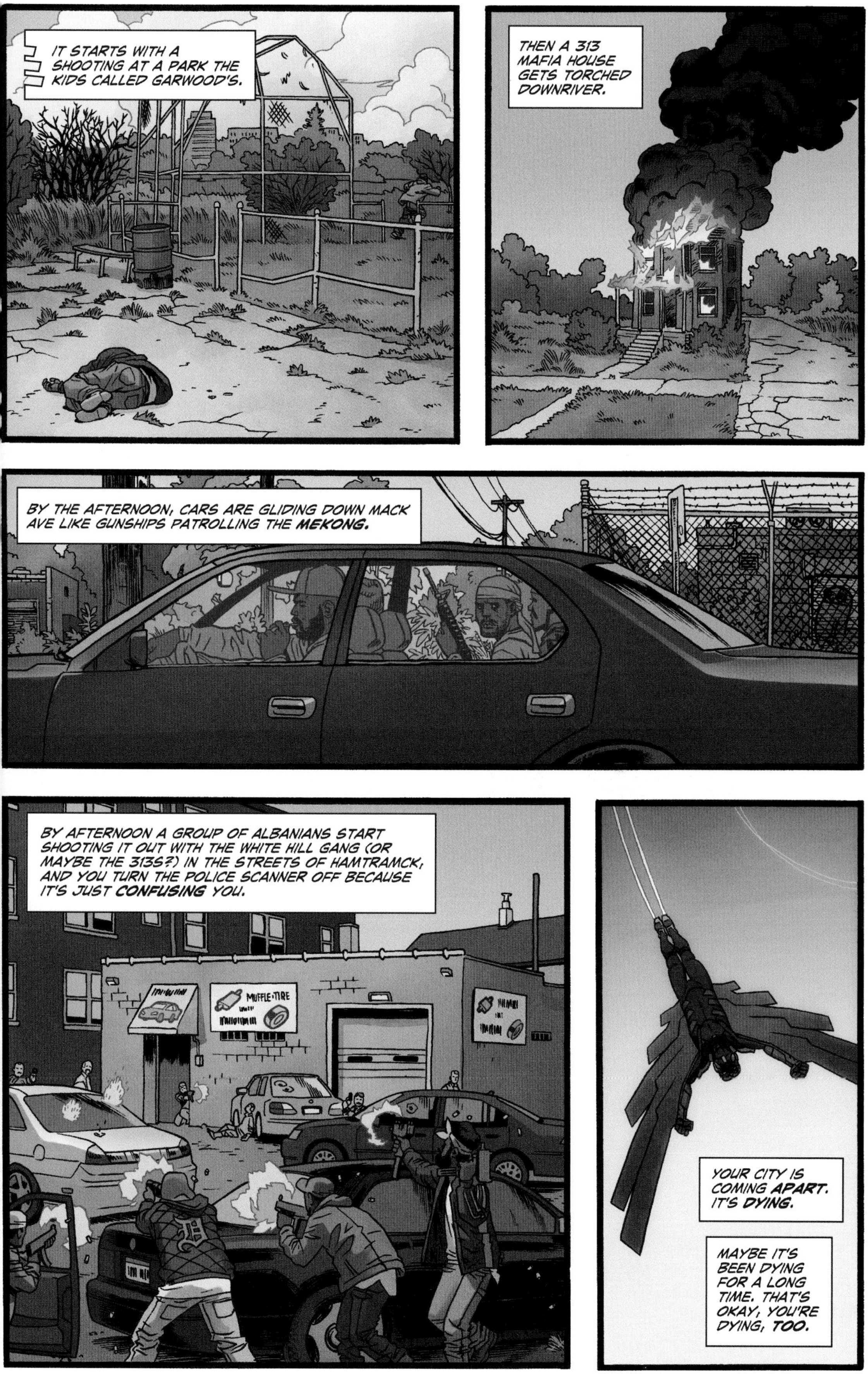
IT STARTS WITH A SHOOTING AT A PARK THE KIDS CALLED GARWOOD'S.
THEN A 313 MAFIA HOUSE GETS TORCHED DOWNRIVER.
BY THE AFTERNOON, CARS ARE GLIDING DOWN MACK AVE LIKE GUNSHIPS PATROLLING THE **MEKONG.**
BY AFTERNOON A GROUP OF ALBANIANS START SHOOTING IT OUT WITH THE WHITE HILL GANG (OR MAYBE THE 313S?) IN THE STREETS OF HAMTRAMCK, AND YOU TURN THE POLICE SCANNER OFF BECAUSE IT'S JUST **CONFUSING** YOU.
YOUR CITY IS COMING **APART.** IT'S **DYING.**
MAYBE IT'S BEEN DYING FOR A LONG TIME. THAT'S OKAY, YOU'RE DYING, **TOO.**

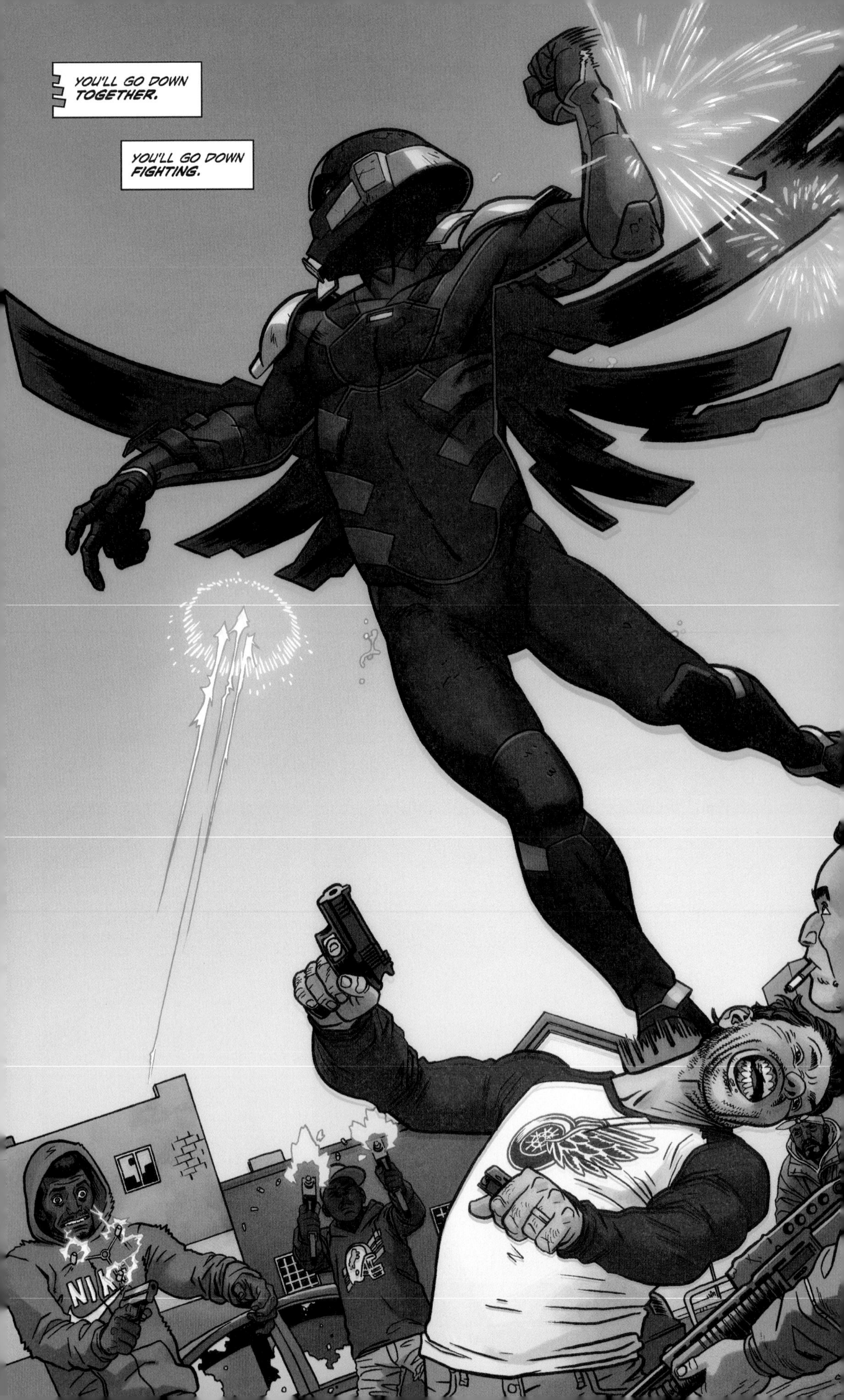
YOU'LL GO DOWN TOGETHER.
YOU'LL GO DOWN FIGHTING.

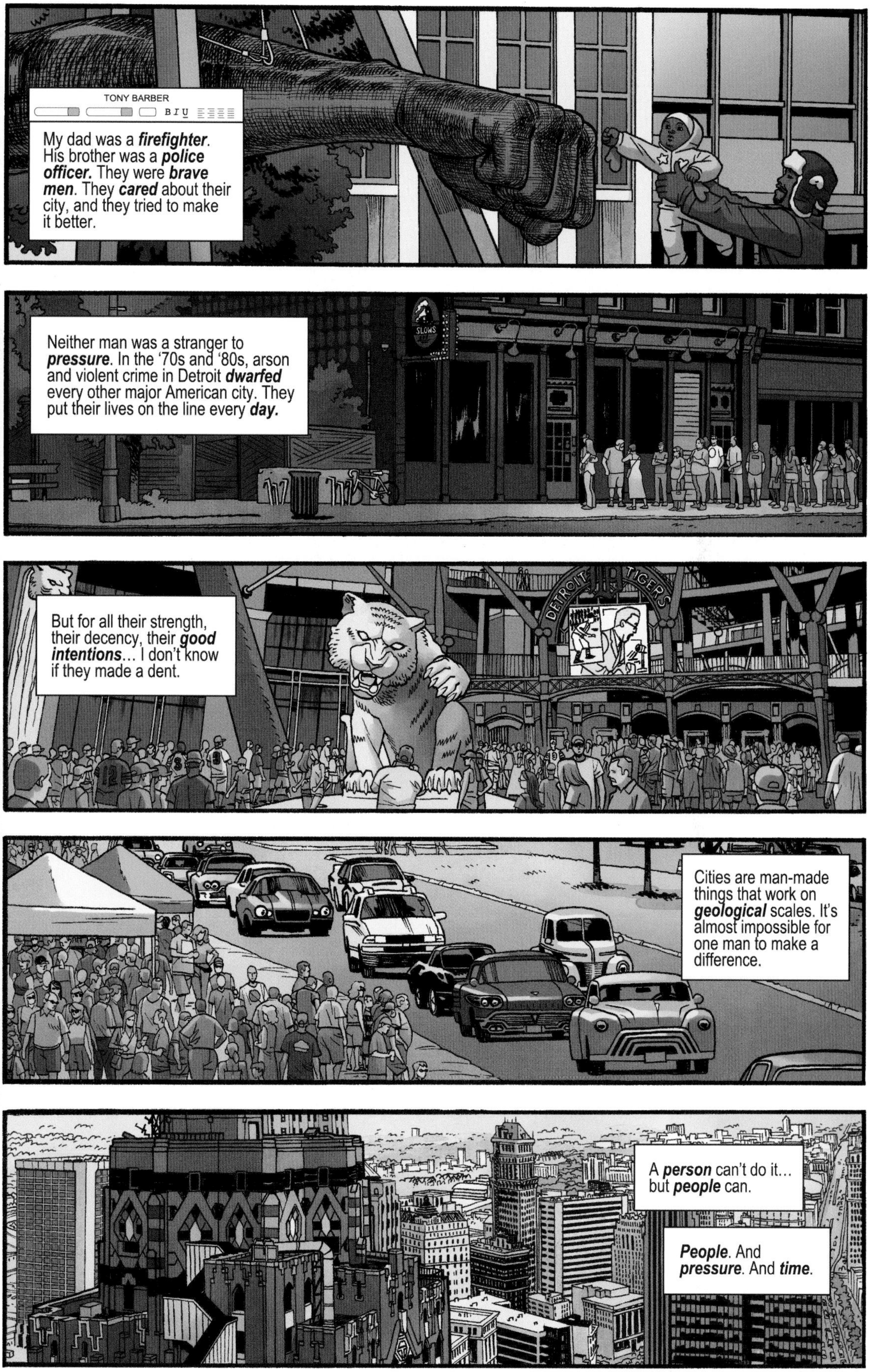
TONY BARBER
My dad was a ***firefighter***. His brother was a ***police officer.*** They were ***brave men***. They ***cared*** about their city, and they tried to make it better.
SLOWS
Neither man was a stranger to ***pressure***. In the '70s and '80s, arson and violent crime in Detroit ***dwarfed*** every other major American city. They put their lives on the line every ***day.***
But for all their strength, their decency, their ***good intentions***... I don't know if they made a dent.
DETROIT TIGERS
Cities are man-made things that work on ***geological*** scales. It's almost impossible for one man to make a difference.
A ***person*** can't do it... but ***people*** can.
People. And ***pressure***. And ***time***.

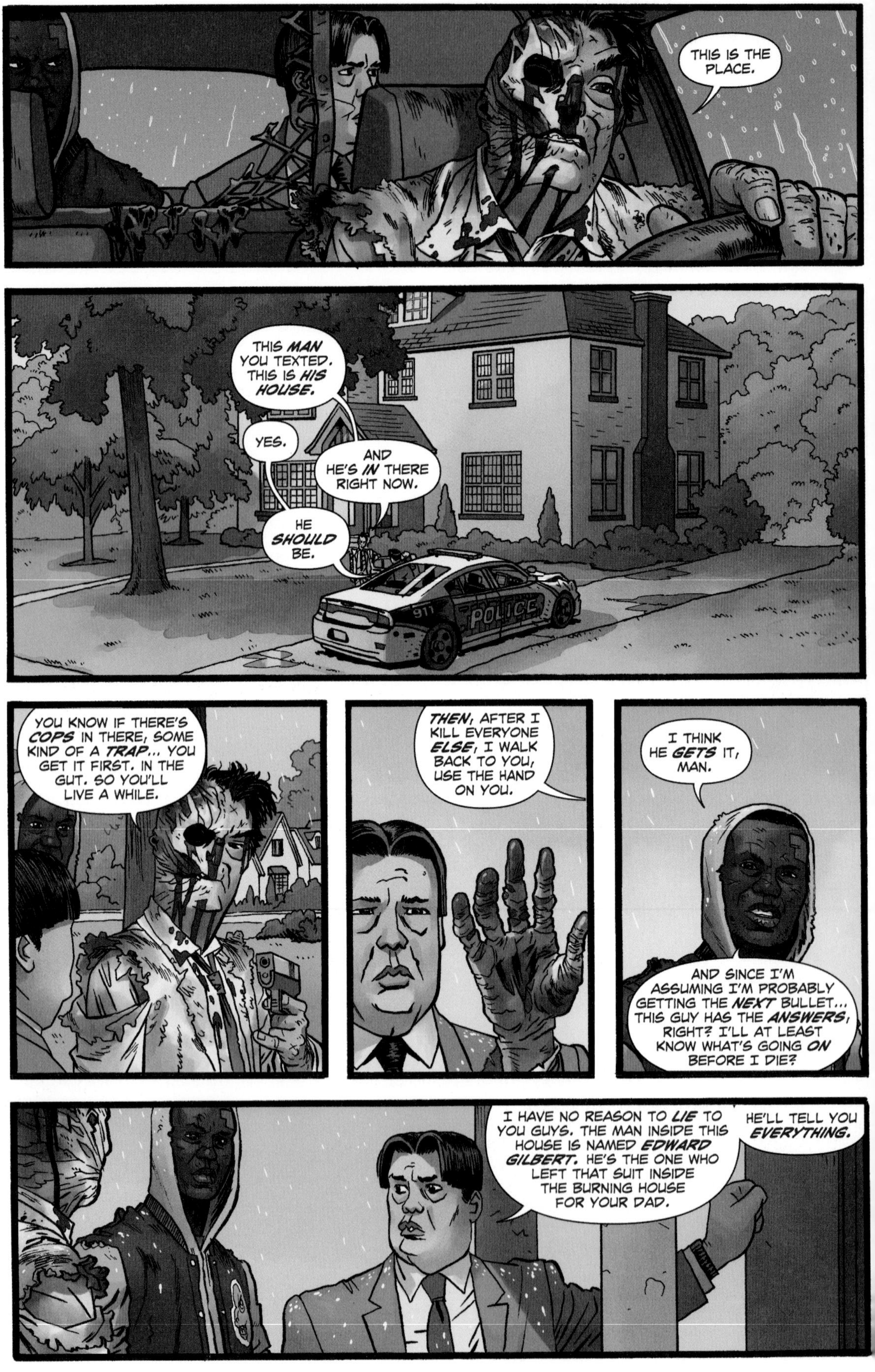

THIS IS THE PLACE.
THIS MAN YOU TEXTED. THIS IS HIS HOUSE.
YES.
AND HE'S IN THERE RIGHT NOW.
HE SHOULD BE.
YOU KNOW IF THERE'S COPS IN THERE, SOME KIND OF A TRAP... YOU GET IT FIRST. IN THE GUT. SO YOU'LL LIVE A WHILE.
THEN, AFTER I KILL EVERYONE ELSE, I WALK BACK TO YOU, USE THE HAND ON YOU.
I THINK HE GETS IT, MAN.
AND SINCE I'M ASSUMING I'M PROBABLY GETTING THE NEXT BULLET... THIS GUY HAS THE ANSWERS, RIGHT? I'LL AT LEAST KNOW WHAT'S GOING ON BEFORE I DIE?
I HAVE NO REASON TO LIE TO YOU GUYS. THE MAN INSIDE THIS HOUSE IS NAMED EDWARD GILBERT. HE'S THE ONE WHO LEFT THAT SUIT INSIDE THE BURNING HOUSE FOR YOUR DAD.
HE'LL TELL YOU EVERYTHING.

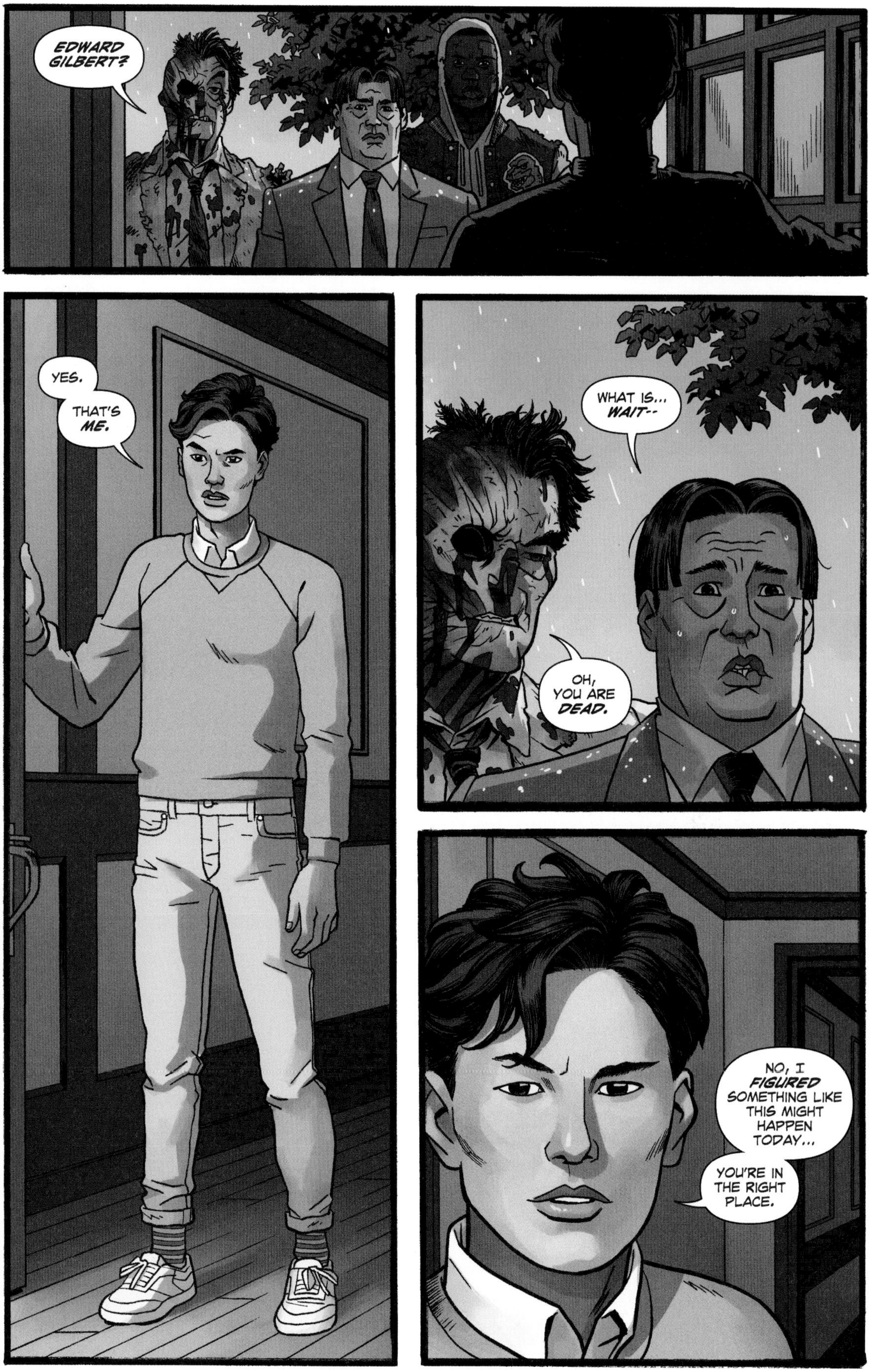
EDWARD GILBERT?
YES.
THAT'S ME.
WHAT IS... WAIT--
OH, YOU ARE DEAD.
NO, I FIGURED SOMETHING LIKE THIS MIGHT HAPPEN TODAY...
YOU'RE IN THE RIGHT PLACE.

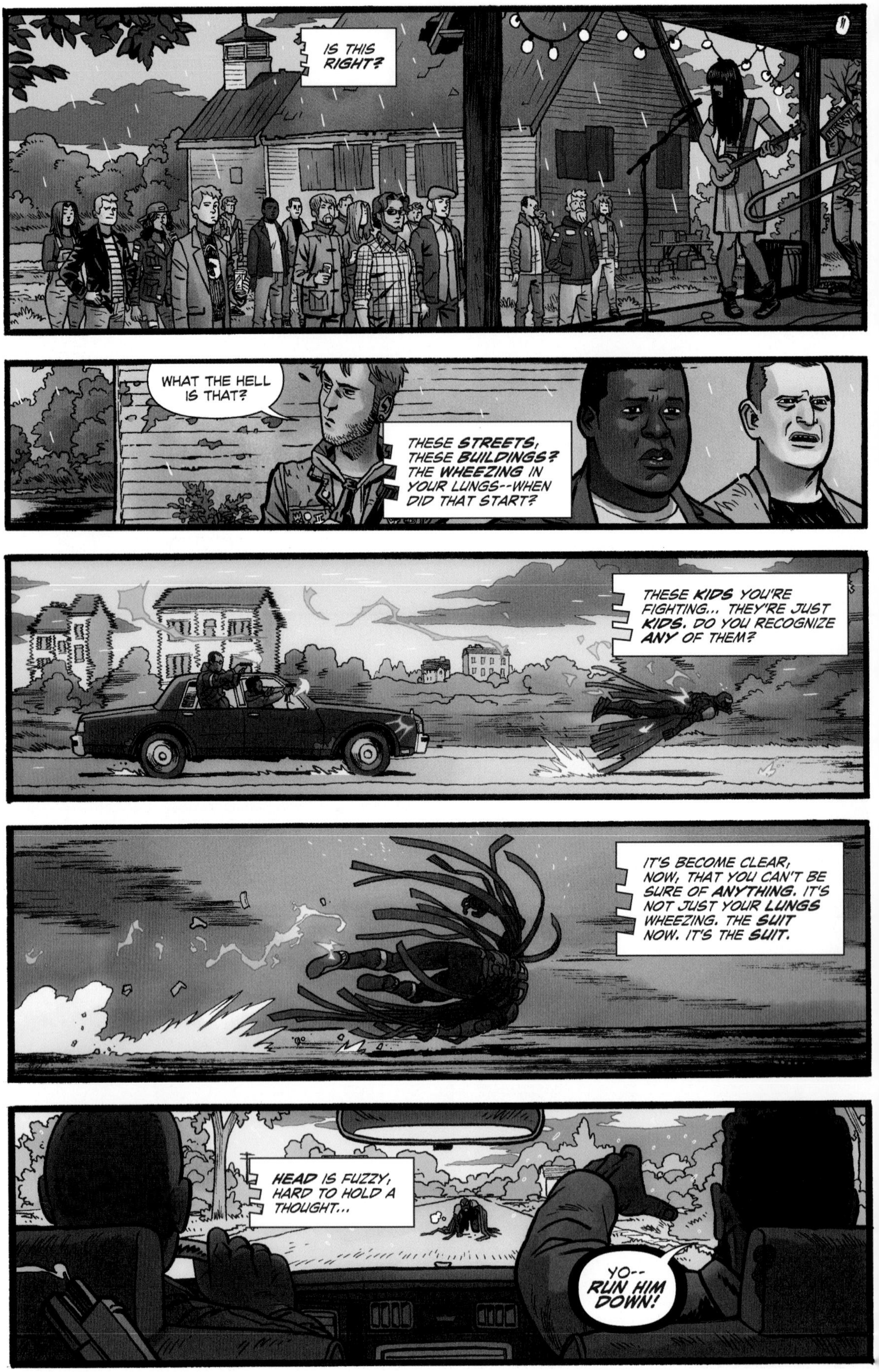
IS THIS RIGHT?
WHAT THE HELL IS THAT?
THESE STREETS, THESE BUILDINGS? THE WHEEZING IN YOUR LUNGS--WHEN DID THAT START?
THESE KIDS YOU'RE FIGHTING... THEY'RE JUST KIDS. DO YOU RECOGNIZE ANY OF THEM?
IT'S BECOME CLEAR, NOW, THAT YOU CAN'T BE SURE OF ANYTHING. IT'S NOT JUST YOUR LUNGS WHEEZING. THE SUIT NOW. IT'S THE SUIT.
HEAD IS FUZZY, HARD TO HOLD A THOUGHT...
YO-- RUN HIM DOWN!

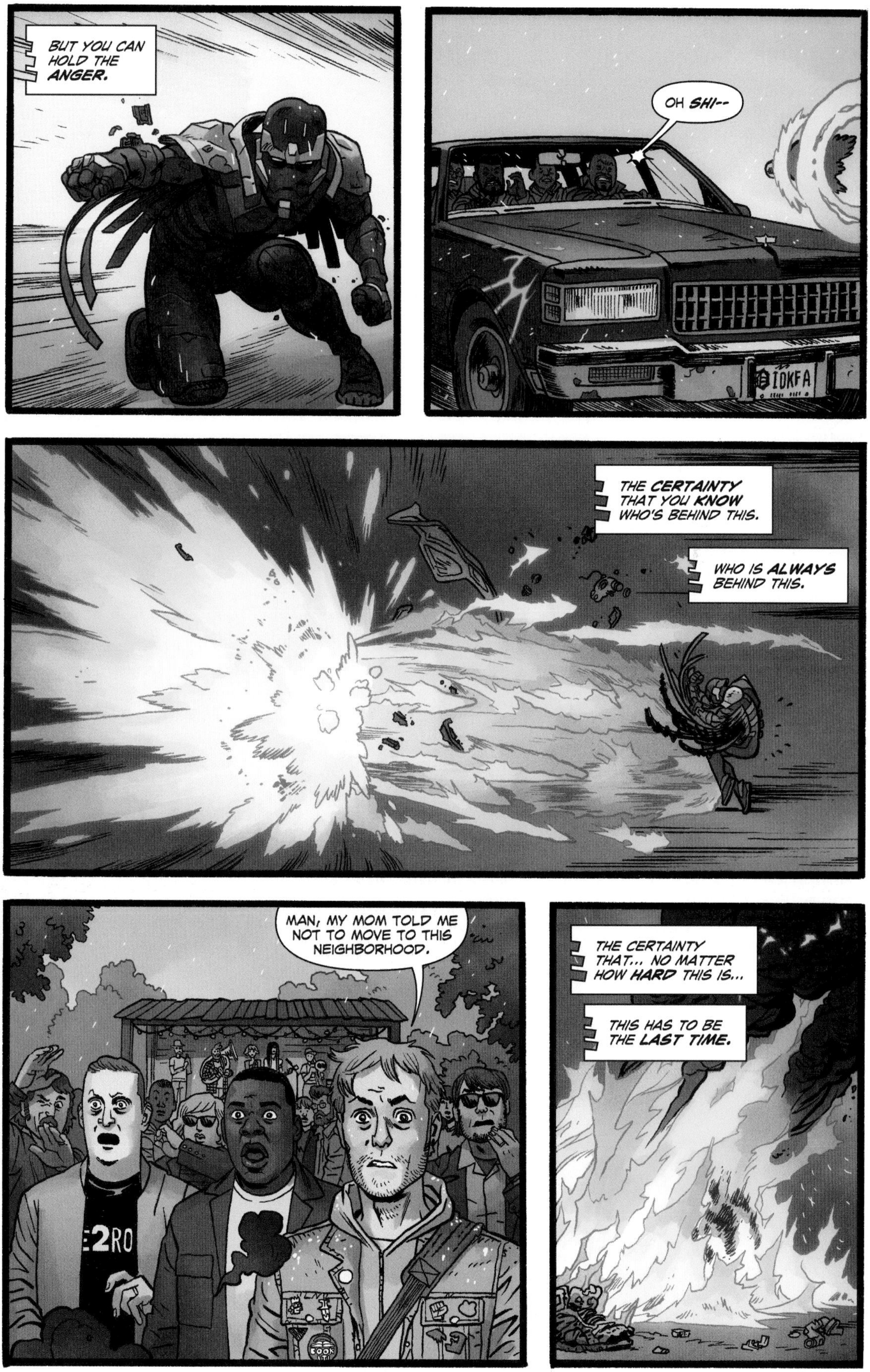
BUT YOU CAN HOLD THE ANGER.
OH SHI--
IDKFA
THE CERTAINTY THAT YOU KNOW WHO'S BEHIND THIS.
WHO IS ALWAYS BEHIND THIS.
MAN, MY MOM TOLD ME NOT TO MOVE TO THIS NEIGHBORHOOD.
THE CERTAINTY THAT... NO MATTER HOW HARD THIS IS...
THIS HAS TO BE THE LAST TIME.

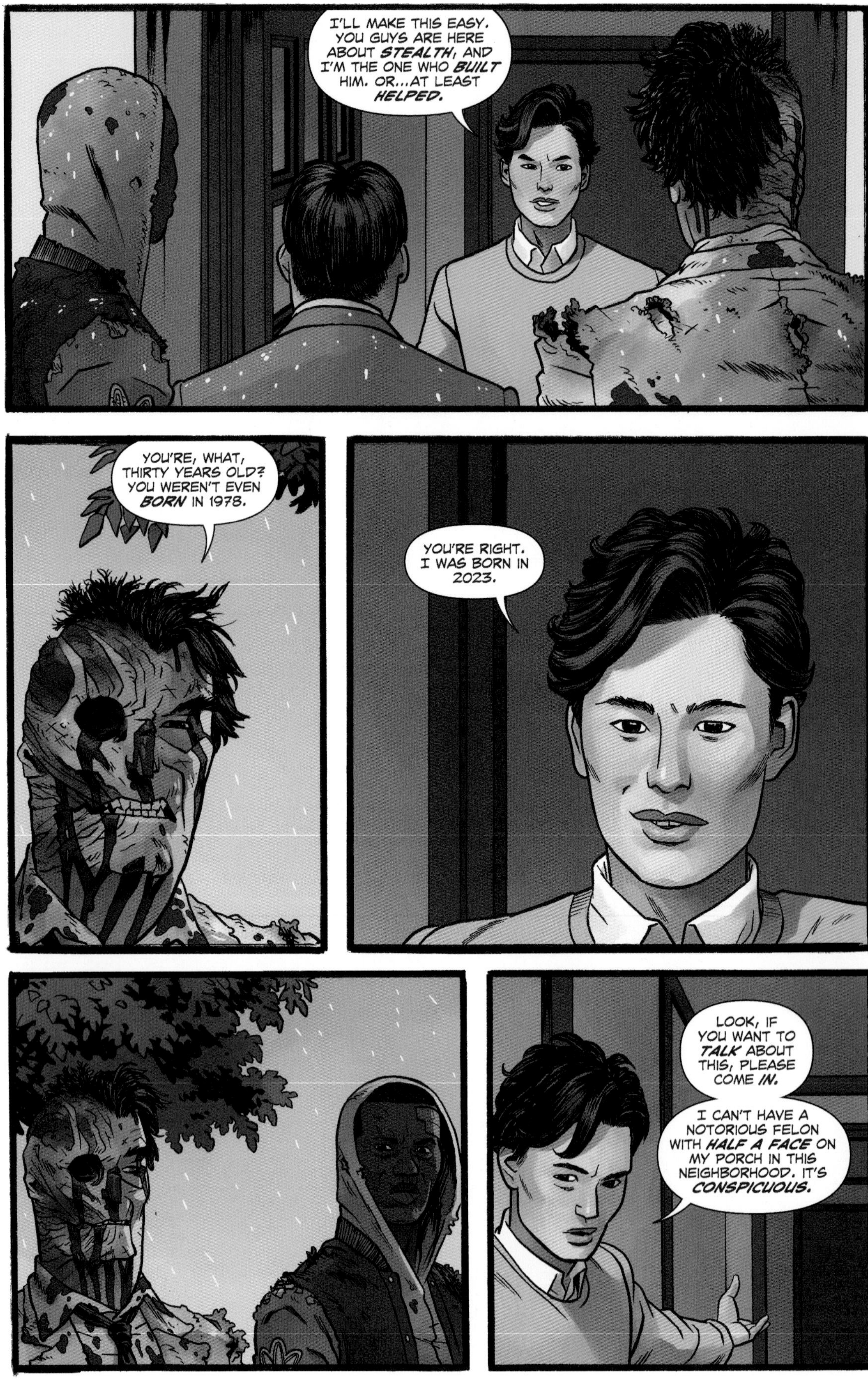
I'LL MAKE THIS EASY. YOU GUYS ARE HERE ABOUT STEALTH; AND I'M THE ONE WHO BUILT HIM. OR...AT LEAST HELPED.
YOU'RE, WHAT, THIRTY YEARS OLD? YOU WEREN'T EVEN BORN IN 1978.
YOU'RE RIGHT. I WAS BORN IN 2023.
LOOK, IF YOU WANT TO TALK ABOUT THIS, PLEASE COME IN.
I CAN'T HAVE A NOTORIOUS FELON WITH HALF A FACE ON MY PORCH IN THIS NEIGHBORHOOD. IT'S CONSPICUOUS.

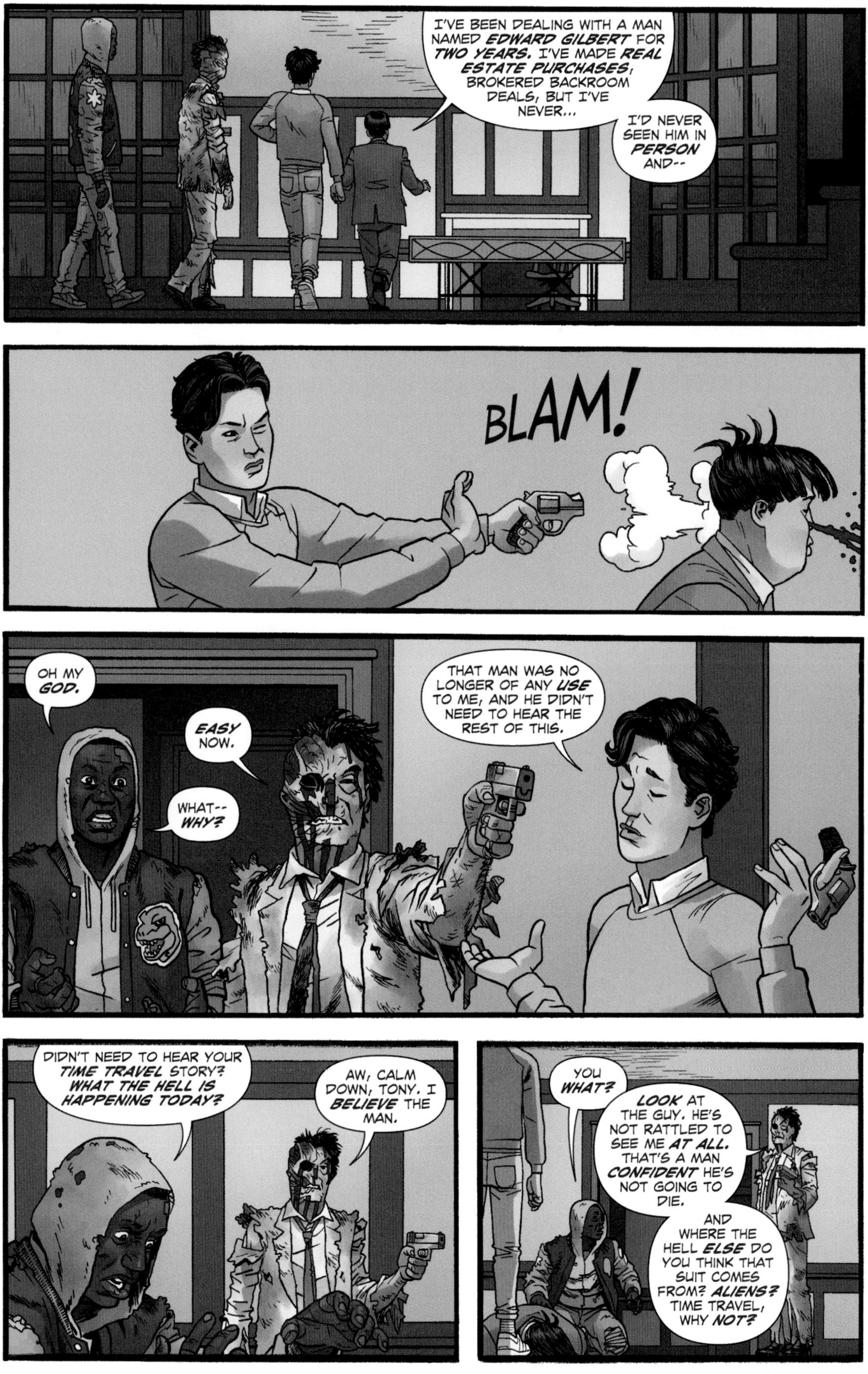
I'VE BEEN DEALING WITH A MAN NAMED EDWARD GILBERT FOR TWO YEARS. I'VE MADE REAL ESTATE PURCHASES, BROKERED BACKROOM DEALS, BUT I'VE NEVER...
I'D NEVER SEEN HIM IN PERSON AND--
BLAM!
OH MY GOD.
EASY NOW.
WHAT-- WHY?
THAT MAN WAS NO LONGER OF ANY USE TO ME, AND HE DIDN'T NEED TO HEAR THE REST OF THIS.
DIDN'T NEED TO HEAR YOUR TIME TRAVEL STORY? WHAT THE HELL IS HAPPENING TODAY?
AW, CALM DOWN, TONY. I BELIEVE THE MAN.
YOU WHAT?
LOOK AT THE GUY. HE'S NOT RATTLED TO SEE ME AT ALL. THAT'S A MAN CONFIDENT HE'S NOT GOING TO DIE.
AND WHERE THE HELL ELSE DO YOU THINK THAT SUIT COMES FROM? ALIENS? TIME TRAVEL, WHY NOT?

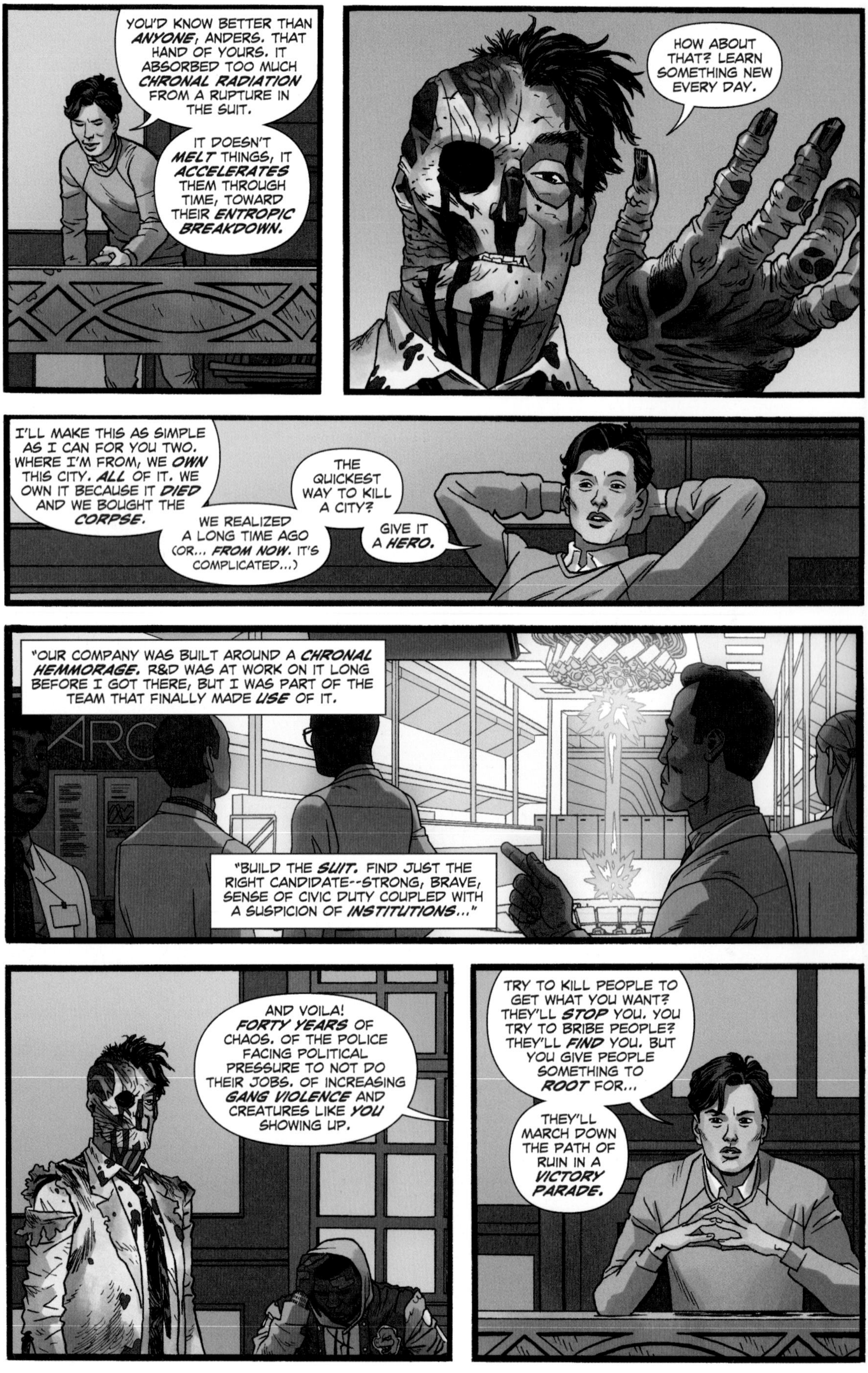
YOU'D KNOW BETTER THAN ANYONE, ANDERS. THAT HAND OF YOURS. IT ABSORBED TOO MUCH CHRONAL RADIATION FROM A RUPTURE IN THE SUIT.
IT DOESN'T MELT THINGS, IT ACCELERATES THEM THROUGH TIME, TOWARD THEIR ENTROPIC BREAKDOWN.
HOW ABOUT THAT? LEARN SOMETHING NEW EVERY DAY.
I'LL MAKE THIS AS SIMPLE AS I CAN FOR YOU TWO. WHERE I'M FROM, WE OWN THIS CITY. ALL OF IT. WE OWN IT BECAUSE IT DIED AND WE BOUGHT THE CORPSE.
WE REALIZED A LONG TIME AGO (OR... FROM NOW. IT'S COMPLICATED...)
THE QUICKEST WAY TO KILL A CITY?
GIVE IT A HERO.
"OUR COMPANY WAS BUILT AROUND A CHRONAL HEMMORAGE. R&D WAS AT WORK ON IT LONG BEFORE I GOT THERE, BUT I WAS PART OF THE TEAM THAT FINALLY MADE USE OF IT.
ARC
"BUILD THE SUIT. FIND JUST THE RIGHT CANDIDATE--STRONG, BRAVE, SENSE OF CIVIC DUTY COUPLED WITH A SUSPICION OF INSTITUTIONS..."
AND VOILA! FORTY YEARS OF CHAOS. OF THE POLICE FACING POLITICAL PRESSURE TO NOT DO THEIR JOBS. OF INCREASING GANG VIOLENCE AND CREATURES LIKE YOU SHOWING UP.
TRY TO KILL PEOPLE TO GET WHAT YOU WANT? THEY'LL STOP YOU. YOU TRY TO BRIBE PEOPLE? THEY'LL FIND YOU. BUT YOU GIVE PEOPLE SOMETHING TO ROOT FOR...
THEY'LL MARCH DOWN THE PATH OF RUIN IN A VICTORY PARADE.

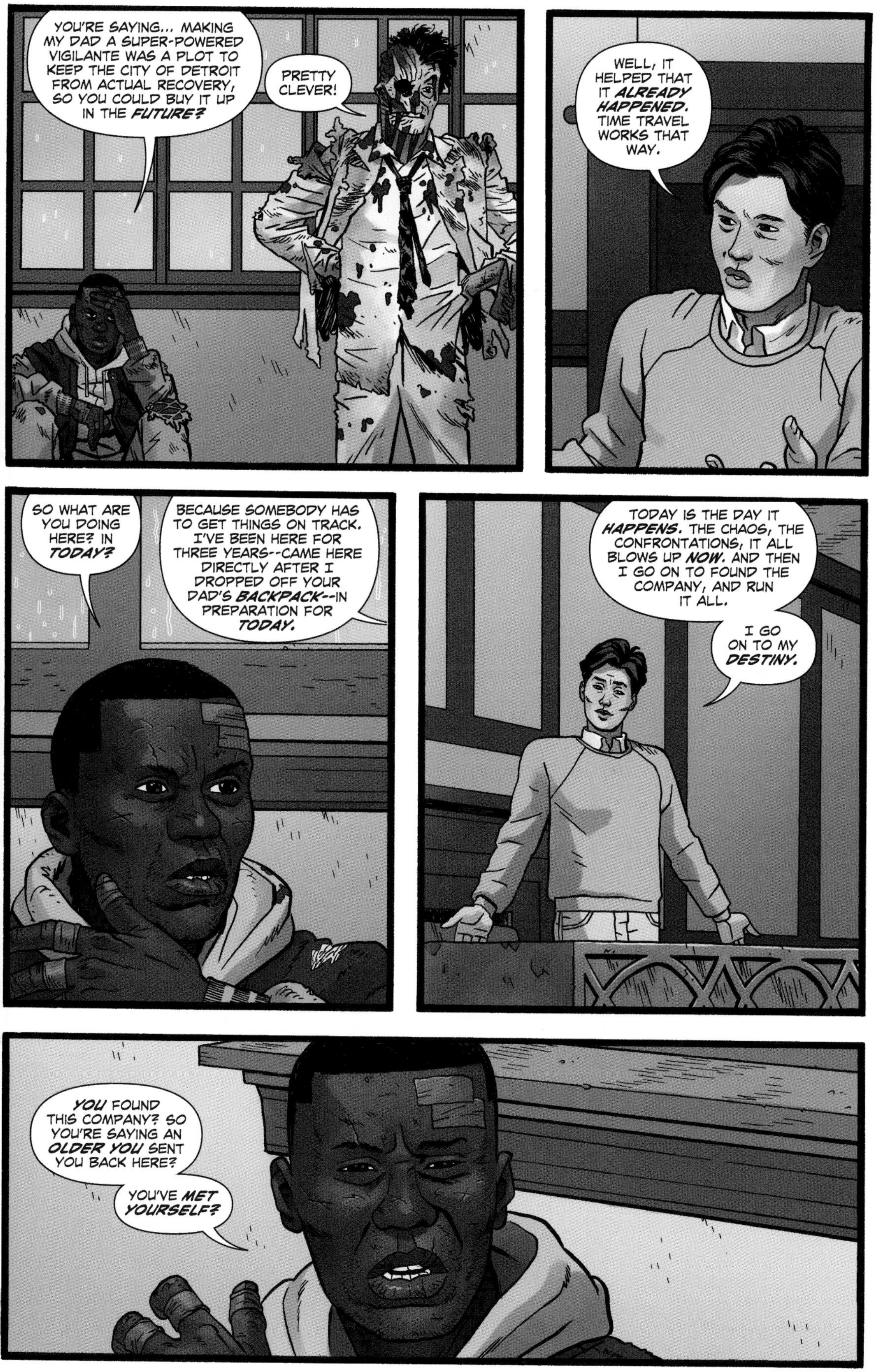
YOU'RE SAYING... MAKING MY DAD A SUPER-POWERED VIGILANTE WAS A PLOT TO KEEP THE CITY OF DETROIT FROM ACTUAL RECOVERY, SO YOU COULD BUY IT UP IN THE *FUTURE?*
PRETTY CLEVER!
WELL, IT HELPED THAT IT *ALREADY HAPPENED.* TIME TRAVEL WORKS THAT WAY.
SO WHAT ARE YOU DOING HERE? IN *TODAY?*
BECAUSE SOMEBODY HAS TO GET THINGS ON TRACK. I'VE BEEN HERE FOR THREE YEARS--CAME HERE DIRECTLY AFTER I DROPPED OFF YOUR DAD'S *BACKPACK*--IN PREPARATION FOR *TODAY.*
TODAY IS THE DAY IT *HAPPENS.* THE CHAOS, THE CONFRONTATIONS, IT ALL BLOWS UP *NOW.* AND THEN I GO ON TO FOUND THE COMPANY, AND RUN IT ALL.
I GO ON TO MY *DESTINY.*
YOU FOUND THIS COMPANY? SO YOU'RE SAYING AN *OLDER YOU* SENT YOU BACK HERE?
YOU'VE *MET YOURSELF?*

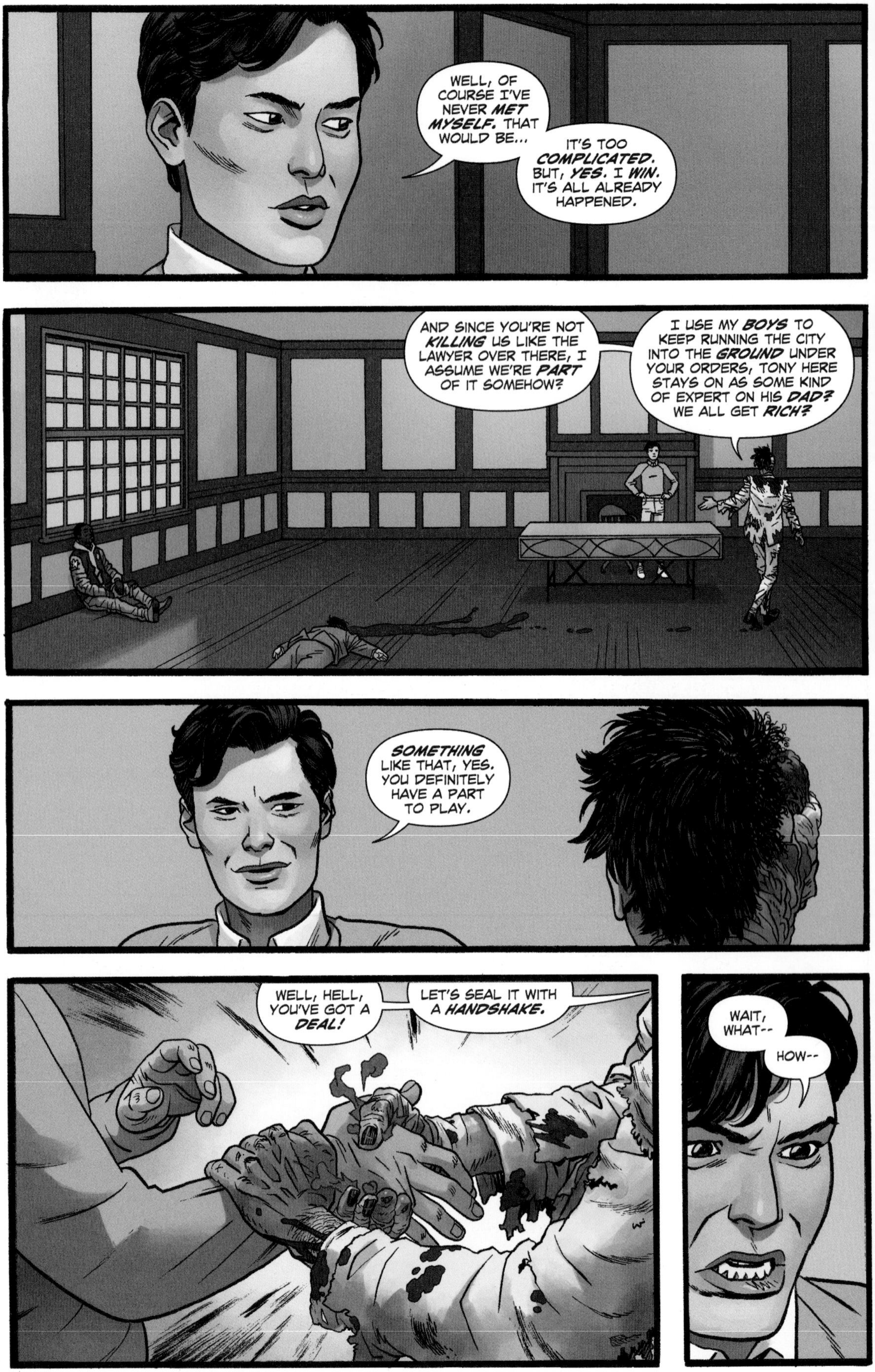
WELL, OF COURSE I'VE NEVER MET MYSELF. THAT WOULD BE...
IT'S TOO COMPLICATED. BUT, YES. I WIN. IT'S ALL ALREADY HAPPENED.
AND SINCE YOU'RE NOT KILLING US LIKE THE LAWYER OVER THERE, I ASSUME WE'RE PART OF IT SOMEHOW?
I USE MY BOYS TO KEEP RUNNING THE CITY INTO THE GROUND UNDER YOUR ORDERS, TONY HERE STAYS ON AS SOME KIND OF EXPERT ON HIS DAD? WE ALL GET RICH?
SOMETHING LIKE THAT, YES. YOU DEFINITELY HAVE A PART TO PLAY.
WELL, HELL, YOU'VE GOT A DEAL!
LET'S SEAL IT WITH A HANDSHAKE.
WAIT, WHAT--
HOW--

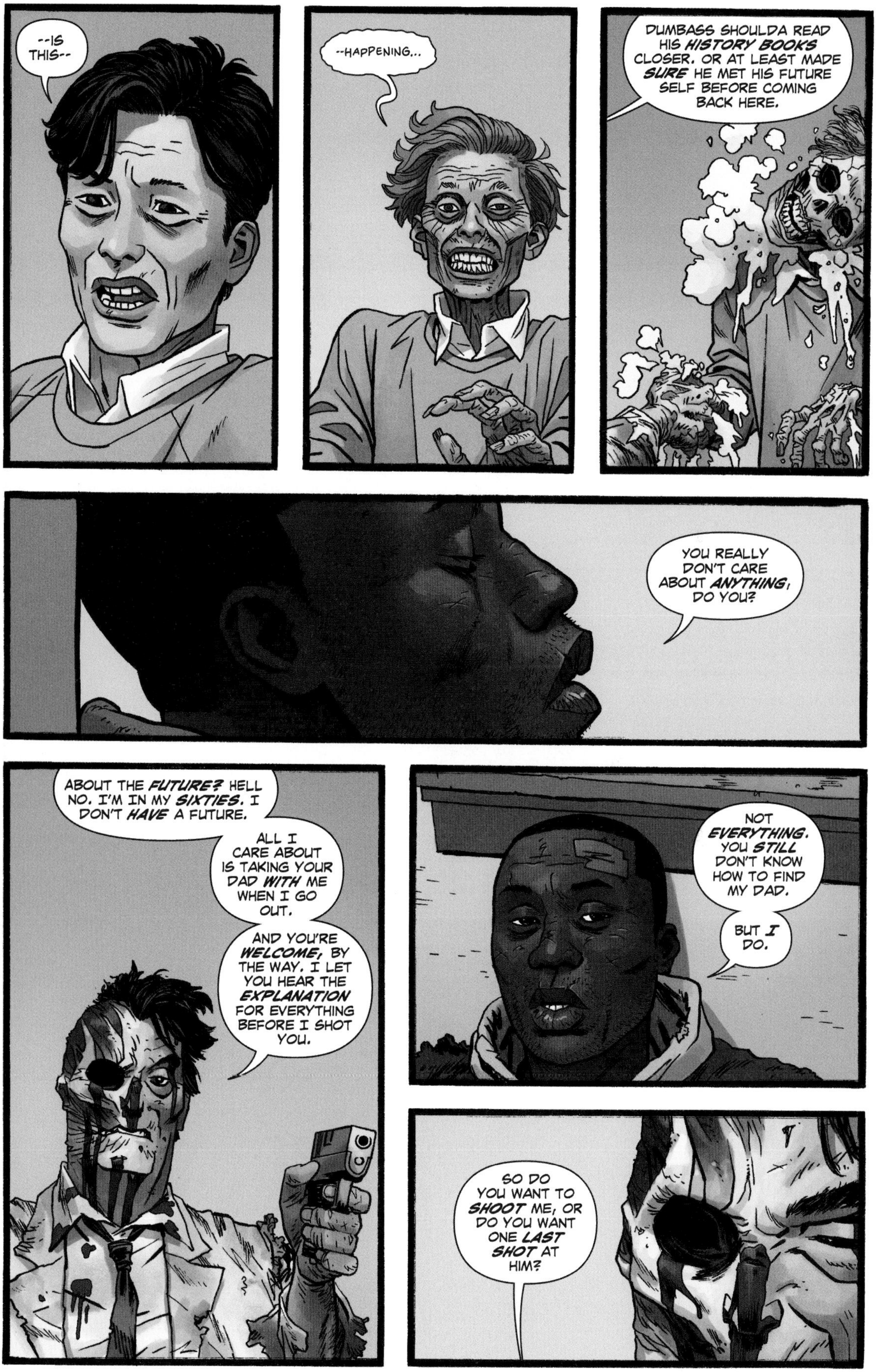

--IS THIS--
--HAPPENING...
DUMBASS SHOULDA READ HIS HISTORY BOOKS CLOSER. OR AT LEAST MADE SURE HE MET HIS FUTURE SELF BEFORE COMING BACK HERE.
YOU REALLY DON'T CARE ABOUT ANYTHING, DO YOU?
ABOUT THE FUTURE? HELL NO. I'M IN MY SIXTIES. I DON'T HAVE A FUTURE.
ALL I CARE ABOUT IS TAKING YOUR DAD WITH ME WHEN I GO OUT.
AND YOU'RE WELCOME, BY THE WAY. I LET YOU HEAR THE EXPLANATION FOR EVERYTHING BEFORE I SHOT YOU.
NOT EVERYTHING. YOU STILL DON'T KNOW HOW TO FIND MY DAD.
BUT I DO.
SO DO YOU WANT TO SHOOT ME, OR DO YOU WANT ONE LAST SHOT AT HIM?

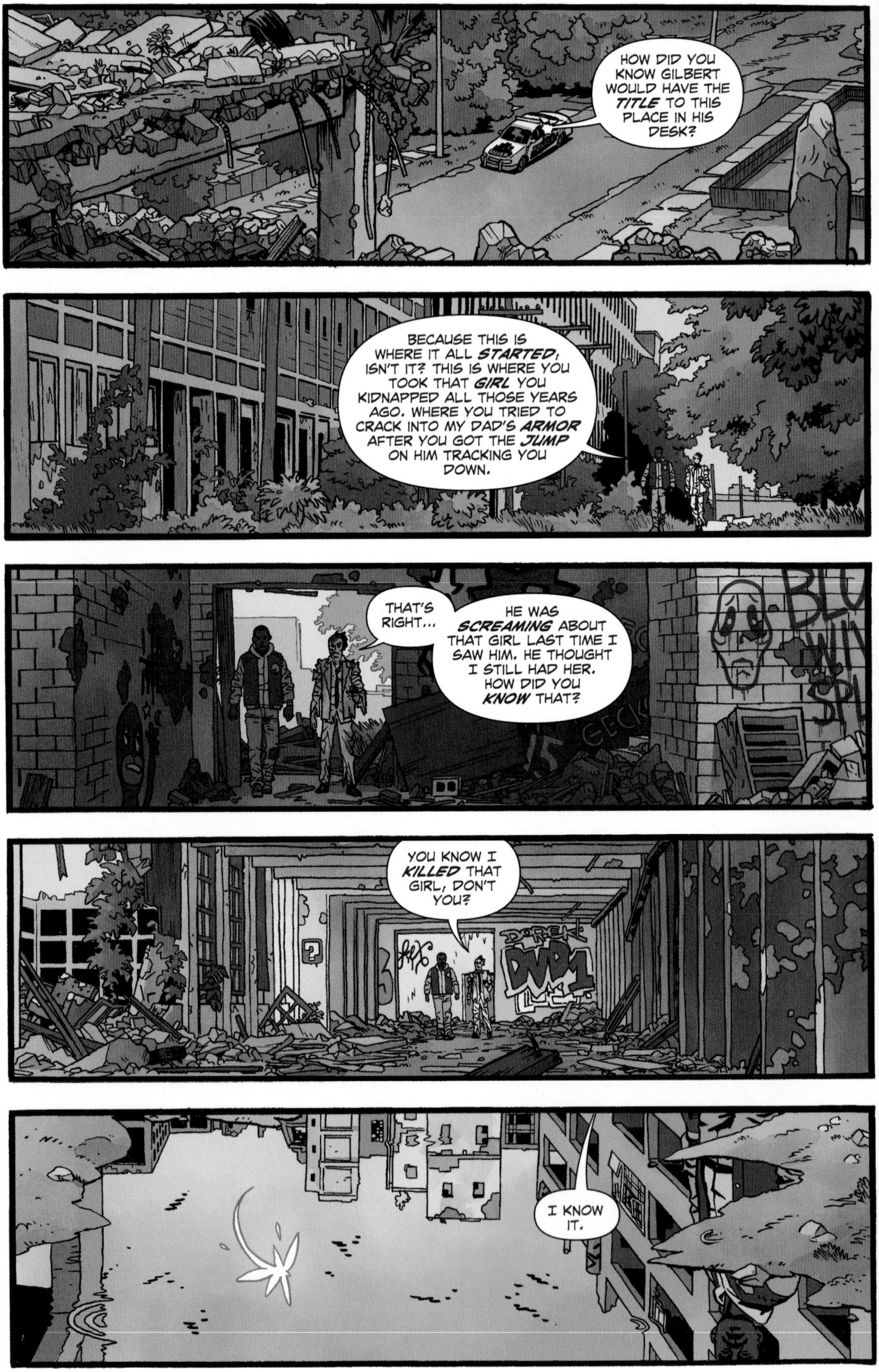
HOW DID YOU KNOW GILBERT WOULD HAVE THE *TITLE* TO THIS PLACE IN HIS DESK?
BECAUSE THIS IS WHERE IT ALL *STARTED*, ISN'T IT? THIS IS WHERE YOU TOOK THAT *GIRL* YOU KIDNAPPED ALL THOSE YEARS AGO. WHERE YOU TRIED TO CRACK INTO MY DAD'S *ARMOR* AFTER YOU GOT THE *JUMP* ON HIM TRACKING YOU DOWN.
THAT'S RIGHT...
HE WAS *SCREAMING* ABOUT THAT GIRL LAST TIME I SAW HIM. HE THOUGHT I STILL HAD HER. HOW DID YOU *KNOW* THAT?
YOU KNOW I *KILLED* THAT GIRL, DON'T YOU?
I KNOW IT.

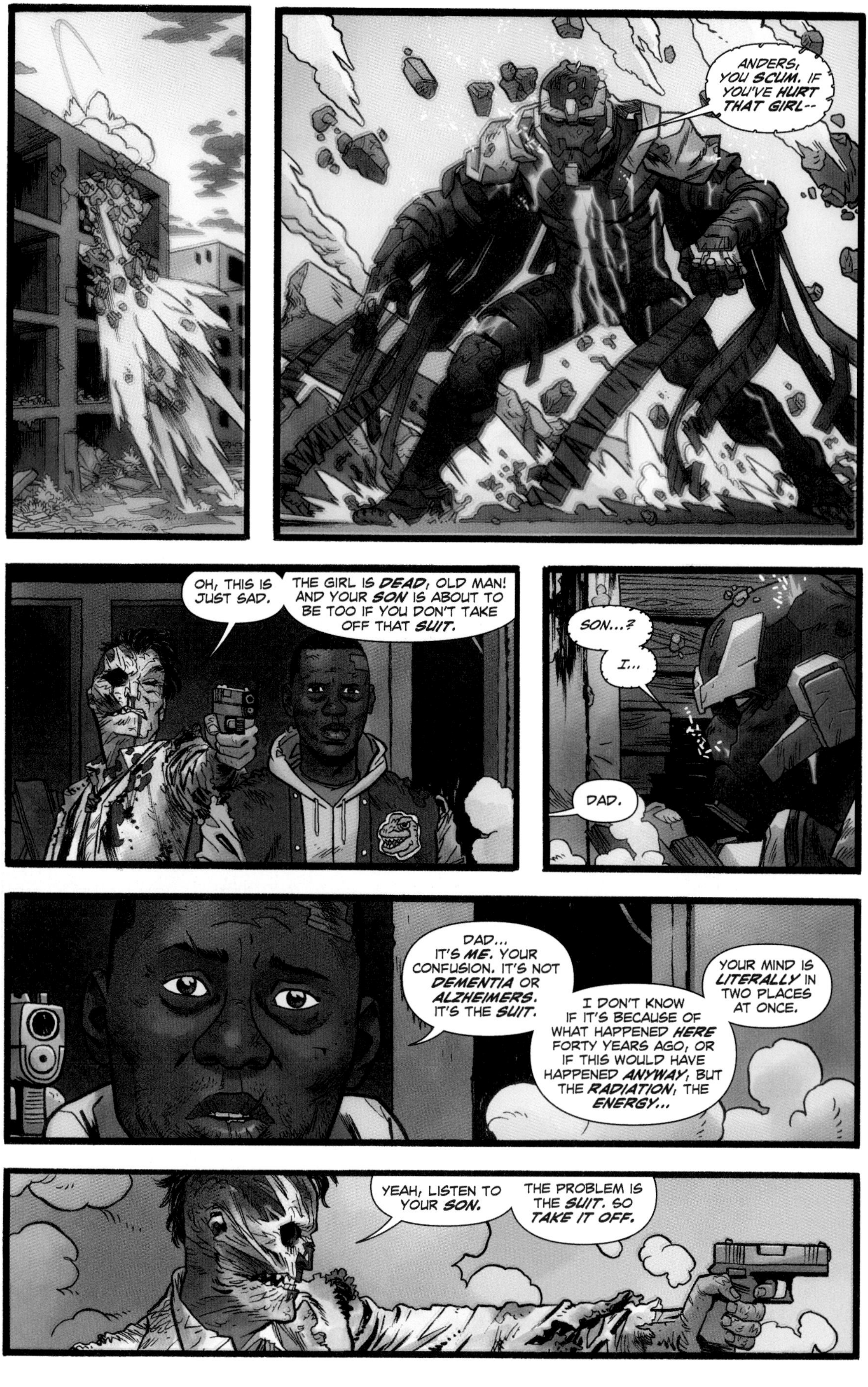
ANDERS, YOU SCUM. IF YOU'VE HURT THAT GIRL--
OH, THIS IS JUST SAD.
THE GIRL IS DEAD, OLD MAN! AND YOUR SON IS ABOUT TO BE TOO IF YOU DON'T TAKE OFF THAT SUIT.
SON...?
I...
DAD.
DAD... IT'S ME. YOUR CONFUSION. IT'S NOT DEMENTIA OR ALZHEIMERS. IT'S THE SUIT.
I DON'T KNOW IF IT'S BECAUSE OF WHAT HAPPENED HERE FORTY YEARS AGO, OR IF THIS WOULD HAVE HAPPENED ANYWAY, BUT THE RADIATION, THE ENERGY...
YOUR MIND IS LITERALLY IN TWO PLACES AT ONCE.
YEAH, LISTEN TO YOUR SON.
THE PROBLEM IS THE SUIT. SO TAKE IT OFF.

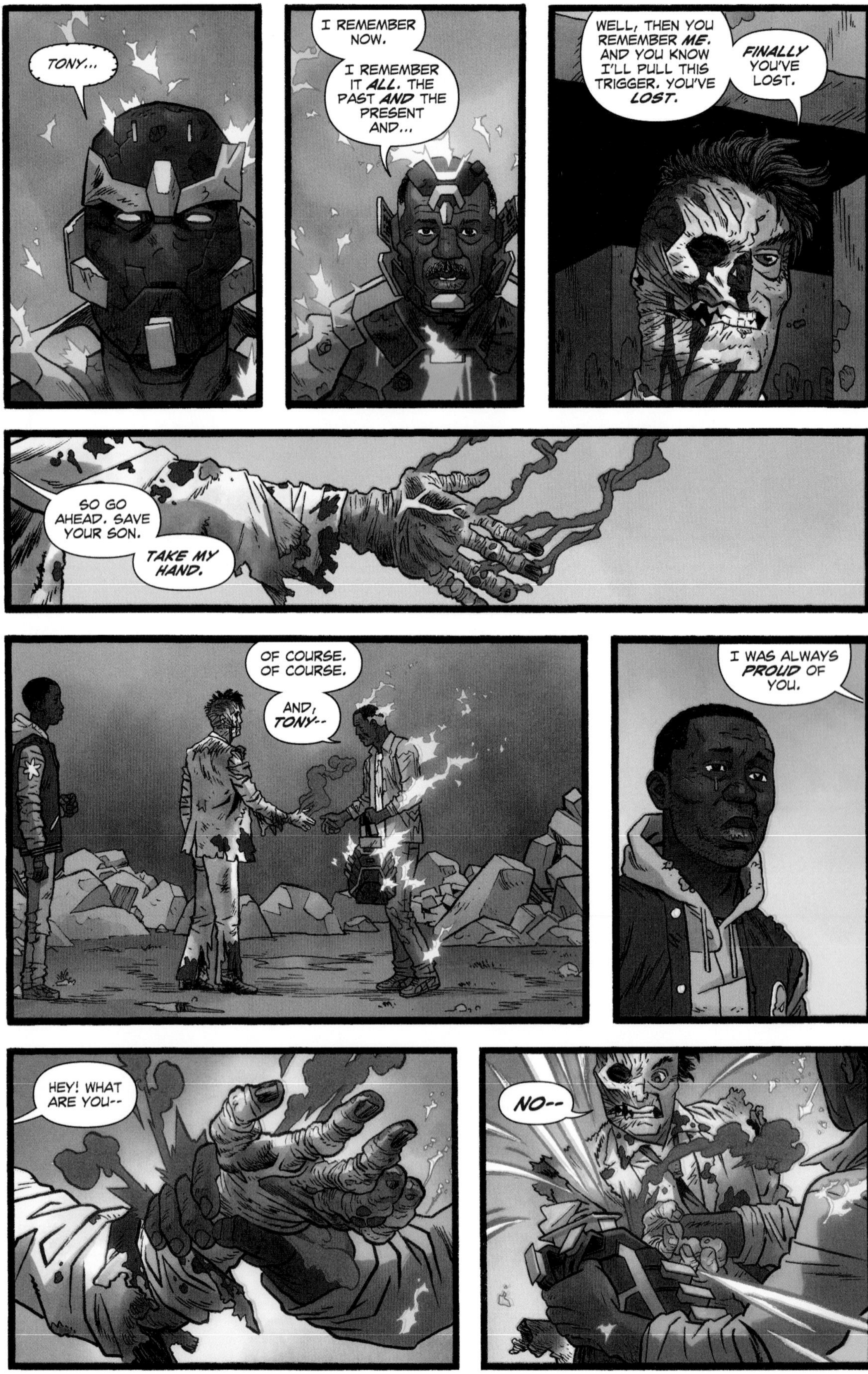
TONY...
I REMEMBER NOW.
I REMEMBER IT ALL. THE PAST AND THE PRESENT AND...
WELL, THEN YOU REMEMBER ME. AND YOU KNOW I'LL PULL THIS TRIGGER. YOU'VE LOST.
FINALLY YOU'VE LOST.
SO GO AHEAD. SAVE YOUR SON.
TAKE MY HAND.
OF COURSE. OF COURSE.
AND, TONY--
I WAS ALWAYS PROUD OF YOU.
HEY! WHAT ARE YOU--
NO--

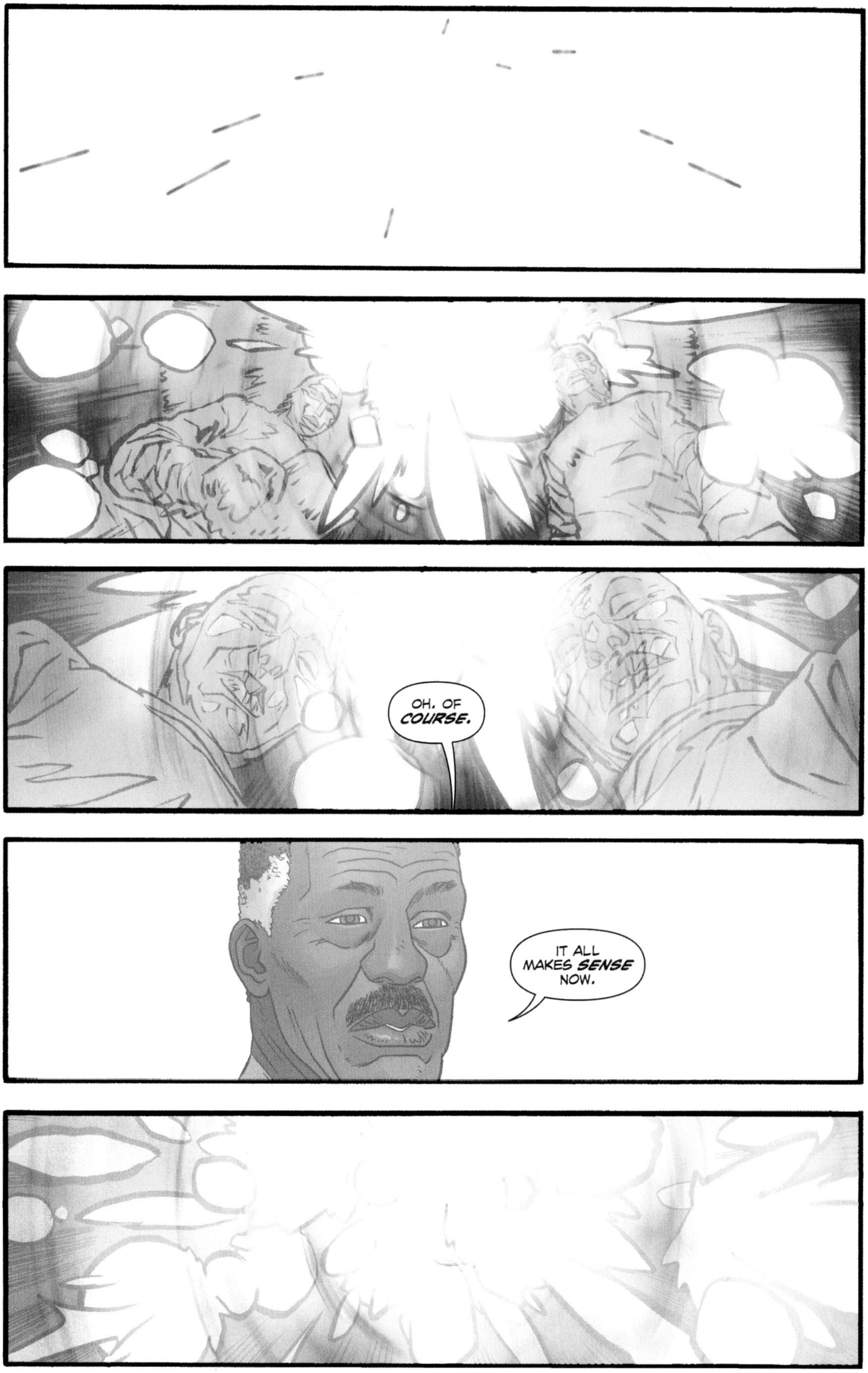
OH. OF COURSE.
IT ALL MAKES SENSE NOW.

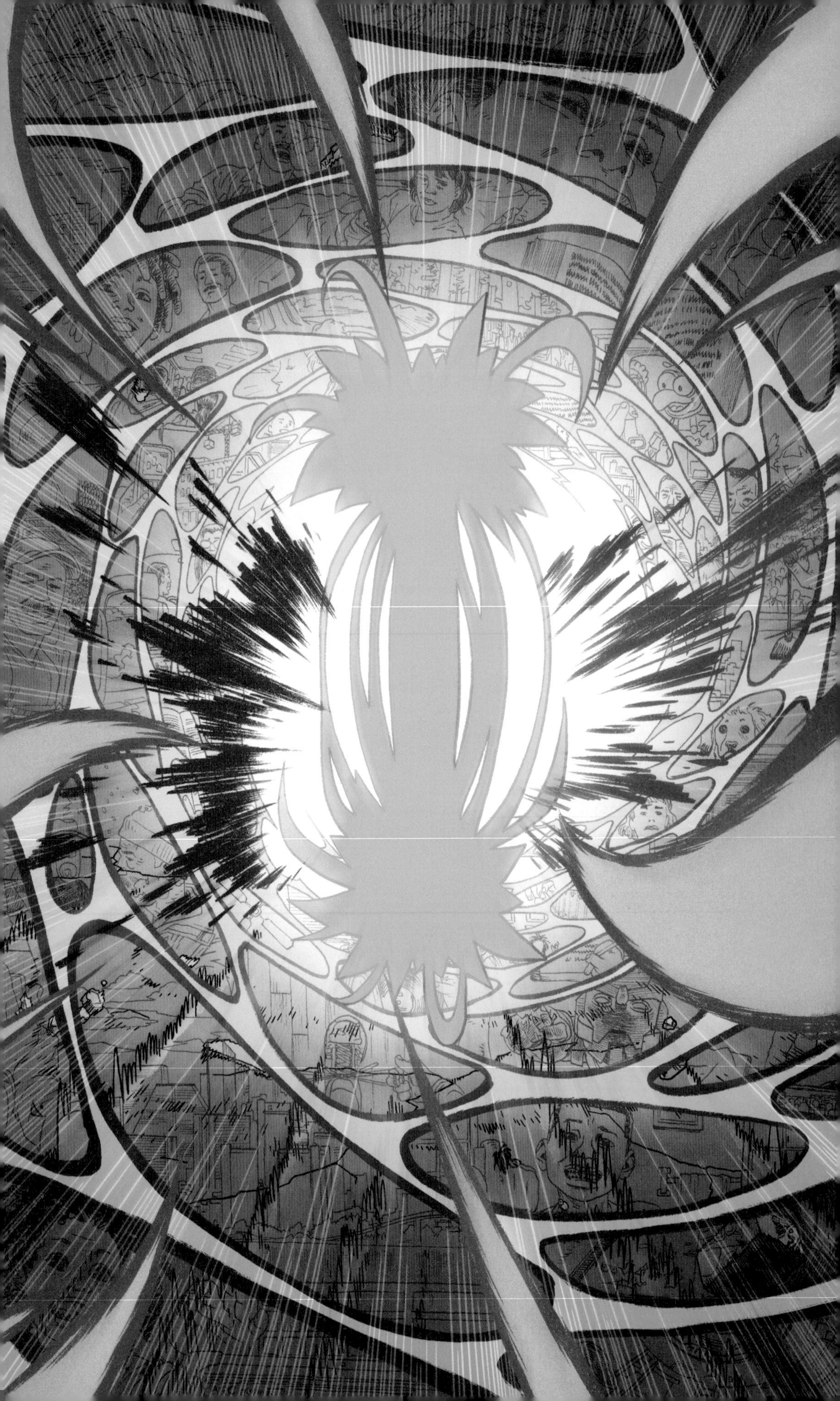

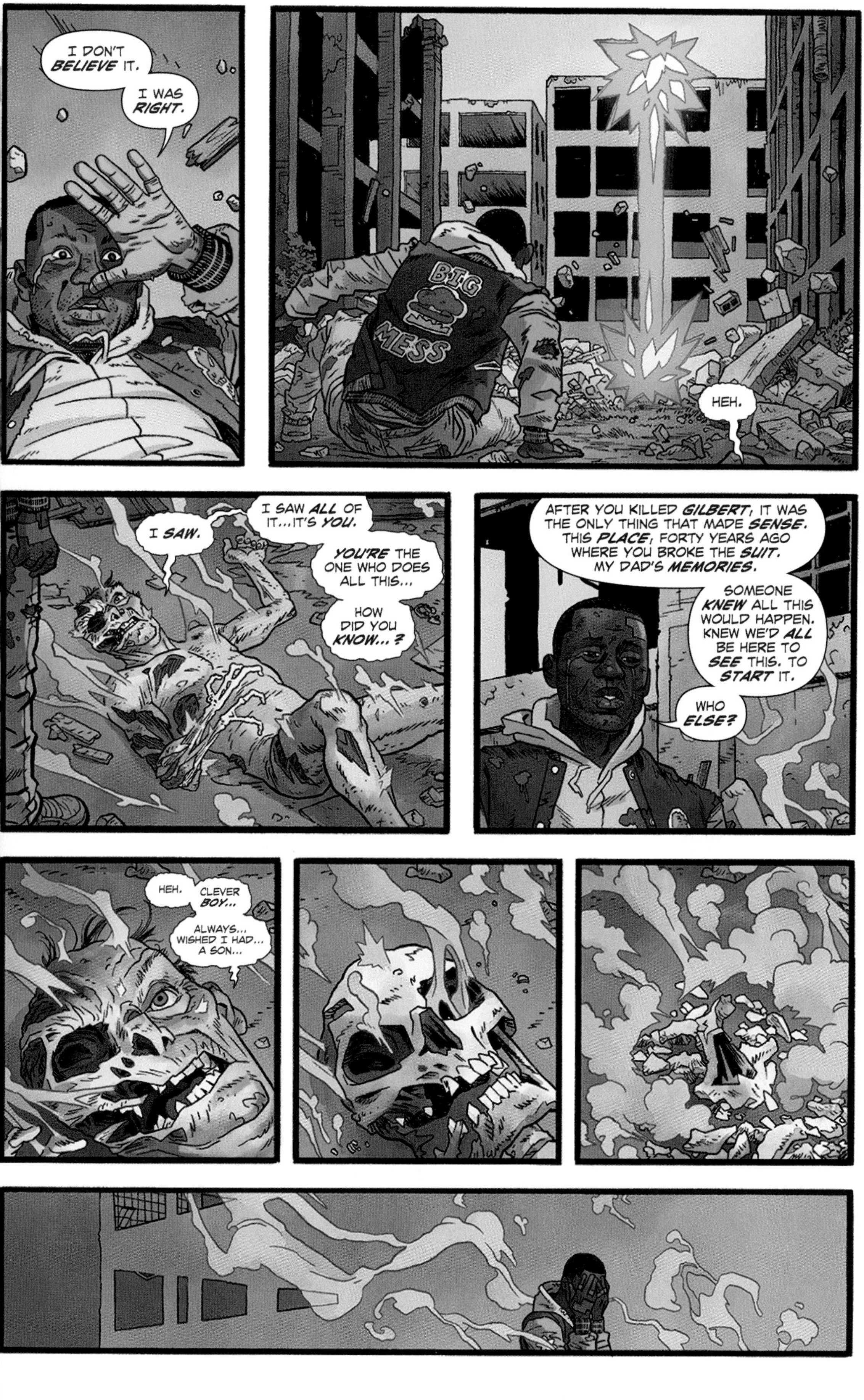

I DON'T BELIEVE IT.
I WAS RIGHT.
HEH.
I SAW.
I SAW ALL OF IT... IT'S YOU.
YOU'RE THE ONE WHO DOES ALL THIS...
HOW DID YOU KNOW...?
AFTER YOU KILLED GILBERT, IT WAS THE ONLY THING THAT MADE SENSE. THIS PLACE, FORTY YEARS AGO WHERE YOU BROKE THE SUIT. MY DAD'S MEMORIES.
SOMEONE KNEW ALL THIS WOULD HAPPEN. KNEW WE'D ALL BE HERE TO SEE THIS. TO START IT.
WHO ELSE?
HEH.
CLEVER BOY...
ALWAYS... WISHED I HAD... A SON...
BIG MESS

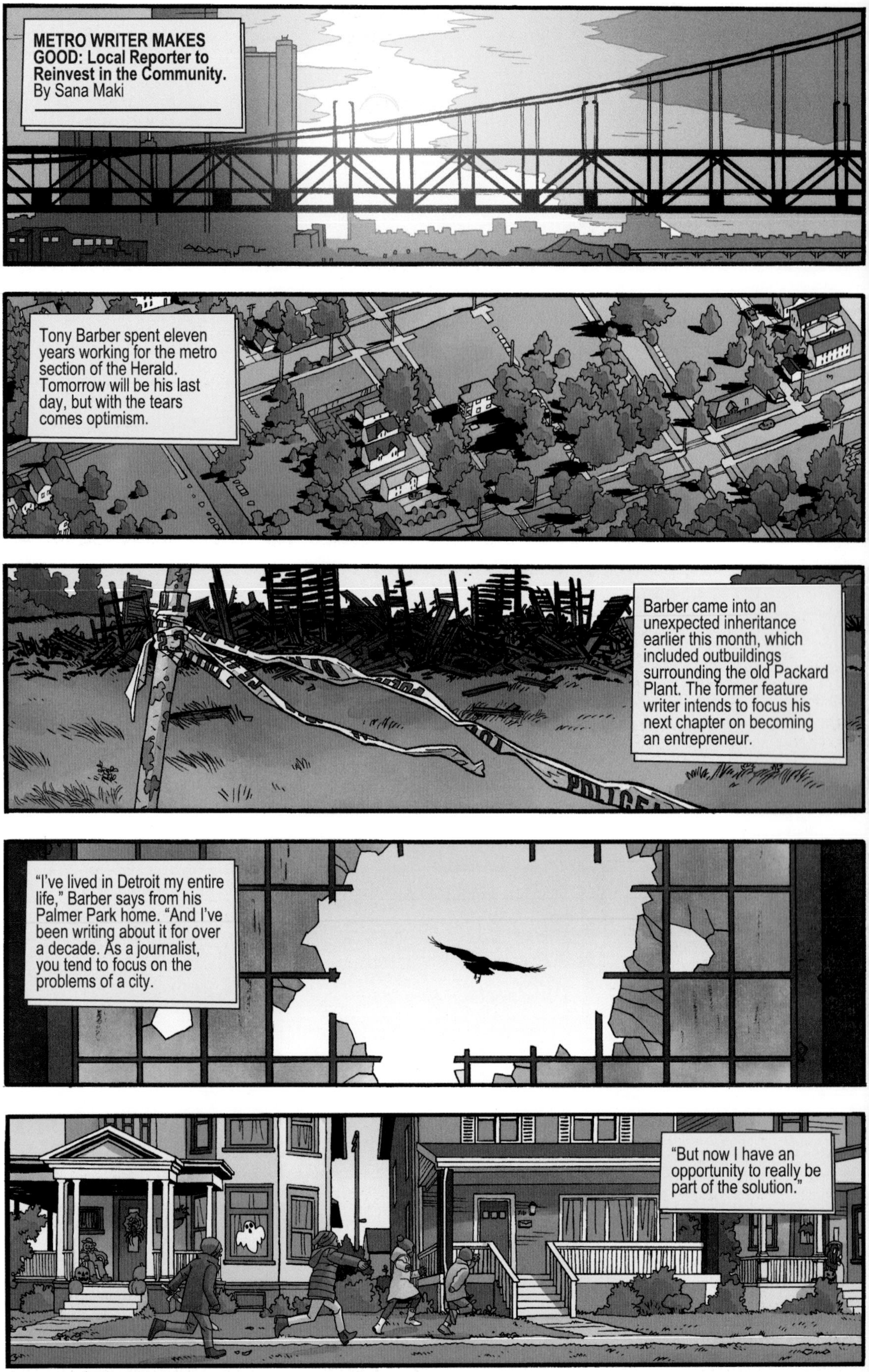
METRO WRITER MAKES GOOD: Local Reporter to Reinvest in the Community.
By Sana Maki
Tony Barber spent eleven years working for the metro section of the Herald. Tomorrow will be his last day, but with the tears comes optimism.
Barber came into an unexpected inheritance earlier this month, which included outbuildings surrounding the old Packard Plant. The former feature writer intends to focus his next chapter on becoming an entrepreneur.
POLICE
"I've lived in Detroit my entire life," Barber says from his Palmer Park home. "And I've been writing about it for over a decade. As a journalist, you tend to focus on the problems of a city.
"But now I have an opportunity to really be part of the solution."

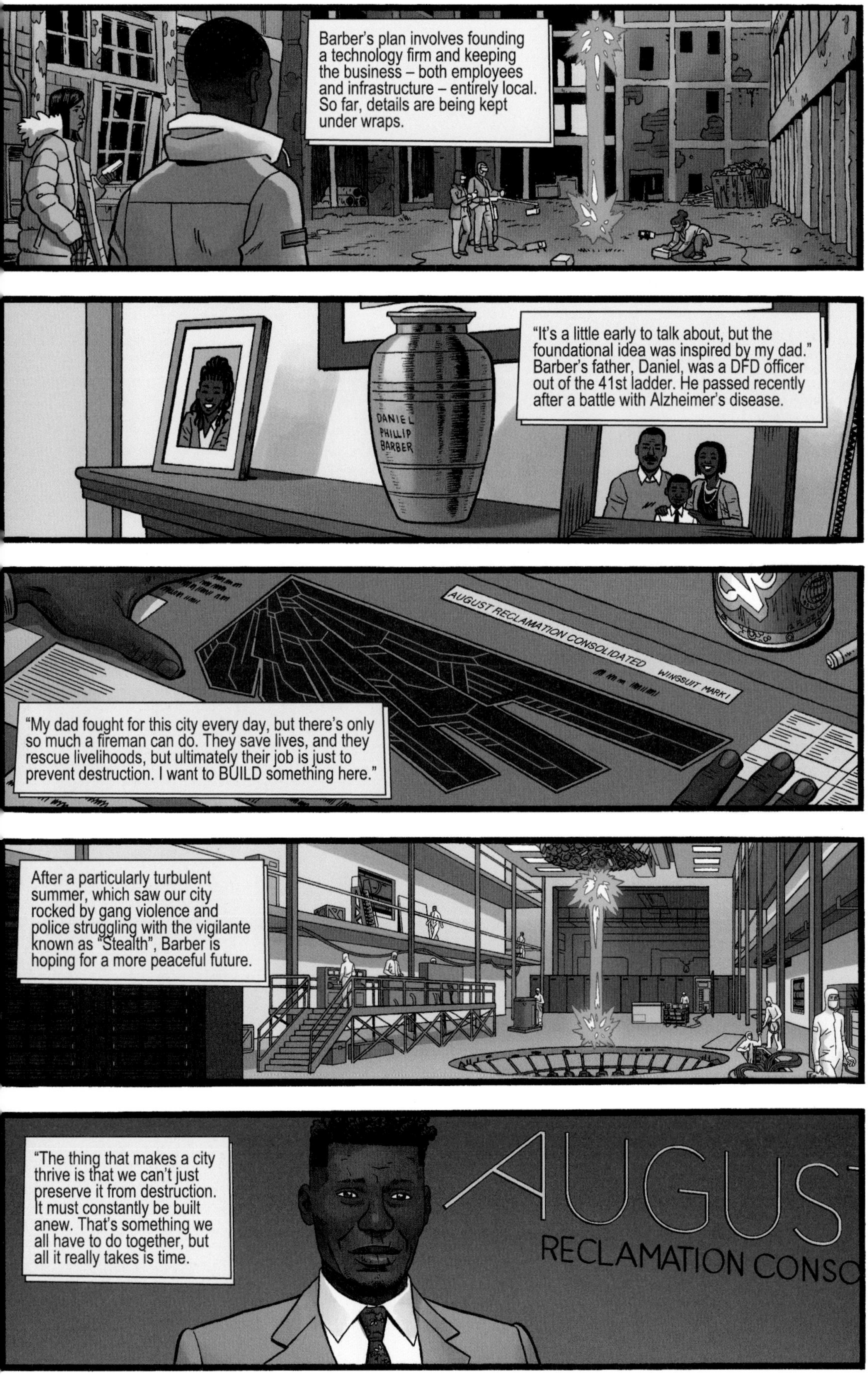
Barber's plan involves founding a technology firm and keeping the business – both employees and infrastructure – entirely local. So far, details are being kept under wraps.
"It's a little early to talk about, but the foundational idea was inspired by my dad." Barber's father, Daniel, was a DFD officer out of the 41st ladder. He passed recently after a battle with Alzheimer's disease.
DANIEL PHILLIP BARBER
AUGUST RECLAMATION CONSOLIDATED
WINGSUIT MARK I
"My dad fought for this city every day, but there's only so much a fireman can do. They save lives, and they rescue livelihoods, but ultimately their job is just to prevent destruction. I want to BUILD something here."
After a particularly turbulent summer, which saw our city rocked by gang violence and police struggling with the vigilante known as "Stealth", Barber is hoping for a more peaceful future.
"The thing that makes a city thrive is that we can't just preserve it from destruction. It must constantly be built anew. That's something we all have to do together, but all it really takes is time.
AUGUS
RECLAMATION CONSO

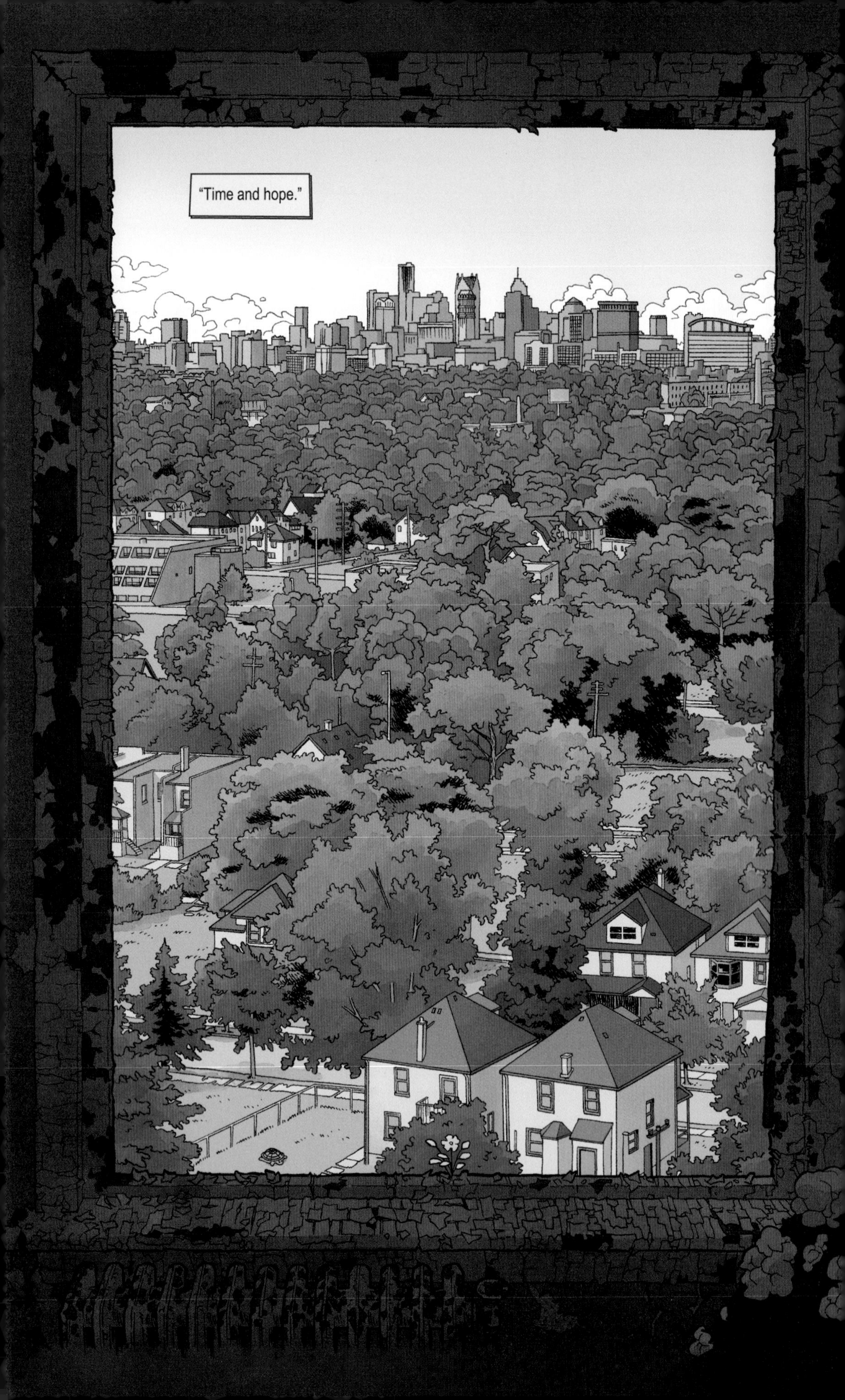
"Time and hope."

THE END

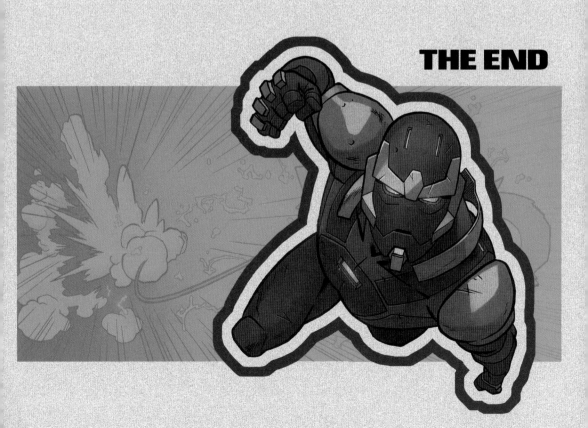

For more tales from ROBERT KIRKMAN and SKYBOUND

BRANDON THOMAS • KHARY RANDOLPH • EMILIO LOPEZ
EXCELLENCE
VOLUME ONE
KILL THE PAST

VOL. 1: KILL THE PAST
ISBN: 978-1-5343-11362-0
$16.99

ROBERT KIRKMAN
CHRIS SAMNEE
FIRE POWER
WITH MATT WILSON AND RUS WOOTON
VOLUME 1 PRELUDE

VOL. 1: PRELUDE
ISBN: 978-1-5343-1655-3
$9.99

WILLIAMSON
BRESSAN
VOLUME NINE
WAR OF THE WORLDS

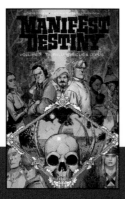

VOL. 1: HOMECOMING TP
ISBN: 978-1-63215-231-2
$9.99

VOL. 2: CALL TO ADVENTURE TP
ISBN: 978-1-63215-446-0
$12.99

VOL. 3: ALLIES AND ENEMIES TP
ISBN: 978-1-63215-683-9
$12.99

VOL. 4: FAMILY HISTORY TP
ISBN: 978-1-63215-871-0
$12.99

VOL. 5: BELLY OF THE BEAST TP
ISBN: 978-1-5343-0218-1
$12.99

VOL. 6: FATHERHOOD TP
ISBN: 978-1-53430-498-7
$14.99

VOL. 7: BLOOD BROTHERS TP
ISBN: 978-1-5343-1053-7
$14.99

VOL. 8: LIVE BY THE SWORD TP
ISBN: 978-1-5343-1368-2
$14.99

VOL. 9: WAR OF THE WORLDS TP
ISBN: 978-1-5343-1601-0
$14.99

MANIFEST DESTINY

VOL. 1: FLORA & FAUNA TP
ISBN: 978-1-60706-982-9
$9.99

VOL. 2: AMPHIBIA & INSECTA TP
ISBN: 978-1-63215-052-3
$14.99

VOL. 3: CHIROPTERA & CARNIFORMAVES TP
ISBN: 978-1-63215-397-5
$14.99

VOL. 4: SASQUATCH TP
ISBN: 978-1-63215-890-1
$14.99

VOL. 5: MNEMOPHOBIA & CHRONOPHOBIA TP
ISBN: 978-1-5343-0230-3
$16.99

VOL. 6: FORTIS & INVISIBILIA TP
ISBN: 978-1-5343-0513-7
$16.99

VOL. 7: TALPA LUMBRICUS & LEPUS TP
ISBN: 978-1-5343-1589-1
$16.99

ROBERT KIRKMAN
LORENZO DE FELICI
ANNALISA LEONI
OBLIVION SONG
FOUR

CHAPTER 1
ISBN: 978-1-5343-0642-4
$9.99

CHAPTER 2
ISBN: 978-1-5343-1057-5
$16.99

CHAPTER 3
ISBN: 978-1-5343-1326-2
$16.99

CHAPTER 4
ISBN: 978-1-5343-1517-4
$14.99

REDNECK
Lone Star

VOL. 1: DEEP IN THE HEART
ISBN: 978-1-5343-0331-7
$16.99

VOL. 2: EYES UPON YOU
ISBN: 978-1-5343-0665-3
$16.99

VOL. 3: LONGHORNS
ISBN: 978-1-5343-1050-6
$16.99

VOL. 4: LONE STAR
ISBN: 978-1-5343-1367-5
$16.99